Praise for *Specters of the Marvelous*

"Fairy-tale studies has needed this book for a long time. With meticulous historical and narrative analysis, Kimberly J. Lau lays out a consummate reckoning of racism in the European tale tradition. The unmarked, naturalized, inevitable whiteness of the tales is thoroughly debunked. This is literary litigation at its finest. A world of assumptions unmasked by a scholar who is also an intrepid investigator working at the highest level of commitment to giving us new truths about the old stories that still shape our worldview."

—Kay Turner, coeditor of *Transgressive Tales: Queering the Grimms* (Wayne State University Press), and founder of the What a Witch project

"In eye-opening ways, *Specters of the Marvelous: Race and the Development of the European Fairy Tale* does for fairy tales what Ebony Elizabeth Thomas's *The Dark Fantastic* did for fantasy and Isiah Lavender III's *Race in American Science Fiction* did for science fiction. We do not have to agree with every one of Kimberly J. Lau's interpretations, but it is impossible after reading this carefully researched book to unsee the workings of racial ideologies and representations in foundational European literary collections of fairy tales, and it is clear how insisting on the power of non-Euro-American wonder genres counters that history—and matters today. This distinctive contribution to viewing fairy-tale history and intersectionality is a must-read in fairy-tale studies."

—Cristina Bacchilega, professor emerita, University of Hawaiʻi at Mānoa, and coeditor of *Marvels & Tales: Journal of Fairy-Tale Studies* (Wayne State University Press)

SPECTERS OF THE MARVELOUS

The Donald Haase Series in Fairy-Tale Studies

Series Editor
Anne E. Duggan, Wayne State University

Founding Editor
Donald Haase, Wayne State University

A complete listing of the advisory editors and the books in this series can be found online at wsupress.wayne.edu.

SPECTERS
OF THE
MARVELOUS

RACE AND THE
DEVELOPMENT OF
THE EUROPEAN
FAIRY TALE

KIMBERLY J. LAU

WAYNE STATE UNIVERSITY PRESS
DETROIT

© 2025 by Wayne State University Press, Detroit, Michigan 48201. All rights reserved. No part of this book may be reproduced without formal permission.

ISBN 9780814341346 (paperback)
ISBN 9780814351536 (hardcover)
ISBN 9780814341353 (e-book)

Library of Congress Control Number: 2024931080

Cover art by Anne Brérot. Used by permission. Cover design by Chelsea Hunter.

Published with the assistance of a fund established by Thelma Gray James of Wayne State University for the publication of folklore and English studies.

Wayne State University Press rests on Waawiyaataanong, also referred to as Detroit, the ancestral and contemporary homeland of the Three Fires Confederacy. These sovereign lands were granted by the Ojibwe, Odawa, Potawatomi, and Wyandot Nations, in 1807, through the Treaty of Detroit. Wayne State University Press affirms Indigenous sovereignty and honors all tribes with a connection to Detroit. With our Native neighbors, the press works to advance educational equity and promote a better future for the earth and all people.

Wayne State University Press
Leonard N. Simons Building
4809 Woodward Avenue
Detroit, Michigan 48201-1309

Visit us online at wsupress.wayne.edu.

CONTENTS

Acknowledgments   ix

Introduction: Specters of the Marvelous   1

1. Italy, 1634–36: Giambattista Basile's *The Tale of Tales*   21

2. France, 1697: Marie-Catherine d'Aulnoy's *Fairy Tales*   53

3. Germany, 1812–57: Jacob and Wilhelm Grimm's *Children's and Household Tales*   89

4. Great Britain, 1889–1910: Andrew and Nora Lang's Colored Fairy Books   129

Conclusion: Spectral Politics and the Return to Wonder   157

Notes   173
References   201
Index   223

ACKNOWLEDGMENTS

Many friends and colleagues provided intellectual community and invaluable support over the long course of this book's becoming. I offer my deepest thanks for their generosity and regret only that language falls short of my immense gratitude. Still, I offer here a few brief acknowledgments and appreciations with the hope that those who have been a part of this project know that I am grateful beyond words.

For financial support, the Committee on Research at the University of California, Santa Cruz.

For time to read, think, and write, the Literature Department and the Humanities Division at the University of California, Santa Cruz.

For permission to reprint previous work, Wayne State University Press (an earlier version of chapter 2) and Bloomsbury Publishing (the section on Helen Oyeyemi in the conclusion).

For the use of her gorgeous, haunting artwork, Anne Brérot.

For editorial care and beautiful bookmaking, Stephanie Williams, Marie Sweetman, Carrie Teefey, Emily Gauronskas, Jude Grant, and the entire Wayne State University Press team.

For careful reviews and astute feedback, series editor Anne Duggan and the anonymous manuscript reviewers.

For meticulous indexing, Wesley Viebahn.

For invaluable help with translations, Kate Olden (Sigrid Weigel's "The Near Stranger" from the German) and Alejandra Monteagudo (assistance with Villeneuve's frame tale).

For generous subject expertise, productively challenging conversations, wisdom, and curiosity, Cristina Bacchilega, Karen Bassi, Dorian Bell, Regina Bendix, JoAnn Conrad, Vilashini Cooppan, Anne Duggan, Carla Freccero, Corrinne Harol, Lindsay Hinck, Christine Jones, Audrey Kim, Sharon Kinoshita, Uli Marzolph, Wolfgang Mieder, Douglas Moggach,

Dard Neuman, Loisa Nygaard, Micah Perks, Jay Rorty, Lewis Seifert, Andrew Teverson, and Kay Turner.

For unrelenting optimism, my mother, Eloise Lau.

For unsurpassed brilliance, truly exceptional editorial counsel, good humor, and ready comfort, Kathy Chetkovich.

For making magic, thank you.

I think of you with wonder.

INTRODUCTION

Specters of the Marvelous

Picture yourself in a fairy-tale world. There you are, among the princes and princesses, peasants and paupers, among the wizened old ladies and roaming peddlers, the vile stepmothers and capricious fairies, among the dwarves and gnomes, witches and ogres, magical animals and enchanted beasts. You might share your last scrap of bread with a downtrodden fellow begging a bite to eat, ignore the arrogant and entitled firstborn making a hash of things, converse with a nearby cat. You might come across an entire village in deep slumber, a wolf charming a girl in the woods, a traveler about to pick a rose from a winter garden.

Perhaps you're struck by a sense of deep familiarity, maybe even déjà vu.

Perhaps you're struck by the ever-present marvelous, the quotidian magic, the ubiquitous, unremarkable fantastic.

Or perhaps you're struck by the fact that everyone around you is white.

The astoundingly white world of the fairy tale is not simply a figment of your imagination. Just as the marvelous constitutes the world of the fairy tale,[1] so too does whiteness. But while the marvelous has been understood as central to the fairy tale's very essence, race has been almost entirely absent in considerations of the genre's formation and development. Despite a long history of subsuming other storytelling traditions in its universalizing reach, "the fairy tale" is a predominantly European genre. As such, it is marked—or, more precisely, *unmarked*—by its whiteness, a whiteness established, naturalized, and perpetuated across centuries of narrative and visual accretion, bolstered throughout by a profoundly racialized otherness. Whether caricatured or metaphorized, patent or tacit, allusive or elusive, race is an ever-present specter haunting the European fairy tale, a haunting all the more disquieting given the genre's colonization of diverse narrative traditions.

My goal is to bring these specters of the marvelous to light by tracing the historically and culturally specific ideas about race that manifest in the familiar worlds of canonical European fairy-tale collections, from Giambattista Basile's early-seventeenth-century *The Tale of Tales* to Andrew Lang's late-nineteenth- and early-twentieth-century Colored Fairy Books. Beyond their canonicity, the collections at the heart of this study—Basile's *The Tale of Tales* (1634–36), Marie-Catherine d'Aulnoy's *Fairy Tales* (1697–98), Jacob and Wilhelm Grimm's *Children's and Household Tales* (1812), and Lang's Colored Fairy Books series (1889–1910)—are held together by intertextualities that suggest a literary genealogy of the European fairy tale. By situating race as a critical dimension of this genealogy, by tracking its presence across the collections, I argue that racial thinking is foundational to the very development of the genre as well as to the imperial impulses that anchor its universalizing tendencies.

This is not to suggest that "the fairy tale" or even "the European fairy tale" is a permanent and unchanging genre. As Donald Haase points out in framing his entry "Fairy Tale" in the widely referenced *Greenwood Encyclopedia of Folktales and Fairy Tales*, the very definition of the genre remains an open question: "Despite its currency and apparent simplicity, the term 'fairy tale' resists a universally accepted or universally satisfying definition. For some, the term denotes a specific narrative form with easily identified characteristics, but for others it suggests not a singular genre but an umbrella category under which a variety of other forms may be grouped" (2008, 1:322).[2] Some of those other forms include *contes de fées* (from the late-seventeenth-century aristocratic French tales), *Märchen* (from the German and itself encompassing a range of genres), *Volksmärchen* (folktale), *Kunstmärchen* (literary tale), and *Zaubermärchen* (a tale of magic or wonder, which has given rise to "wonder tale" as another way of naming "the fairy tale" and similar-seeming tales). The fact that "the fairy tale" continues to defy attempts to pin it down does not mean that the genre hasn't settled into a recognizable popular form, however, and it is precisely that commonsense understanding of "the fairy tale" that undergirds my claims about the genre, even as I work to undo the hegemonic beliefs that contribute to such an understanding.

Genres, like all social and cultural constructions, have particular histories shaped by the ideological contexts of their emergence and development, a development that often accounts for their naturalized and seemingly immutable forms. Indeed, it is the very impression of immutability that gives a genre its hegemonic power, and the fairy tale is no exception.

And yet, even as popular understandings of "the fairy tale" assume an essentialized form, the genre's relation to the marvelous helps work against an overwhelming tendency toward fixity. As Lewis Seifert has established in his complex reading of the *merveilleux* (marvelous) in the fairy tales and culture of late-seventeenth- and early-eighteenth-century France, "[t]he *merveilleux* is capable of reproducing familiar realities, but also of revealing their incoherences and suggesting, in however schematic a way, a different future" (1996, 23). By invoking "specters of the marvelous" in the book's title, then, I hope to conjure the racializations haunting the fairy tale while also conveying the possibilities for other tales of wonder that such hauntings might inspire, tales like those discussed in the concluding chapter.

At the same time, I also hope that *Specters of the Marvelous* will do for fairy-tale studies what a number of transformative works have done for the study of fantasy and its racial underpinnings.[3] Despite the fact that the fairy tale is an established genre of both fantasy literature and the fantastic more broadly, it has been notably missing from contemporary discussions of race and fantasy, whether in critical analyses (e.g., Iton 2008, Rieder 2008, Young 2016, Jerng 2017, Rifkin 2019, Thomas 2019, Cornum 2021), decolonizing works (e.g., Thomas 2000, Dillon 2012, Roanhorse et al. 2017), or popular debate among fans. The reframing, historicizing, and nuanced (re)readings at the center of such critiques of fantasy, along with the ongoing conversations they have inspired about fantasy as a multimodal genre, have contributed to a critical orientation in which *not* considering race is simply impossible. In this context, especially, the fairy tale's marginalization—indeed, its absence—is particularly unsettling and highlights a troubling lacuna, one that I seek to address in ways that make thinking about the fairy tale without thinking about race similarly impossible.

Of Genres and Genealogies

Origin stories and genealogies always entail some degree of myth-making and speculation. As a result, they also tend to encourage alternative accounts and invite scholarly controversy. The genealogy at the heart of this book is no different. Privileging Basile's *The Tale of Tales* as the foundational text on which the European fairy-tale tradition is built necessarily forecloses other compelling histories. An alternative genealogy might begin with *The Arabian Nights*, for instance. Based on Antoine Galland's early-eighteenth-century "translations" of a fourteenth-century Syrian manuscript, the collection that has come to be known as *The Arabian Nights* was part of the contemporary French vogue for fairy tales, fueled in large part by the *contes de fées* authored by aristocratic salon women.[4] From the outset, the *Nights* was a European production intended for European readers, and the many published versions of the *Nights* emphasized and embroidered tales to showcase the fantastic elements with strong affinities to European fairy tales. In this sense, *The Arabian Nights* seems a persuasive starting point for a European fairy-tale canon. For European audiences, however, *The Arabian Nights* was consistently circumscribed by an Orientalist otherness. Born of seventeenth-century European cultural imaginaries and racial formation projects, the *Nights* was indelibly marked in ways that signaled its cultural difference, even when specifically framed as a collection of fairy tales. As such, *The Arabian Nights* has, since its European inception, always been closely allied with but distinct from the European fairy tale, especially as the genre has come to be understood in the popular sense, and for this reason it remains adjacent to the genealogy at the center of *Specters of the Marvelous*.

My decision to begin with Basile's collection also obscures the earlier publication of a dozen or so fairy tales by Giovan Francesco Straparola in his 1550–53 *Pleasant Nights*.[5] Interspersed among the seventy-four tales in the two-volume compendium of predominantly "urban tales of artisans, the bourgeoisie, and the nobility," Straparola's fairy tales clearly anticipate and influence the versions that follow (Bottigheimer 2002, 1; see also Magnanini 2015).[6] "Costantino and His Cat" (11.1), for instance, recounts the now-familiar story of Puss-in-Boots, versions of which appear in Basile's *The Tale of Tales*, Charles Perrault's *Tales from Times*

Past (1697), and the Grimms' *Children's and Household Tales*. Quite a few of Straparola's other fairy tales also make their way into Basile's collection—Nancy Canepa (2007b) identifies nine tales with strong affinities to Straparola's stories as well as several others that adhere to narrative subplots and motifs—and some of the lesser-known tales, like "Prince Pig" (2.1) and "Peter the Fool" (3.1), provide inspiration for the *conteuses*, the aristocratic French women who wrote fairy tales for publication as well as for performance in late-seventeenth-century salons.[7] In *Fairy Tales* (1697) and *New Tales, or Fairies in Fashion* (1698), for example, d'Aulnoy offers her versions of the two tales, "Prince Marcassin" ("Prince Pig") and "The Dolphin" ("Peter the Fool"), and Henriette-Julie de Murat's 1699 *Sublime and Allegorical Stories* includes "The Pig King." Nonetheless, I have chosen to begin this genealogy with Basile's *The Tale of Tales* because it is widely recognized as the first European *collection* of fairy tales and because of its clear influence on later collections (see, e.g., Canepa and Ansani 1997; Canepa 1999, 2007b; Barchilon 2009; Magnanini 2023).

If the originary status of Basile's *The Tale of Tales* is open to debate, so too is d'Aulnoy's place in this genealogy, especially given the later popularity and eventual canonization of Perrault's *Tales from Times Past* and the simultaneous cultural erasure of stories by the *conteuses*. Despite their near invisibility and critical marginalization for most of the twentieth century, however, d'Aulnoy's stories—which established the term *fairy tale*—were wildly popular in her time and continually published through the early twentieth century. In addition to their publication in France, d'Aulnoy's fairy tales, along with her novels and travel narratives, were almost immediately translated into English and reissued with regularity for the next two centuries. According to Melvin Palmer (1969), there were thirty-six British editions of d'Aulnoy's ten works by 1740; even more, her fairy tales appeared in three different translations and multiple reprints, beginning as early as 1699, thirty years before the first English translation of Perrault's *Tales from Times Past* (see also Palmer 1975; Jones 2008; Barchilon 2009). Thus, although nineteenth-century fairy-tale scholars such as the Grimms and Lang embraced and promoted Perrault's tales for their ostensible relationship to oral tradition, thereby further contributing to the *conteuses*' marginalization in increasingly hegemonic accounts of the genre's development, Palmer's bibliographic history reveals d'Aulnoy's unequivocal importance to the history of the European fairy tale: "Mme d'Aulnoy's fairy tales constitute a major chapter ... in the late seventeenth-century French vogue for fairy tales, but she constitutes almost the entire history of the corresponding though less ambitious vogue in England in the early eighteenth century" (1969, 25).[8]

The line from Basile to d'Aulnoy involves more than d'Aulnoy's contemporary renown and her centrality to the eighteenth-century proliferation of the fairy tale, however. As Nancy Canepa and Antonella Ansani demonstrate in the introduction to *Out of the Woods: The Origins of the Literary Fairy Tale in Italy and France*, Basile's use of the fairy tale to engage "a series of social and literary concerns ... was to be fully exploited by the first generation of French tale-writers (especially female authors such as Marie-Catherine d'Aulnoy) who skillfully manipulated the various marginalities associated with the fairy-tale genre to address their own issues of marginality" and to stage "polemical social dramas" (1997, 11, 13). In addition to the fact that "Basile was a concrete point of reference for at least some of the later French authors" and that d'Aulnoy "drew from previous collections (notably those of Giovan Francesco Straparola and Giambattista Basile)" (Barchilon 2009, 353), Canepa and Ansani highlight the sociopolitical similarities between early-seventeenth-century Naples and late-seventeenth-century Paris and suggest that the fairy tale was perfectly suited for "[exploring] alternate literary languages and ideological visions and [developing] with relative freedom critiques of literary traditions and social institutions" (1997, 13). In both cases, shifting monarchical policies and financial needs inspired dramatic and detrimental social and cultural change, not only lowering standards of living for all classes but also curtailing sociopolitical power for court intellectuals like Basile and aristocratic women like d'Aulnoy. The "polemical social dramas" at the heart of their tales thus animate the consequences of royal folly while also, especially in the case of the *conteuses*, imagining utopian alternatives (see, e.g., Zipes 1991 [1983]; Seifert 1996; Canepa and Ansani 1997; Duggan 2005; Canepa 2007b).

Less explicit than these antimonarchical political critiques is another set of polemical social dramas—social dramas driven by ideas about race, racial difference, and white superiority—and it is in this convergence that the genealogical relationship between Basile and d'Aulnoy emerges most clearly. Jacques Barchilon (2009), in his brief catalog of d'Aulnoy's *contes*, notes that of the twenty-four tales in her two collections ten fall under the ATU 425 type (Search for the Lost Husband), five are related to ATU 402 (The Animal Bride), and two involve ATU 403 (The Black and the White Bride).[9] The thematic emphasis articulated in the racialized nexus of these tale types corresponds, in remarkably striking fashion, with Basile's frame tale (a combination of ATU 425 and ATU 403) and the subset of recurring tale types that together reveal the collection's overriding ideological investment in racial difference and white superiority. While the following chapters on Basile's *The Tale of Tales* and d'Aulnoy's *Fairy Tales* and *New Tales, or Fairies in Fashion* delve into the particularities of how these tale types jointly engage the specific cultural languages, discourses, and politics of race surrounding each collection, I mention the association here because it highlights both the literary lineage from Basile to d'Aulnoy and the enduring import of race in the development of the European fairy tale.

In claiming that race is critical to the development of the European fairy tale, I mean more than that it is a persistent motif across different historical periods and cultures. Rather, I am arguing that race—in different manifestations from literal to metaphoric, allusive, and ethnographic—undergirds the European literary fairy tale as it slowly coheres and settles into the familiar genre so easily recognizable today in its popular iterations. This is not to suggest that all fairy tales adhere to precisely the same structure, nor that all are shaped by centuries of racial thinking, only that some of the most iconic ones, tales with a metonymic power to represent the genre, were elaborated and consolidated in and through the racial logics that saturated the cultural and political worlds in which Basile, d'Aulnoy, the Grimms, and Lang wrote. "Beauty and the Beast"—and the broader tale type, ATU 425 (Search for the Lost Husband), of which it is a variant—provides an especially clear example. The two versions in Basile's *The Tale of Tales*, "The Padlock" (2.9) and "The Golden Trunk" (5.4), are essentially Cupid and Psyche stories (ATU 425B, Son of the Witch), and both feature "handsome slave[s]," who welcome the protagonist into their palaces and come to them as unseen nocturnal lovers. That the handsome slaves are Black becomes evident in the course of both narratives, explicitly so in "The Golden Trunk," when the heroine lights a candle to gaze upon her lover and finds that "the ebony had turned to ivory, the caviar to the milkiest milk, and the coal to whitewash," and implicitly in "The Padlock" when, in the same scene, the heroine is surprised to discover that her lover is "a flower of beauty, a young man who was all lilies and roses," the language frequently invoked in the collection to mark white beauty (Canepa 2007a, 406, 201).

While Basile's tales track the Cupid and Psyche tradition quite closely, they differ in one significant way: in each tale, the unseen nocturnal lover is not a god but a man cursed to live as a Black slave, at least by day. In d'Aulnoy's "The Green Serpent," a version of Cupid and Psyche in which the heroine understands her own experience through explicit references to the myth, the unseen lover is neither god nor man but a frightful green serpent, thus combining the animal bridegroom and Cupid and Psyche subvariants in ways that not only anticipate the Beauty and the Beast tradition but also make clear its racialized subtexts. That is, in replacing Basile's Black slaves with animals—a green serpent here, a wild boar in "Prince Marcassin"—d'Aulnoy metaphorizes the literal racializations driving "The Padlock" and "The Golden Trunk." At the same time, d'Aulnoy's animal bridegrooms—with their far stranger, decidedly fantastic, or simply more animalistic environments—bridge the motifemic transition from Basile's handsome Black slaves to the accursed, but still clearly aristocratic and civilized, Beast of the first literary version of "Beauty and the Beast" by Gabrielle-Suzanne Barbot de Villeneuve, whose 1740 novella was adapted and shortened to its canonical form by Jeanne-Marie Leprince de Beaumont in 1756. By the mid-eighteenth century, then, the dominant motifs of the animal bridegroom and the Cupid and Psyche traditions were consolidated in "Beauty and the Beast," one of the most recognizable and widely reproduced of all European fairy tales, further entrenching the tacit (and relentlessly stubborn) affiliation of human Blackness and animality.

Paradoxically, the metaphors that suture Blackness to animality simultaneously render the equivalence exceedingly obvious and increasingly obscured. It is thus no surprise that, while unmarked in the narrative itself, the Beast's racialization continually materializes in the tale's history of illustration and performance. Michelle Smith and Rebecca-Anne Do Rozario's (2016) extensive analysis of Beauty and the Beast portrayals in British children's books, pantomimes, and fairy extravaganzas across the long nineteenth century reveals the imbrication of Orientalism, scientific racism, speciesism, and imperialism as fundamental to the Beast's otherness. Although the Beast's cultural markers of otherness vary depending on whether they appear in print or in performance as well as on the historical timing of their production, they all depict racial difference. As such, according to Smith and Do Rozario, while Orientalism persists as the dominant register of otherness in book illustrations throughout the century, it wanes in stage productions around midcentury when it is "commonly replaced by depictions of, and topical references to apes and black men" (39). Tracing the shifting nineteenth-century representations of the Beast onstage, Smith and Do Rozario read his otherness as a synthesis of Victorian ideologies of difference: "Reflecting anxieties about the maintenance of racial superiority in the age of empire and human superiority in light of theories of evolution, stage adaptations of 'Beauty and the Beast' respond to various categories of Otherness by emphasising the racial difference between black and white, the species difference between human and animal, and sometimes by fusing the two ideas to associate racial difference with animality" (40).

Of course, the racially othered Beast and his animal bridegroom brethren are not the only constructions of racialized human difference in the canonical fairy-tale collections. Basile's frame tale, for instance, positions racial difference—in the form of the Moorish slave girl Lucia and the white princess Zoza—as *the* pivotal conflict motivating the entire storytelling occasion that constitutes *The Tale of Tales*. A literalization of the Black Bride and the White Bride tale type (ATU 403), Basile's frame tale condenses a number of contemporary stereotypes about Black female slaves in the ugly, conniving, abusive Lucia, who usurps Zoza's rightful place as Prince Tadeo's bride. This patently raced conflict is so significant to the meaning of the collection that Basile reiterates the dominant themes of the Black Bride and the White Bride—again literalized—in the collection's penultimate tale, "The Three Citrons" (5.9), essentially a version of the frame tale writ small and an invitation for Zoza to recount her trials, thereby bringing the frame tale to a close with Lucia's outing and violent death. The Black Bride and the White Bride tale type, like Beauty and the Beast, is among the most common fairy tales and appears in multiple variations in d'Aulnoy's *Tales of the Fairies*, the Grimms' *Children's and Household Tales*, and Lang's Colored Fairy Books, all of which I discuss in detail in the chapters that follow.[10] The fact that motifs, tale types, and individual tales recur, carrying forward racialized figurations across this genealogy of the European fairy tale, is not to suggest that they convey the same meanings, however. Rather, each iteration of a motif or tale or character resonates differently depending on its social, historical, and political contexts. As such, even the same beastly lovers, black brides, and stock casts of supporting characters signify different racial logics.

The Grimms' *Children's and Household Tales* and Lang's Colored Fairy Books also include an abundance of lesser-known European tales and tales from other storytelling traditions that speak to the racial and racist concerns particular to the social and political contexts of their production. In the Grimms' collection, for instance, two notoriously antisemitic tales—"The Good Bargain" and "The Jew in the Thornbush"—as well as several others that invoke antisemitic caricatures and tropes not only racialize Jewish identity but also create a paradigm for the anti-Black racism that inhabits tales like "The Three Black Princesses," "The Prince Who Feared Nothing," and the various versions of the Black Bride and the White Bride. Lang's twelve-volume Colored Fairy Book series brings together some of the most canonical and some of the more esoteric European fairy tales and complements them with "savage" tales collected by ethnographers, missionaries, and colonial administrators. This expansion of tales under the explicit sign of "the fairy tale" not only lends further insight into the highly nuanced relationship between race and the development of the European fairy tale but also makes clear the universalizing impulses that emerge in the latter half of the genre's genealogy.

Thus, although the Grimms' *Children's and Household Tales* was motivated by German nationalism, exacerbated by French occupation, it also—ironically—contributed to the universalizing of the genre by virtue of the brothers' extensive notes outlining other versions, variants, and sources. Even more, the early English translation and subsequent popularity of the Grimms' collection in Victorian Great Britain encouraged Lang's belief that tales are essentially universal with local changes occurring over time as cultures "evolved" along a unilinear trajectory, a belief he reiterates in the prefaces to the Colored Fairy Books. The indisputable canonicity of the Grimms' *Children's and Household Tales* and Lang's fairy books, together with the other collections they inspired, only extends and naturalizes the European fairy tale's ostensible universality. Indeed, so thoroughly unquestioned is the assumption of the genre's universality that contemporary scholars continue to perpetuate the belief. Canepa and Ansani, for example, close their introduction to a volume exploring the intertwined histories of the seventeenth- and eighteenth-century Italian and French fairy tales with such a claim: "These tales are, then, the elegant and convincing examples of the fact that the universality of the literary fairy tale consists precisely in its remarkable capacity for being reworked by individual authors into stories of their own times" (1997, 26). Here, Canepa and Ansani articulate beautifully the epistemological imperialism that continually establishes and reestablishes for successive generations the white world of "the fairy tale."

Visualizing the Invisible

Not surprisingly, the whiteness of the fairy-tale world is especially evident in the genre's visual interpretations and adaptations, from fine art and book illustrations to pantomimes, plays, and animations. More than simply translating words into images and performances, however, such portrayals reveal the taken-for-granted nature of the fairy tale's whiteness while also actively adding meaning to the tales, in the process further securing their implicit racism and racial thinking. Sara Hines (2010) provides an outstanding example of this dynamic in her analysis of Henry J. Ford's illustrations for "The Glass Axe" in Lang's *Yellow Fairy Book* (1894). Adapted from Hermann Kletke's Hungarian tale, "The Glass Axe" recounts the story of a prince who is cursed to a terrible fate should his feet ever touch the ground; though protected by every accommodation imaginable, the prince is eventually thrown from his horse while out hunting, only to awaken in a strange land ruled by a fairy who gives him a glass axe with which he must clear a forest before sunset. The fairy also "[cautions] him with many angry words against speaking to a black girl he would most likely meet in the wood" (*Yellow Fairy Book*, 142). When the glass axe shatters upon striking the first tree, the prince wanders the forest in a state of despair until he finally exhausts himself and falls asleep; he awakens to find a Black girl who explains that she, too, is under the fairy's curse, that the fairy is her mother (and that if he lets on that he knows, the girl will die), that she can help him accomplish the impossible tasks her mother sets for him, and that he can eventually free her from her curse by bearing her away. After the prince surprises the fairy by completing a number of her hopeless trials, she spies on him and, upon learning that her daughter is aiding him, lets out a ferocious shriek and gives chase. The girl uses magic to transform them into various objects, thus facilitating their escape. After a series of frightening encounters with the increasingly enraged fairy, the prince disenchants the "black girl"—who becomes "the most beautiful girl he had ever seen"—and together they drown the evil fairy before marrying and "[living] happily for ever afterwards" (147–48).

Ford's illustrations for "The Glass Axe" depict two key scenes. The first, captioned "The black girl stops the witch with a bit of rock," features the dark-skinned girl in loose tunic and harem-style pants and the white prince in royal European hunting garb. The second, captioned with a line from the story ("But the waters seized [the fairy's] chariot and sunk it in the lowest depths"), creates a backdrop of the drowning fairy and her doomed dragon while highlighting, in the foreground, the prince and a young white woman in royal European clothing as they swim away from the dark scene of destruction. As Hines notes, the second illustration is not placed with the text describing the scene, which occurs on the next page; instead, it is positioned such that it "immediately follows the line in the text that indicates the girl has become 'beautiful'" (2010, 43). Hines's reading of this "out-of-sequence" placement is completely persuasive: "The illustration capitalizes on an implication that is latent in the text. . . . Although there is no direct suggestion in the text . . . that the girl changes skin color, these Victorian illustrations, strategically placed in the story, interpret the text for us, and they support the assumption that contemporary readers would have understood the girl to have been transformed from a black woman to a white woman" (43–44). While Hines's careful analysis of the placement of the two illustrations is especially convincing, they need not be positioned in exactly that way to expose the ideologies of race and beauty underpinning the tale. Indeed, the assumption that Blackness is an accursed state in the European fairy tale is clear as early as Basile's "handsome black slave[s]," as is the corollary that disenchantment and its related superlative beauty involve becoming white.

Hines's claim that the "ideologies present in the images are ingrained in the culture to such an extent that they require neither textual definition nor explanation" (44) is further supported by Veronica Schanoes's (2019) reading of several modern retellings of Rumpelstiltskin in relation to the naturalized ethnocentrism of the Grimms' tales. Before focusing on adaptations by Jane Yolen and Naomi Novik, Schanoes highlights the tension between Rumpelstiltskin's presumed Jewishness—not only by Jewish writers but also by participants in online white supremacist fora—and the fact that references to Jews are entirely absent from the Grimms' tale as well as from the scholarly literature about the tale. In the framing notes for their stories, both Yolen and Novik call attention to the details that cast Rumpelstiltskin as a Jew: for Yolen, "he has an unpronounceable name, lives apart from the kingdom, changes money, and is thought to want the child for some unspeakable blood rites," while Novik recalls him as "the sinister caricature of the hunched, long-nosed man whose hands run with gold and who wants to steal golden-haired babies" (quoted in Schanoes 2019, 293).[11] Schanoes speculates that because Rumpelstiltskin is only ever described as a "little man" in the Grimms' tale, "it is illustrations that move Rumpelstiltskin from merely being small to being gnarled, long-nosed, and long-bearded in Yolen's and Novik's understandings" (293). Similarly, the Grimms' tale describes the queen's baby only as "a beautiful child" (Zipes 2003, 195), and Novik's characterization of the child as a "golden-haired [baby]" is thus also likely rooted in the tale's illustrated history as well as the abiding ideological conflation of beauty and whiteness so clearly articulated through the illustrations for "The Glass Axe."

 These examples make clear that fairy-tale meanings emerge from the mutually constitutive relationship of text and image (see also Bodmer 2003; Bottigheimer 2010b; Conrad 2018). Tacit, but clearly present, ideological dimensions of fairy tales are materialized in the accompanying illustrations while the illustrations—and their visual assumptions of race, ethnicity, beauty, character—add to the tale's established meanings and connotations. While such an imbrication of text and image surfaces and solidifies the unarticulated values circulating in and around European fairy tales, the visual register is not a static one. As Smith and Do Rozario establish in their aforementioned analysis of portrayals of Beauty and—especially—the Beast in Victorian and Edwardian illustrated books and stage productions, representations vary according to the particular social, political, and scientific concerns of the era: "The general shift in the ways in which the Beast is Othered—from race to species and back again in the early twentieth century—in part evidences the increasing questioning of the human-animal divide in the second half of the nineteenth century, as well as the ways in which racialised hierarchies were imbricated with questions of species" (2016, 48), an articulation made particularly evident in Jeanne-Marie Leprince de Beaumont's frame narrative for her 1756 "Beauty and the Beast," when Miss Molly compares the Beast to her father's lackey, "a little boy who was all black" (Duggan 2016, 1184).[12] Tracing changes to the Beast's representation over the long nineteenth century in England, Smith and Do Rozario's historical account underscores the fact that as much as illustrations change, they nevertheless continue to render visible the dominant ideas and ideologies of race that continually haunt the European fairy tale.

Although fairy-tale illustrations and performances clearly join literary collections and collectively play a significant role in the historical naturalizing of whiteness in canonical European fairy tales, an in-depth analysis is beyond the scope of *Specters of the Marvelous*, which attends to the literary dimensions of this multifaceted phenomenon.[13] Even so, I include these brief examples because they demonstrate so beautifully how race and racial thinking are structured into many European fairy tales despite their seeming absence. As Toni Morrison (1988, 1993 [1990]) has convincingly demonstrated in her landmark readings of canonical American literature, race need not be figured as an explicit theme, character, or idiom to exert a profound, even fundamental, influence. She assumes that absence does not necessarily signal a lack of presence, "that invisible things are not necessarily 'not-there'; that a void may be empty but not be a vacuum" (1988, 136), and she goes on to describe her project of rereading the American canon as a search for "ghosts in the machine" (138), a project akin to Saidiya Hartman's desire to imagine individual histories out of the archive's silences: "listening for the unsaid, translating misconstrued words, and refashioning disfigured lives" (2008, 3). The long history of fairy-tale illustrations and performances materializes some of those ghosts and ghostly silences, in the process making clear that, far from being a hidden code awaiting critical translation, ideologies of race are so present and pervasive in the European fairy tale that they go wholly unremarked.

The Work of This Book

The work of this book is to make those ideas and ideologies of race remarkable, to render visible the specters long haunting the European fairy tale, and to lay bare the specific workings of race on and in a genre invested with a certain universalism. In so doing, I am not suggesting an interpretive exclusivity, however; rather, I imagine *Specters of the Marvelous* in dialogue with the extensive world of fairy-tale scholarship that seeks to identify and contextualize the misogyny, heterosexism, classism, and ableism (to name some of the critical analyses garnering the most attention) encapsulated and naturalized in the European fairy-tale tradition. Only collectively can fairy-tale studies attend to the genre's hegemonic work from an intersectional perspective, and I hope that the readings that follow contribute another, long overlooked dimension to the critical conversation.

Each of the following chapters revolves around one of the aforementioned canonical collections, connecting close readings of its tales to the specific cultural discourses, scholarly debates, and imperial geopolitics that continually facilitated and renewed ideas about racial difference and white superiority. Read together, the chapters also establish a genealogy of literary influence by tracing key narrative elements and tales as they recur and develop across the collections. I hope that this convergence of literary influence and comparative histories of racialization highlight both the principal role of race in the development of the European fairy tale and the naturalized role of the fairy tale in the development of Western racisms and racial formations.

Chapter 1 focuses on Giambattista Basile's early-seventeenth-century *The Tale of Tales*, widely recognized as the first European collection of fairy tales as well as one of the earliest literary works written in the Neapolitan vernacular. Basile's commitment to publishing in the vernacular signals his awareness of the power and politics of language, and I suggest that this awareness influences the collection's language of slavery at a moment when slavery was becoming increasingly racialized. More specifically, Basile's *The Tale of Tales* animates the historical transition in the language of slavery from a nonracialized, figurative language rooted in the *servitium amoris* (slave to love) tradition of the Roman elegists to a racialized, literal language rooted in the commerce of human bondage.

While naturalized "slave to love" metaphors provide an everyday backdrop for Basile's collection, literal slaves are racially marked and cast as vilified or cursed characters.

The collection's frame tale—and, consequently, the collection itself—is driven by the actions of one such slave, described and referenced only through racist stereotypes and dehumanizing caricatures until the collection's close, when her name is revealed to be Lucia, itself a generalized moniker for female slaves of the period. Basile's frame tale is also writ small in the collection's penultimate tale, "The Three Citrons," a tale whose telling unsettles those present when they recognize that its parallels to their own gathering, over which the socially inappropriate Black queen presides, may cut too close to the bone. Indeed, "The Three Citrons" essentially invites Zoza, the frame tale's true bride, to recount her story, thus leading to Lucia's unmasking and subsequent punishment as well as to the close of the collection. The fact that *The Tale of Tales* opens and closes with two *literalized* versions of the Black Bride and the White Bride tale type (ATU 403)—that the doubled struggle between Black slave and white princess occupies the privileged narrative positions—indicates that race, embodied and emblematized in the figure of the slave, is of critical significance to this foundational collection of European fairy tales. In addition, as mentioned above, *The Tale of Tales* also includes two versions of the Cupid and Psyche and Beauty and the Beast tale types (ATU 425B/C), in which the "beast" characters are Black slaves by day and white princes by night. Based on these mirrored pairings and other tales in the collection, I contend that the transition from figurative "slave *to* love" to literal "slave *in* love" demonstrates not only the undeniable role that such racialized figurations play in the earliest texts but also how such figurations contribute to the future development of the genre.

Many of Basile's characters, narrative elements, and tale types appear in the elaborate literary fairy tales of the French *conteuses* so popular at the turn of the eighteenth century. In *Fairy Tales* and *New Tales, or Fairies in Fashion*, d'Aulnoy invokes these tropes and tale types to create stories that resonate with the philosophies of assimilation and the ideologies of race implicit, and sometimes explicit, in late-seventeenth-century French imperial policy and colonial practices pertaining to New France. In chapter 2, I situate d'Aulnoy's tales—and especially her animal bridegroom stories—alongside contemporary philosophy, early modern articulations of racial difference, New World travel narratives, and the French *Jesuit Relations* in order to draw out their ideological convergences. "Prince Marcassin," for instance, showcases the religious belief in perfectibility and the cultural belief in "Frenchification" that cohere around imperial discourses of the *sauvage*. Alongside "Prince Marcassin," tales like "The Dolphin," "The Ram," and "Belle-Etoile" animate the French imperial fascination with the New World's utopian possibilities—its precious metals and gems, its abundant food supplies, and its "noble savages."

In the chapter's final section, I turn to the latter part of the French fairy-tale vogue in the mid-eighteenth century, when France's colonial priorities had shifted to the Caribbean. Comparing d'Aulnoy's animal bridegroom tales with Gabrielle-Suzanne Barbot de Villeneuve's "Beauty and the Beast" (1740), a lengthy and complicated novella embedded in a collection whose frame tale recounts the rise of a French plantation owner on the island colony of Saint-Domingue, I suggest that the "beastly" husbands make material the different racializations of New World and French Caribbean others.[14] That is, d'Aulnoy's and Villeneuve's tales track the ideological transition from a belief in the inherent assimilability of *les sauvages* in New France to a sense of complete unassimilability of African slaves in the French Caribbean, and this ideological transition is especially evident in the transformation of the sexual dimensions of the Beauty and the Beast tradition, which now requires the beast's complete disenchantment and return to human form before sexual contact occurs, a notable difference from d'Aulnoy's tales and an obvious embrace of the antimiscegenation position formalized in the *Code Noir*.

Eighteenth-century Europe saw a proliferation of scientific and philosophical theories of race and human variability, and chapter 3 sets the Grimms' *Children's and Household Tales* against this backdrop while also attending to the brothers' investment in a German romantic nationalism bolstered by political and cultural antisemitism. Putting the Grimms' explicitly antisemitic tales in conversation with the collection's tales equating Blackness with an accursed or villainous state, I argue that, for the Grimms, German nationalism involves the collapsing of racialized antisemitism and anti-Black racism. The ideological conflation of the two comes to the fore in an extensive catalog of shared stereotypes as well as in the call—made most vigorously by Johann David

Michaelis in the 1780s—for Germany to establish its own "sugar islands," which would not only provide a destination for exiled Jews, "naturally" suited to hard labor in climes intolerable for white gentile Germans, but would also free Germany from its dependence on other imperial powers.

The Grimms' explicitly antisemitic "The Jew in the Thornbush" and "The Good Bargain" thus provide interpretive keys to the collection's tales featuring Black characters, like "The Three Black Princesses" and "The Prince Who Feared Nothing," while also exposing the ways that Blackness is metaphorized and coded in a number of other tales such as "Mother Holle," "The Three Little Gnomes in the Forest," and "The White Bride and the Black Bride." Given the convergence of racialized antisemitism and anti-Black racism, such metaphoric codes also point to the less explicit antisemitism running through *Children's and Household Tales*, and privileging both in my reading of the Grimms' tales reveals a largely unrecognized dimension of the genre's racialized underpinnings. Even more, because the Grimms initiated both a passion among scholars for collecting tales in the spirit of romantic nationalism and an enthusiasm for translations of their fairy tales among popular audiences, *Children's and Household Tales* has had a signal importance in the universalization of the European fairy tale, antisemitic and racist warts and all.

Andrew Lang's twelve-volume Colored Fairy Book series, the focus of chapter 4, extends the European fairy tale's universalization by bringing together tales from western and eastern Europe, Scandinavia, the British Isles, the Mediterranean, East Asia, India, Africa, Oceania, Aboriginal Australia, and the indigenous Americas, all under the sign of "the fairy tale." Beyond the epistemological imperialism inherent in collapsing the world's narrative genres into that of the European fairy tale, the Colored Fairy Books also promote social evolutionary theory, one of Lang's lifelong intellectual commitments. As he explains in most of the series' prefaces, social evolutionary theory posits that all cultures develop along the same trajectory such that a "civilized" society, like Great Britain, is simply at a more advanced evolutionary stage than that of a "savage" society, like those of the indigenous Americas. In the specific case of narrative, Lang contends that tales differ primarily in the degree to which their supernatural and magical elements are both comprehensible and believable by their audience; that is, what a "savage" listener may find sacred or meaningful in a tale is likely to appear nonsensical or curious to a "civilized" listener, for whom the oddity is simply a remnant from an earlier developmental stage. This particular form of universalizing obviously indexes global hierarchies of power, exposing the Colored Fairy Books' tight coupling of epistemological imperialism and real-world empire-building.

The Colored Fairy Books were not the work of Lang alone, however. By his own account, the series was "almost wholly the work of Mrs. [Nora] Lang," who translated and adapted a majority of the tales for a white British audience (*Violet Fairy Book*, 1901, vii). Like her husband, Nora Lang was invested in British imperial ideology, as evidenced most clearly in her geography primers, pedagogical texts that mapped the empire for children. Chapter 4 thus considers the Langs' abiding enthusiasms, their intellectual commitments, and their other projects as interpretive guides to their adaptations of several tales from colonized peoples in Australia, Africa, and North America. Ultimately, I argue, the prefaces to the individual volumes, the strategic adaptations, and the overall arc of the Colored Fairy Books consolidate the British empire and, in showcasing examples of the empire's varied cultural "possessions," paradoxically universalize the European fairy tale by subsuming a diversity of wonder genres under the sign of "the fairy tale."

As I hope the following chapters make clear, the fairy-tale world is white not by chance but by design. Racist beliefs and racialized thinking contributed to the beginnings of the genre as a literary form in the early modern period, from there worked and reworked across time and space, across cultures and languages, until the ideas are so familiar and ubiquitous, so engrained and natural as to go entirely unnoticed. To see the fairy-tale world anew—to notice its remarkable whiteness—involves a seismic shift in perceptions of the genre, a jolt, a shake, a series of unsettling ripples, perhaps some rubble. The concluding chapter celebrates what comes after. More a commencement than a conclusion, the final chapter moves from the historical to the contemporary and introduces a collection of Indigenous, Creole, and postcolonial fairy-tale adaptations, engagements, and contestations—Hawaiian activist storytelling described by Bryan Kamaoli Kuwada and Aiko Yamashiro (2016); short stories by Nalo Hopkinson (2001) and Bolu Babalola (2020); the visual art of Sarindar Dhaliwal (2009); and novels by Helen Oyeyemi (2009, 2011, 2019)—that restore race to the universal and begin the long process of decolonizing both the European fairy-tale canon and fairy-tale studies more generally. Drawing on the spectral politics that emerges across these collected works, I argue that they help return us to wonder by resisting, resituating, and/or reworking European fairy tales in ways that articulate the unmarked racisms haunting the genre, thus transforming not only the world of the fairy tale but also the very world we inhabit.

1
ITALY, 1634–36

Giambattista Basile's
The Tale of Tales

The first European collection of literary fairy tales hinges on a slave. Composed in the early seventeenth century and published posthumously between 1634 and 1636, Giambattista Basile's *The Tale of Tales* presents five days of storytelling set within a fairy-tale frame featuring a melancholy princess, an enchanted prince, and a "false bride" in the form of a Moorish slave. Closer in structure to that of the *Arabian Nights* than Boccaccio's *Decameron*, Basile's frame tale provides both a diegetic logic for the enclosed tales and an opportunity for metacommentary in each tale's preface before it ultimately converges with the final tale. The story begins with the princess Zoza, whose father finds her lack of laughter so troubling that he invites and invents endless entertainments to delight her. When none succeed, he installs a public fountain of oil, imagining that such a slippery creation might lead to any number of hilarious incidents. And indeed it does: an old woman stops to soak up the oil; a court page throws a stone at her, breaking her jar; they fall into a colorful exchange of insults and curses; and the old woman, now angry beyond words, "[raises] her stage curtain and [reveals] a woodsy scene" (Canepa 2007a, 37). Finally, the princess laughs. While Zoza's laughter may thrill the king, it just compounds the old woman's rage, and she literally curses Zoza to a single potential husband, Prince Tadeo of Round Field, who has himself been cursed into an enchanted sleep from which he can be awakened only by a woman who fills a dedicated pitcher with her tears in three days' time, a seemingly impossible task. Melancholy Zoza is up to the challenge, however, and she sets out for Round Field, along the way meeting three fairy sisters who give her magical objects to be used in time of extreme need; after seven years, she finds the enchanted prince and begins filling the pitcher with her tears. In a mere two days, the pitcher is nearly full, and Zoza, exhausted from so much crying, falls asleep.

Cut to the slave.[1]

As it turns out, a "cricket-legged slave girl" (39) has been patiently watching Zoza, plotting to "wrench that fine booty from Zoza's hands and leave her with a fistful of flies" (39). After gently removing the pitcher of tears from the sleeping Zoza, the slave tops it off with a few of her own, thus returning Tadeo to life; true to the letter of the curse, upon awakening Tadeo "[takes] hold of that mass of black flesh, and [carries] her off to his palace where, amid festivities and royal fireworks, he [makes] her his wife" (39). Zoza, after awakening to the empty pitcher and subsequently learning of the royal wedding, realizes that "two black things had brought her to her downfall: sleep and a slave" (39). Hoping for a second chance to win the only man she can marry, Zoza moves into a house across from the palace, where "one day she was sighted by Tadeo, who like a bat was always flying round that black night of a slave but became an eagle when he fixed his eyes upon Zoza" (39). The slave princess is quick to recognize Tadeo's attraction to Zoza, and she threatens him with injury to their unborn child: "If you no move from windowsill, me punch belly and little Georgie kill" (40). At this point, Zoza turns to her magical objects, each of which the slave desires with such tremendous passion that she threatens to kill their unborn child if Tadeo does not acquire it for her. Zoza generously gifts each object to the royal couple, but in the final case she first asks the magical doll to "instill in the slave's heart the desire to hear tales" (41). *The Tale of Tales* is the unfolding of that desire, animated by ten old women who come to tell stories to the royal couple over the course of five days.

The "cricket-legged slave girl" may be the frame tale's driving force, but she is not the only slave in *The Tale of Tales*. Slaves feature prominently in "The Padlock" (2.9), "The Golden Trunk" (5.4), and "The Three Citrons" (5.9), and Lisa, the protagonist of "The Little Slave Girl" (2.8), while not a slave, is treated as one. Collectively, these characters—especially the female slaves—condense dominant beliefs about slaves in the contemporary Italian cultural imagination:[2] prone to duplicity and thievery, generally untrustworthy, often willing to use pregnancy to better their situations, linguistically deficient, and deserving of unchecked physical and verbal abuse (see, e.g., Origo 1955; Epstein 2001). At the same time, their ethnic and religious otherness—Moor, Saracen, "Allah lover" (Canepa 2007a, 438)—is reified in their Blackness and punctuated by racialized physical markers such as "cricket-legged" (39, 438), "thick-lipped" (197, 438), "wiggle ass" (438). Beyond this culturally recognizable language of racial and ethnic difference, Basile's endless devotion to metaphor further amplifies the association between blackness and a dehumanized otherness: a "mass of black flesh"; a "black thing"; a "black night of a slave"; a "statue of jet" (439); an "ink blot" (439); the "black mourning" draped on the "freshly whitewashed house" (439). In the few instances where Basile extends his descriptions of slaves beyond metaphors of blackness, he still dehumanizes them by invoking a language of animality—monkey, bitch, horse, crow. Whether through Basile's metaphors of blackness or through readily identifiable cultural markers of racial difference, *The Tale of Tales* is replete with an undeniably material language of slavery.

Echoes of this material language of slavery reverberate throughout *The Tale of Tales* in another, much more figurative, language of slavery. Human and animal characters—as often royal as common, as often magical as not—regularly pledge themselves as "slaves" to others: "I give myself to you like a little slave girl in chains, now and forever after" (186); "I could give myself to the one and the other like a slave in chains" (232); "command me as you wish, since I'll be your bought slave" (354); "we want more than ever to be your slaves" (250). When characters are not directly expressing their devotion to each other by figuratively enslaving themselves, Basile metaphorizes slavery's tropes to convey their intense sexual attraction and amorous bonds. In "The Green Meadow" (2.2), for instance, the narrator Ceca describes the prince's pursuit of Nella as his throwing "the hook of amorous servitude to that bream so many times that he finally stuck her in the gills of her affection and made her his" (153), and Ciulla, the narrator of "The Two Little Pizzas" (7.4), concludes her tale with the king freeing Marziella from the sorceress's literal chains and "fabricating another, even stronger chain in his own heart" (349).

Even more, Basile's distinctive metaphoric characterizations ensure that this figurative language of slavery permeates the collection in both explicit and implicit ways. In one complexly layered description from "The Two Little Pizzas" (7.4)—"when that black Moor of a Night came out to play *tubba catubba* with the stars" (348)—a metaphor of racialized ethnic difference encodes a series of associations inherent in its cultural references and eventually leads to the slave at the center of the figuration. *Tubba catubba*, according to Nancy Canepa's footnote, is a "dance similar to the Sfessania" (348n11), often conflated with the "dance of Lucia," commonly known as "bitchy Lucia" (36 and 36n6), as Canepa's further reference to an earlier footnote in the frame tale makes clear. That earlier footnote quotes from Roberto De Simone's 2002 Italian edition of *The Tale of Tales*:

> In the sixteenth and seventeenth centuries, the Moorish "dance of Lucia" was widely performed in Naples. It derived from the ecstatic dances of possession characterized by continuous spinning, like those that today are still performed by dervishes. Already "desacralized" in the sixteenth century, it was transformed into a ritualistic Carnival performance.... The ambiguous character of Lucia was played by a man in blackface, dressed as an Oriental woman, whose song and movements referred to the sexual act, birth, death, and resurrection. The accompanying chorus insulted Lucia with the epithet of "bitch." ... Later this dance was confused with the dance of Sfessania, which took its name from the city of Fez in Morocco. (36n6)[3]

Lucia is more than simply the name—clearly not a "Moorish" one—given to this dance of parodic otherness, however. Rather, Lucia was among the two or three most common names assigned to female slaves in Italy during the medieval and early modern periods (Epstein 2001, 26–27), and by Basile's time it had clearly come to serve as a generic term for a female slave. Even more, as Suzanne Magnanini notes, such cultural associations also sexualized the female slave by aligning her with the promiscuous stock character from Neapolitan street theater (2023, 213). In "The Three Citrons" (5.9), for instance, the Moorish slave girl, clearly an avatar of the frame tale's slave princess, twice calls herself "unfortunate Lucia" (Canepa 2007a, 438) as she bemoans her life as a slave; that this is not her proper (slave) name becomes clear when she later refers to herself as Giorgia. The ironic humor of Giorgia referring to herself as Lucia certainly would not be lost on Basile's contemporaries: as Paul Nettl points out, in the sixteenth- and seventeenth-century "Mauresque"—"the dance of the black man" and the pantomimes derived from those dances—"[t]he regular Negro characters were the comical Negresses Giorgia and Lucia" (1944, 111). Giorgia's use of the generic Lucia to refer to her slave status, occurring as it does in the collection's penultimate tale, sets the stage for the princess slave's unmasking on the final day of storytelling when she is for the first time referred to by her proper (slave) name: Lucia. And, in both instances, it is the slave girls' improper sexuality—their status as "false brides"—that drives the story. Like so many fairy-tale names, Lucia thus functions as an aptronym, which Basile makes undeniably clear when he writes that "Lucia truly acted like a Lucia" (Canepa 2007a, 443) while listening to Zoza's tale.

Carmela Bernadetta Scala suggests that Basile's use of the name Lucia to refer to the frame tale's false bride "exemplifies his typically Baroque inversions by coupling the 'black, ugly, deceitful slave' with Saint Lucy, a celebrated Christian saint who represents 'illuminating grace'" (2014, 72);[4] the tension implicit in such a coupling depends on the doubled inversions of religion (Christian and Moor) and color-based character ("black"/ "deceitful" and "illuminating grace") and underscores the slave bride's complete otherness. Through these layered significations—Blackness, Moor, Lucia as a common slave name—Lucia condenses physical and psychological characteristics that convey quite clearly the emergent racializations underpinning slavery in the early modern Neapolitan and Italian contexts, cultural contexts still informed by complex histories of Mediterranean slavery in which "Europeans, Ottomans, North Africans, and sub-Saharan Africans enslaved, traded, and ransomed or freed each other" (Magnanini 2023, 208).[5] As such, the layered associations implicit in Basile's metaphor of "that black Moor of a Night" playing the *tubba catubba* call attention to the fact that the figurative language of racialized ethnicity cannot be separated from ideologies of slavery in *The Tale of Tales*, and this particular movement from metaphor ("that black Moor of a Night") to materiality (Lucia, the slave princess) highlights the tightly bound nature of the collection's two languages of slavery.

In *Speaking of Slavery: Color, Ethnicity, and Human Bondage in Italy*, Steven Epstein (2001) identifies the ways in which Italian might itself be considered a language of slavery. Excavating the slave at the heart of that most familiar of Italian salutations—*ciao!*—Epstein argues that histories and ideologies of Italian slavery are deeply imbricated with everyday language and culture, and his brief explanation of *ciao*'s etymology inspires a number of important cultural questions:

> Ciao! This familiar greeting and salutation derives from the expression "(vostro) schiavo," "(your) slave." Probably first used in Venice, the word recalls the elaborate courtesies of past centuries, when refined people spoke as though they were slaves or servants, without irony or comradely solidarity with their inferiors. And yet, why a slave? Why would a free person want to be a slave in any context? The meaning of this type of reversal is hard to recover, but a small problem of etymology prompts larger questions about slavery. (xi)

While Epstein primarily focuses on Italian slavery in the medieval and early modern periods, he situates that history within the broader context of Italian understandings of "race," *avant la lettre*, and contends that setting aside modern ideas about race—focusing instead on medieval and early modern ideas about skin color and ethnic labels—might help pinpoint both the emergence of racialized thinking and the origins of racism in Europe. For Epstein, the medieval and early modern periods represent a transition between two distinctly different forms of slavery—on the one hand, Roman slavery, which he characterizes as "nonracist, especially in the western Mediterranean," and, on the other hand, the slave trade of early modern Europe, which he characterizes as "profoundly racist" (81). Somewhere between the two, he argues, "lay the roots of racism" (81).

Between the two also lay the creation and publication of *The Tale of Tales*. As such, the questions that Epstein raises with regard to slavery's influence on Italian language and culture—"[W]hy a slave? Why would a free person want to be a slave in any context?" (xi) and, implicitly, where, in time and space, might we locate the origins of European racism?—are especially productive for understanding the collection's doubled language of slavery. Against the backdrop of Epstein's conjoined questions, the coexistence of these languages and the coexistence of figurative and literal slaves in *The Tale of Tales* calls attention to the ways that racial thinking simultaneously underpins and drives the collection as well as the emergent genre of the literary fairy tale itself. Despite the fact that *The Tale of Tales* hinges on a slave, that it is saturated with the figurative and literal languages of slavery, Suzanne Magnanini's "Ogres and Slaves: Representations of Race in Giambattista Basile's Fairy Tales" (2023) is the only critical engagement with the collection to address race in any substantive way. This general disciplinary shortcoming limits critical and interpretive histories of the collection as well as an understanding of the full extent to which *The Tale of Tales* has influenced the development of the European literary fairy tale as a genre.

Slaves to Love

Situating Epstein's perplexing questions—"Why a slave? Why would a free person want to be a slave in any context?"—alongside Basile's *The Tale of Tales* suggests a correspondence between the earliest European fairy tales and Roman love elegy, a genre commonly defined by the poet-speaker's adoption of the *servitium amoris* (slave to love) trope, a trope Gian Biagio Conte considers "the center of [elegy's] . . . ideological system" (1994, 37) and one fully developed "only in the Augustan elegy" (Lyne 1979, 121). Although Epstein traces several medieval and early modern ideologies of Italian slavery to the Roman Empire and emphasizes the cultural continuities between classical Rome and medieval and early modern Italy, he overlooks Roman love elegy and the *servitium amoris* trope as possible inspirations for a free person's willing self-characterization as slave to another. And yet, as Barbara Gold points out, despite the fact that the genre existed for only about forty years, it had "an extraordinary and long-lived influence on subsequent art and literature" (2012, 1).

Thematically, Roman love elegy is a decidedly gendered performance of emotional turmoil as expressed by the speaker-poet, "a young man in love, suffering the vicissitudes of enslavement to desire for his elusive mistress" (Janan 2012, 376).[6] In profoundly intertextual and allusive ways, the principal Roman elegists—Gallus, Propertius, Tibullus, and Ovid (whom most scholars have read as ironically engaged with the tradition)—invoke, consolidate, and institutionalize the *servitium amoris* trope as their poet-speakers share their diegetic experiences of being anguished lovers, their experiences of servile humility and humiliation, of grief and suffering, abasement and degradation at the hands of their mistresses. Within this context, love's chains are a dominant metonym and, according to Frank Copley, a uniquely Roman one (1947, 299), but more than the physical torment of love's chains or the pain from love's other punishments by torch or whip, it is the ontology of slavery that truly anchors the *servitium amoris* trope. Along these lines, Copley argues that "it is not so much that the lover suffers; rather it is the peculiarly slavish manner in which he suffers, and the spirit with which he accepts his sufferings that are brought out by these features of *servitium amoris*" (299). R.O.A.M. Lyne makes a similar point that "the crucially relevant aspect of slavery for the image is . . . the *servility* of the slave as a social institution" (1979, 118, emphasis in the original).

For the Roman elegists, servility was thus more than a language to communicate their personal experiences of love as suffering and torture. It was also an ideology, perhaps the very definition, of love—Copley contends that for the Roman elegists "*servitium* is virtually a synonym for *amor*" (1947, 291)—and they "taught that in line with their own behavior all lovers should be prepared to be slaves and, better still, willing and eager slaves" (Murgatroyd 1981, 604). Given this pedagogical impulse and the remarkable and lasting cultural influence of Roman love elegy, it is easy to imagine that the *servitium amoris* tradition would have been widely known in the medieval and early modern periods, especially among those that Epstein identifies as most likely to be engaged in "the elaborate courtesies of past centuries when refined people spoke as though they were slaves or servants" (2001, xi). According to Hérica Valladares, "Latin love elegy had, by the second century C.E., become part of a popular Roman discourse on the emotions" (2012, 335).

In addition to a naturalized familiarity with the language of slavery implicit in the *servitium amoris* trope, elites of the medieval and early modern periods would have also recognized the many demeaning—often emasculating—tasks elegiac lover-poets frequently imagined and described themselves undertaking for their mistresses: "[H]e is to carry her parasol, make way for her in the crowd, pull out her footstool, take off or put on her shoes, hold her mirror, run her errands, escort her home by night, hasten through heat or cold to do her bidding" (Copley 1947,

293). As duties typically assigned to female slaves, these tasks would have been incredibly shameful and humiliating for a free man to perform in the service of a woman during the Roman era; over time, however, many have become commonly associated with polite "gentlemanly" behavior (so gentlemanly, in fact, as to now be considered sexist).

The parallels between the behaviors and linguistic practices associated with being a slave to love suggest that the *servitium amoris* trope may have been taken up by "refined people" in the salutation *votro schiavo* (your slave)—and eventually collapsed into the salutation *ciao!*—in the same way that formerly demeaning tasks were transformed into elite behaviors. In this way, elites might draw on the familiar language of the elegiac poet-lover's enslavement to his beloved in order to express to each other the depth of their relationships. Indeed, when Filadoro says to the prince in "The Dove" (2.7), "I give myself to you like a little slave girl in chains" (Canepa 2007a, 186), Canepa refers the reader to Benedetto Croce's footnote, in his 1925 Italian translation, that this was a formulaic way of signing letters, evidence of the ubiquity of voluntary enslavement as a theme in the vernacular expression of intimacy.

Reading *The Tale of Tales* in conversation with—and as shaped by—Roman love elegy and the *servitium amoris* trope is particularly helpful in distinguishing Basile's figurative language of slavery from the prodigious use of metaphor that he indulges throughout the collection. When Basile's characters invoke chains, fetters, and yokes to convey their love and attraction, when they willingly offer themselves as slaves to others, they are participating in an established and systematic cultural language of slavery to love formalized and elevated by the Roman elegists, in whose hands "it reached its highest development" (Murgatroyd 1981, 596). The striking correspondences between Basile's figurative language of slavery and the *servitium amoris* trope thus clearly suggest more than historical resonances and indirect cultural influence; rather, they point to an extensive intertextual relationship, one that highlights the ways that naturalized ideas about slavery profoundly influence *The Tale of Tales*.

Basile's intertextual engagement with Roman love elegy is perhaps most explicit in "The Crucible," the eclogue that follows the first day's entertainments. In this staged dialogue—presented in verse in Italian—the courtiers Fabiello and Iacovuccio imagine what an enchanted crucible with the power to separate reality from appearance might reveal about different members of society, from high-ranking lords, counts, and knights to obedient servants, from swashbucklers and flatterers to prostitutes and women whose cosmetics hide their true appearances. Among those they subject to the crucible is the lover:

> Here we have the lover: he believes the hours he spends and squanders in the service of Love to be happy ones. The flames and chains are sweet to him; the arrow that pierces him because of a great beauty is dear to him. He confesses that he craves death and barely manages to live; he calls suffering joy, delirium and torment amusement, heartbreak and lovesickness pleasure. He eats no meal that brings him benefit, gets no sleep that is worth anything: half-baked sleep and meals without gusto. Though he earns no pay he patrols outside the beloved doors, though he is no architect he makes sketches and builds castles in the air, and though he is no executioner he tortures his own life without end.... But if you put him in the crucible, you'll realize there's a substratum of madness, a sort of consumption, a state ever uncertain between fear and hope ever suspended between doubt and suspicion.... And even if he finally warms the ice and chips away at the stone of the one he loves, she who is nearest to him when she is farthest away, he no sooner tastes the sweetness than he repents! (Canepa 2007a, 136)

Iacovuccio's description of the lover consolidates Roman elegy's dominant images, upheld as distinctive markers of the genre in the critical literature. Copley, for instance, emphasizes the poet-lover's subjection to chains and flames (as well as whips and lashes): "Tibullus, his hands bound behind his back, has learned the lesson of love's power from the lash of Venus herself; he will never refuse to submit to her chains and whips; his *saeva puella* [cruel girl] burns him with the torch; the proud and the unfaithful lover alike, he says, must expect the fire, the rack, the steel, and the twisted lash across his back" (1947, 296). Relatedly, Murgatroyd sees in Tibullus's line "the chains of a beautiful girl hold me bound" (1.1.55) the Roman elegists' most original contribution to the *servitium amoris* trope (1981, 596–97), and Mathilde Skoie likewise highlights love's chains as the trope's privileged metonym: "The poet/lover is all along shackled in the chains of love in the figure of the *servitium amoris*" (2012, 92). As Iacovuccio suggests, however, the lover nonetheless finds a certain joy, amusement, and pleasure in the pain of his enslavement, what David Wray characterizes as the lover-poet's practice of "adding the spice of masochistic thrill to the sweetness of the (impossible) bliss he envisions" (2012, 35–36), and it is this masochistic pleasure that ensures the poet-lover "eagerly offers to reduce himself to servile status" (Murgatroyd 1981, 604) despite the tortures, doubts, and suspicions that constantly plague him. Indeed, Joseph Farrell stresses that doubt and suspicion are themselves defining features of the lover-poet, who "lives in a state of constant jealousy, enthrallment, and inability to satisfy the whims of his *domina* ['mistress' in the literal sense of a woman in a position of domination over others]" (2012, 13).

Perhaps the most direct citation of the *servitium amoris* trope is Iacovuccio's portrayal of the lover watching his *domina*'s door: "Though he earns no pay he patrols outside the beloved doors," an obvious echo of Tibullus's self-representation as sitting like a "slave guardian before her hard doors" (1.1.53–6). A highly debased and idiosyncratic demonstration of devotion, the paraclausithyron or "song of the locked-out lover" is "a defining *topos* of elegy" (Sharrock 2012, 75), and numerous critics call attention to the poet-lover "hanging about her door, wheedling and whining to be let in" (Miller 2012, 56), "weeping outside her door, pleading to be admitted" (James 2003a, 101).

If the locked door and the chains of love are the recurring metaphors at the heart of Roman elegy and the *servitium amoris* trope, love's arrow is in many ways its originary figuration, at least insofar as Ovid writes himself into the tradition by articulating form and content in a retrospective claim to the genre's creation (Bowditch 2012, Leach 2012, Sharrock 2012, Wray 2012). By stealing a foot from Ovid's verse, Cupid forces the poet into writing love elegy instead of the more respectable epic: "The Ovidian corpus begins with an act of vandalism by the god of Love against the poet's attempts to write in continuous hexameters (equal lines of six metrical feet) and thus in the lofty vein of epic: Cupid steals a foot from every second line and forces the poet into a different mode" (Sharrock 2012, 70). In this context, Iacovuccio's description of the lover holding dear to the "arrow that pierces him because of a great beauty" is productively ambiguous, calling to mind at least two effects that Cupid's arrow might have on the lover-poet—binding him to the *domina* of elegy and binding him to elegy itself.

The fact that Iacovuccio and Fabiello choose to subject the poet to the crucible immediately after the lover suggests that Basile is playing not only with the cultural conventions of the *servitium amoris* trope but also with the dual effects of Cupid's arrow on the lover-poet. Even more, as Canepa notes, Iacovuccio uses Italian—not Neapolitan—when offering examples of the "thousands and thousands of new turns of phrase" (2007a, 136) with which the poet preoccupies himself, and for Canepa, the use of Italian in this context signals Basile's parodying of the Petrarchan love lyric. Given Petrarch's importance to the neo-Latin return of Roman love elegy (Hooley 2012, 493) and the interconnections among Roman love elegy, Petrarchan love lyric, and modern European elegy (Ludwig 1971), Basile's parody underscores the foundational significance of the genre to the long genealogy of European love poetry (and broader "love genres," such as the literary fairy tale), although no subsequent forms cohere around the *servitium amoris* trope with the same intensity, nor are their poetic love objects such cruel mistresses.

Roman elegy is, of course, focalized through the male poet-lover, but it necessarily revolves around his female beloved, a *puella* (girl) or *domina* to whom he has figuratively enslaved himself. While modern critics are divided as to whether such enslavement and its associated social inversions translate into a genuine agency for the *domina* (Gold 2012, 3; Greene 2012, 370), the *trope* of the *domina* portrays her as powerful, domineering, and cruel above all else.[7] In addition, as Sharon James persuasively argues, "[t]his generic woman can be nothing other than a courtesan of formidable intelligence, education, and independence" (2003b, ix), a *docta puella* or "'learned girl' who can understand, appreciate, and evaluate the literary strategies of a given poet" (7). As a courtesan, she is by her profession always already fickle, thus inciting doubt and jealousy in the poet-lover, and while often physically attractive beyond compare, the ever-fleeting beauty of youth demands that she secure her economic future while she can, a tendency the poet-lover often perceives as her greedy desire for gifts, the bestowing of which he believes should give him unpaid access to her bed. Despite his willing servitude to such a *puella* and his seemingly enthusiastic and masochistic embrace of the suffering she inspires, the lover-poet also harbors a "constantly submerged but subconsciously felt" desire to punish and hurt her (James 2003b, 188); thus, according to James, "he regularly expresses, and occasionally indulges in, an urge to violence against his beloved . . . that belies the passivity of *servitium amoris*" (147).

Although Roman love elegy is predicated on the impossibility of an enduring romantic relationship between poet-lover and *domina* and is thus antithetical to the emergent European literary fairy tale with its predominantly happy endings, the dynamic between poet-lover and *domina* nonetheless adds an important dimension to Basile's figurative language of slavery. In "Sapia" (5.6), for instance, the titular character is the quintessential *docta puella*, and she acquires her name by virtue of the "great knowledge she had accumulated in thirteen years" (Canepa 2007a, 419). Hoping to educate his "thick-headed" son, the king of Closed Castle sends the boy to Sapia, imagining that she will have a positive effect on the prince (418); Sapia, however, finds the prince unwilling to learn anything, and in her frustration she gives him "a nice slap on the face" (419). Gravely humiliated by Sapia's action, the prince is inspired to learn everything, and he soon becomes the wisest man in the kingdom. Still, his humiliation at Sapia's hand continues to torment him to the point where he decides "either to die or to avenge himself" (419). With this in mind, he marries Sapia, installs her in a locked room, and deprives her of ample food and drink. Confused as to the reason for his punishing behavior, she asks, "What was the point of asking me to be your wife if you wanted to keep me worse than a slave?," and when he reminds her of his humiliation, she doesn't apologize but rather reproaches him for his stupidity: "If I slapped you, I did it because you were an ass and I thought it would wisen you up: you know that those who love you make you cry, and those who do not make you laugh" (420). Although the prince and Sapia are eventually united in romantic love (after several ruses orchestrated by Sapia's mother and the prince's acceptance of Sapia's great wisdom), the tale reads like a parable—or perhaps parody—of the *servitium amoris* tradition, including the lover-poet's predilection for humiliation and tears and his urge to violence, here actually realized.

If "Sapia" stages a version of the *servitium amoris* tradition, "Pride Punished" (4.10) provides a compelling example of how the trope not only informs the figurative language of slavery in *The Tale of Tales* but also reveals its racialized underpinnings. In this tale, the king of Long

Furrow seeks an eligible husband for his daughter, Cinziella, "as beautiful as a moon" but also so proud as to "[give] heed to no one" (371). The king of Lovely Land is especially taken by her, but his tireless efforts are to no avail: "[T]he more he weighed the scales of his servitude in her favor, the more she measured out crooked rewards" (372). Weighed down by his increasing (figurative) servitude and full of despair, his daily laments clearly position her as *domina*:[8] "When, O cruel lady, after so many melons of hope that I've found to be white squash, will I be able to taste a red one? When, O cruel bitch, will the tempests of your cruelty calm?" (372). Like the prince of "Sapia," the king of Lovely Land takes his revenge through an elaborate series of ruses. He first disguises himself as a peasant and gains access to Cinziella's bed by exchanging three beautiful garments for three consecutive nights with her, during which she becomes pregnant; he then takes her to his kingdom, still in disguise, and ostensibly begs a place for them to stay in the king's stables. Once there, his punishments are unusually cruel: he helps her get work in the palace and encourages her to steal small items—pieces of bread, scraps of cloth—so they can survive; while she is doing so, he enters as king, "catches" her in the act of stealing, and demands she be punished. His mother, in on the ruse, finally intervenes when Cinziella goes into labor, and the sight of the newborn twin sons is enough to reunite the two in romantic love, although not before the king gives Cinziella an explicit lesson in humility.

While the tormented lover's address to his cruel mistress and the exchange of gifts for sex certainly reproduce the dominant features of the *servitium amoris* trope, it is in the king's earlier vow of revenge that the underlying racialization of Basile's figurative language of slavery becomes clear: "[H]e solemnly swore to take a revenge on that dark Saracen that would force her to repent for having so tormented him" (372). Nowhere in the tale is Cinziella described in terms that would indicate her identity as a literal Saracen; indeed, by Western conventions, the comparison of her beauty to the moon suggests her pale complexion, and while some Saracens were unquestionably light skinned, in *The Tale of Tales* they are always Black slaves.[9] Here, then, Basile's characteristic Baroque inversion is in effect on both the diegetic and extradiegetic levels: the king of Lovely Land inverts the gender dynamic at the heart of the *servitium amoris* trope when he exacts his desire for violence and revenge, and Basile inverts the trope's most identifiable figuration such that the *domina* becomes the slave when he equates the "cruel mistress" with "dark Saracen." Through this elision of "cruel lady" / "cruel bitch" and "dark Saracen," Basile introduces race into the *servitium amoris* trope and, in so doing, also reconfigures its gendered politics of power in a foreshadowing of the tale's remaining action as well as in his figurative language of slavery.

Slaves in Love

The racialization of the *servitium amoris* trope through Basile's conflation of the *domina* and the Saracen is not an idiosyncratic nor innocent slippage, as Lucia's characterization in the frame tale makes abundantly clear. In contrast to Cinziella, Lucia is, of course, a literal slave positioned as *domina*, not *domina* figured as slave; nonetheless, the effect on Basile's figurative language of slavery is the same and highlights the deeply imbricated nature of his two languages of slavery. While understanding Lucia as *domina* may seem counterintuitive given the *domina*'s classical representation as "intelligent, educated, elegant, charming, sexually attractive, and financially needy but socially independent" (James 2003b, 26), Basile's prodigious talent for the literary inversion and subversion characteristic of Baroque style and innovation opens up such a reading. Indeed, as Canepa argues, Basile's deep investment in metamorphosis—emblematic of the Baroque problematic concerning the tensions between appearance and reality—is such that "reality ultimately assumes the aspect of a continuum in which everything can eventually and inevitably become its other" (1999, 220). *Domina* as slave; slave as *domina*.

The idea of Lucia as *domina* is evident in more than Basile's literary inversions, however. Given Roman love elegy's self-presentation as a genre of lament,[10] it should be no surprise that the dynamic between poet-lover and *domina* is one marked by weeping—and especially male weeping. Thorsten Fögen claims that "in Roman love elegy, there is weeping everywhere" (2009, 181), and James underscores the particularly gendered nature of that weeping: "The weeping male lover is a hallmark of the genre, and his talent for tears is prodigious.... Male tears are thus a property of elegiac love, and they generally derive from the *puella*'s cruelty, the misery of love, the separation of lover from *puella*, and quarrels. Men weep because elegiac love naturally engenders tears, these being a generic symptom of passive servility to a hard, demanding woman" (2003a, 99, 103–4). James goes on to argue that the male poet-lover has a complex desire—a complex need, even—to see his *puella* weep precisely because he blames and resents her for his suffering, because he harbors a (perhaps) suppressed longing for revenge, and because her tears are evidence of her love for him. As such, he "enjoy[s] the fantasized prospect of [his] mistress weeping on [his] account" and "seek[s] reassurance in female tears" (99–100). Fögen, by contrast, contends that the genre's abundant weeping is very often "stripped of its seriousness and deployed for humorous ends" (2009, 181), and while he certainly offers persuasive textual evidence to support such a reading, his dismissal of James's nuanced interpretation as simply "not proven to be convincing" (196) ignores both the likely psychological dimensions of such a *fantasy* of female tears and the fact that the two readings are not incompatible.

Although there are undeniably ironic and satiric uses of weeping in Roman love elegy—particularly in Ovid's *Ars amatoria*, which critics tend to read as an ironic take on the tradition as a whole—James's interpretation is significant for any consideration of the place of tears in *The Tale of Tales* because it accords with the *tropes* of Roman love elegy. Weeping, according to James, is "part of a strategic program in the complex game of elegiac love affairs" (2003a, 100), and the *domina*'s reputation for deception leaves the poet-lover wondering whether her tears are genuine, whether they are "invented or purposeful rather than expressions of feeling" or "a stratagem (*insidiis*) for affecting his emotions" (104). Fögen also highlights the elegiac discourse on false tears, reiterating the cynical emphasis on female deception and situating it within a long history of male suspicion of female tears, which he traces at least to Aristotle (2009, 187). Tom Lutz, in his *Crying: The Natural and Cultural History of Tears*, cites examples of the belief in strategic female tears from late antiquity: "Publius Syrus wrote in the first century A.D. that 'women have learned to shed tears in order that they might lie the better,' and Cato, in the second century, offered the maxim: 'When a woman weeps she is constructing a snare with her tears'" (1999, 56). Clearly, as Donald Lateiner points out, such disingenuous and calculated female tears prove "a favoured topic of cynical male authors through the centuries" (2009, 280) and are ubiquitous in the European cultural imagination.

The theme of false female tears necessarily implicates Lucia, who steals prince Tadeo from Zoza by topping off the pitcher of tears she had earlier filled to near completion. More than simply marking her as a conventionally deceitful female weeper, however, Lucia's false tears are central to her figuration as *domina* in Basile's Baroque inversion and subversion of the Roman love elegy. Clearly capable of producing tears on demand, Lucia seems to have learned well from Dipsas, Ovid's female *praeceptor amoris*, who advises the *puella* that if she wants to "capture a man for herself alone," she must become an actress with "the ability to weep at will," among other things (Fögen 2009, 194). Lucia's gift for strategic tears condenses the multiple forms of deception associated with the *puella*—especially one who has embraced the talents of an actress—and ensures that she is characterized by her deceitfulness above all else: "she who deceitfully took from others what was theirs" (Canepa 2007a, 35); "she had seen in the tale of the other slave the spitting image of her own deceits" (443); "the slave's deceit in taking [Zoza's] good fortune out of her hands" (444).

Once Lucia secures Tadeo with her false tears, she continues to act as his *domina*, evidenced in the language of servitude that Basile invokes to describe the prince: "[t]he prince, who had let himself be harnessed by the Moorish slave" (40); "Tadeo, who let this bitch give him the runs and pull on his tail" (40); "Tadeo let himself be wound like wool and pulled by the nose by the arrogance of this wife who rode him like a horse" (41). In addition to such metaphors of domination describing Lucia's command over Tadeo, her relentless demands for the enchanted objects Zoza displays on her windowsill and for the storytelling that will satisfy her magical desire to hear tales further align her with the *domina* of Roman love elegy: "If me no have singing devil from sill, me punch belly and little Georgie kill"; "If you no hen get from sill, me punch belly and little Georgie kill"; "If you no buy me dolly from sill, me punch belly and little Georgie kill" (40); "If people no come and with tales my ears fill, me punch belly and little Georgie kill" (41). Here, Lucia's formulaic demand translates the behavior of the classical *domina* into the Neapolitan-Moorish patois associated with slaves of the period, simultaneously parodying the love elegy while also underscoring the literalness of Lucia's slave status. Indeed, as Carmela Bernadetta Scala points out, "[f]rom a historical point of view, she [Lucia] stands as the representative of the many slaves present in Naples during Basile's time" (2014, 16).

If Lucia's false tears and her demand for gifts figure her as *domina*, her doubling through Giorgia's character in "The Three Citrons" (5.9) reinforces her status as literal slave. Both girls' stories open with the phrase "In the meantime," highlighting their function as interludes to their respective tales' primary narratives of the white protagonists whose love is thwarted by the Black false bride. Giorgia's story, like Lucia's, takes place at a fountain where she has been sent to fetch water. Unbeknownst to her, a beautiful white fairy is waiting in a tree above the fountain for her betrothed, the prince, to return. When Giorgia goes to fill her jug, she mistakes the fairy's reflection for her own and, keenly aware of the color-coded logic of slavery, begins to question her status: "What you see, unfortunate Lucia, you be so beautiful and mistress send you to get water and me put up with this, O unfortunate Lucia?" (Canepa 2007a, 438). In an act of resistance, she breaks the water jug before returning home empty-handed. The next day, she is sent back to the fountain, where she again sees what she believes to be her reflection and resists her slave status: "Me no thick-lipped slave, me no Allah lover, me no wiggle ass; me so beautiful and me bring barrel to fountain?" (438). She breaks the water barrel, but when she returns home her mistress isn't buying Giorgia's lies: "When the poor mistress heard this she could no longer keep her calm, and she grabbed a broom and bruised the slave up so good that she felt it for quite a few days afterward" (438); literally adding insult to injury, the mistress follows with a verbal attack: "[Y]ou ragged slave, cricket leg, broken ass. . . . Fill this with water and bring it back immediately, or I'll grab you like an octopus and give you such a beating that you'll always remember my name!" (438). Fearing a further beating, Giorgia returns to the fountain, but upon seeing "her" reflection, she once again refuses her status as slave: "Me be stupid to get water: better if Giorgia marry! This no beauty for to die angry and serve cross mistress!" (438). And with this, Giorgia uses a hairpin to poke holes in the goatskin, the sight of which makes the fairy laugh, thus revealing to Giorgia the underlying source of her beatings.

The fairy, "who was the mother of courtesy" (438) (and probably also naive, given that she had only a short while before been born from a citron), shares her story with Giorgia, who connives to win the prince's hand. Offering to comb the fairy's hair, Giorgia ascends the tree, where she uses her hairpin to pierce the fairy; at this, the fairy turns into a dove and flies off. When the prince returns, he unleashes a torrent of racialized metaphors to express his despair: "Who put this ink blot on the royal paper where I planned to write my happiest days? Who draped with black mourning the freshly whitewashed house where I thought I would take all my pleasures? Who would have me find this touchstone where I left a silver mine destined to make me rich and blissful?" (439). At this, "the cunning slave said, 'Not to marvel, my prince,' for presto! Me be enchanted, one year white face, one year black ass!'" (439). Despite Giorgia's patois—a clear marker of her slave status—and the prince's being "swollen with rage and incensed beyond belief" (439), he returns with her to his kingdom where his parents bestow their crowns upon the newlyweds. As the royal cooks are preparing the celebratory feasts, a dove appears and says: "Cook in the kitchen / What is the king doing with the Saracen?" (439). The dove's repeated query initiates a chain of events that ultimately lead to the rebirth of the fairy—again from a citron—and to the false bride's exposure and death by means she has herself articulated in response to the king's question of how one who harmed the fairy ought to be punished.

Giorgia's depiction in "The Three Citrons" closely mirrors Lucia's, and together they coalesce and animate a range of cultural signifiers and beliefs about slavery in the early modern period. Her direct dialogue, for instance, echoes Lucia's Neapolitan-Moorish patois, both a real historical dialect commonly used by slaves living in Naples and other Italian port cities and a culturally recognizable exaggeration of that language used to parody racially othered slaves in comic theater of the period (Canepa 2007a, 39n18; Magnanini 2023, 211). By limiting this patois to Lucia and Giorgia, Basile consolidates slavery and racial otherness despite the fact that not all slaves of the period were racial or ethnic others.[11] Similarly, Giorgia's epithets—those she herself invokes ("thick-lipped slave," "Allah lover," "wiggle ass") and those hurled by her angry mistress ("ragged slave," "cricket leg," "broken ass")—not only emphasize her doubling of Lucia, thereby reducing the individual female slave to generic type, but also trade in the general ethnic and religious stereotypes of slaves to expose the period's essentially unassailable racialization of slavery.

Even more, while Giorgia's choice of epithets reveals an internalized racism, her characterizations remain at the level of religious and ethnic stereotype whereas the mistress's insults have the effect of diminishing Giorgia's and Lucia's individual personhood by collapsing them into the same figure—an act of domination as much literary as historical. Later in the story, the prince and the fairy extend Giorgia's—and thus the slave's—racial and religious difference, he by obsessively cataloging her Blackness and she, in dove form, by referring to her as "the Saracen" (Canepa 2007a, 439). Here, as in "Pride Punished" (4.10), "Saracen" clearly serves as a synonym for "Black slave" and makes clear the racial thinking underpinning the cultural logic of slavery in the early modern Italian context.

Alongside its articulation of this particular cultural logic of slavery, "The Three Citrons" also conveys some of the material reality of slavery in its rendering of Giorgia's physical and verbal abuse. Beaten and bruised "so good that she felt it for quite a few days afterward" (438) and threatened with another thrashing if she again fails to fetch the water ("I'll grab you like an octopus and give you such a beating that you'll always remember my name!" [438]), Giorgia returns with haste to the fountain to fulfill her mistress's command, "for she had experienced the lightning and was afraid of the thunder" (438). That this is not an idiosyncratic episode of violence nor an idle threat but rather Giorgia's life as a slave becomes especially clear when she anticipates her fate: "to die angry and serve cross mistress" (438). The physical and verbal abuse that Giorgia imagines escaping when she mistakes the white fairy's reflection for her own is more fully elaborated in "The Little Slave Girl" (2.8), a tale that turns on the innocent Lisa's treatment as a slave by her evil aunt: "[S]he immediately cut off Lisa's hair, gave her a juicy beating, put her in a ragged dress, and every day unloaded lumps on her head, eggplants on her eyes, brands on her face, and gave her a mouth that looked like she had eaten raw pigeons" (197). Although Lisa's race and ethnicity are unmarked, thus signifying her whiteness according to the conventions of the collection, her aunt's exclamations assign her a figurative Blackness. Upon first discovering the enchanted crystal casket containing Lisa, the aunt refers to her as "the Mohammed that he [Lisa's uncle] was worshipping in the caskets" (197); here, Canepa cites Croce's footnote explaining that "Mohammed's body, according to a legend common in Europe, was preserved in Medina in a coffin that was suspended in the air by the force of a magnet" (197). Later, when Lisa's uncle—who doesn't realize the "slave" is his niece—asks what each member of the household, even the cats, would like from the fair, his wife's invective similarly identifies Lisa with a figurative Blackness, reverberating with the insults to which Giorgia's mistress subjects her: "Go ahead, put this thick-lipped slave in the same bag as us; let's have one rule for everyone, and then we'll all want to piss in the same chamber pot. Leave her alone, damn it, and let's not award so much importance to an ugly animal like her!" (197).

Surely inflected with the Baroque excess that distinguishes *The Tale of Tales*, Basile's colorful descriptions of Lisa's abuse are nonetheless informed by and reflective of the historical fact of violence against slaves. Epstein, who turns to Basile for a "useful view of [Italian] slavery in its last major phase," suggests that "[p]erhaps inadvertently, Basile gives us a vivid impression of what it was like to be a mistreated slave, down to the swollen purple bruises under Lisa's eyes" (2001, 41). Indeed, the materiality underlying Basile's descriptions of Giorgia's and Lisa's beatings—the pains that Giorgia feels for days afterward, the blood and bruises that mark Lisa—foregrounds the reality of slavery as a system of authorized violence enacted on the bodies of slaves. By the early fourth century, Constantinian edicts already protected the rights of masters to beat their slaves with near complete impunity: "[M]asters had the right to beat a slave to induce better behavior, and even if the slave died, there should be no investigation to determine whether the owner's intent was to correct or to kill. Simple punishment remained the absolute right of masters" (63). Such rights, ensconced in law as well as in cultural productions like literature, changed very little as systems of slavery extended through the centuries and around the globe.

The brutal punishments that Giorgia and Lisa endure also exacerbate the ideological slippages between Basile's slaves and their Blackness, whether literal, as in Giorgia's case, or figurative, as in Lisa's. That is, beliefs about slaves are deeply entangled with beliefs about Blackness, and it is the collapsing of the two that catalyzes the narratives at the heart of *The Tale of Tales*, a point made especially clear in the fact that slavery as a system of human bondage in the early modern Mediterranean was much more complex as it was lived and practiced. The most common beliefs about slaves—and women—were very likely cultural inheritances from antiquity, when "women and slaves were similarly viewed as duplicitous and given to excess in ways that might endanger the person and property of free male citizens" (Joshel and Murnaghan 1998, 4). By the fourteenth century, the necessary intimacy and dependency of domestic slavery translated cultural ideas about the duplicity of women and slaves into images of terror: Petrarch defined slaves as *domestici bostes* (domestic enemies), and Margherita Datini referred to her own slaves as *femmine bestiali* (bestial women), who "might at any moment rise up against you" (Origo 1955, 322, 342). Medieval color prejudices—Epstein notes that "[m]edieval Italians were conscious of color and associated bad traits and things with darker people" (2001, 23)—and early modern ideas about race, ethnicity, and religion were mapped onto representations of slaves as deceitful, treacherous, and potentially violent by writers like the Dominican friar Matteo Bandello (1485–1561), who claimed "that the worst slaves were Moors from North Africa" and who wrote a story expressing a fear of Moorish slaves who might turn violent at any moment (Epstein 2001, 44–45).

Basile, for his part, reifies these layered ideologies of racialized slavery, as Epstein's reading of the collection's frame tale makes clear: "The frame story, where the nameless black slave ensnares the handsome prince, perpetuates stereotypes about blacks, and shows just how durable these images of bad black things had now become in parts of Italian culture. Again the slave is a domestic enemy: plotting, devious, and evil—willing to harm a baby in the womb in order to gratify her whims" (47). Simultaneously reifications and narrative characters, Lucia and Giorgia are at once exaggerated *femmine bestiali*—women who connive to steal the royals betrothed to others, endanger their respective princes by causing them emotional turmoil, and feel no remorse at the thought of harming the innocents who obstruct their desires—and very real slaves in whom complex histories of race and slavery converge. This dual representation, the way Giorgia and Lucia straddle the divide between fiction and reality, is made manifest in the collection's metanarrative structure, which invites diegetic conversation regarding the parallels between fiction and reality. While the frame tale ensures narrative continuity across the collection by providing such commentary in the introductory remarks for each embedded tale, it is not until the transition from "The Three Citrons" to the final tale, when tale and frame converge, that those remarks turn to the group's immediate circumstances: "[P]art of the group praised the ability with which [Ciommetella] told it, while others murmured and accused her of poor judgment, since she shouldn't have broadcast the disgraceful actions of someone so similar to the slave princess" (Canepa 2007a, 443). Here, the storytellers consider the fine line between the fictional slave, Giorgia, and the real slave, Lucia; in so doing, they reiterate the point that the two are not only doubles of each other, one on each side of the fiction/reality divide, but that they are also, extradiegetically, doubled representations that foreground the interlocking nature of slavery's figuration and its materiality.

Basile's portrayals of Lucia and Giorgia may trade in exaggerated stereotypes of the racial and religious otherness central to early modern Italian ideas of slavery, but the two women are nevertheless rendered in greater detail than many other characters in *The Tale of Tales*, a distinction made particularly clear in the collection's representation of its literal male slaves. While the collection's two primary male slaves and their tales—"The Padlock" (2.9) and "The Golden Trunk" (5.4)—are doubled in ways similar to the twinning of Lucia and Giorgia and their stories, the conditions of their slavery differ in dramatic ways. Both tales are variants of the ATU 425 cycle (Search for the Lost Husband / Cupid and Psyche / Animal Bridegroom / Beauty and the Beast), and the "handsome slaves" (200, 405) are positioned in the Cupid / animal bridegroom role; as such, their slave status is temporary, the result of a curse or an enchantment that not only foreshadows an end to their servitude but also allows them to return to whiteness at night, although this fact remains hidden from their female lovers who are prohibited from looking upon them. In contrast to Lucia and Giorgia, the male slaves are never reduced to derogatory physical descriptions, never speak in the Neapolitan-Moorish dialect, and are never subject to the demands and punishments of masters because they are free of such rulers.

The differences between Basile's male and female slaves may be a reflection of contemporary sexism or of the historical reality of gendered slavery in Italy in the early modern period—by the fifteenth century, male slaves were becoming increasingly rare, constituting "less than 3 percent of the slave population in Genoa in 1458," for instance (Epstein 2001, 30)—or both.[12] Regardless, given the primacy of Lucia and

Giorgia to the narrative progression and underlying logic of *The Tale of Tales*, their doubling in the male slaves suggests that the handsome pair is equally significant to the collection. Whereas the female slaves are literal, however, the male slaves are liminal; that is, they exist between slave and free as well as between literal and figurative. Situated at the nexus of Basile's two languages of slavery, the handsome slaves and their tales, discussed in detail below, embody the movement from "slave to love" to "slave in love," from *servitium amoris* to the material experiences of Lucia and Giorgia. At the heart of this transition and in the striking representational differences between the paired slave girls and the doubled handsome male slaves is, of course, race, naturalized in the fantastic sensibilities of the European literary fairy tale.

From "Slaves to Love" to "Slaves in Love"

The fact that the only two male slave protagonists in *The Tale of Tales* appear in ATU 425 variants reveals the subtle workings of racial thinking in Basile's collection and in the early development of the fairy tale as a European literary genre. Positioned in the tale type between Cupid—whom Ovid associates with the origins of Roman love elegy—and the animal bridegroom, these handsome, enchanted Black slaves are complex characters, fabulously wealthy and independent while also embodying an otherness that will only be fully realized in later versions of the tale when their racialized slave status is metaphorized in the beastly bridegrooms for which the tale type is most well known. In "The Padlock," which follows "The Little Slave Girl" (2.8) in the collection, Luciella (a diminutive for Lucia), the youngest daughter of a poor woman, goes to fetch water from a fountain; there, she meets a handsome slave who invites her to accompany him to a grotto where he promises to give her "a lot of nice little things" (Canepa 2007a, 200). Passing through the grotto, they arrive at a magnificent underground palace, where she lives in luxury: a splendid table is set for her; she is dressed beautifully by two servant girls; she sleeps in an embroidered and bejeweled bed, where "as soon as the candles were put out, someone came and lay down beside her" (200). When she asks to visit her mother, "the slave" provides her with a "large sack of money" as a gift for her mother and requests only that she return soon and not disclose where she has been staying. After several more visits home, each of which further intensifies her sisters' envy, they convince her that her "happiness will always be incomplete" unless she learns the identity of her "husband," and they provide her with a plan for doing so (201).

Astounded by the sight of her husband—"a flower of beauty, a young man who was all lilies and roses" (201)—Luciella opens the magical padlock her sisters have given her to secure him forever and finds therein a group of women to whom she cries out, thus waking her lover, who promptly banishes her for having discovered his secret. Now pregnant, she wanders through the world, begging, and is finally taken in by a kind lady-in-waiting at the palace, where Luciella gives birth to a beautiful son. Each night after the boy's birth, a handsome young man sneaks into Luciella's chambers, speaks to his son, and slips away before the rooster's first song; after several nights, the lady-in-waiting reports his actions to the queen, who has all the roosters killed, hides in Luciella's chamber, and eventually recognizes the young man as her son, who had been cursed by an ogress to remain a slave until his mother embraced him and the rooster remained silent. Once disenchanted, he and Luciella are reunited.

Although "The Padlock" is a truncated version of ATU 425 and lacks the titular search for the lost husband sequence, the narrative clearly incorporates many of the tale type's common motifs, featuring aspects of the Cupid and Psyche tradition (e.g., the unseen lover, the jealous sisters who urge her to look at him, and the lover's abandonment when she does) and anticipating aspects of the Beauty and the Beast tradition (e.g., the opulent palace, meals, and clothing, the gifts of money for her family, and the jealous sisters' inducement to disobey the slave/beast's wishes, even if unspoken). The seemingly odd choice to cast a Black slave in the role of mysterious lover—especially given the fact that the plot does not depend on his status as a slave—becomes clearer when "The Padlock" is read alongside its twinned tale, "The Golden Trunk," a more complete version of the tale type.

Like "The Padlock," "The Golden Trunk" begins with the youngest daughter of an impoverished family. Forsaken by her two older sisters, Parmetella takes her sow to graze in a secluded pasture where she discovers a tree with golden leaves. Returning each day with a leaf for her father to sell, she eventually strips the tree bare, at which point she decides to remove its golden trunk. In the process of moving the trunk, she finds beneath it a beautiful staircase made of porphyry; unable to resist her curiosity, she follows it to a dark cave and, eventually, to a "splendid palace, where your feet trod on nothing but gold and silver and you saw nothing before you but pearls and precious stones" (405). Upon entering, she finds a table set with a lavish meal, and as she is enjoying its bounty, a handsome slave enters, declares that he wants her for a wife, and promises that he will make her the happiest woman in the world; when night falls and she is in bed, "the slave" instructs her to put out the candle and to "be careful to do as [he tells her] if [she doesn't] want to tangle things up" (405). Waking alone after a night of sex that she can only conceptualize in terms of brutality—"her wool being carded without a comb"; "a civil war" during which she decides she can "keep still under the blows" (406)—Parmetella wonders about the identity of her nocturnal companion; the following night, after her companion has finished his "romping around" (406) and fallen asleep, she lights a candle, looks under the covers, and is stunned by what she sees: "the ebony had turned to ivory, the caviar to the milkiest milk, and the coal to whitewash . . . the most beautiful brushstroke that Nature had ever given to its canvas of marvels" (406). Roused by the candle, the "beautiful young man" curses Parmetella, chastising her for her curiosity, blaming her for the additional seven years' penance he must now do, and banishing her before he himself "[slips] away like quicksilver" (406).

Outside the palace, Parmetella meets a fairy who, cognizant of the girl's fate, equips her with advice for surviving her various travails until she finds her way into the house of an ogress, who also happens to be the mother of her handsome slave lover, whose name turns out to be Thunder-and-Lightning. Infuriated at Parmetella's trickery, which prevents her from being eaten, the ogress sets a series of impossible tasks for the girl, threatening to eat her should she fail to complete each day's work by sundown of that day: separate twelve sacks of mixed beans into individual piles by type; fill the ticks for twelve mattresses with feathers; retrieve a box of enchanted musical instruments from the ogress's sister. Weeping and bemoaning her dire predicament—"and all because [she] saw a black face become white!" (408)—Parmetella attracts Thunder-and-Lightning's attention, and although he addresses her as "Traitor," he is not without sympathy. First, he calls forth a "river of ants" (409) to sort the beans; then he tells her to "moan and scream that the King of Birds is dead," which causes an enormous flock of birds to come beat their wings, thus providing the feathers required to fill the mattresses. Finally, he shares with her instructions for securing the box of enchanted instruments, emphasizing that she must not open the box. When she sees that Parmetella has completed each of the first two tasks, the ogress exclaims, "That dog Thunder-and-Lightning did me this nice service" and "Thunder-and-Lightning is starting to get on my nerves, but I'll be dragged around on a monkey's tail if I don't trap her someplace where she won't be able to get away from me!" (409). Despite once again indulging her curiosity and opening the box of enchanted instruments, Parmetella survives the third task, only to learn that the ogress has arranged a marriage for Thunder-and-Lightning; after a series of events involving the bride's insults, however, Thunder-and-Lightning kills the bride and takes Parmetella to bed instead. When the ogress sees them together in the morning, she rushes to her sister's house, only to find that she has thrown herself into the oven in grief over Parmetella's having done the same to her child. At this, the ogress transforms into a ram and batters herself to death, and Parmetella lives happily ever after with Thunder-and-Lightning. Many of the details in "Thunder and Lightning" clearly adhere to the most extensive versions of the ATU 425 tale type and especially to subtype 425B (Cupid and Psyche / Son of the Witch): the prohibition against viewing the mysterious lover and the girl's transgression; the lover's disappearance and the girl's search for him; the seemingly impossible tasks set forth by the lover's mother and the lover's assistance in completing them; the final request to fetch a closed box from the lover's aunt; the prohibition against opening the box, the girl's transgression, and the lover's assistance; the mother's attempt to marry her son to another; and, finally, the marriage of the lover and the girl.

Apuleius's "Cupid and Psyche" is the most obvious intertext for both of Basile's ATU 425 tales featuring Black slaves as mysterious, enchanted lovers, and yet the classical Roman source leaves many details unexplained. Perhaps most perplexing is Basile's transformation of Cupid, god of love and son of Venus, to Thunder-and-Lightning, enchanted Black slave and son of an ogress, even in the context of subtype 425B, which joins the two variants. With respect to "The Padlock," which of course also features an enchanted Black slave as protagonist, Canepa adds information from Penzer's 1932 English translation to her own note that the tale is one of a number in *The Tale of Tales* that share motifs with the story of Cupid and Psyche: "Penzer discusses a very similar Greek tale and hypothesizes that Basile may have derived his from it. There are also variants from Turkey and Crete, and Basile could have heard one of these while in Venice or Crete (where he was stationed during 1604–07), though it does not seem that he knew either Turkish or modern Greek (1: 200–01)" (2007a, 199). Given Basile's travels through Italy and the Mediterranean, beyond just Venice and Crete, and "the pivotal role that many Italian cities had in international commerce (thereby facilitating contacts, mercantile and cultural, with other geographical areas . . .)" (Canepa 1999, 16), it seems entirely reasonable to assume that Basile would have been familiar with Greek and/or Turkish variants of ATU 425. It is not clear, though, that those variants account for some of the most striking details and motifs in "The Golden Trunk."

Variants from North Africa, however, bear a striking resemblance to "The Golden Trunk," and Emmanuel Plantade and Nedjima Plantade (2014) argue convincingly, on philological grounds, that Apuleius's "Cupid and Psyche" is in fact derived from the Berber oral tradition, perhaps not so surprising given Apuleius's own Berber background.[13] Moreover, they suggest that Apuleius perhaps modeled *The Golden Ass* on "the process that had given the oral fables of Libya the stature of Greek and Latin poems" and further hypothesize that "the oral fables of Libya were translated into Greek and written down at Cyrene, a colonial city where Greek men often married Libyan women" (175). Colonialism and commerce in and around the Mediterranean, from classical antiquity through the early modern period, undoubtedly fostered and facilitated the sorts of cultural exchange that might explain the rich repertoire of ATU 425 tales that Basile brings together in *The Tale of Tales* as well as some of the seemingly idiosyncratic motifs that diverge from his more readily recognized intertexts like Apuleius's "Cupid and Psyche." Indeed, Basile's "The Golden Trunk" tracks much more closely with the North African variants of "The Son of the Ogress" described by Plantade and Plantade than with Apuleius's tale.

In addition to sharing the general plot structure—the mysterious nocturnal visits, the prohibition against looking at the lover and the girl's transgression, the mother as ogress, the son's help with the mother's tasks, the eventual death of the mother and aunt, and, finally, the couple's marriage—Berber versions of "The Son of the Ogress" include the same tasks: not only bean or seed sorting, as appears in "Cupid and Psyche," but also feather collecting. To assist with the sorting, the lover calls forth ants, as Cupid does; when it comes to feather collecting, absent from Apuleius's tale, both Thunder-and-Lightning and the lovers in the North African tales tell the heroine how to enlist the birds by invoking their master, or the "King of Birds." While in the Berber versions, the "King of Birds" is often the royal name of the mysterious supernatural lover, Basile's use of the same title and persona for fulfilling the same task seems more than coincidental.[14] Other names in "The Golden Trunk" similarly resonate with details in several Berber versions. In one tale cited by Plantade and Plantade, the lover's name is "*Asfer n Ihwa*, which can be translated as 'Whistling of the Rain' and which is referred to in our eastern Moroccan version as *Seffar Ihwa* ('Whistling of the Wind,' in s 185)" (2014, 180); these names certainly evoke Basile's Thunder-and-Lightning and provide a possible context for the enchanted Black slave's ostensibly random name. In another tale, also referenced by Plantade and Plantade, the supernatural lover, "surprised and bitterly disappointed" at the heroine's initial transgression, exclaims: "Ah! Moonlight [the heroine's name], I trusted you and you betrayed me!" (181). Here, the lover's sense of betrayal provides a rationale for Thunder-and-Lightning's referring to Parmetella by the proper name "Traitor" from the moment they are reunited at the ogress's house through the end of the tale.

This broader ATU 425 tradition reveals the undeniable significance of early racial thinking for Basile's introduction of the handsome (temporary) slaves as the protagonists of "The Padlock" and "The Golden Trunk," an addition to the tale type that exists only in his two versions.[15] Given Basile's clear interest in race and the general racialization of slaves throughout *The Tale of Tales*, it is easy to imagine his associating a North African tale with Black African slaves and thus writing his handsome Black slaves into these two versions of ATU 425. At the same time, dominant ideas about Blackness—so clear in Basile's descriptions of Lucia and Giorgia as ugly, deceptive, servile—reinforce the tales' equation of Blackness with being punished or living in a cursed state, an equation echoed in longstanding ideologies that justified slavery on purely racial and ethnic grounds. Epstein conveys these ideological elisions in beautifully succinct fashion: "And so there is a kind of declension, from bad luck to sin to force as evolving, overlapping, even mutually confirming explanations for slavery.... Ethnicity or color came to be a proxy for bad luck.... In more complex ways color also became a proxy for sin itself, as people came to believe that belonging to certain ethnic groups, or even being a particular color, justified enslavement" (2001, 197). While later versions of ATU 425, such as d'Aulnoy's 1697 "Prince Marcassin," Villeneuve's 1740 "Beauty and the Beast," and Beaumont's 1756 didactic retelling of the latter, provide a diegetic rationale for the prince's animal birth or transformation into beast, Basile's tales never articulate the reason for the ogress's curse or punishment, thus implying that Blackness was already a broad, culturally comprehensible, and even naturalized form of punishment. That Blackness—and not slavery—is the real curse or punishment in these tales is clear in the fact that the handsome slaves retain their humanity and male privilege throughout: they continue to function as masters of their palaces, including having slaves of their own, and they return to whiteness at night when they join the heroines in bed.

Attending to the figure of the slave—whether the slave to love or the slave in love—in *The Tale of Tales* reveals the collection's unacknowledged origins at the nexus of slavery as a racialized cultural phenomenon and Roman elegy as a hyperbolic expression of romantic love. Although never specifically addressing Basile's extensive intertextual treatment of the Roman love elegy, Canepa argues that it is precisely through such intertextual practices that Basile "[engages] polemically with convention" (2007a, 21), rewriting high literary traditions in order to "[effect] a displacement of rhetorical hierarchies that complements the rewriting of social hierarchies" (1999, 224). While rewriting social hierarchies obviously structures a great deal of Basile's project, the implicit and explicit racializations inherent in his doubled languages of slavery also make clear that race is a much more nuanced and complex cultural phenomenon and hierarchy in the collection. On the one hand, his depictions of Lucia and Giorgia only reinforce race-based social hierarchies; on the other, his handsome slaves suggest a sort of racial fluidity that destabilizes hegemonic elisions of Blackness and slavery. Regardless of such complexities, however, the racialization of Basile's slaves establishes a paradigm that gets metaphorized in later European literary fairy tales, even as its racial and racist underpinnings persist. As Epstein so cogently points out with regard to the language of slavery (and equally relevant for Basile's literary slaves), "[l]ong after slaves disappear, the heritage of the words and the ideas they struggle to express is the ultimate reckoning. The hypocrisies, the racism, the sexism, the brutality bound up with the daily practice of slavery live on in language" (2001, 61).

Moreover, because the figurative language of slavery is in many ways constitutive of the hyperbolic nature of Roman love elegy, Basile's invocation of that language throughout *The Tale of Tales* seamlessly sutures the two genres. The exaggerated romance of the European literary fairy tale—exemplified in the happily-ever-after ending that eventually comes to define the genre and that is already present in many of Basile's tales—is widely recognized; the influence of racialized thinking, first instantiated in the figure of the slave in Basile's collection, is not. If, as Canepa contends, *The Tale of Tales*, as a consummate Baroque text and example of dialect literature, recodes high literary tradition to "construct a thematics of difference" (2007b, 12), race is the unacknowledged but indisputable privileged signifier of such a thematics. Thus, while Roman love elegy and the *servitium amoris* trope may give form to the literary fairy tale as elaborated by Basile, their coupling with his material language of slavery ensures that the literary fairy tale is a specifically racialized form, albeit one that gets remetaphorized in ways that invisibilize and increasingly naturalize its racialized dimensions as the European literary fairy tale continues to evolve.

2
FRANCE, 1697

Marie-Catherine d'Aulnoy's Fairy Tales

If Basile's *Tale of Tales* animates the convergence of literal and figurative in the European fairy tale's foundational racial logics, the fantastic worlds of Marie-Catherine d'Aulnoy's marvelous tales showcase the growing power that metaphors of race exerted in the development of the genre as an implicitly politicized cultural form. Holding together the marvelous and the quotidian, d'Aulnoy's *contes de fées*—alongside those of the first French fairy-tale vogue (1690–1715)—facilitate a deep engagement with cultural politics. Lewis Seifert's (1996) persuasive reading of these *contes* as simultaneously nostalgic *and* utopian discourses emerging out of contemporary negotiations over the boundaries of gender, class, and sexuality highlights their implicitly political nature. Elaborating on Seifert's foundational work, Patricia Hannon (1998), Elizabeth Wanning Harries (2001), and Anne E. Duggan (2005) all offer similarly nuanced interpretations of the *conteuses*' tales as contesting social and political efforts to limit women's rights and freedoms, constrain their voices, and marginalize their cultural influence. Although largely overlooked in critical literary and fairy-tale scholarship until the late 1980s—perhaps because of their omission from the classical canon despite their wild popularity in their own time and the centuries that followed—these *contes de fées* are today widely understood as early modern writings about the gender politics of the day, particularly in terms of the issues that most affected the educated and aristocratic *salonnières* who authored them.

Within this context, Christine Jones (2003) has argued, the *conteuses* developed a "poetics of enchantment" that opened into a *politics* of enchantment. Cultivating a new grammar of the frivolous as the basis for their particular aesthetic style, the *conteuses* reframed one of the most contentious cultural debates of the period—the Quarrel of the Ancients and the Moderns—so as to position themselves as more modern than even Charles Perrault, a leading proponent of the modern position. Attending to the prefatory epistles with which many *conteuses* framed their tale collections and extending Gabrielle Verdier's (1993) and Elizabeth Harries's (2001) comparative readings of the frontispieces accompanying Perrault's *Conte de ma mère l'oye* and Marie-Catherine d'Aulnoy's *Les Contes des fées* and *Suites des contes nouveaux, ou Des fées à la mode*, Jones (2003) foregrounds the ways that several notable *conteuses* used aesthetic commentary and visual imagery to challenge Perrault's equation of the storyteller with the old peasant woman. Instead, Jones contends, the *conteuses* invoked playful metacommentaries—discourses about their own literary production—through which they both assumed the role of the modern female storyteller and recast Perrault's Mother Goose as ancient, outmoded, and stodgy.

Of the *conteuses*, Madame d'Aulnoy was the most widely known, not only for her *contes de fées*[1]—which initiated the first French vogue for fairy tales—but also for her novels and (very likely fictionalized) travel writings. Extremely popular in their own time, d'Aulnoy's works also enjoyed a certain prestige. Indeed, most were issued by Claude Barbin, an influential bookseller who also published works by La Fontaine, Racine, and Molière (McLeod 1989, 94); they were then almost immediately translated into English in multiple editions as well as numerous formats beyond books, including chapbooks, pamphlets, and magazine serials (Palmer 1975). However, while d'Aulnoy's novels and travel writings had a lasting appeal well beyond her lifetime, it is really her fairy tales that have endured across the centuries. Simultaneously iconic of the first French fairy-tale vogue and yet distinct from other *contes de fées* in their length, ornate description, and narrative complexity, d'Aulnoy's tales also offer the most sophisticated intertextual engagement with Perrault's *contes* and, as such, with his politics—especially his gender politics.[2] In addition to their popularity through the eighteenth and nineteenth centuries, d'Aulnoy's *contes* have also been among the most well studied of the French tradition since their critical "rediscovery" in the late 1980s, perhaps because they offer the richest sites for analysis of the fairy tale in relation to an early modern feminist sensibility.

If d'Aulnoy's *contes de fées* clearly unfold against a cultural backdrop of explicit gender politics, they also suggest another, more implicit politics—one influenced by nascent ideas and ideologies of "race" as informed by early European exploration and travel and by France's expanding colonial empire, first in "New France" and later in the Caribbean.[3] Although largely excluded from dominant paradigms of early modern French culture, colonization figures prominently in the cultural imagination of the period. Sara Melzer contends that "culture and colonization were always conjoined, so interdependent that each enabled and shaped the other" (2012, 3), and she reads France's discourses of its early colonization by the Ancient World and its contemporary colonization of the New World as mirrors of each other that exemplify this point. As such, Melzer reads the Quarrel of the Ancients and the Moderns as "the primary locus where the nation's colonial and cultural discourses merged" (3).

Drawing on Melzer's elaboration of the Quarrel of the Ancients and the Moderns to account for the colonial underpinnings of France's cultural debates, I consider this other politics—this politics of race—as it resonates in d'Aulnoy's fairy tales. Excavating traces of early modern racial logics in d'Aulnoy's *contes*—expressed in the fantastic landscapes of the European imperial imagination, in the ethnographic descriptions of *les sauvages* in the French *Jesuit Relations* and other travel writings, in the New World colonial policies of assimilation and Frenchification, and in the early racial typologies beginning to circulate at the end of the seventeenth century—I argue that race has been (and continues to be) critical to the development of the fairy tale as a literary genre despite its near complete invisibility.

Fantastic Travels

While d'Aulnoy is today primarily known for her *contes de fées*, she enjoyed unprecedented success as a travel writer in her own time. Of her three travel narratives, *Mémoires de la cour d'Espagne* (1690) and *Relation du voyage d'Espagne* (1691) became instant sensations throughout Europe, and Melvin Palmer speculates that the *"succès fou"* of these works (which were translated into English, German, and Dutch) might be attributable to the fact that "[a]ll of Europe was interested in travel literature, the exotic, and Spain in particular" at that historical moment (1971, 223). To contextualize this popularity numerically: *Mémoires de la cour d'Espagne* went through eight editions by 1695 and was issued twice more by 1740; *Relation du voyage d'Espagne* was issued five times by 1695 and eleven times total by 1740 (222). Glenda McLeod points out that d'Aulnoy wrote "the single most famous seventeenth-century French account of a journey into Spain" (1989, 91); she also reveals the fact that "the greatest debate on her works is whether she ever went there" (91).[4]

Fantasy and travel have long enjoyed an intimate relationship—fantasy transports readers to new worlds while travel conveys fantasies of otherness—and that relationship ensures that voyage literature, as Erica Harth (1983) refers to it, is always seeded with some degree of fiction. D'Aulnoy's works may be (much) more fictive than the genre generally accommodates, but Palmer argues that their borrowings as well as their fictive underpinnings and stylistic devices should be understood within a literary context demanding verisimilitude at the very moment that writers were also struggling to bring about two new genres—the memoir and the epistolary novel (1971, 229); as such, he encourages a reading of *Mémoires de la cour d'Espagne* and *Relation du voyage d'Espagne* as early experiments in prose fiction rather than as hoaxes or plagiarisms.

Regardless of the veracity of d'Aulnoy's travels, her travel writing indicates a deep familiarity with the genre of the *relation*, the most common designation for voyage literature in France. As a *salonnière*, d'Aulnoy would very likely have been caught up in what Harth characterizes as the "new rage [sweeping] the French reading public" in the 1660s: "everyone, so it seemed, was reading voyage literature" (1983, 224). Of course, voyage literature—primarily in the form of early discovery narratives and the annual *Jesuit Relations*—was popular well before the 1660s, and according to Melzer, it had a "surprisingly large impact on 17th-century thought" (2006, 36). Dating back to the sixteenth century, *relations* were a fundamental part of the imperial imagination, and, as such, they advanced France's colonial projects through religious, commercial, and political conquest and expansion. Melzer's reminder that the *relations* "need to be seen as *relational*, in the religious sense of *reliare*, meaning to tie together" (36) underscores the cultural power they exerted in forging bonds—real and fantastic—between France and "the worlds beyond it" (36). The wide availability and best-selling nature of such voyage literature, together with d'Aulnoy's specific interest in authoring her own *relations*, suggests that she likely read a diversity of travel accounts, including those published prior to the 1660s, many of which had become canonical in their own right. Thus, as I hope is clear, I am less concerned with the "truth" of d'Aulnoy's travel narratives and more interested in their discursive continuity with her *contes de fées*, the ways in which they share registers of wonder and vocabularies of the fantastic while also resonating with the descriptions of exotic and marvelous new worlds characteristic of early modern European voyage literature.

Reading d'Aulnoy's *contes* alongside European travel literature points to specific historical contexts and geographic sites as anchors for the imaginary landscapes that give rise to an implicit politics of race in her fairy tales. Ideally, such intertextual analysis adds nuance to "the imperial imagination" so that it signifies more than a generalized encounter with otherness and difference. Thus, for instance, while much has been made of d'Aulnoy's sumptuously opulent fairy-tale settings and her decadently bejeweled characters as a nostalgic longing for "the certainty of aristocratic essence" (Seifert 1996, 84),[5] I follow Patricia Hannon in her claims that "the fairy tales' inscription of wealth is far more complex and surely more dynamic than has been recognized by contemporary scholarship" (1998, 214). Hannon's own interpretation turns on the tensions implicit in the *conteuses*' use of such extravagance, which valorizes the monarchy even as it appropriates luxury as a "political power base from which to challenge authority" (149). While I find Hannon's argument quite compelling, I also want to consider what such riches might mean if read alongside early travel literature and its celebration of the New World's fantastic abundance.

The fabled islands of gold and silver, Cryse and Argyre, were already well established in the European cultural imagination by the time Christopher Columbus stumbled onto the American continent and presumed he had reached the Orient, the supposed locale of these islands (Dickason 1984, 9). Even more, Olive Dickason contends, "Columbus's conviction that he had reached the Orient would have been reinforced by the sight of Amerindians wearing gold ornaments" (9). Columbus's reports of his journeys and the publicity surrounding them—among the earliest travel writing but already inspiring a "new fashion in literature" (6)—thus instantiated a lasting image of the New World as one of almost mythological riches. A half century or so later, Francisco López de Gómara, Cortés's personal chaplain and secretary, wrote with some regret of the Spanish practice of taking gold, silver, and pearls from the inhabitants of the New World since those riches were far less valuable, in his mind, than what the Spanish were leaving—Christian teachings—and since such riches were easily available from the land itself: "[I]t is certainly true that we would have done better not to have taken their goods and property from them, and to have contented ourselves with what we obtained from the mines, from the depths of their tombs and the rivers. That amounted to more than sixty millions in gold, without counting the pearls and emeralds . . . all of which represents a far greater value than what we took from them" (quoted in Dickason 1984, 40). Regardless of his regret and the ostensible value of Christian evangelizing, Gómara's description extends earlier beliefs in the excesses of New World wealth.

Dickason recounts a number of anecdotes—culled from sixteenth- and seventeenth-century travel narratives published in French—about the natives' seeming indifference to the value of gold and silver because of its sheer abundance:

> Early accounts abound in references to Amerindians fishing with golden fish hooks, wearing golden breast plates or golden rings in ears and noses, not to mention pearl necklaces and bracelets. Perhaps the culmination was the tale of the conquistadors shoeing their horses with gold because there was no iron to be had. Spaniards reported counting eighty houses in Cuzco that were not only roofed with gold but also lined with it. A house in Collao was said to be roofed with pure gold worked to resemble straw. The legend of the gilded chieftain El Dorado dates from about 1535. . . . The chieftain lived in a land so rich in gold that each day he covered his body with a fine film of the dust, removing it at night and letting it lie where it dropped. . . . In quite another mood was the story of Amerindians commiserating with the Spanish horses for having iron bits in their mouths, and bringing gold for a substitute because they thought it would be better for the animals. According

to Lescarbot, Spanish women living in Peru had their shoes plated with gold and silver and garnished with pearls. (1984, 55)

Such fantastic accounts of the New World's profusion of gold and precious stones reverberate through d'Aulnoy's *contes*. For instance, Prince Ariel finds a "palace of pure gold" (2003 [1895 (1697 and 1698)], 72) on the Isle of Calm Delights, and once inside he marvels at its endless wonders, particularly the gold and diamonds, which are even more impressive "for their workmanship than for their intrinsic worth" (72). Babiole's palace—magically created by an endless stream of workmen who emerge from a hazelnut given her by a fairy—similarly "[shines] with gold and azure" (225), and the White Cat's chateau is "the most magnificent imaginable" (348) with a gate of gold as well as a golden door adorned with jewels. In addition, just as early Spanish travel accounts were replete with examples of the supposed use of gold for the production of everyday objects—fishhooks, earrings, nose rings, horseshoes—d'Aulnoy's tales offer a similarly impressive catalog of gold trifles and household items, including "a little golden plate" for the princess's cat, Bluet, in "Prince Ariel" (74); "a balustrade which was of worked gold" (121) in "The Golden Branch"; golden bells for doors, horses, and cats in several tales; and "a table laid for two, with gold knife, fork and spoon for each" in "The White Cat" (348). Throughout d'Aulnoy's fairy tales, gold building materials and domestic objects are complemented by similar objects decorated with, sometimes even rendered whole from, diamonds, pearls, rubies, emeralds, and a diversity of semiprecious stones. "Finette Cendron," in particular, resonates with early descriptions of how the New World's riches were put to luxurious use: her "beautiful Spanish jennet" is in one instance "saddled and bridled, with more diamonds on its saddle-cloth than would buy three whole towns," and in another "all covered with golden bells and ribbons . . . its saddle cloth and bridle priceless" (201); likewise, her red velvet slipper—so crucial to her eventual identification—is "embroidered with pearls" (199) in similar fashion to the Spanish women living in Peru whose shoes were "plated with gold and silver and garnished with pearls" (Dickason 1984, 55).

Beyond these marvelous worlds of gold, d'Aulnoy's imagined landscapes are characterized by a natural abundance—or, perhaps, an unnatural, fairy-generated one—that echoes common tropes of early voyage literature about the New World as a land of plenty. Samuel de Champlain's 1604–18 travel narratives, for instance, offer extensive descriptions of rivers, waterways, fertile meadows, and countless varieties of trees and wild fruits along with seemingly endless lists of birds, sea mammals, and fish in such numbers that the travelers never fear for hunger:

> [W]e saw so great a quantity of birds . . . that we killed them easily with sticks. On another [island] we found the shore completely covered with sea-wolves, of which we captured as many as we wished. At the two others there is such an abundance of birds of different sorts that one could not imagine it, if he had not seen them. There are cormorants, three kinds of duck, geese, marmettes, bustards, sea-parrots, snipe, vultures, and other birds of prey; gulls, sea-larks of two or three kinds; herons, large sea-gulls, curlews, sea-magpies, divers, ospreys, appoils, ravens, cranes, and other sorts with which I am not acquainted. . . . In May and June, so great a number of herring and bass are caught there that vessels could be loaded with them. (Grant 1959, 29, 41)

The New World's natural plenitude—the land's seeming ability to provision and feed the voyagers with ease—surfaces in excessive and highly civilized style in d'Aulnoy's description of King Ram's underground domain, so far beneath the earth that Merveilleuse believes she "must at least be going to the Antipodes" (2003 [1895 (1697 and 1698)], 180):

> At last she suddenly discovered a vast plain variegated with a thousand different flowers, the scent of which was sweeter than any she had ever felt. A great river of orange-flower water flowed all around, while streams of Spanish wine, of rossolis, of hippocras, and a thousand other sorts of liqueurs formed cascades and charming little streams. This plain was covered with strange trees. There were whole avenues of such, where partridges, better larded and better cooked than you find them at La Guerbois's, hung from the branches. There were other walks where the trees were laden with quails, young rabbits, turkeys, chickens, pheasants, and ortolans. In certain places where the air seemed darker, it rained lobsters

and soups, ragouts of sweetbreads, white puddings, sausages, tarts, pastries, preserves (dry and liquid), sovereigns, crowns, pearls, and diamonds. (180)

Although it is difficult *not* to read King Ram's marvelous land as anything but a parody of Champlain's travel writings and other early New World voyage literature, I am not suggesting a direct intertextual relationship between d'Aulnoy's *contes* and such accounts. Rather, I highlight the ways that d'Aulnoy's fairy tales seem to reiterate the register of wonder and the grammar of a different marvelous so critical to New World *relations* in order to emphasize the significance of that specific site of difference to the implicit racial underpinnings of her 1697 *Les Contes des fées* and her 1698 *Suites des contes nouveaux, ou Des fées à la mode*, two of the most influential and canonical fairy-tale collections through the nineteenth century. This is not to imply that d'Aulnoy was not also influenced by other voyage literature, such as the "Oriental" *relations*, and by other cultural longings for the exotic, such as the vogue for *chinoiserie* and other Orientalist fashions of the time. Indeed, several of her golden chateaux have interior walls of "transparent porcelain painted in many colours" (d'Aulnoy 2003 [1895 (1697 and 1698)], 348) or "porcelain, so fine that you could see the light through them" (72); palace rooms are "full of exquisite china vases" (72), and entertaining monkeys are "dressed as Chinese" (331). As Christine Jones claims in her reading of porcelain's seventeenth- and eighteenth-century social and political networks as they evolved in France, Versailles "inspired a décor known as *lachinage*, or chinamania" (2013, 36), and like Louis XIV, d'Aulnoy seems to have "understood that porcelain had a compelling power attached to its beauty that was at once regal, romantic, and fantastical" (36). Nonetheless, her tales reveal a much deeper—perhaps subconscious—engagement with the New World, its explorers, and its native inhabitants than with China or "the Orient" more broadly conceived. In this, she would have been wholly consistent with both the ethnographic and the colonial priorities of the day. According to Dickason, despite the fact that Oriental *relations* vastly outnumbered New World ones, "as far as ethnology is concerned, these statistics are misleading; in all the literature, surprisingly little was written on the people of the Orient, whereas in that on the New World, a comparatively large amount of space was devoted to its peoples" (1984, 38). While Europe perceived the East to be highly civilized,[6] the New World and its native inhabitants "seemed to present a *tabula rasa* ready to be inscribed in any way that Europeans wished" (38).

Marvelous New Worlds

Resonating with precisely these possibilities for imperial inscription, d'Aulnoy's "Belle-Etoile" and "The Dolphin"—two tales involving (unwitting) sea travel—offer idiosyncratic and provocative details that might be read as articulating a politics of French empire, and, as such, they provide an interpretive framework for understanding several of d'Aulnoy's other *contes* within the context of increasing colonial expansion. In "Belle-Etoile," a princess, her brothers, and their cousin are abandoned to the sea by the evil Queen-Mother's lady-in-waiting, who has been charged with killing them. At sea, they are rescued and adopted by a pirate and his wife, Corsine, who happily forgo a life of plundering when they discover that jewels fall from the children's hair whenever combed. In the logic of the tale, the pirate's intervention makes sense since the children are left to die at sea; however, d'Aulnoy grants the pirate a significance beyond the demands of the plot by elaborating on his previous life and his motivations for turning to piracy: "The man had been well educated, and it was less from inclination than from the forwardness of fortune that he had become a pirate. He had met Corsine in the house of a princess, where her mind had been properly cultivated; she was well-bred, and, although she inhabited a kind of desert, where they subsisted on the booty he brought home from his voyages, she had not forgotten the usages of society. Thus their joy that they were no longer forced to expose themselves to all the dangers inseparable from a pirate's life, was very great, and they were getting rich all the same" (d'Aulnoy 2003 [1895 (1697 and 1698)], 450–51). Recognizing in the children a "charming disposition" that he takes as a sign of their noble birth, the pirate provides them with clever tutors so that they are well educated in "the various branches of knowledge" (451). When the children leave home to discover their true lineage, "never was there a sadder parting" (455), not because of the pirate and Corsine's "interested motives, for they had amassed such a quantity of treasure that they did not want any more," but rather because of the mutual love that has developed between the children and their "benefactors" (454).

In the second half of the seventeenth century, the French attitude toward piracy was a conflicted one, particularly in relation to the Caribbean, where European countries were contending for colonial power. On the one hand, piracy challenged state authority. As Doris Garraway points out in her work on libertinage as a ruling paradigm in the French Caribbean, "[p]irates claimed the right to violence while balking at the supposedly noble virtues of selflessness, love of country, and loyalty to the king" (2005, 117). On the other hand, piracy "represented in the extreme the ethos of colonialism itself, that is, a search for profit in which conventional morality and social structures are radically undermined" (117). Even more, Garraway argues that piracy was often critical to the success of the colonies insofar as it could provide new and struggling settlements with provisions when official French suppliers could not (100–101). The ideological tensions associated with piracy come to the fore in Alexandre Olivier Oexmelin's sensationally successful *Histoire des aventuriers*, a personal account of his life as a pirate around Tortuga, Saint-Domingue, and the Spanish Main, first published in Holland in 1678. An immediate international bestseller, *Histoire des aventuriers* was published in five European languages—the first French edition dates from 1686—with numerous editions by the end of the seventeenth century (Garraway 2005, 96–103). Oexmelin's *Histoire des aventuriers* is perhaps most noteworthy for its transformation of the pirate into an *honnête homme* (honorary noble) and unofficial statesman. For instance, despite his common birth and lack of education, Oexmelin's French editor characterizes him as having not only "a bit of both [good birth and education], if one pays attention to common sense," but also the "liberty of a noble man" as evidenced in his writing (quoted in Garraway 2005, 105). According to Garraway, as popular literary figures, pirates "emerge as veritable military heroes," and "[b]y relating piracy to more socially acceptable forms of honorable warfare, the literary text advanced the interests of the state" (117).

That "Belle-Etoile" advances the same ideology of the heroic pirate statesman is especially clear in the name d'Aulnoy gives the pirate's wife, Corsine. At the end of the seventeenth century, there were two words for piracy in French: *pirate*, which referred to "someone engaging in unlicensed theft and pillage on the high seas," and *corsair*, which referred to "a pirate sailing with a state commission" (Garraway 2005, 100). Were she herself a pirate and not simply a pirate's wife, Corsine would certainly act on behalf of the state, as her name makes clear. And, indeed, Corsine and the pirate, like the transformed Oexmelin, prove themselves invaluable to the state as they facilitate truth, justice, and rightful order in the kingdom of their adopted children's birth. Not only do they outfit the children with a "very stout and magnificent vessel" (d'Aulnoy 2003 [1895 (1697 and 1698)], 455) that sees them safely to the kingdom, but they have also prepared them well for assuming the life of royalty. In Garraway's reading, Oexmelin's *Histoire des aventuriers* suggests that "the destiny of pirates is just as often to serve the king and receive compensation for their sacrifices in the form of social prestige and high office" (2005, 119), and d'Aulnoy reiterates this claim in the conclusion to "Belle-Etoile" when "[t]he pirate and his wife [are] sent for in order that they might be rewarded for the excellent education they had given the children" (d'Aulnoy 2003 [1895 (1697 and 1698)], 480). Moreover, despite the fact that the pirate and Corsine speak to the children at length about the evils of court that have made it hateful to them—a critique that parallels the machinations that led the Queen-Mother to order the deaths of the children—d'Aulnoy returns them, at least symbolically, to a purified and honorable court at the end of the tale. Thus recuperating piracy *and* the state, d'Aulnoy imagines Corsine and her husband as Oexmelin's heroic pirate statesmen, aligned with state goals and, as such, implicitly justifying the expanding French empire.

While "Belle-Etoile" seems most directly resonant with France's nascent empire in the Caribbean, the colonial policies and discourses pertaining to Canadian New France tend to exert a greater presence in d'Aulnoy's collection as a whole, and this is especially clear in "The Dolphin." "The Dolphin" is a complex tale of ugly Prince Alidor's unrequited love for Livorette, his ability to transform himself into her beloved canary with the aid of a magical dolphin whose life he has spared, the pregnancy that comes of Livorette allowing her canary to sleep in her bedroom at night, their banishment from the kingdom and rescue at sea by the dolphin, Alidor's transformation into a handsome prince, Livorette's eventual clearing of her name, and their final ascension to the throne. This tale, the final *conte* in d'Aulnoy's second collection, is particularly striking in its privileging of the magical and benevolent dolphin as the animal savior. Not only was the dolphin relatively rare as a rescuing figure in fairy tales and mythology at that time—for instance, Rudolf Schenda in the *Enzyklopädie des Märchens* (1981–2015) cites examples from only two Greek myths, one story in the *Arabian Nights*, d'Aulnoy's *conte*, a story in a collection of Madagassi tales, and the folk beliefs of fishermen in southern France—but it was also the symbol of the French monarchy. The heir or heirs apparent were referred to as *le dauphin*, and the dolphin had a place of prominence on their coat of arms. Louis XIV was the 19th Dauphin of France until he assumed the throne in 1643; he also sired four *dauphins*. Thus, the fact that the benevolent dolphin takes "the shape of a young monarch of marvelous beauty and wit" (535) in order to attend Prince Alidor's and Princess Livorette's wedding ceremony indicates that the association is not a coincidental or accidental one for d'Aulnoy.

Despite the dolphin's implicit royal status, he remains beholden to Alidor and continues to serve as a magical benefactor. When Alidor, Livorette, and their son are in danger of drowning in the sea (where they have been cast in a barrel to die for Livorette's transgression), Alidor calls to the dolphin and transfers his powers of command to the princess, who requests that he "bear them away to the loveliest island in the world, and to build on it the finest palace that ever was seen, with exquisite gardens, surrounded by streams, one full of wine and another of water, with a garden full of flowers and a tree in the middle, whose stem should be silver and its branches gold, with three oranges growing on it, one of diamond, another of ruby, and a third of emerald. The palace was to be painted and gilded, and all her story represented on its walls" (526). Like so many of d'Aulnoy's descriptions of extravagant golden castles and bountiful lands, this one also reproduces the language of New World plenitude, but here it is explicitly brought about through the actions of the dolphin—*le dauphin*, the young monarch. Through such word play, d'Aulnoy's marvelous world converges with the utopian possibilities of New France as rendered in the early voyage literature at the heart of the imperial imagination.

If such descriptions of the dolphin's island evoke New France, that relationship is even more clearly articulated in the dolphin's orders that Alidor and Livorette be acknowledged as king and queen of the island by the local inhabitants. As was the case with colonies the world over, the dolphin's island offers all the possibilities of remaking oneself. No longer a banished and dishonored princess (pregnant out of wedlock without a clue as to the father's identity) and a deranged prince, Livorette and Alidor are transformed—literally, in Alidor's case, when he overcomes his derangement and is changed into a handsome and witty prince—upon their arrival in this new land where they are treated with the deference due their new station. Indeed, Livorette's and Alidor's transformation into the island's royalty literalizes the French colonial fantasy of being taken for gods and installed as emperors upon first contact (Dickason 1984, 273). Beyond the respect and honor paid them by the island's inhabitants, Alidor and Livorette also find themselves the recipients of an infinite stream of wealth, and this wealth furthers the correspondences between the marvelous island and France's New World colonies: "[S]treams of metal flowed into these wells, and when money was wanted one had nothing to do but to let down a bucket and say: 'I wish to draw up louis, pistoles, quadruples, crowns, or other coins.' At the word the water took the wished-for form, and the bucket came up full of gold or silver or coins, and yet the spring never dried up for those who made good use of it" (d'Aulnoy 2003 [1895 (1697 and 1698)], 528). Upon testing these streams and finding their buckets full of golden grains, Alidor and Livorette ask why the gold is not yet coined, only to learn that "they [are] waiting to know the arms of the prince and princess so as to stamp them" (528). Alidor, however, chooses another insignia for the coins, claiming "'we are too much indebted to the generous dolphin to have any other image on them than his.' In an instant all the grains were changed into gold pieces, with a dolphin on each" (529). Alidor's and d'Aulnoy's decision to have the coins stamped with the image of the dolphin is especially noteworthy since the only French coins bearing the mark of the dolphin in the sixteenth and seventeenth centuries were those intended for circulation in New France ("French Coinage for Canada and Louisiana," n.d.).[7]

If "Belle-Etoile" and "The Dolphin" seem to conceive of the marvelous world and the New World through a shared imperial imaginary, they also reveal a certain utopianism common to both d'Aulnoy's *contes* as a whole and the early colonial hopes for New France. The utopian impulses in d'Aulnoy's fairy tales are well documented, especially in terms of a politics of gender and sexuality (Seifert 1996; Duggan 1998), but such a utopianism also infuses the implicit racial and colonial politics of her *contes*. Although French colonial projects in North America were vexed at almost every turn, early explorers and religious missionaries wrote with great hope of the possibilities for New France and its native peoples. For instance, in a 1642 letter to "a lady of rank," Marie de l'Incarnation, the famous Ursuline missionary whose letters were published in France in 1677 and 1681, writes, "It seems that the fervor of the primitive Church has descended to New France and that it illuminates the hearts of our good converts, so that if France will give them a little help . . . in a short time a much further progress will be seen" (Marshall 1967, 70). Later that year, in a letter to the Mother Superior of Tours, she described the changes brought about by Christian baptism: "[O]nce they are [baptized], the grace with which their souls have been made beautiful renders them very grateful and almost all their prayers and communions are made for the preservation of the persons in France that do good to them and by their charity have delivered them from infidelity" (109). Father Paul Le Jeune, one of the first Jesuit missionaries to New France, conveys a similar hope in the *Jesuit Relations* of 1632–33: "[S]ince they ['our poor Savages'] interest themselves in the glory of God, in the spread of the Gospel, in the conversion of souls, we feel an inexplicable and affectionate interest in their affairs; so much so that, if things would go according to our wishes, they would gain more in one month than they have lost in all the years that their plans have been thwarted. . . . I hope that in a few years they will see the fruits of Heaven and of earth growing from the seeds which they have planted with so much trouble" (1901 [1632–33], 85). It is precisely this belief in the possibility of human transformation—characterized here by Christianity but certainly not limited to that domain—that lends a utopian quality to d'Aulnoy's tales and to the fantastic metamorphoses of her fairy-tale animals in particular.

Animals and Assimilation

For d'Aulnoy, the boundary between human and animal[8] is a porous one, and metamorphosis—the movement back and forth across that fluid divide—figures prominently in her *contes*.[9] While most critics have read d'Aulnoy's animal-human metamorphoses and hybridities metaphorically or allegorically through the lenses of psychology, gender, and sexuality,[10] Lewis Seifert attends closely to the "nonhuman dimension of her hybrid characters" (2011, 246) in order to underscore the fact that "animals—no matter how anthropomorphic—always pose an existential problem for humans" (244). Focusing on "Babiole" and "Prince Wild Boar," Seifert argues that the tales' opposing approaches to the human-animal boundary—"Babiole" reasserts a stable boundary between human and animal while "Prince Wild Boar" concludes by calling that very stability into question—condense seventeenth-century cultural debates about the nature of humans and animals and gesture toward the possibility of a "hybrid subjectivity" (257) denied by Descartes's theory of the animal-machine. Patricia Hannon similarly highlights metamorphosis's potential for "alternative representations of subjectivity" (1998, 82) in d'Aulnoy's tales of human-animal transformation. Like Seifert and Hannon, I also situate d'Aulnoy's metamorphosis tales in a contemporary cultural context preoccupied with the boundary between "human" and "animal"—specifically, New France, especially as forged in the imperial imagination, a fantastic site where *animal* was often conflated with *sauvage* (the term most commonly used for the land's native inhabitants) and necessarily racially inflected.

Although *sauvage* signified "wild," "uncultivated," and "not domesticated" more than "savage," as it is frequently translated into English, the term's range of meanings—explicit as well as implicit—indexes contemporary concerns as to where *les sauvages* should be positioned in relation to (European) man and animal. For instance, Europeans in New France compared native people's ability to navigate the wilderness as "suspiciously animal-like," "an innate instinct, the same as that possessed by animals" (Dickason 1984, 91). Similarly, François Bernier, most famous for his travel writings about India but also a Gassendist philosopher interested in current debates about "animal mechanism" inspired by Descartes's theory of the animal-machine, suggested "the possibility that some animals may use a very primitive language, and he compared them to 'Canadians and those other Savage Nations with a very limited vocabulary'" (Stuurman 2000, 9). Even more, lacking state and political formations that Europeans could easily identify or understand, natives were frequently deemed nonhuman or prehuman by those, like Hobbes and later Montesquieu, for whom human society did not exist without the state (Dickason 1984, 53). Such examples converge in what Gordon Sayre describes as a "romantic or racist primitivism that maintained that the *sauvages américains* were radically new, possibly nonhuman" (1997, 81).

And yet, even as *les sauvages* were inscribed into this liminal position between (European) man and animal, they were also invoked in contemporary philosophies and discourses of human perfectibility. By the seventeenth century, human perfectibility was no longer determined solely by God, as Pelagians believed, nor by one's free will, as Augustinians believed; instead, it could be achieved through the "deliberate intervention of their fellow-men" (Passemore 2000, 226). This belief in human perfectibility undergirded French colonial policy through the elision of perfectibility and assimilation. As Saliha Belmessous argues in her theorization of assimilation's pivotal role in French and British colonization, "through the pursuit of assimilation, empire was driven by the utopian project of transforming colonized peoples not only into Europeans, but more particularly into *improved* Europeans.... Colonizers... wanted colonized peoples to be what they themselves were not yet" (2013, 2–3).[11] In seventeenth-century New France, assimilation—which included everything from dress and bodily discipline to religious belief and action—was known as *francisation* (Frenchification), and it played a critical role in the French colonization of North America from the outset. In that particular colonial setting, *francisation* centered on the interrelated conversion of natives to both Catholicism and French "civility."

Although the policy of *francisation* was, of course, predicated on an understanding of local Indigenous peoples as *sauvages* who were culturally and economically inferior to Europeans, it nonetheless assumed the possibility of their becoming French citizens. Thus, in a 1627 charter, Cardinal Richelieu decreed that Christianized Native Americans "will be deemed and considered natural-born French, and, as such, could come and settle in France when it shall seem good to them, and acquire property, bequeath, inherit and accept donations and legacies like any other true subjects and natural-born French and without having to apply for letters of declaration or of naturalization" (quoted in Belmessous 2013, 30). In addition, the policy of *francisation* was also intended as a means of renewing French civilization. As Belmessous explains, "in establishing Christian and virtuous colonies, French settlers would not only extend God's empire but also restore virtue amongst the French people" (14). In essence, *francisation* was a multifaceted strategy for building the French empire, and metamorphosis was its underlying paradigm.

In similar fashion, d'Aulnoy's fairy-tale metamorphoses participate in the transformation of "animals" into idealized humans, thus centering race at the nexus of the marvelous and the imperial. Like *les sauvages*, d'Aulnoy's "animal" characters tend to occupy ontologically ambiguous positions because their animal states generally result from fairy enchantments. As a quintessential marker of the marvelous, enchantment captures the fairy tale's complex relationship to the era's dominant literary principle of *vraisemblance* and in so doing highlights the ways that an implicitly racialized metamorphosis extends beyond the thematic in d'Aulnoy's *contes*. Seifert argues that d'Aulnoy's use of metamorphosis underscores the fairy tales' "ambivalent treatment of *vraisemblance*" (1996, 35), and he further contends that "representations of the body become a fundamental means by which moral, social, and ontological *vraisemblance* are both upheld and transgressed" (35).[12] Through literal and figurative metamorphosis in d'Aulnoy's *contes* as well as in the broader colonial imagination, the bodies and habits—along with the minds and souls, the cultural practices and beliefs—of animal-like others become specifically French idealizations of human perfection. Ontological *vraisemblance*—which "implied perfecting real individual species in accordance with a true original" (Seifert 1996, 27) and "extending what is true, bringing it to perfection" (Kibédi-Varga, quoted in Seifert 1996, 27)—draws out and articulates most clearly the metarelationship that conjoins metamorphosis and the fairy tale, theme and structure, to reiterate the imperial ideologies of *francisation*, assimilation, and human perfectibility at play in d'Aulnoy's *contes*.

Of d'Aulnoy's many tales of metamorphosis, "Babiole" and "Prince Marcassin"[13]—two stories in which the protagonists assume their animal being immediately following their births—best exemplify the convergence of fairy-tale metamorphosis, colonial policies of *francisation* and assimilation, and ontological *vraisemblance*.[14] Babiole, for instance, is "dressed like a princess" (d'Aulnoy 2003 [1895 (1697 and 1698)], 213), "taught to walk only on her feet" (213), and even learns to speak "in a sweet and clear voice, and so distinctly that not a word was lost" (213). Indeed, as her human qualities become more apparent, she is forced to reside in the queen's court and to "reply like a sybil to a hundred witty and learned questions that she did not always understand" (213); even more, "she was no longer permitted to eat what was to her taste" (213). Similarly, although Prince Marcassin initially "fed like a wild boar in whom the desire of life is strong" (482), he is provided with six nurses, including three dry nurses who were "always giving him Spanish wines and cordials to drink, which taught him early to be a judge of the best wines" (483). His mother, the queen, covers him in ribbons and has his ears pierced; he is dressed in "long garments covering his limbs, and an English cap of black velvet to conceal his head, his ears, and a part of his snout" (484). Even more, he is taught—or forced—to walk on his hind legs, to wear shoes and silk stockings (484). In essence, "no pains were spared to teach him dainty ways and good manners" (484), and "he was beaten when he grunted. In short, in so far as it was possible, they weaned him from his wild-boar habits" (483).

Calling to mind the imperial fantasies of assimilation and perfectibility—the remaking of the other into a perfected French citizen through language, education, dress, and foodways—the attempts to transform Babiole and Prince Marcassin also echo the frustrations about the "nature" of *les sauvages* so often recounted by Catholic missionaries in their letters and reports. After thirty-five years in Canada, the Ursuline missionary Marie de l'Incarnation's early utopian zeal had been heavily tempered: "[I]t is a very difficult thing, not to say impossible, to make the little Savages French or civilized.... We find docility and intelligence in these girls, but when we are least expecting it, they clamber over our wall and go off to run with their kinsmen in the woods.... Such is the nature of the Savages; they cannot be restrained" (Marshall 1967, 341). Similarly, although Babiole is a sweet enough monkey not to bite her childhood companion, the prince, she nonetheless "could not get rid of the evil disposition natural to her race" (d'Aulnoy 2003 [1895 (1697 and 1698)], 214), and Prince Marcassin asks his mother, "Why ... do you always insist that there is no difference between a wild boar and me, that I inspire terror, and that I should go and hide myself?" (494). Here, as in the French colonial missionary reports, d'Aulnoy's references to "the evil disposition natural to [Babiole's] race" and the lack of difference between "a wild boar and [Prince Marcassin]" suggest that, beneath the new clothes, new habitus, and new language, the underlying "nature" of these races continually interferes with the process of *francisation*.

While *race* did not acquire its modern meaning until the eighteenth century, some of its early uses centered on what we would today recognize as the biological—the "nature" referenced by d'Aulnoy as well as by colonial missionaries. When the term *race* first entered the French lexicon in the late fifteenth century, for instance, it referred to the traits valued in breeding animals for the hunt and for warfare; not long after, it also came to apply to the nobility—those believed to have inherited similarly valuable qualities—and eventually to royal lineage (Boulle 2003, 12). In 1684, the essay "A New Division of the Earth, according to the Different Species or Races of Men Who Inhabit It"—published anonymously but rightly attributed to François Bernier—extended such theories of *race* well beyond the nobility. Here, Bernier classifies humanity into four categories based on distinct, fixed physical traits—he distinguishes between inherent skin color and that resulting from exposure to the sun, for example—thus anticipating the later dominance of racial typologies and systems of classification so critical to the consolidation of *race*'s modern meaning.

Largely based on his personal aesthetics, his travels through northern Africa and India, and the published *relations* of the period, Bernier's "A New Division of the Earth" exemplifies the arbitrariness of how *race* and *nature* were deployed in the early modern period. Bernier defines the four races as "1. The 'first' race; 2. The African negroes; 3. The East and Northeast Asian race; 4. The Lapps," and for him "the major axis of difference is between the 'first' race and the Africans" (Stuurman 2000, 4). Contrary to modern racial classification, however, the "first" race includes not only Europeans but also North Africans, Middle Easterners, Indians, some Southeast Asians, and *les Amériquains*, although Bernier equivocates quite extensively on this final inclusion. Moreover, the arbitrariness and personal aesthetics underlying his classification are particularly clear in the naturalized hierarchies of whiteness that permeate all his descriptions and distinctions. Nonetheless—and despite the fact that "A New Division of the Earth" is more "seventeenth-century anthropological essay" than "later, more theoretically-elaborated racial [typology]" (Stuurman 2000, 2)—both Pierre Boulle (2003) and Siep Stuurman offer persuasive evidence of Bernier's essay as significant to what Stuurman calls the "long and complex intellectual trajectory of modern racial thought" (2000, 2). Although "A New Division of the Earth" first appeared in the prestigious *Journal des sçavans*, the journal of the French Academy of Sciences, it is generally treated as a curiosity, relegated to footnotes and passing references in the history of the origins of modern racial thought. Even in its day and in the Buffon-esque development of racial classification that followed not too long after, its influence was limited. Boulle speculates that this may be due to the fact that Bernier "remained a man of the salons" and his prominence in Parisian salon society may have "impeded the broad circulation of his thought" (2003, 20).

While I have not found any evidence to indicate that d'Aulnoy was personally acquainted with Bernier—he was a member of Marguerite de la Sablière's salon during the years that d'Aulnoy seems to have been absent from Paris—her *contes* suggest a familiarity with the idea of racial classification outlined in "A New Division of the Earth."[15] Indeed, the language of race infuses d'Aulnoy's fantastic details and descriptions: a "race of monsters" (d'Aulnoy 2003 [1895 (1697 and 1698)], 117); ogres as a "terrible people" (141); monkeys as a "race" (214); a princess's encounter with *les pagodes*, or "the pagoda race" (256);[16] a battle with the Marionettes, another fantastic race and the "eternal enemies" of the Pagodinas (260–61); a king's fear that the "Marcassin race would be perpetuated in the royal house" (489). As an especially elaborate example, d'Aulnoy's characterization of *les pagodes* transports the language of racial classification into the realm of the marvelous: "she saw coming towards her a hundred pagodas, adorned and built in a hundred different ways. The biggest were about an arm's length in height, and the smallest not more than four fingers; some beautiful, graceful, and pleasant looking; others hideous, and of a terrible ugliness. They were of diamonds, emeralds, rubies, pearls, crystal, amber, coral, porcelain, gold, silver, brass, bronze, iron, wood, clay; some without arms, others without feet, with mouth reaching from ear to ear, squint eyes, flat noses. In short, there is not greater unlikeness between the creatures who inhabit the world than there was between those pagodas" (254). Here, d'Aulnoy's attention to the Pagodinas' material constitution, their facial features, and their bodily forms, together with her acknowledgment of the variation among them, replicates Bernier's classificatory style and ambiguity, his "way of classifying human beings according to physical characteristics such as skin color, facial type and bodily shape" and his claim that "internal variation is also found among the other three races [in addition to the 'first' race]" (Stuurman 2000, 3–4). Similarly, d'Aulnoy's description of an Ethiopian princess's "jet black complexion, [her] flat nose and thick lips" (330) echoes Bernier's characterization of Africans as having "thick lips and that squashed nose" (Boulle 2003, 16), although such descriptions of Africans were certainly not limited to Bernier. At the same time, d'Aulnoy invokes the Ethiopian princess's features in a culturally relative way as the princess wonders, "'is anything wanting that makes a woman handsome?'" (330). That d'Aulnoy's *contes* resonate with a number of different—potentially contradictory—ideas about race highlights the fact that she was writing during a transitional moment in the development of race as a modern concept. If *race* was sometimes associated with biology in the late seventeenth century, it was nonetheless still seen as flexible and unfixed (Boulle 2003, 12).

In drawing together early racial classification and dominant ideas about *francisation*, civility, and human perfectibility, "Prince Marcassin," more than any other metamorphosis tale in d'Aulnoy's collection, moves beyond the themes of assimilation mentioned above to exemplify the ways her *contes* not only reflect, but also participate in, the various discourses circulating in and around contemporary ideas of race and racial difference. As Seifert has demonstrated in his comparative reading of d'Aulnoy's and Murat's rewritings of Straparola's sixteenth-century pig prince tale, d'Aulnoy's "Prince Marcassin" is distinct in its emphasis on the animal protagonist's wild nature. That is, d'Aulnoy names the porcine prince "Marcassin" (young wild boar) and refers to him as "le sanglier" (wild boar) whereas Straparola and Murat both opt for the domesticated "cochon" or "porc" (both meaning "pig").[17] Seifert persuasively interprets d'Aulnoy's choice as "[situating] the prince's animal instincts squarely outside the domesticated and anthropomorphic realms of the 'cochon' and the 'porc'" (2002, 195), and he further argues that such liminality parallels the "tensions within the civilizing process," which are "revealed to be the driving force in masculine subjectivity" (187).[18] Without contesting Seifert's reading, I want to suggest that "Prince Marcassin"'s narrativization of the tensions implicit in the civilizing process might also be productively understood in relation to the formation of colonial subjects in New France. In this context, d'Aulnoy's choice of *marcassin* and *sanglier* takes on even greater significance since Huron—the name given to the natives with whom French colonists built alliances and about whom colonial authorities and missionaries wrote their most extensive ethnographic works—"[alluded] to the practice of shaving the head except for a few small tufts or 'straight locks, like the bristles of a wild boar . . . as this is what *hure* signifies in French'" (Sayre 1997, xii, quoting *Jesuit Relations* 38). With "bristles [that] stood up in a fearsome way" and a "proud" look (d'Aulnoy 2003 [1895 (1697 and 1698)], 484), Prince Marcassin is more than the universal uncivilized other of the French imagination; rather, he is a very specific other whose story condenses the dominant cultural fantasy of colonization as civilizing mission.

Despite Prince Marcassin's dress, education, and training in courtly manners, his animal "nature" continually prevents his complete assimilation to French culture. After two disastrous attempts at marriage—he kills each bride on their wedding night when he learns of their duplicities—Prince Marcassin leaves the court for the forest, "where he began to lead the life of his wild-boar kindred" (499). There he learns that "nothing in the world demands more freedom than the heart," and he "[sees] that all the animals are happy because they live without constraint" (500). Here, Prince Marcassin's appreciation of the forest as symbol of freedom recalls Marie de l'Incarnation's regret that the Ursuline's seminarians continually escaped the convent for the woods, their "nature" not allowing them to be "restrained" (Marshall 1967, 341); clearly, Prince Marcassin's *sauvage* nature prevails over the extensive attempts to "humanize" him. And yet, such an understanding of the heart's need for freedom strikes a particularly human note, and it is with this newfound sensibility that Prince Marcassin woos Marthésie, the youngest sister of his first two brides, only to find that, once again, his animal nature exerts itself: "'There must be,' he said to her, with a wild-boar smile, 'something human mingled with the animal in me. This breaking of my promise for which you blame me, this little trick by which I gained my end, these show the man in me, for, to speak frankly, there is more honour amongst animals than amongst men'" (d'Aulnoy 2003 [1895 (1697 and 1698)], 502–3). The constant blending of animal and human natures in Prince Marcassin exposes the conflicted ideologies implicit in the colonial project of *francisation*. No simple allegory of successful imperial metamorphosis, "Prince Marcassin" highlights instead the often divergent beliefs about *les sauvages*—at times proud, noble, and courageous and at others animalistic, barbaric, and filthy.

The complexity and nuance with which d'Aulnoy renders Prince Marcassin's animal-human hybridity throughout the tale also attests to the tensions at play in the era's mirrored discourses of "civility" and "civilizing." Toward the end of the seventeenth century, civility's historical function as an indexical code for social status was losing its efficacy; somewhat paradoxically, civility had become a "mark of vulgarity" for the nobility because of its capacity to obscure social distinctions "through conformity to common rules," accessible to increasingly diverse segments of the French population through guides to "proper" behavior and manners (Revel 1989, 199–201). No longer an exclusive sign of the elite, civility was now associated with insincerity, appearances, and flattery, particularly among aspiring courtiers, and it is precisely this sense of civility that Prince Marcassin's mother, like many of d'Aulnoy's other protagonists,[19] incisively critiques: "'The former [courtiers] do nothing but sing praises, the latter [princes] hear nothing but praises sung. How is it possible ever to know one's faults in such a labyrinth?" she asks him while trying to persuade him from marrying a second time (d'Aulnoy 2003 [1895 (1697 and 1698)], 494). For d'Aulnoy, like Prince Marcassin, the forest offers an escape from a court ruled by the vulgarities of civility.

And yet, the forest is also the realm of *les sauvages*, characterized above all by its lack of civilization. Here, then, the critique of civility converges with the need to civilize the other. Elaborating on Michèle Farrell's interpretation of the figure of the old, female peasant storyteller as symbolically symptomatic of asymmetrical class relations, Seifert contends that she instantiates an "'aristocratic romanticism,' the elitist, idealized vision of peasant life enabling members of the upper classes to capitalize on the advantages of what Norbert Elias called 'the civilizing process' . . . while simultaneously retreating from its constraints" (1996, 75). That is, according to Seifert, the "originary" storyteller was invoked for strategic reasons related to the socioeconomic politics of *mondain* culture and a "nostalgic fixation on social hierarchy" (75). In similar fashion, the New World *sauvage* provides a figure through which d'Aulnoy can legitimate her understanding of an elite civility free of the vulgarities of courtly life. As such, Prince Marcassin's move to the forest calls attention to the importance of the French civilizing mission while simultaneously dismissing the insignificance of courtly civility. Moreover, as in New France, Prince Marcassin's civilizing process relies on a deeply gendered ideology. As Seifert points out, all three literary versions of "The Pig King" interrogate the "civilizing influence of women upon the prince, masculinity, and the court at large," and despite attempts to highlight the imbrication of "nature and culture, the uncivilized and the civilized, the deformed and the refined," the three literary tales ultimately show how the former are subsumed in the latter (2002b, 187).[20]

In the New World context, Native women were likewise seen as the key to colonial civilizing efforts since it was assumed that "assimilated women would pass on a culture based on French civility to their husbands and children, a culture promoting male authority, controlled sexuality, and stable married households" (Belmessous 2013, 39). Such gendered ideologies also encouraged miscegenation—and specifically intermarriage between French settlers and Native women—as a colonial policy to advance *francisation* in the Canadian territories. According to the colonial logic, intermarriage and cohabitation would facilitate the process by which *les sauvages* took on French cultural practices and integrated into colonial society. At the same time, such liaisons would also prevent Frenchmen "from falling into savagery (*ensauvagement*) as they had in Brazil about fifty years earlier" (36). Even more, the ideological understanding of both settlers and natives as commoners further encouraged such relationships and circumvented any concerns about the possibility of *mésalliance*, the troubling—especially for nobles—union of people across class lines (26).[21]

As was the case for the missionaries and the natives in New France, Marthésie's civilizing of Prince Marcassin is a gradual process—when he greets her, he "[crouches] at her feet, to let her know that wild boars when they wish have most courteous forms of salutation" (d'Aulnoy 2003 [1895 (1697 and 1698)], 502); when she expresses revulsion at the pile of slaughtered animals he offers her for their wedding feast, he is inspired to create a charming presentation of fruits displayed on three hedgehogs instead; when she accuses him of giving his place to a man each night, he controls his anger and reasons with her, no longer reacting with the violence he indulged with her sisters. Before the civilizing process is complete, however—that is, before Prince Marcassin is fully transformed into a human—Marthésie learns that "the Marcassin race was to be perpetuated" (504). Given the possibility of immediate fairy-tale metamorphosis, the time involved in Marthésie's civilizing of Prince Marcassin is particularly significant insofar as it allows for the pregnancy that highlights their cross-species miscegenation—or what *appears* to be a cross-species miscegenation. In reality, Prince Marcassin is transformed into a man each night; however, neither he nor Marthésie seem aware of this nocturnal disenchantment. In this regard, their tale calls to mind two other stories in d'Aulnoy's collection: "The Dolphin," in which Livorette is unknowingly impregnated when she playfully "marries" her beloved canary (the transformed ugly Prince Alidor, whom she despises) and allows him to sleep in her chamber where he turns himself into a man each night, and "The Blue Bird," in which the imprisoned princess and the transformed blue bird carry on an entirely naturalized and passionate love affair. These examples of enduring cross-species erotics—rather than instantaneous disenchantment—suggest that an openness to interracial marriage and miscegenation was central to the imperial imagination of New France.[22]

The happy endings—marriage and transformation into idealized humans—with which d'Aulnoy concludes "Babiole" and "Prince Marcassin," her major metamorphosis tales, suggests a faith and investment in human perfectibility, in the *francisation* and assimilation of *les sauvages*. At the same time, however, "Prince Marcassin" concludes with an ambiguous lesson from the fairies concerning the nature of appearances: while the deaths of the first two brides turn out to be mere illusions, the emphasis on the untrustworthiness of appearances turns back on Prince Marcassin in an ontological muddle, a permanent blurring of human and animal. As Seifert writes with regard to the conclusion, "Neither the animal nor the human are all they seem at face value, and the prince recognizes this long before the end of the tale" (2002b, 202). As such, d'Aulnoy seems to argue, human metamorphosis is marked by a certain fragility. Underlying the fragility of such transformations is a tension between desire and disdain—the prince's constant caressing of Babiole coupled with his mockery when she proclaims her love; the queen's adoration of her son, Prince Marcassin, coupled with her insistence that he should not pursue the women of the court—and this tension points to the complicated project of assimilating a colonial other imagined to be simultaneously exalted and debased.

Beasts, from *Sauvage* to Slave

Given the paradoxes and contradictions underlying *les sauvages* in the colonial imagination, it should not be surprising that official support for French-Native miscegenation and cohabitation was fairly short lived, especially when it became apparent that such relationships frequently resulted in Frenchmen—often fur traders—living among native populations, thus subverting French cultural and religious goals for New France. By the late seventeenth century, intermarriage was no longer encouraged, even if it had not yet been prohibited. Indeed, colonial policies and ideologies of miscegenation in New France continued to spark debate well into the first decades of the eighteenth century. As early as 1686, however, Governor General Jacques René de Brisay de Denonville issued one of the first official statements against cohabitation as part of colonial policy, and by 1709, Governor Vaudreuil argued that "[o]ne should never mingle a bad blood with a good one. Our experience in this country shows that the French who married savage women have become dissolute, idle and have an unbearable independence. And their children are as lazy as the savages themselves. This must prevent us from permitting such marriages... Every child from these unions seems to try constantly to do a lot of harm to the French" (quoted in Belmessous 2013, 47). Here, then, the failures of miscegenation—and of *francisation* more broadly—introduce not only a shift in policy and discourse but also a significant shift in ideology. As Belmessous makes clear, colonial authorities explained these failures through the racialization of Indigenous Americans, evidenced so clearly in Vaudreuil's arguments against "mingl[ing] bad blood with a good one." Although Vaudreuil's discourse of good and bad blood draws on the language of nature or biology—which would obviously constitute the foundation of later theories of race—he was most likely referring to blood as lineage, as was the common usage of the time; nonetheless, his comments are complicated by the fact that blood seems also to refer to *les sauvages* as a group, thus confusing the biological and social meanings of the word and revealing the beginnings of a more modern racial ideology.

In this regard, the emergent discourses of race surrounding New France begin to converge with the ongoing racial formation projects in France's other primary colonial setting, namely the Caribbean. Clearly,

French settlers and colonists were engaged in intimate relationships with Native American and African women across the French empire, and yet official perspectives on these interracial relationships varied significantly. Although colonial authorities and metropolitan officials continued to debate the importance of French-Native marriages for the viability of New France well into the first decades of the eighteenth century, the *Code Noir* of 1724—a revision of the 1685 *Code Noir* and explicitly motivated by the case of Louisiana—strictly "forbid[s] our White subjects of either sex from contracting marriage with Blacks . . . [and] also forbid[s] our said white subjects . . . from living in concubinage with slaves." While historians have posited a number of complex social, cultural, religious, and economic reasons why French authorities might support Native-French relationships in trade-based colonies while outlawing African-French relationships in slave-based colonies,[23] I am more interested in tracing their effects on the development of the animal groom tale in the French tradition.

If these increasingly racialized discourses of otherness and antimiscegenation failed to overwhelm d'Aulnoy's utopian impulses—the marvelous appeal of metamorphosis—they seem to have exerted a decidedly different influence on Gabrielle-Suzanne Barbot de Villeneuve's 1740 "Beauty and the Beast" and its famous rewriting by Jeanne-Marie Leprince de Beaumont in 1756. Villeneuve foregrounds the imperial fantasies of her version of "Beauty and the Beast" by granting it the privileged position in her collection *La Jeune Américaine*, a collection whose frame tale involves the return journey of a plantation owner's daughter to Saint-Domingue upon the completion of her education in France. More than a simple pretext for the collection, Villeneuve's frame tale is deeply imbricated with its two novella-length tales. According to Barbara Cooper's analysis of Villeneuve's complete oeuvre, Villeneuve "takes great care to develop" her frame tales, designing them "in such a way that the fairy tales become a concrete and integral part of the frame plot" (1985, 112–13). In the particular case of *La Jeune Américaine*, Cooper underscores Villeneuve's overall use of French colonial "realism, concreteness, and authenticity" to "[imbue] the otherwise impersonal narrator with the expert authority of a world traveller" (115): the poor air quality in America; the legendary Saint-Dominguan hospitality; the Creole temperament and love of the island environment; the local diseases;

and the negative stereotypes about the inferiority of American manners (115–16).[24] Such detail suggests that Villeneuve had more than a cursory interest in Saint-Domingue; indeed, she wants her readers to "imagine themselves on the trip to Saint-Domingue" (Biancardi 2008 [1740], 94).[25] As Élisa Biancardi points out, the narrator's invitation implies a conflation of exotic and marvelous transport (2008, 94),[26] and such a doubled, fantastic voyage highlights the powerful—albeit implicit—traces of colonial Saint-Domingue and its cultural and political associations in Villeneuve's "Beauty and the Beast."[27]

The French presence in Saint-Domingue began in the second half of the seventeenth century with buccaneer outposts, which were quickly followed by slave-based plantation agriculture and then imperial recognition by Louis XIV in 1665. By the early eighteenth century, Saint-Domingue was the centerpiece of France's empire: as the world's largest producer of sugar, the island generated immense wealth and was "considered by some the most valuable province in France" (Garraway 2005, 8). Although France's Caribbean colonies all benefited from the Atlantic slave trade and from the horrific forms of slave labor on which sugar production, in particular, depended, Saint-Domingue was superlative in its exploitation of slave labor for colonial wealth. Indeed, the island had the largest slave population of any of France's colonies. Doris Garraway cites one statistic that helps put Saint-Domingue's utter reliance on slavery into perspective: "Between 1686 and 1720, the population of slaves in the Lesser Antilles quadrupled, while in Saint-Domingue their numbers increased fourteen times" (2005, 8).

The degree to which colonial slavery—and the scientific and philosophical discourses of "race" that emerged around the same time as its growth, perhaps even through its growth[28]—was discussed in the metropole in the first half of the eighteenth century is unclear. Garraway contends that few books about the Caribbean colonies were popular successes, and she attributes this to the "late date at which colonial slavery became a topic of interest for metropolitan readers and writers" (4); for Garraway, it is only with the 1748 publication of Montesquieu's *De l'Esprit de lois* that colonial slavery began to influence French literature (4). Madeleine Dobie largely agrees, although she argues persuasively that the notable lack of cultural attention to colonial slavery in the New World in the first half of the eighteenth century actually manifests itself, through displacement, in the fascination with "the Orient" (2001, 38–43; 2012, 40). Andrew Curran, in his work on the scientific foundations of race in eighteenth-century investigations of skin color, claims that racialized discussions of human diversity began somewhat earlier: "[B]y the 1730s an increasing number of naturalists, anatomists, and religious writers began debating this question [of the origin of the *nègre*] much more intensely and from a variety of perspectives" (2011, 2). While Dobie critiques Curran for "[conveying] the impression that skin color and the difference embodied by Africans were prominent subjects of discussion in eighteenth-century France" when, she asserts, the works he considers were actually "fairly isolated" (2012, 41), Curran himself points out that "the subject of the *nègre* initially remained irrelevant to most people in France and Europe . . . until the 1750s" (2011, 11). Nonetheless, the fact that in 1739 the prestigious *Journal des sçavans* publicized a prize, sponsored by the Académie royale des sciences de Bordeaux, for the best essay on the "physical causes of *nègre*'s color" (Curran 2011, 2) suggests that, among educated elites, there was substantial interest in both colonial slavery and racial difference. Similarly, Sue Peabody dates public discussion of colonial slavery to midcentury, but her detailed analyses of the Edict of 1718 and the Declaration of 1738—two key pieces of legislation that sought to define the status of slaves in France—likewise imply some degree of public attention to the increasingly imbricated questions of race and slavery (1996, 3–56). Given the prominence and specificity of beliefs about Saint-Domingue in *La Jeune Américaine*, it seems more than likely that Villeneuve was among those who took an interest in such social, political, and philosophical debates.

Regardless, Villeneuve's version of "Beauty and the Beast" is haunted by the presence of race and colonial slavery. From the outset, the tale is motivated by the reality of France's colonial economy: a wealthy merchant loses his fortune to shipwreck and piracy, and, as Aurora Wolfgang contends, when he comes across the Beast's seemingly uninhabited domain, "he imagines, in the spirit of the colonizer, that all the wealth before him must be his for the taking" (2020, 62). In keeping with Villeneuve's perhaps paradoxical tendency to imbue her fairy tales with a "realistic view of the world" (Cooper 1985, 42), the colonial economy is evident throughout the marvelous setting. Among Beauty's favorite enchantments in the Beast's castle, for instance, are an aviary full of rare birds, a group of parrots of all species and colors, and a troop of monkeys of various shapes and colors, several of whom come to form her cortège. While certainly more magically adept in their singing, conversing, entertaining, and courtly mannerisms than the average bird or monkey, Beauty's exotic companions nonetheless represent colonial trade more than fairy magic. As Louise Robbins notes in her work on exotic animals in eighteenth-century Paris, many such animals "were geographically linked to France's colonies" (2002, xiii); in particular, "[m]ost small birds and animals were imported into France from Africa and the Caribbean, reflecting the predominance of these trade routes" as well as the fact that sailors involved with the slave trade "would often buy or trade for parrots, parakeets, finches, and monkeys" (27). In eighteenth-century France, exotic birds and monkeys were status symbols, prized gifts, and rare collectibles, and their value was enhanced by the difficulty of transporting—and sustaining—them across the Atlantic. Thus, the lively diversity of the Beast's birds and monkeys are an especially impressive testament to his incredible wealth, born of both colonialism and fairy magic.

If the Beast's exotic animals call to mind the colonial economy undergirding Villeneuve's tale, he himself is associated with its very engine: the slave. In the context of Caribbean slavery, the categories of slave and African collapse into each other and often slip into the category of the animal. As such, Africans, slaves, and beasts find themselves in an ideological tangle that coheres during the Atlantic slave trade, the justification for which further entrenched earlier stereotypes and beliefs. In her work on representations of Black men in eighteenth-century visual culture, Mary Bellhouse refers to *The Sugar Mill*, an engraving in De Tertre's 1667–71 *Histoire générale des Antilles habitées par les François*, to offer an example of how the Black plantation slave and the beast of burden are rendered symbolically equivalent (2006, 746). Not limited to visual representations, such an equivalency also extended to salon literature of the period; in his overview of François Bernier's "New Division of the Earth" and the emergence of racial typologies in the late seventeenth century, Pierre Boulle describes a passage from Fontenelle's 1685 *Lettres galantes du chevalier d'Her* that underscores the racialization implicit in the association of man and monkey: "[T]his distancing of Africans from Europeans finds its way even into contemporary salon literature, as in a letter from a gallant, accompanying the gift to a lady of 'the two ugliest animals that it [Africa] has produced . . . the stupidest of Moors and the most mischievous [*malicieux*] of monkeys,' in which Fontenelle suggests in an obvious sexual double entendre that what capacity to reason the African possesses, he obtained from 'the long practice' he's had of the monkey" (2003, 19). Here, several ideologies of the African and the slave come to the fore: transgressive sexuality, stupidity, ugliness. For some, like Bernier, such cultural representations of Africans and slaves as easily dominated, animalistic, and stupid legitimated "natural slavery, 'by which those who excel in the powers of the mind command those who only excel in brute force, just as the soul governs the body, and man rules the animals; all the more because it is useful for them to be governed by others, as it is useful for some animals to be domesticated by men'" (quoted in Stuurman 2000, 10).

With "a kind of trunk, similar to an elephant's" (Wolfgang 2020, 95), the Beast's frightful appearance connects him to Africa, and like the African/slave/animal,[29] Villeneuve's Beast is not only ugly but also potentially violent (as Beauty's father discovers after pilfering the Beast's roses) and prone to cannibalism (as Beauty and her father assume as they make their way to his castle).[30] After their first night's conversation, however, Beauty finds that he was "more inclined to be stupid than fierce" (109) and, as she soon learns, something of a "docile Beast" (109). While the descriptions of the Beast and the African/slave/animal share an ideological vocabulary, their alignment is most clearly realized in the hovering sexual threat that the Beast poses throughout the main part of the tale.[31] Suellen Diaconoff characterizes this threat in terms of desire and self-control, thus foregrounding the shared ideological dimensions of the Beast and the slave's supposed hypersexuality: "With each passing day, Belle becomes concerned that the Beast's desire for sex is growing stronger than his self-control and that the threat of sexual violation looms before her" (2005, 166). In essence, the Beast's characterization conforms to "the standard [by midcentury] inventory of vices commonly attributed to the *nègre*: hypersexuality, dishonesty, and a stunning lack of either common sense or intelligence" (Curran 2011, 69).

Addressing the explicit sexuality of the tale, Cooper stresses that "Madame de Villeneuve is no false prude" (1985, 15), citing not only the Beast's blunt and unrefined nightly question of whether Beauty will sleep with him but also the fact that Villeneuve "does not eschew the manifest erotic connotations of 'lit' [bed]" (150). Clearly, Cooper's analysis is a defense of Villeneuve against Jacques Barchilon's assertion that "[t]he chief fault [of the Villeneuve text] consisted in stating in frank and vulgar terms that the Beast was seeking sexual intercourse. Every night the Beast would 'ask Beauty without manners if she wanted to sleep with it (the Beast).' These words recur often enough in the Villeneuve text to become mildly obnoxious" (quoted in Cooper 1985, 150). And yet, Cooper also recognizes the impossibility of a sexual union between Beauty and the Beast due to the "code of *bienséance*" (151). Thus, she reads the scene in which they literally (and chastely) share a bed as Villeneuve's "implicitly feminist" adaptation of "the topos of the wedding night" (151); that is, where the wedding night traditionally initiates female metamorphosis, it here brings about male transformation (151). Most significantly, as both Cooper and Diaconoff point out, the implicit legality of the vows Beauty and the Beast exchange upon her return to the castle and Villeneuve's humorous rendering of their wedding night—in which Beauty's internal anxieties that the bed will not hold the Beast's weight are met by his deep snoring—make it clear that "[t]he monster's intentions . . . were pure. . . . If physical violation or loss of virginity or even rape had been the unspoken threat throughout the tale, it is now revealed as unfounded" (Diaconoff 2005, 168). While the Beast as seeming sexual threat might ultimately be assimilated to the tale's lesson about appearances, the fact remains that while he is the Beast, he figures the threat of animal sexuality, a sexuality that challenges the limits of his self-control and, in this way, channels increasing fears of miscegenation.

If the specter of miscegenation looms large in Beauty's consenting to "these strange nuptials" (Wolfgang 2020, 129; "cet étrange hymen," Villeneuve 2008 [1740], 155), Villeneuve is careful to dissociate the prince from the Beast through the language of liberty, a language that reiterates the tale's relation to France's Caribbean empire and its colonial systems of plantation slavery. While imprisonment is thematized throughout the tale—Beauty's, the exotic birds in the Beast's aviary, even the prince in the body of the Beast—it is in two of Beauty's declarations that the language of colonial slavery really comes to the fore. In both instances, Beauty announces her willingness to pay any price for her beloved Unknown's freedom: "Je voudrais à quelque prix que ce fût vous rendre la liberté" (Villeneuve 2008 [1740], 131; "I would do anything to set you free" [Wolfgang 2020, 114]; literally "I would like, *at any price*, to free you" [my emphasis]) and "c'était un bonheur qu'elle eût acheté du prix de sa liberté" (Villeneuve 2008 [1740], 136; "it was a happiness for which she would have sacrificed her freedom, and even all the luxury that surrounded her" [Wolfgang 2020, 118]; literally "it was a happiness she would have bought with the price of her freedom" [my translation]). In both cases, the price of the transaction depends on an implicit calculus of the cost of liberty and human life. Finally, lest there be any question, Beauty declares "le prince est libre" (Villeneuve 2008 [1740], 162; "the prince is free" [my translation]) in response to the fairy's inquiry as to whether she will renounce her status as the prince's wife when his mother contests the marriage on the grounds of its *mésalliance* after learning that Beauty is the daughter of a merchant.[32] According to Garraway, the juridical terms for *slave* and *free* are predicated on an ideological and linguistic distinction "between 'naturally free person' (*libre naturel*) and 'freed person' (*affranchi*)" (2005, 207). Thus, even though the prince is freed from his beastly existence, Beauty categorically marks him as a free person.

Race—made marvelous by beastly otherness—is no longer flexible and unfixed as it was in d'Aulnoy's tales, and as such it is essentially excised from the animal groom tale—or, from a complementary perspective, it entirely dominates the tale. That is, the prince is now born into royalty and is transformed into a beast only in his adolescence; as a result, his disenchantment is a return to his "natural" civilized and free status. The quixotic possibilities of d'Aulnoy's animal-human couplings are entirely foreclosed in Villeneuve's and Beaumont's "Beauty and the Beast" tales, where the beast must be transformed *prior to* any significant interaction with the virginal maiden and certainly before their relationship is consummated; moreover, his disenchantment is much less involved, the consequence of a single night's enchanted slumber or a simple kiss that distinguishes Villeneuve's and Beaumont's moralizing lessons about appearances from d'Aulnoy's more ambiguous ontological and epistemological conclusion that derives from a much longer process of transformation. More than simple narrative choices, these changes reflect France's shifting imperial priorities—from seventeenth-century New France to the increasingly lucrative Caribbean holdings of the late seventeenth and eighteenth centuries—and, most significantly, the distinctive racializations of their colonial subjects.[33] While already in Bernier's early theory of race Native Americans are subsumed (albeit equivocally) into the "first" race and "the major axis of difference is between the 'first' race and the Africans" (Stuurman 2000, 4), the systems of plantation slavery that generated vast wealth for the French Caribbean islands only exacerbated and further entrenched these early distinctions and the stereotypes at the foundation of such racial formations.

The sixteen-year interval between the publication of Villeneuve's "Beauty and the Beast" and Beaumont's much shorter, highly didactic version is precisely the period in which early modern ideas about race were consolidated into a scientific system that continues to exert a lingering influence today. The middle of the eighteenth century saw the publication of several racial typologies, including Buffon's incredibly popular *Histoire naturelle* (1749–89), which positioned man and animal in a shared taxonomic system, often drawing comparisons between the two, and proved foundational to a science of race.[34] At the same time, the philosophical debate concerning slavery also began to cohere and to exert a greater presence in public discourse, while the start of the Seven Years' War heightened general awareness of France's colonial stake in the Caribbean. The burgeoning interest in race science and the increased attention to colonial slavery intersect in contemporary concerns about "animal slaves," common representations of "the domestic animal as overworked slave, the wild animal as mercilessly harassed fugitive, and the captive animal as unhappy prisoner" (Robbins 2002, 190). Although first used in the positive sense, by midcentury "animal slaves" became a negative description in literature as well as in natural history books, and—depending on the implicit emphasis (*animal* or *slave*)—they were invoked as commentaries on animal cruelty or colonial slavery (and sometimes both) (190). In this context, Beaumont's abbreviated tale and the complete erasure of the Beast's explicit sexuality might be understood as more than simple bourgeois prudery; rather, such erasure (or, perhaps more likely, repression) also suggests the increasingly strong prohibitions against miscegenation and the underlying fear of Black male (hyper)sexuality, especially given the explicit racialization of the Beast by Miss Molly in Beaumont's frame narrative: "I believe that I would have accustomed myself to seeing him, just like Beauty. When Papa took on a little boy who was all black to be his lackey, I was afraid of him. I would hide myself when he would enter a room. To me he seemed uglier than a beast. And then, little by little, I accustomed myself to it. He lifts me when I get into the carriage, and I no longer think of his face" (Duggan 2016, 1184). With Beaumont's "Beauty and the Beast"—which has become so canonical that critics often cite it as the original literary version (Cooper 1985, 2–3)—the French animal groom tale comes to represent not the utopian possibilities of assimilation but the racial anxieties of miscegenation, a trend made abundantly clear in the fairy tale's Edwardian and Victorian dramatic adaptations (Smith and Do Rozario 2016).

It is not uncommon for fairy-tale scholars and critics to read in the fantastic beasts and ogres of the European fairy tale a generalized other. I am arguing, however, that the French animal groom tales—so iconic of *the* European fairy tale in the popular imagination and so central to fairy-tale scholarship—are informed by very specific ideas and ideologies of race and colonization circulating in the French imperial imagination of the late seventeenth and eighteenth centuries.[35] That said, I am not suggesting a coherent ideological project in any of the *conteuses'* animal groom tales but rather an ongoing negotiation—perhaps even a subconscious one—with discourses of empire, assimilation, and otherness. D'Aulnoy's collection, as a whole, reveals racial formation in process while Villeneuve's and Beaumont's "Beauty and the Beast" tales suggest more established ideologies of race. Insofar as their *contes de fées* were canonical and influential, however, they demonstrate that early modern and modern ideas about race played a fundamental role in the development of the European fairy tale, a genre whose fantastic and utopian possibilities were largely foreclosed as the demands of empire intensified and race came to assume its modern meanings.

3

GERMANY, 1812–57

Jacob and Wilhelm Grimm's
Children's and Household Tales

The long century between the 1740 publication of Villeneuve's "La Belle et la Bête" and the final, highly crafted seventh edition of Jacob and Wilhelm Grimm's *Kinder- und Hausmärchen* in 1857 was dominated by a European preoccupation with questions of human difference and its associated cultural, economic, and moral implications. Although early typologies of human variability, such as François Bernier's "New Division of the Earth by the Different Species or 'Races' of Man that Inhabit It" (1684), emerged prior to the eighteenth century, the eighteenth century saw a real burgeoning of scientific theories of race as well as the heated philosophical, religious, ethnological, and scientific debates they aroused. German thinkers—among them Immanuel Kant, Johann Gottfried Herder, Johann Gottlieb Fichte, Johann Friedrich Blumenbach, Christoph Meiners, Friedrich Wilhelm Joseph von Schelling, Johann David Michaelis—were foundational to the development and critique of these new conceptualizations of human difference, often articulating their positions with nationalist and/or antisemitic politics, with Romantic literature and art, with the nascent discipline of ethnology, with scholarly Orientalism, and with fantasies of colonial power.

Unfolding against a backdrop of fervid European imperialism—contests for control of the highly lucrative Caribbean islands, extensive colonial systems in India and Southeast Asia, the ongoing conquest and colonization of the Americas—eighteenth- and nineteenth-century racial thinking and theorizing was, of course, equally inflected by the global stirrings and eventual successes of revolution. Within this context, the French and Haitian Revolutions had profound effects on German philosophy and literature. Susan Buck-Morss argues convincingly, for instance, that the Haitian Revolution contributed significantly to G. W. F. Hegel's theory of the master-slave dialectic, as elaborated in his *The Phenomenology of Mind* (1807), which also bears the influences of the French Revolution (2009, passim).[1] More directly related to scientific and ethnological discourses of race and human variability, Christoph Meiners's 1790 series of articles outlining the "natural inferiority" of Asians, Africans, and Americans relative to white Europeans is, according to Susanne Zantop, an undeniable reaction to the "slave uprisings in the French colony of St. Domingue, the first serious challenge to European colonial rule" (1997b, 23). In a slightly later series of articles published in 1792, Meiners extends his racial taxonomy to differentiate and rank white Europeans in a classificatory system that firmly establishes the "Germanic type" as the pinnacle of the racial hierarchy, and Zantop contends that this further stratification of human difference even among white Europeans represents a shift in Meiners's racial anxiety from colonial uprisings to the contagious potentialities of the French Revolution, the "threat of revolutionary ideas and armies that might spill across the Rhine" (29).

Meiners was not alone in his anxieties: although his ideas were "reductive" and "at times shrill," they also tapped into the "despair and frustration" many German intellectuals experienced in the 1790s as a result of internal "German" fragmentation and weakness relative to the French menace (Zantop 1997a, 90). Along these lines, Zantop highlights the particular threat of "feminization" through "French 'rape' of German territories" as a disquieting concern for many such German intellectuals (1997b, 29), a concern that Meiners translated into a masculinist dimension of his racial hierarchy. While not articulating exactly the same fears of feminization associated with the French Revolution, Ludwig Achim von Arnim reveals a similar desire for Germany to protect itself from the ostensibly threatening elements at the revolution's heart. In "Von Volksliedern," the 1805 essay he published together with *Des Knaben Wunderhorn* (coedited with Clemens Brentano), von Arnim distinguishes the revolutionary "alienated poor of modern society" from the "pre-modern, pre-capitalist, and rural" *Volk*, maintaining that "it was actually the extinction of folk-song in France (i.e., by implication, the conversion of its Volk into a deracinated modern mass) which made the revolution of 1789 possible" (Perraudin 2000, 8). The alarming prospect of German "deracination" was only one of the cultural dangers von Arnim—like other Romantic writers of the period—identified with the French Revolution, as Michael Perraudin makes clear in his enumeration of the impressive range of grievances in von Arnim's "elaborately regressive . . . Romantic cultural-political critique": "rationalist academicism and the decadence and enervation of the current political regime in Germany . . . cosmopolitanism, urbanization, taxation, bureaucratisation, the cult of private property, liberal economics and its neglect of the lower classes, pernicious policies of universal education, the attempts to found a national theatre, mercenary soldiering, and a range of further issues" (2000, 7–8).

In contrast to von Arnim, some Romantics, like Friedrich Wilhelm Joseph Schelling, initially hoped that the French Revolution would "inspire rather than dictate the course of cultural change in Germany" (Williamson 2006, 150), but the Napoleonic invasion of Prussia in 1806 and the subsequent Confederation of the Rhine soon quelled any such hopes and, for many German intellectuals, replaced them with nationalist aspirations.[2] Despite philosophical, literary, and political differences, such nationalist aspirations often cohered around Johann Gottfried Herder's work on "national poetry"—or folk poetry—as an expression of a group's collective spirit, its *Volksgeist* or *Nationalgeist*. For Herder, early German literature had been "truly close to the people" before it was infiltrated by "foreign cultural influences by way of an aristocracy committed to suppressing any expression of a national community spirit"; as such, the "true spirit of national democracy could only develop within the framework of a free and national state" (Hermand 1992, 8). While folk poetry was foundational to Herder's theorization of human variability and constituted an early form of cultural relativism—he famously conjectured that Black Africans might see white Europeans as albinos and devils (Sikka 2005, 328; Schmiesing 2016, 212)—his broader understanding of human difference was nonetheless typically (for the period) Eurocentric and certainly never precluded his own nationalist inclinations nor the ways his work inspired other, more extreme nationalists, especially after "the French Revolution and the Napoleonic Wars served both to spread and politicize [his] ideas" (Hare and Link 2019, 580).[3]

In this context, Herder's theories of *Volksgeist* opened cultural spaces for political and artistic movements centered on a celebration of the "old Teutons," a "decidedly mythologized people often compared to the ancient Romans in terms of courage, loyalty, virtue, nobility, and love of freedom" and whose status as "'free men,' unfettered by feudal lords or taxes," resonated with the egalitarian values of the revolution across the Rhine (Hermand 1992, 2, 10). While less radically democratic, even segments of the intellectual elite "looked to ancient models to shape a new Germanic destiny" (Marchand 2009, 55), and Suzanne L. Marchand calls attention to the influence of Herder's work on a "remarkable contingent of young scholars—including the brothers Grimm, Humboldt, and Schlegel," who "sought in the rewriting of universal cultural history a narrative that would explain and validate German-Christian culture's world-historical mission in the present" (55). Scholars of German Orientalism, like Marchand and Todd Kontje (2004), highlight the imbricated histories of nationalist interest in Germanic "*Volkslieder, Märchen,* and neglected works of the Middle Ages" (Kontje 2004, 119–20), Oriental religions and languages, comparative linguistics, and the emergent discipline of *Germanistik*, and Kontje articulates the specific way nineteenth-century scholars enacted a "double [move]" to "simultaneously align Germany with Europe in its development away from an unchanging Orient and distance Germany from the rest of Europe by claiming priority in the race to modern times" (115).

These frequently related, sometimes crosscutting, scholarly, social, and political discourses, debates, and movements—tethered in various ways to historical upheavals and transnational empires, to German universities and social organizations, to literature and popular culture—convey a sense of the intellectual energy and political urgency driving much of the racial thinking so central to late-eighteenth- and nineteenth-century German letters and science. As scholars of German legal history and language and Herderian collectors of ostensibly German legends, folktales, and fairy tales, as sometimes political appointees and resistors, and as antisemitic sympathizers and avowed Romantic nationalists, Jacob and Wilhelm Grimm were immersed in this cultural world.[4] As Ruth B. Bottigheimer notes, the brothers were attuned to "the major political traumas of the day," beginning with the French Revolution and the subsequent Thermidorian Reaction (1987, 3). Perhaps even more significantly, as J. Laurence Hare and Fabian Link suggest, the Grimms also contributed—at least indirectly—to the "salient political questions of the day" by virtue of their scholarship on the German *Volk* and, simultaneously, their status as political appointees, which helped ensure "that the cultural notion of *Volk* and the political idea of the nation-state . . . overlapped from the outset, as contemporaries realized that defining the former was necessary to constructing the latter" (2019, 583–84). Given this cultural surround, it can be no surprise that the increasingly detailed and didactic editions of *Kinder- und Hausmärchen* are undeniably marked by the ideologies of race circulating in and through the Grimms' scholarly and political worlds, ideologies I seek to lay bare in my reading of their tales alongside these historical events and discourses.

The Racialization of Jews and "Jewishness"

The confluence of nascent scientific and ethnologic theories of race, European imperial expansion, transnational revolutionary fervor, German nationalism, and scholarly Orientalism also brought into particularly sharp focus contemporary questions surrounding Jewish emancipation. European Jews had, of course, been subject to tremendous prejudice and oppression for centuries, but much of that prejudice was motivated by religious difference and by an enduring sense of Jews as "the archetypal non-national, the 'state within a state'" (MacMaster 2000, 70), an understanding that led to their marginalization in many eighteenth-century theories of race predicated on a correlation between human variability and geography (Hess 2006, 205). As Jonathan M. Hess points out, however, the earliest debates about Jewish emancipation together with a growing attention to "Semitic" languages, peoples, and cultures in Orientalist theological scholarship—both dating to the 1780s—helped establish a "specific link between theological antagonism toward Judaism and a racially conceived, politically charged antisemitism" (2000, 56–57).[5] While Jews' "Oriental" origins had long factored in European anti-Judaism, Nina Berman contends that in the context of late-eighteenth- and early-nineteenth-century Orientalism this association provided a foundation for an explicitly racial antisemitism (2011, 175–76). Germany's relationship to the Middle East—especially, but not exclusively, manifest in scholarly and literary Orientalism—thus proved critical to the ideological development and eventual solidifying of a racialized antisemitism, a *"biologically* determined Otherness" in the hegemonic service of "building a Christian German nation" (Hewitt-White 2003, 122, emphasis in original).

The expressly Christian nationalist movement in Germany shared deep, at times overlapping, affinities with Romantic nationalism, and the desire among such Romantic thinkers as Adam Müller, Joseph Görres, and Jacob Grimm to "return to a medieval and/or feudal society or a religiously mystified 'German essence' or 'elementary power'" was implicitly—if not explicitly—antisemitic at its core (Hermand 1992, 18). If one source of a "religiously mystified 'German essence' was to be found in the mythologized 'Old Teutons,'" Berman suggests that another might be the "timeless yet clearly premodern Orient," at once a nostalgic and a utopian site offering potential solutions for a postrevolutionary Europe (2011, 168). Within this context, Berman calls attention to the fairy tale as "one of the most popular forms used to express the various changes associated with the political and social transformation in the postrevolutionary period" (170) and suggests that the "Oriental tale"—in collections like the *Arabian Nights*; in French and British translations, adaptations, and inspirations; and in *Kunstmärchen* by early Romantics like Wieland, Goethe, and Wackenroder—is entangled, through influence, inspiration, and incorporation, with "the German fairy tale," a "genre facilitating the articulation of a German national consciousness" (170).

Following Berman's privileging of the German fairy tale as an especially significant genre for the period's Christian Romantic nationalism, it can hardly be surprising that the explicitly antisemitic Christlich-Deutsche Tischgesellschaft was cofounded by the folk song collector Achim von Arnim in 1811 and counted among its initial members his *Des Knaben Wunderhorn* collaborator, Clemens Brentano, as well as Friedrich von Savigny, Wilhelm Grimm's "revered mentor" (Bottigheimer 1987, 141). Despite von Arnim's characterization of the Christlich-Deutsche Tischgesellschaft as a "Freßgesellschaft" (eating society) founded "partly in 'Scherz,' partly in 'Ernst,'" Charlene A. Lea makes clear that von Arnim had "serious political and cultural aims for his creation" (1993, 89). One of the group's first actions was to determine its membership, and von Arnim proposed banning "philistines, non-converted Jews, Frenchmen, and women" (Lea 1993, 92); although he later claimed that his inclusion of

Jews in that list was a "Scherz" (joke), his cofounder, the conservative and jingoistic Adam Müller, not only lent it credence but also extended the list to include even converted Jews, and it was this amended proposal that ultimately passed (Lea 1993, 92). While the Grimms were not members of the Berlin-based Christlich-Deutsche Tischgesellschaft, they were undeniably aware of its activities: von Arnim wrote of the group in a letter to the brothers (Lea 1993, 89), and von Arnim, Brentano, and von Savigny were part of the Grimms' closest social and intellectual circles (Zipes 2002, 8). Even more, as Lea notes, the Christlich-Deutsche Tischgesellschaft was known and taken seriously by those outside of the society, and though its members were so diverse as to render political consensus impossible, the group's undivided antisemitism and its ban on Jews was well recognized (1993, 92, 94).

At an early meeting of the Christlich-Deutsche Tischgesellschaft, Brentano presented what he deemed to be an amusing paper titled "Der Philister vor, in und nach der Geschichte" (The philistine before, in, and after history), which superficially contrasted philistines and Jews in a "vicious" attack on both groups (Lea 1993, 94). Lea describes "Der Philister" as dominated by "hatefulness and ethnocentrism," and she catalogs Brentano's religious, economic, social, and philosophical antisemitism, which he integrates in a paragraph critiquing the Jewish nouveaux riches:

> In this bitter passage, Brentano intends to remind the reader to hate all Jews because Jews were present at the crucifixion of Christ. He mentions the supposed dirtiness of Jews, who he says were still accompanied by flies from the Egyptian plague. Brentano even brings in the old clothes which poor Jews sold, contrasting those Jews with the theater-going Jews in Berlin who work at the stock market. For him, these bankers are still holding the dreaded letters of credit for which Jewish moneylenders had been known since the Middle Ages, when Jews were barred from other professions. (94–95)

Brentano's paper was not initially intended for publication, but within a couple months of his presentation to the Christlich-Deutsch Tischgesellschaft he had two hundred unsigned copies printed. The lack of author attribution led to speculation among angry liberals and Jews that von Arnim had penned "Der Philister" (an indication of how thoroughly he was associated with antisemitism), and this assumption caused a very public quarrel and imbroglio with Moritz Itzig, a converted Jew in Berlin's high society. The attention the affair garnered—alongside the circulation of "Der Philister" and von Arnim's own antisemitic writings—contributed to the group's "indelible anti-Semitic stamp" (Lea 1993, 94) and underscores the centrality of antisemitism to Christian Romantic nationalism and to contemporary understandings of the German *Volk*, not only for von Arnim and Brentano but also for other folk narrative collectors and editors like the Grimms.

Although overtly Jewish characters feature in only three of the Grimms' tales[6]—one of which has been read as somewhat ambiguous in terms of its antisemitism (Bottigheimer 1987, 141; Helfer 2009, 33)—Wilhelm's decision to include the two unquestionably antisemitic tales in the Small Edition of *Kinder- und Hausmärchen*, "where they would and did get maximum exposure among particularly impressionable young readers" (Bottigheimer 1987, 141), lends credence to Martha B. Helfer's contention that a "conscious anti-Jewish agenda arguably informs the Grimms' *Kinder- und Hausmärchen*," even if it is not the collection's primary motivation (2009, 32). So too does the fact that variants of all three tales exist without Jewish characters. A particularly telling example involves "The Jew in the Thornbush," the most egregiously offensive of the collection's three overtly antisemitic tales. In her analysis of Wilhelm's 1815 notes to this tale together with its publishing history, Bottigheimer calls attention to the fact that Wilhelm "[skirts] any analysis of how the figure of the Jew came to be substituted for that of the monk two hundred years before" (1987, 140) and asks why the tale is even included in *Children's and Household Tales* given that there are versions of the tale in mid-nineteenth-century German collections featuring the monk as victim.[7]

Despite its title, "The Jew in the Thornbush" revolves not around the Jewish character but around the former servant of a miserly rich man. Industrious, cheerful, and, as it turns out, rather naive, the servant works without pay for three years, at which point he finally requests his earnings in order that he might go out into the world. The miser makes a false show of magnanimity, pays the servant three farthings, and the servant goes off feeling like a wealthy man. He soon meets a dwarf who begs the three farthings from him, and, when the servant readily hands them over, the dwarf grants him three wishes: a gun that never misses its mark, a fiddle that compels everyone to dance, and the power to make others grant his demands. Shortly after taking possession of his new acquisitions, the servant encounters "a Jew with a long goatee" marveling at a singing bird and wishing someone could salt its tail (Zipes 2003, 368). At this, the servant shoots the bird with his charmed gun and then tells the Jew, whom he calls a "lousy swindler," to fetch the bird from the thornbush where it has fallen; the servant then begins to play his magic fiddle, causing the Jew injury as he is forced to dance among the thorns. The Jew gives the servant his bag of gold to stop fiddling, and after the servant leaves, the Jew reports the incident to the local judge, who sends a party after the servant, finds his account less than believable, and sentences him to hang. Ascending to the gallows, the servant asks that he be granted a final request—to play his fiddle one last time—which the judge allows. In the midst of the furious dancing, the judge spares the servant's life in exchange for an end to the fiddling. The servant then approaches the Jew, who had asked to be tied up when the servant requested a last chance to play his fiddle, again calling him a "lousy swindler" and demanding, under threat of more fiddling, that he "confess and tell us where you got the money from" (369). The Jew then screams, "'I stole it, I stole it!' . . . 'but you earned it honestly'" (369), at which point the judge has him hanged as a thief.

"The Jew in the Thornbush" is an absurdly confounding tale that, in Bottigheimer's words, "avoids rational causation and obfuscates responsibility for actions, perhaps to dim the reader's perception of its purposefully unjust conclusion" (1987, 138). Indeed, the logic of the tale is accessible only when read through an antisemitic lens that allows the unscrupulous and miserly master to go unremarked, the maliciously mischievous and extortionist servant to be called "honest," and the Jew to claim the servant earned the bag of gold honestly. As Bottigheimer establishes, such a lens also required Wilhelm's increasingly antisemitic editing of the tale between its first appearance in 1815 and its final form in 1839: the servant, "faithful" and "diligent" in 1815, becomes "really faithful" in 1819 and, finally, "diligent" and "honest" by 1839; the Jew goes from being "old" in 1815 to being "a Jew with a long goat's beard," thus associating him with the devil and with other scapegoats (1987, 139).[8]

Consistent with Wilhelm's often pedantic elaborations to the tales, he also adds nuance to the servant's ostensible motivations for forcing the Jew to dance among the thorns: during their first meeting in 1815, the servant "thinks to himself that the Jew has cheated enough people and the narrative adds that the 100 gulden the Jew offered the servant to stop playing the fiddle had just been squeezed out of a Christian" (Bottigheimer 1987, 139); by the final edition, the servant's justification is made ever clearer: "You've skinned plenty of people, so now the thorns will give you some of your own treatment in return" (Zipes 2003, 368). Similarly, the 1815 tale concludes with a simple summarizing sentence— "Then my servant let his fiddle rest and the scoundrel was hanged on the gallows in his place" (Bottigheimer 1987, 139)—whereas the final version closes with the Jew's confession and declaration of the servant's having "earned" the money "honestly" (Zipes 2003, 369).

Wilhelm's evocative additions and revisions do more than intensify the antisemitism at the heart of "The Jew in the Thornbush," however; they also introduce a number of antisemitic subtexts absent from the 1815 version. As Helfer points out, for instance, the servant's rationale for his malicious fiddling while the Jew is in the thornbush—the thorns-for-thorns exchange based on an eye-for-an-eye logic that seems too sophisticated for the naive servant—calls to mind "the Jew's true crime" by "[invoking] the figure of another Jew famously crowned in thorns," thereby ultimately suggesting that "the just punishment for the Jew for allegedly crucifying Jesus is the elimination of the Jew from Christian society" (2009, 40–41). While the antisemitism driving "The Jew in the Thornbush" is thematically abundant, Helfer's reading of the tale's antisemitic subtexts supersedes the thematic and focuses instead on the structural dimension of the thorns-for-thorns exchange. In so doing, she identifies in that particular exchange an example of what she terms a *"Tausch-Täuschung* problematic typical of many Enlightenment texts," including the antisemitic fairy tales in the German Romantic tradition that she analyzes for her case study: "[T]rue Christian morality is constructed through a series of narrative trades or exchanges (*Tausch[e]*) that expose deception (*Täuschung*) . . . coded as the quintessential 'Jewish' trait" (2009, 38–39). Reading "The Jew in the Thornbush" through Helfer's *Tausch-Täuschung* problematic helps translate the tale's seeming lack of "rational causation" into a coherent, albeit disturbingly antisemitic, logic while also drawing out its intertextual resonances with the other two antisemitic tales in *Kinder- und Hausmärchen*.

"The Good Bargain" offers a particularly clear example of the underlying antisemitic structure of the *Tausch-Täuschung* problematic as the tale revolves around a series of exchanges undertaken by a simpleton farmer. The series of trades begins when the farmer sells two cows for seven talers and, passing a pond on the way home, mistakes the frogs' croaking—*aat, aat, aat*, which he hears as *Acht* (eight)—as a challenge to the sum he acquired; in order to settle the dispute, he throws the coins into the pond and waits for the frogs to count and return them. A while later, after acquiring and slaughtering another cow, he heads to the city to sell the meat to the butcher; along the way, he encounters a pack of dogs and mistakes their barking—*wuff, wuff, wuff*—as a request for a whiff of the meat, which he leaves with them to sniff and then deliver to the butcher. After three days, he goes to the butcher and demands payment for the meat, only to be chased off by the angry butcher and his threatening broomstick. The farmer then seeks an audience with the king so he can report the perceived injustice, and when the king and his daughter hear the farmer's tale of the frogs, the dogs, and the butcher, the daughter bursts out laughing. Because she is a princess who never laughs, the king rewards the farmer by giving her to him in marriage, but the farmer—already married—declines, which angers the king. The king then offers the farmer another reward—"five hundred in full measure" (Zipes 2003, 28)—if he will return in three days to collect it. A sentry who witnessed the princess laughing asks the farmer about his reward, and when he learns that the farmer is to receive "five hundred," he begs a share; a Jew, who happens to overhear their conversation, offers to change three hundred of the promised reward into small coins, whereupon he cheats the farmer by giving him "the sum in bad groschen, three of which were worth two good ones" (28). When the farmer returns to the king to claim his reward, the king orders his coat be removed so that he may receive the five hundred, at which point the farmer reveals that they no longer belong to him as he gave two hundred to the sentry and three hundred to the Jew, who are forced to take his lashings; the king is so entertained by what the farmer has done that he offers him yet another reward, inviting him to take as much money as he wants from the king's treasure chamber. Later, when the Jew overhears the farmer maligning the king, whom he believes may have shorted his reward, he runs to tell the king, talks the farmer into returning to the kingdom, and, as a way of getting the farmer to go immediately, offers to lend him his beautiful coat. When the king threatens to punish the farmer for his remarks, the farmer replies: "Jews always tell lies. There's not a word of truth that comes out of his mouth. Why, that fellow's even capable of claiming that I'm wearing his coat" (29). Seeing no reason to question the farmer's claim that "Jews always tell lies," the king declares that "[t]he Jew has certainly deceived someone, either me or the farmer"; he then "had the Jew given his due again in *hard* talers" while the farmer leaves "in the good coat with good money in his pocket" (29).

For Helfer, the main characters' underlying structural equivalency condenses the *Tausch-Täuschung* problematic so clearly thematized in "The Good Bargain": "The peasant goes home 'good,' pleased that he has finally closed a good deal, with good money in his pocket and a good coat on his back. The Jew, in contrast, deals in 'bad' coins and remains 'bad' throughout the text" (2009, 38). Even more, as Helfer points out, the Jew's trading in "bad faith" aligns him with the tale's other "bad faith" trading partners—the "dishonest, thick-headed frogs with big mouths and bulging eyes, and the thieving dogs," whose descriptions rely on "semantic markers derived from theological and moral registers to present antisemitism as amusing and just, as entirely keeping with a Christian ethos" (38). The metaphoric dimension of the purportedly "Jewish" behavior represented by the animal "traders" is even more clearly rendered in "The Bright Sun Will Bring It to Light," the least overtly antisemitic tale, in which a journeyman tailor attempts to rob a Jew who claims to have only eight farthings. Believing, per dominant antisemitic stereotypes, that the Jew must have "a lot of money with him" and that he is lying about being poor, the tailor beats and kills him only to find that the Jew does, indeed, have only eight farthings; as the Jew is dying he says, "The bright sun will bring it to light!" (Zipes 2003, 383). Years later, when the tailor is married with children, his wife finds him considering the sun's reflection on the wall and asks what he means when he says, "Ah, yes, the sun wants very much to bring it to light, but it can't" (383); after some cajoling, he finally tells her about killing the Jew, swearing her to secrecy, but (in keeping with the misogynist depictions of female characters throughout *Kinder- und Hausmärchen*) she tells her neighbor, who tells someone else, until the entire city learns the story and the tailor is tried and convicted.

Here, as Helfer argues, what the *Tausch-Täuschung* problematic makes particularly evident through the tailor as a metaphoric Jew— "[he] travels, Wandering Jew-like, in the world plying his trade; he will do anything for money; he threatens innocent people; he murders; he deceives even his closest relatives; and he tries to hide his true nature" (2009, 36)—is the deceptively insidious nature of potential Jewish assimilation and "passing" in Christian society. In this sense, "The Bright Sun Will Bring It to Light," while not as overtly antisemitic as the other two tales included in *Kinder- und Hausmärchen*, is perhaps the most political, effectively warning those who might favor Jewish emancipation of the dangers associated with assimilated—that is to say, hidden—Jews. At the same time, although "Jewish" behavior is "exposed" and ultimately condemned in "The Bright Sun Will Bring It to Light," the antisemitism of these three tales is not necessarily always anchored to stereotypical "Jewish" behaviors. The rich, miserly, duplicitous master in "The Jew in the Thornbush" escapes any censure and narrative commentary, for instance, and the malicious, deceitful, extortionist acts perpetrated by the servant and the simpleton farmer are celebrated and rewarded. Such seeming inconsistencies thus establish "Jewishness" as a free-floating signifier and indicate that the diffuse quality of the Jewish threat exists not in "Jewish" behavior but in the Jew's "very nature" (Helfer 2009, 39). Implicit in that "nature," of course, is a racialized understanding of both "Jewishness" and antisemitism, and I want to suggest that this explicitly racialized logic structures much of *Kinder- und Hausmärchen* in often implicit—but highly significant—ways.

Racialized Antisemitism and Colonial Anti-Black Racism

While the question of Jewish emancipation certainly played a pivotal role in the Grimms' overtly antisemitic tales, it was by no means the only pressing question to emerge from the crucible of late-eighteenth- and early-nineteenth-century European race science, philosophy, ethnology, and imperialism. Indeed, the question of slavery—and its abolition—inspired even greater moral and political debate across the continent as well as the Atlantic.[9] Although seemingly distinct, Jewish emancipation and Black abolition were often politically and culturally linked through parallel stereotypes of Jewish and Black racial difference from white Europeans as well as through conceptual and ideological relays between colonialism and nationalism. The long-standing belief that Jews had "interbred with Arabs and Africans before migrating to Europe" helped instantiate the idea of Jewish "blackness" in European race science as early as the late eighteenth century (Davis 2012, 80), and so compelling was this idea that by about 1860 Jews were regularly characterized in specifically racialized ways as "black Negroes," "black Africans," and "white Negroes" (MacMaster 2000, 66; Gilman 1985, 31). At the same time, characterizations of Black Africans reverberated with the language and logic of antisemitism, and Christian S. Davis argues that the prevalence of such discourses provided colonial radicals and racial antisemites with "an antirace" on which "to project their worst fears and hatreds" while also facilitating the naturalization of affinities between German antisemitism and anti-Black racism for ordinary Germans (2000, 130, 132). Within this context, Jews and Blacks were subject to a number of the same derogatory stereotypes, beliefs, and anxieties, including an "inability to speak proper German, an obscene and ridiculous love of finery, and an inherent laziness," the latter often invoked in contrast to German industriousness (Davis 2000, 90, 115); in addition, fears of miscegenation also pertained to both groups.[10]

The profound ideological correspondences between late-eighteenth- and nineteenth-century antisemitism and anti-Black racism are perhaps best exemplified in Johann David Michaelis's 1782 "fantasy of Jewish colonial deportation" to longed-for German "sugar islands" (Hess 2000, 59). Michaelis was a late-eighteenth-century Orientalist scholar at the University of Göttingen, a leading authority on ancient Judaism, and the author of a six-volume treatise on Mosaic law, *Mosaisches Recht* (1770–75). He was also a great admirer of *ancient* Judaism. When it came to modern Jews and the question of Jewish emancipation, however, Michaelis turned to his area of expertise to advance an antiassimilationist position: because Mosaic law was premised on ensuring Jewish separatism, he argued, it was impossible for Jews to be integrated into modern, secular society (Hess 2000, 57–58). Michaelis quickly extended his opposition to Jewish emancipation beyond his immediate area of expertise, marshaling professional resources and committing much of the rest of his career to the fight. In 1782, for instance, he used his well-regarded scholarly *Orientalische und exegetische Bibliothek* (Oriental and exegetical library) as a platform to counter Christian Konrad Wilhelm von Dohm's 1781 systematic proposal for Jewish "civic improvement" based on "Prussian internal colonialism" (Hess 2000, 57–58, 61). Propelled largely by "climate"-based understandings of human difference first developed by Montesquieu, Kant, Blumenbach, and Meiners, Michaelis's rejoinder to Dohm revolves around his claim that Jews are an "unmixed race [*ungemischte Race*] of a more Southern people" who will never have the bodily strength required to render military service to the German state (quoted in Hess 2000, 58). There is a way for Jews to serve the state, however, and, for Michaelis, it is a particularly fitting one given their origins in a southern climate: "Such a people can perhaps become useful to us in agriculture and manufacturing, if one manages them in the proper manner. They would become even more useful if we had sugar islands which from time to time could depopulate the European fatherland, sugar islands which, with the wealth they produce, nevertheless have an unhealthy climate" (quoted in Hess 2000, 58). Here, in the proposal to deport Jews to a climate intolerable for Germans but inherently bearable for Jews, a proposal predicated on the idea that "degenerate" Jews are a source of ready slave labor capable of freeing Germans from a reliance on other European powers for commodities like sugar, the conflated logics of antisemitism and colonial anti-Black racism emerge with particular force.

Even more, as Hess makes clear in drawing out the interlocking dimensions of Michaelis's proposal, Orientalism is not incidental to his colonialist antisemitism: "With his vision of sugar island Jews, Michaelis articulates a racial antisemitism with a theological pedigree that marks the ultimate embodiment of German Orientalist fantasies of both intellectual hegemony *and* colonialist power" (2000, 93, emphasis in original). In situating Michaelis's proposal at the nexus of Orientalism, biblical scholarship, and questions of colonial expansion, Hess is careful to delineate the ways that, for Michaelis, deporting Jews to fantasized sugar islands is a matter of both German "economic self-sufficiency" and "peaceful expansion of interior power" and not a form of imperialism, which he opposed in polemical fashion as part of his efforts to establish scholarly Orientalist hegemony (2000, 62, 83).[11]

While Michaelis's proposal, anchored in a fantasy of German sugar islands, offers an especially trenchant example of the late-eighteenth- and nineteenth-century convergence of antisemitism and anti-Black racism, his fantasy of German colonialism—and the array of racialized and racist ideologies implicit in such a fantasy—was far from unique. In her sweeping analysis of German colonial fantasies in the precolonial era, Susanne Zantop argues persuasively that, although Germany's colonial period was relatively brief, its *fantasies* of colonialism—"stories of sexual conquest and surrender, love and blissful domestic relations between colonizer and colonized, set in colonial territory, stories that made the strange familiar, and the familiar 'familial'" (1997a, 2)—were much more expansive and enduring. Privileging colonial fantasies over political and philosophical debates and discourses of colonialism, Zantop demonstrates the varied ways that popular literature, travel writing, and children's fiction encouraged Germans to imagine themselves as part of a colonial project, an imaginary belonging that fostered a sense of "national identity in opposition to the perceived racial, sexual, ethnic, or national characteristics of others, Europeans and non-Europeans alike" (7). Here, in fantasies of German colonialism, scholarly, political, and popular iterations of race theory, racialized antisemitism, and anti-Black racism combine to naturalize German superiority over Jews and Blacks, thereby saturating late-eighteenth- and nineteenth-century German culture with ideologies of human difference that positioned the two groups as singularly "more foreign and repellent than any of the other human races" (Davis 2000, 80).

Among the many German colonial fantasies that "formed a cultural residue of myths about self and other(s)" during the first half of the nineteenth century, Joachim Heinrich Campe's 1779–80 *Robinson der Jüngere: Ein Lesebuch für Kinder* (Robinson the Younger: A reader for children), an adaptation of Daniel Defoe's *Robinson Crusoe* (1719), was perhaps the most widely consumed and enduring, the epitome of *Robinsonade*, a new genre rooted in eighteenth- and nineteenth-century Germany's "[i]nnumerable rewrites, adaptations, sequels, and retranslations" (Zantop 1997a, 3, 103). Resonating with characterizations typical of *Kinder- und Hausmärchen*, Campe's *Robinson der Jüngere* has been described as a "Bible of the bourgeoisie" and "a practical and moral guidebook for the whole Family of Germans in the years of national consolidation," and Zantop contends that "[m]ore than any other text, *Robinson Crusoe* shaped the minds of German children, youths, and hence adults, from the eighteenth well into the twentieth century" (Promies, quoted in Zantop 1997a, 103–4; Zantop, 103–4). Perhaps the two most influential texts in the pedagogical promotion of bourgeois nationalism, *Kinder- und Hausmärchen* and *Robinson der Jüngere* share a number of structural and discursive features: both cultivate a sense of oral tradition (the Grimms by introducing their collection with a celebration of the purportedly oral sources of the tales and Campe by organizing the book's chapters into thirty-one domestic storytelling evenings); both privilege the fairy-tale genre (*Robinson* opens with "once upon a time," traces Krusoe's personal development over the course of his adventure, and ends with a "happily ever after" when he returns, with Freitag, to Hamburg, where the two work as "brother carpenters"); and both engage "the readership and society at large in multiple and interlocking pedagogical projects, in which teaching/reading generates 'doing,' and vice versa" (Zantop 1997a, 105–29). Zantop maintains that, for Campe, "education is metaphorically equated with colonization and colonization with education, the domestication of little savages," and within this context, Krusoe "anticipates the ideal German, as he appears in the racial/cultural theories of Herder, Kant, and others . . . a stepping stone in the formation of a German self-image based on colonialist fantasy" (105, 120). Such an explicitly colonial logic may be undeniably manifest in Campe's *Robinson der Jüngere*, but the imbrication of education, race, nation, and colonial fantasy pertains to *Kinder- und Hausmärchen* as well, especially given the philosophical-scientific ideas about human variability surrounding both texts.

While some theories of human variability were inflected with shades of cultural relativism, others were much more strident and reductive.[12] On the decidedly reductive end of the continuum, the Göttingen philosopher and historian Christoph Meiners published a series of articles (1786–92) that collectively establish a simplistic human typology based on Germanic superiority. Beginning with his *Grundriß der Geschichte der Menschheit* (Sketch of the history of mankind) in 1786, Meiners divides humanity into two basic categories: the "culturally superior" beautiful and the "mongolized," and thus inferior, ugly (Kontje 2004, 3–4; Zantop 1997b, 23). Not surprisingly, only whites—indeed, only certain whites (the Germanic ones)—occupied the category of the beautiful, thus relegating all dark and darker-skinned peoples to the category of the ugly, which Meiners articulates with a litany of contemporary stereotypes about Germany's Jewish, Gypsy, African, Asian, and American others such that the ugly are also "stupid and vicious" (Kontje 2004, 4) as well as lazy, cowardly, animalistic (especially simian), promiscuous, and prone to violence and treachery (Zantop 1997b, 24). Structured by a series of binary oppositions—beautiful/ugly, strong/weak, hardworking/lazy, moral/immoral, white/dark (Zantop 1997a, 88; 1997b, 28)—Meiners's racial taxonomy essentially translates racial and racist formations into a language primed for bourgeois nationalist pedagogical projects like *Robinson der Jüngere* and *Kinder- und Hausmärchen*.

In language that seems straight out of a fairy tale, Meiners describes those of Germanic stock—the inhabitants of northern Germany, Denmark, Sweden, Norway, Holland, Great Britain and the adjacent islands—as having "the whitest, most blooming and most delicate skin"; in the specific case of female beauty, Meiners imagines a somewhat less rigid hierarchy in which Greek women might be "superior to Slavic women," although "rarely or never do they attain, as to delicacy and whiteness of skin, the rosy cheeks of beautiful Englishwomen or German women and *Jungfrauen*" (quoted in Zantop 1997a, 88). In her reading of Meiners's claims about Germanic superiority and skin color, Zantop, too, notes the resonances between his language and that of traditional fairy tales: Germans are the "'fairest of them all'—a kind of 'Snow White' syndrome" (1997a, 87). For Meiners, skin color and beauty are more than superficial marks of national chauvinism, however; rather, they are the visible effects of blood, and blood is the "primary and ultimate cause of difference" and the determinant of "racial 'families'" as well as the "intellectual, moral, or economic differences between races" (Zantop 1997a, 89–90; 1997b, 28). As such, Meiners's assumption that blood dictates skin color extends Zantop's "Snow White" analogy even further by privileging the power of blood in fantasies of white beauty that exist at the heart of both "Snow White" and Meiners's typology.

Meiners's amalgamation of beauty, blood, nation, and racial superiority comes to life in Caitlin Hewitt-White's argument that the Grimms' stepmother figure represents "a Black Jewish outsider" (2003, 129). While Hewitt-White's reading of such characters as condensations of antisemitism and colonial anti-Black racism may be something of an overstatement, her point that stepmothers pose a threat to the family in the same ways that Jews and Blacks pose a threat to the nation is a compelling one, particularly given the common metaphorization of nation as family. Within this context, blood is a principal factor in the calculus of racial superiority because it runs through the metonymic association between family and nation, social constructs "established through an ideology of biological sameness" and, for nationalists like the Grimms, threatened by often interlocking contemporary forces—a sense of German effeminacy resulting from French occupation, the possibility of Jewish emancipation, and anxieties about an imaginary Black threat (121). Triangulating the Grimms' Romantic nationalism with their explicit investment in the patriarchal (and implicitly biological) family and with contemporary discourses of anti-Black racism and racialized antisemitism, Hewitt-White contends that the brothers mobilize older myths of white supremacy to create in the figure of the stepmother "a Black Jewish outsider to the authentic family/nation," thereby amplifying her already menacing otherness (129). Moreover, well-documented cases of the Grimms' replacing mothers with stepmothers in several major tales—"Hansel and Gretel," "Mother Holle," "Snow White"—further attests to the distinctly ideological nature of their project (see, e.g., Ellis 1983; Tatar 2019 [1987]; Hewitt-White 2003). The fact that the tales substituting stepmothers for biological mothers are all included in the Small Edition and that "Mother Holle" and "Snow White" are two of the tales in *Kinder- und Hausmärchen* that most explicitly thematize beauty, blood, and race foregrounds both the pedagogical impulses underlying the collection's racial formations and the racist nature of the pedagogical project, even if the stepmother figure is not literally a Black Jewish outsider.

Antisemitism and the Racialization of Blackness

Read together, Michaelis's colonial fantasy of Jewish deportation to imagined German sugar islands and the parallelism between the Grimms' stepmother and Black Jewish threats to the family and the nation make clear that the convergence of colonial anti-Black racism and racialized antisemitism was of fundamental import not only to late-eighteenth- and nineteenth-century German thought and politics but also to the very development of *Kinder- und Hausmärchen*. Despite the distinct influence of wide-ranging racial formation projects on the Grimms' collection, however, discussions of race in *Kinder- und Hausmärchen* are astoundingly scarce. While the explicitly antisemitic tales have garnered some critical attention—only a small number of which posit a *racialized* antisemitism—other forms of racism and racialized thinking have been largely overlooked. Hewitt-White's aforementioned analysis of the stepmother as a radically othered threat is a notable exception, as is Ann Schmiesing's (2016) subtle exploration of Blackness in *Kinder- und Hausmärchen*. Focusing primarily on the four tales that feature Black human protagonists,[13] Schmiesing offers a nuanced study of Blackness at the nexus of Western color symbolism and contemporary ideas about race, generally suggesting that the overwhelmingly negative associations articulated with Blackness in *Kinder- und Hausmärchen* can be understood as both reflecting and reinforcing "colorist attitudes" while also tempering such claims by highlighting examples of positive black associations—Snow White's hair, a black dwarf who proves to be a magical helper (211).

Throughout, Schmiesing is careful to avoid attributing racist intentionality or racialized thinking to the Grimms, despite her conclusion that triumphant (white) male authority connects these tales, thematically, to "prevailing nineteenth-century European constructions of race, ethnicity, and skin color" (228). Tracing the Grimms' editing of these particular tales and situating them alongside the variants noted in the appendixes to the first two volumes of *Kinder- und Hausmärchen*, for instance, Schmiesing points out that the final versions "either reveal black and white color symbolism where none exists in the non-KHM [*Kinder- und Hausmärchen*] variants . . . or they contain more pronounced black and white color symbolism than the non-KHM variants typically do" (220). While acknowledging the possibility that contemporary readers may have associated the blackness portrayed in these tales with colorist stereotypes linking blackness with disease, degeneracy, and deformity, Schmiesing generally attributes the Grimms' introducing (or intensifying) Black characters to their "interest in and deep knowledge of color symbolism in literature and folklore and their attraction to (and frequent editorial efforts to enhance) pictorial language" (228, 220). Even in the undeniably colonial-inflected case of "The Three Black Princesses," a tale set in "East India," Schmiesing's attentive analysis—grounded in a history of colonial conflict involving the Dutch and British East India Companies in Mysore, the tale-teller's familial connections to those conflicts, and the story's general "layer of Orientalism"—suggests only that "[t]he color symbolism in 'The Three Black Princesses' may principally be derived from early allegorical associations of white and black with purity and the diabolical" and that the East Indian setting likely would have led the Grimms' readers to understand such allegorical associations "at least in part within the context of colonial imaginings of race and ethnicity" (223, 225). To be sure, color symbolism—particularly the long history of negative associations with blackness in Western culture—informs the Grimms' tales, but the fact that racist typologies of human difference like the one elaborated by Meiners often relied on extant color symbolism, that questions of racialized human variability saturated late-eighteenth- and nineteenth-century thought and politics, and that the Grimms edited the tales according to their personal prejudices suggests that these tales (and, I would argue, the collection as a whole) reveal a much more active engagement with the racial thinking and racist ideologies of the period.

Of the four tales featuring Black characters, "The Three Black Princesses" stands out in two distinct ways: its named setting outside of German-speaking Europe and the permanence of the three princesses' Blackness. The story is rife with odd, at times nonsensical, details and plot elements, and the rather rough nature of its narrative progression gives it the feel of a tale cobbled together from the tropes and motifs of other tales. The story begins when "East India" is invaded by an enemy and held ransom for six hundred talers; in order to raise the ransom, the city leaders announce that whoever provides the ransom shall become mayor. At the same time, a poor fisherman is working the sea with his son when the enemy comes upon them, takes the son prisoner, and gives the father (a convenient) six hundred talers in return. The father becomes mayor. Meanwhile, the son manages to escape and eventually makes his way to a mountain that opens up to reveal an enchanted castle. Within the castle, everything is draped in black, including three princesses, also entirely black but for "a little white on their faces" (Zipes 2003, 449). Apparently in need of saving, the princesses explain to the young man that he can rescue them if he refrains from looking at or speaking to them for an entire year; strangely, they also add that should he want for anything, all he has to do is ask, and they will answer if so permitted. Before the end of the year, he asks to visit his father, and the princesses provide him with money and clothes, elicit a promise that he will return in a week, and magically transport him to East India. Reunited with his parents, he tells them of his encounter with the three princesses; his mother warns him that it might not be such a good idea to save the princesses and provides him with a consecrated candle for protection, advising that he allow some of the wax to drop on their faces. Upon his return, his fear causes him to do exactly that, at which point the princesses turn half white and lash out at him in anger, crying, "You cursed dog, our blood shall cry out for vengeance! There is no man born now or anywhere nor ever will be who can save us. But we still have three brothers bound by seven chains, and they shall tear you to pieces" (450). A shrieking then permeates the castle, the young man escapes out a window, and the castle sinks back into the earth, never to be seen again.

"The Three Black Princesses" is perhaps most remarkable for its opening two words: "East India." More than an idiosyncratic setting,[14] more than the "layer of Orientalism" that Schmiesing sees as connecting the tale to contemporary concerns about race, ethnicity, and skin color, "East India" is the site of a racialized slippage: although the fisherman's son is the one who is East Indian, the three Black princesses, with their ferocious, animalistic brothers and their vulnerability to the consecrated candle, to Christianity, are the ones who are ideologically and stereotypically aligned with East India and its assumed radical otherness. Although there were, of course, Christians living in Asia and the Middle East during the eighteenth and nineteenth centuries, the "Oriental" locale of "East India" was much more likely to function as a signifier of racial, religious, and racialized religious difference than as an historical geographic reference. Extending Berman's aforementioned claim that the nineteenth-century emphasis on Jews' Oriental origin was foundational for contemporary racialized antisemitism, Marchand summarizes German Orientalism's sweeping ethnic and racial prejudices: "residual hatred for the Turks, resentment toward the Jews, and indifference toward all other cultures of the East" (2009, 56). Kontje likewise underscores the geopolitical dimensions of German Orientalism in his claim that it was "directed both outward and inward, motivated by a desire to conquer as much of Europe and the rest of the world as possible and to eliminate racial 'inferiors' within the homeland" (2004, 8). These are some of the attitudes put into circulation by the signifier "East India," and its free-floating nature—the easy slippage by which it adheres to the three Black princesses—reveals one dimension of the fantastic, entangled, and completely naturalized processes by which Blackness was racialized in the Grimms' tales, much as antisemitism's racialization was facilitated by "Jewishness" as a free-floating signifier in "The Bright Sun Will Bring It to Light."

As an anchor for the tale's racialization, the East Indian setting is also imbricated with the story's other singular feature: the permanence of the princesses' blackness. Despite the princesses' instructing the fisherman's son as to how he might rescue them, they never explain the state from which they must be freed nor the cause of that state. The hero, like the Grimms' readers, assumes that the princesses must be rescued from their blackness, but their outrage at being touched by the wax of the consecrated candle opens a range of possibilities. If blackness is, indeed, the condition from which they must be rescued, there is no hope for them. Their blackness is immutable; it exists in their blood, "blood that will cry for vengeance" after they are awoken by the drippings of the consecrated candle. Within this context, the East Indian locale provides the ready associations necessary to smooth over the tale's distinctly atypical fairy-tale features. Broad Orientalist tropes, antisemitic and otherwise, rationalize the hero's failure, the impossibility of "saving" diabolical Blacks, who ultimately return—irate, vengeful, chained, subhuman—back into the earth, to the depths of hell. Whatever their plight, Christianity cannot save them because race and all its attendant forms of inferiority exist in the blood. Thus, despite Germany's history of Christian missionary work, race was widely understood as an absolute and unalterable marker of difference, and the enduring proverbial sentiment that "regenerating" Jews through baptism would be as effective as "trying to wash a blackamoor white" attests to the especially trenchant nature of such ideas about race when they involved Jews and Blacks (Hess 2000, 88; MacMaster 2000, 74).

The clearly racialized idiosyncrasies of "The Three Black Princesses" come into even sharper focus when the tale is read alongside "The Prince Who Feared Nothing," another of the four tales featuring Black characters and one with which it shares several central motifs. In this tale, an adventuring prince meets a giant, who—impressed by the prince's strength and courage—beseeches him to fetch an apple from the Tree of Life for the giant's bride. The giant warns the prince that nobody has ever accomplished such a feat because the Tree is in a garden surrounded by an iron fence and protected all around by wild animals; he also reveals that the prince must put his arm through a ring hanging from the Tree in order to pick an apple. The prince succeeds in acquiring the apple, gains great strength from the ring, which tightens around his arm, and earns the devotion of one of the wild lions guarding the garden. When the giant presents the apple to his bride, however, she demands to see the ring since she knows that the ring will be on the arm of the one who fetched the apple. This leads to a seemingly endless fight between the giant and the magically fortified prince until the giant tricks the prince into removing the ring and runs off with it, only to have the faithful lion chase him down and return the ring. Not to be bested by the prince and his lion, the giant attacks and blinds the prince before attempting to lead him off a cliff; once again, the lion intervenes, saving the prince and pushing the giant to his death below. The lion then leads the prince to a spring, where he splashes the prince's face, eventually restoring his sight with the magical waters. Soon after, the prince happens upon an enchanted castle, where he meets a "maiden with a beautiful figure and fine appearance . . . *but* [who] was quite black" (Zipes 2003, 397; my emphasis). She tells him that an "evil spell" has been cast over her and that he can release her from it if he spends three nights in the great hall of the castle without showing any fear and without uttering a sound as he is being tortured; he readily accepts the challenge, assuring her that he's not afraid and that "[w]ith God's help," he'll try to free her (397). Each successive night is more torturous, leaving the prince closer and closer to death in the mornings, but the "black maiden" always appears and washes him with the Water of Life, reinvigorating him for the next night's torments. After the first night, the prince notices that her feet have turned white, and, after the second, "she had already become white to the tips of her fingers" (399). When he is revived from his unconscious state on the third morning, he sees the maiden who is now "white as snow and as beautiful as the day is bright" (399). Once they disenchant the castle, she "turn[s] into a rich princess," and they celebrate their wedding (399).

"The Prince Who Feared Nothing" follows the highly conventional narrative structure typical of the European fairy tale. As such, it is also an almost perfect inversion of "The Three Black Princesses." Not only is the prince successful in releasing the enchanted maiden from the "evil curse" of Blackness, transforming her into a beautiful white princess, while the fisherman's son fails in his attempt to rescue the three (immutably) Black princesses, but his success is also attributed, at least in part, to his seeking God's help whereas the fisherman's son's failure is brought about by the consecrated candle. The opening sequence, which seems incongruous with the second half of the story and perhaps irrelevant for a comparative reading of the two tales, suggests their mirrored coupling as well. The "miraculous garden," the Tree of Life with its "red apples glistening on the branches," the wild animals sleeping peacefully around the garden—all evoke the Garden of Eden, imagined to be located in the celebrated *ancient* East, a clear contrast to the *contemporary* East Indian setting of "The Three Black Princesses." Even the lion, "neither furious nor ferocious," who follows the prince "meekly" and repeatedly saves his life before disappearing entirely from the tale stands in contrast to the three Black princesses' implicitly violent and animalistic brothers, "bound by seven chains" and ready to "tear [the fisherman's son] to pieces" (396, 450).[15]

Read together as an inverted pair, these tales highlight the thorough integration and extensive reach of racialized antisemitism and anti-Black racism in *Kinder- und Hausmärchen*: thus, where "The Three Black Princesses" posits permanent Blackness as both racialized and opposed to Christianity, "The Prince Who Feared Nothing" anchors the tale's Christian overlay to the maiden's transitory Blackness. The maiden is beautiful "but" Black, a clear reference to the "black but beautiful" maiden in the Song of Solomon, "whom early Christian and Jewish commentators interpreted as an allegory for the soul that can be saved despite its fall from grace" (Schmiesing 2016, 216–17). Such an allegorical understanding certainly accords with the Grimms' ideological project, but the largely literal nature of Origen's third-century exegesis resonates even more acutely both with the maiden's temporary Blackness and with Grimms' Christian pedagogy: "[B]eginning with the verses in Song, that saw the 'daughters of Jerusalem' (the born Jews) mock the black maiden for her blackness (her gentile birth), who, although indeed black, is beautiful ('black but beautiful') through faith in Jesus and conversion to Christianity. Eventually, the maiden's blackness diminishes and she 'becomes white and fair' (based on a reading of Song 8.5 found in the Old Greek translation: 'Who is she that comes up having been made white?')" (Goldberg 2003, 48).[16]

If the Grimms' tales featuring Black characters bear the unmistakable imprint of racialized Christian ideology, even more striking is the racial legacy of their fairy-tale inheritance. In particular, "The White Bride and the Black Bride"—and the constellation of related tales of true and false brides, kind and unkind girls in *Kinder- und Hausmärchen*—reverberates, in sometimes stark and sometimes allusive fashion, with the overtly racialized motifs in Basile's early literary variants. "The White Bride and the Black Bride" is simultaneously a tale of kind and unkind girls and a tale of true and false brides. It begins when God, disguised as a poor man, asks directions of a woman and her daughter and stepdaughter. The woman and her daughter respond with haughty disregard and sass, while the stepdaughter offers to show him the way. Angered by the insolence of the woman and her daughter, the Lord "turned his back on them and cursed them so that they became black as night and ugly as sin" (Zipes 2003, 440). Appreciative of the stepdaughter, God offers her three wishes, and she asks to be as "beautiful and pure as the sun" (upon which God makes her "as white and beautiful as the day"); to have an ever-full money purse; and to ascend to heaven after her death (440). When the mother sees that she and her daughter are "black as coal and ugly, while the stepdaughter was white and beautiful," she begins to plot ways of harming her.

Meanwhile, the stepdaughter has a loving brother, Reginer, who works as the king's coachman. Reginer loves his sister so dearly that he asks to paint her portrait in order that he might see her constantly; she consents but on the condition that nobody else view it. When the king's wife dies, he is inconsolable, not at the loss of his wife but because "her equal" could not be found. Jealous of Reginer, the king's servants report that the coachman gazes upon a beautiful portrait every day. After viewing the portrait himself, the king decides to marry Reginer's sister and sends him, along with golden clothing, to fetch her. This is the moment for which the stepmother has been waiting, and she uses her witchcraft to cloud Reginer's eyes and to stop up his sister's ears; during the return journey, the stepmother takes advantage of the siblings' magically induced disabilities to clothe her daughter in the golden bridal garments and to toss her stepdaughter out of the carriage and into a nearby river, where a "snow white" duck appears at the very moment the stepdaughter sinks beneath the surface. The king is furious when he sees how "abysmally ugly" his betrothed is, and he orders Reginer be thrown into a pit full of adders and snakes. Here, too, however, the stepmother intervenes with her witchcraft such that the king not only allows them to stay but also comes to find the Black bride nice enough in appearance that he eventually marries her. Soon after, the white duck makes its way to the castle kitchen, where it asks the kitchen boy questions regarding Reginer's whereabouts and what the "black witch" is doing in the house. After three nights of this, the kitchen boy reports everything to the king, who proceeds to the kitchen on the following night and, upon seeing the duck, uses his sword to decapitate it; naturally, the king's action causes the duck to turn into the beautiful maiden from the portrait. She then recounts her story, requests that Reginer be removed from the pit of snakes, and marries the king after he has killed the stepmother and her "black daughter" according to their description of how the perpetrator of such deception ought to be punished.

The Grimms note the tale's similarities to a number of European versions of "The Kind and Unkind Girls," including d'Aulnoy's "Rosette" and Basile's "The Two Little Pizzas," but they overlook or ignore the tale's equally pronounced relationship to Basile's "The Three Citrons" and *Lo cunto*'s frame tale, two false bride stories that turn on the machinations of conniving Black slaves. Given the brothers' familiarity with *Lo cunto*, which they had early on planned to translate, the undeniable significance of skin color to "The White Bride and the Black Bride," and the absence of racial marking in the versions they reference, their omission seems particularly remarkable. As Schmiesing notes, the Grimms comment only on the tale's color symbolism, which they explain as a "simple opposition of blackness and whiteness for ugliness and beauty, sin and purity," an opposition they situate in relation to "overarching myths of day and night" (Grimms quoted in Schmiesing 2016, 216; Schmiesing 2016, 216), even though their description of the women's transformation—"he [the Lord] turned his back on them and cursed them so that they became black as night and ugly as sin" (Zipes 2003, 440)—recalls the curse of

Ham and the biblical origins of Blackness and slavery.[17] Implicit in the Grimms' explanatory comments is, of course, a racialized understanding of Blackness and whiteness that accords with contemporary theories of human difference such as Meiners's. Regardless of the Grimms' stated interpretation, the fairy-tale genealogy of "The White Bride and the Black Bride" exposes the tale's undeniable racialization. Indeed, one of the most striking motifs of "The White Bride and the Black Bride" is the white duck's questioning of the kitchen boy: "'What's the black witch doing in the house?'" (Zipes 2003, 442). Here, both the motif and the question echo those in Basile's "The Three Citrons" when the "pretty dove"—avatar of the true bride ("a beauty without measure, a *whiteness* beyond all imagination")—asks, "Cook in the kitchen, / What is the king doing with the Saracen?" (Canepa 2007a: 437, 439; my emphasis). That "Saracen" is a racial designation is substantiated by the king's later referring to the false bride as "the black queen" as well as by historical and intertextual details in the tale and the collection as a whole.[18]

This fairy-tale genealogy also lends insight into the ways that race—often figurative—informs the entire group of tales about kind and unkind girls and true and false brides in *Kinder- und Hausmärchen*: "Mother Holle," "The Three Little Gnomes in the Forest," "The Singing Springing Lark," "The Goose Girl," and, of course, "The White Bride and the Black Bride." An intertextual reading of these tales, together with Basile's "The Three Citrons," "The Two Little Pizzas," and *Lo cunto*'s frame tale, thus opens relays that suggest a racial logic extending well beyond the four tales featuring Black characters. In "Mother Holle," for instance, the black pitch that permanently covers the unkind girl as punishment for her laziness and impudence not only metaphorizes the unkind girl's literal Blackness in "The White Bride and the Black Bride" but also highlights the raced nature of the descriptions the Grimms invoke for this particular unkind girl: "the lazy maiden," a "[loafer]" who "[does] not want to get out of bed in the morning," a "dirty maiden" (Zipes 2003, 90–91). This cascading set of signifiers also reframes the descriptions of the unkind girl (and eventual false bride) in "The Three Little Gnomes in the Forest" such that her "wicked and greedy heart," her "[stinginess]," and—thanks to the "gifts" the gnomes bestow—her "[growing] uglier with each day that passes," and her spitting toads from her mouth with every word she utters all take on racial (and racially antisemitic) dimensions (48). Here, while not overtly sutured to black skin, character traits such as ugliness, laziness, sloth, and greed call to mind many of the common eighteenth- and nineteenth-century stereotypes of Blacks and Jews cited above, and the unkind girl's 'speaking in toads' literalizes in the most egregious and visceral way the dominant belief that Blacks and Jews could never speak German properly (Davis 2012, 115).[19] The chain of signifiers that secures the literal Black bride to the unkind girl covered in black pitch to the unkind girl who grows uglier by the day and all to their laziness, deceit, and general impudence—in contrast to the beautiful, white, innocent, hardworking kind girls and true brides—brings Meiners's taxonomy of human variability to life, its reductive, binary simplicity, and its division of people into the beautiful and the ugly easily incorporated into the Grimms' pedagogical project.

More than just stories of the beautiful and the ugly, the German and the other, this subset of tales also carries forward—in often metaphorized and fantastic ways—the accumulated racial formations that inhere in earlier versions of the tales. In so doing, they also reveal the complicity of the genre itself: that is, as a genre, the European fairy tale, with its unquestioned immersion in the marvelous, its everyday acceptance of the eccentric detail, naturalizes the underlying racial formations of the earliest literary versions. Thus, for example, Hans My Hedgehog's initial Blackness might seem like an odd element to the story, an inexplicable detail smoothly whitewashed much as Hans My Hedgehog is magically whitened by an unknown ointment, but situating the tale in its fairy-tale genealogy connects his temporary Blackness to Prince Marcassin's figuration as racialized *sauvage*, a connection that suggests a (perhaps subconscious) rationale for the Blackness that results when he is first disenchanted from his hedgehog state.[20] Similarly, the reference to the Red Sea in "The Singing Springing Lark" stands out for its highly unusual geographic specificity until the tale is read alongside its literary ATU 425 antecedents, beginning with Apuleius's "Cupid and Psyche" and Basile's related "The Padlock" and "The Golden Trunk," two versions with probable roots in the North African oral tradition that likely informed Apuleius's tale and both featuring handsome Black slaves as the disguised lovers. Here, the inheritance from the Libyan oral tradition, Apuleius's classical tale, and Basile's, d'Aulnoy's, and Villeneuve's differently racialized versions not only makes sense of the "Red Sea" as an othering boundary separating the domains of the true and false brides but also exposes the tacit racializing of the dragon princess (false bride) and her obviously non-Christian sorcerer father. Thus, while the ready acceptance of seemingly inexplicable or nonsensical details in the Grimms' fairy tales might simply be attributed to genre expectations, their grounding in the genealogy of the European literary fairy-tale tradition suggests otherwise: far from nonsensical, such details are, in fact, laden with meaning, and those meanings call attention to the fact that the European fairy tale is at its heart an enduring racial formation project and that racial thinking is fundamental to the development of the genre.

From Jews and Blacks to Women, Apes, and Others

Of the six Black characters in *Kinder- und Hausmärchen*, five are female: the Black bride, the princess rescued by the prince who fears nothing, and the three immutably Black princesses. The single male character—Hans My Hedgehog—also happens to be the only one privileged with a name and, most astounding, one of the few characters in the entire collection whose christening is explicitly noted. While it might be tempting simply to attribute these gendered differences to the overall sexism of the collection, to do so would be to ignore the significant ways in which late-eighteenth- and nineteenth-century racial antisemitism, anti-Black racism, and the convergence of the two in taxonomies of human variability were also thoroughly inflected with sexism.[21] In his classification of the "naturally inferior," for instance, Meiners includes Blacks, children, women, servants, criminals, and Jews, none of whom can, or should, "aspire to equality with their natural superiors, the white male Christian masters" (Zantop 1997b, 24). Meiners was by no means alone in linking women, Blacks, Jews, and a range of socially marginalized others in his theory of male German superiority, and Neil MacMaster notes that "[a]nalogies were constantly drawn between 'races,' women, children, criminals, the insane and the lower classes (the European workers as 'savages' in the 'jungle' of the urban slum)" (2000, 67). As Sander Gilman points out, the ideological collapse between Blacks and Jews originated in a "need to externalize the anxiety generated by change in European (read Christian) middle-class society"; moreover, the externalization and material instantiation of this anxiety meant that, with Jews, "[t]he black, the proletarian, the child, the woman, the avant-garde [were] all associated in a web of analogies" in the nineteenth century (1985, 35, 37). Such associations were further bolstered by shared discourses of women and "savages" in Enlightenment philosophy, particularly as women (and femininity more generally) came to substitute for the "savage" in male subject formations that depended on the conquest and civilizing of "nature" (Weigel 1987, 181–89). In the German context, Zantop argues, similar colonial fantasies not only "assigned the white European/German male a position of power and authority over all kinds of feminized others, be they wives/children/servants, colonized women/feminized natives/colonized territory, or the 'effeminate' aristocracy," but also ensured that "race and gender became superimposed, reinforcing each other to determine the position of each individual in the universal rosters created by natural history and comparative anthropology" (1997a, 43, 66).

Considered together, the stark gender differences in the Black characters and the deep ideological conflation and naturalization of misogyny and racism in pseudoscientific and ethnological theories of human variability expose the ways racial thinking is complicit in *Kinder- und Hausmärchen*'s sexist representation of female characters. Hewitt-White's interpretation of the Grimms' stepmothers as specifically *gendered* Black Jewish threats to the family and the nation offers one example but is by no means singular: witches, "shrews," and ignorant, often childlike, wives similarly reiterate the compelling need, in the tales, for white, Christian patriarchal authority, a need that also legitimizes the white Christian patriarch's rightful place in the family, the nation, and the contemporary hierarchies of human difference so critical to the evolution of the period's racialized patriotism. Threaded through this nexus of patriarchal, nationalist, racialized, and (fantastic) imperialist projects is an assumed civilizing mission, and Sigrid Brauner contends that the long histories of cannibals, witches, and shrews as civilization's others fix them in a raced and gendered constellation critical to the elaboration of a "superior, elite, (masculine) European identity" (1994, 20). Additionally, she argues, the historical demonization of both witches and cannibals is of special importance to Germany: the author of the *Malleus melficarum* (1487), the notorious treatise on the extermination of witches, was a German Dominican who initiated the first programmatic witch trials in the German provinces, and German artists seeded the earliest images of "New World cannibals" in the German editions of Vespucci's *Mundus Novus* (1503) and *Quattuor Americi navigationes* (1504) (Brauner 1994, 2). Even more, as Yvonne Owens makes clear in her study of witchcraft iconography in the work of sixteenth-century artist Hans Baldung Grien, early modern beliefs about witchcraft were underpinned by the same logics that sustained Jewish persecution, and cannibalism was the trope that fully secured their ideological binding: "Indeed, only Jews and witches were considered capable of the atrocities of cannibalistic infanticide" (2014, 56).[22]

This historical, perhaps especially German, alignment of witches and cannibals is, of course, a recurring motif in the Grimms' tales, often animated in the figure of the cannibalistic witch, although cannibals and witches obviously exist independently in the tales as well. The witches, stepmothers, and witchy stepmothers in tales such as "Hansel and Gretel," "The Juniper Tree," and "The Foundling" all seek to cook (or succeed in cooking) the male child in the brother-(step)sister pairings, thus making undeniably clear their threat not only to the patriarchal family but also to the future of the patriarchal family. While cannibalistic witches intent on devouring young men might serve as an exaggerated or caricatured reminder of the danger that such feminine, sometimes racialized outsiders pose to the patriarchal family and the nation, threatening as they do infants, children, and pregnant women in particular, even noncannibalistic witches and sorceresses imperil the reproduction of the patriarchal family and, by extension, the nation. The witches, sorceresses, and ogresses in tales like "Hansel and Gretel" (where both the stepmother and the witch-ogress threaten the family), "Rapunzel," and "Jorinda and Joringel," for instance, literally destroy and disrupt familial bonds:[23] in "Rapunzel," the sorceress extracts a promise for the couple's newborn in exchange for access to the rapunzel growing in her garden and, later, forcibly separates Rapunzel, pregnant in the earliest version, and her (baby daddy) prince; in "Jorinda and Joringel," the overtly racialized witch—"a haggard old woman, yellow and scrawny, with large red eyes and a crooked nose that almost touched her chin with its tip" (Zipes 2003, 249)—transforms Jorinda into a nightingale and imprisons her along with hundreds of other young women she has transformed and caged in their avian forms. Although racial thinking is certainly not alone responsible for the overriding sexism and misogyny of the Grimms' tales, the shared logics driving late-eighteenth- and nineteenth-century taxonomies and theories of human difference—along with the social, cultural, and political anxieties they sought to quell—can be understood as racializing the figure of the witch (as well as other female characters, especially villainous ones such as sorceresses and ogresses) regardless of whether she is explicitly marked as such.

The ideological correspondences that bind women, children, natives, slaves, servants, peasants, criminals, Jews, and Blacks in a knot of affiliated and overlapping signifiers also lend insight into the ways racial thinking frequently drives multiple, commonly linked, forms of otherness and monstrosity in *Kinder- und Hausmärchen*. "Eve's Unequal Children," for example, translates Meiners's fundamental organizing principle—white beauty as an index of racial, social, and moral superiority—into a Christian etiological parable that completely naturalizes Meiners's racist logic. The tale takes place a considerable time after the Fall, when the Lord has let Adam and Eve know that he plans to visit their home. In preparation, Eve gathers her "most handsome" children—the story notes that some of the children were "beautiful" and some "ugly"—and bathes them, combs their hair, dresses them in freshly laundered clothing, and warns them to mind themselves in the presence of the Lord. The "ugly children," by contrast, are told to "keep out of sight," and Eve hides them under the hay, under the roof, in the straw, in the oven, in the cellar, under a tub, a wine barrel, an old fur, a pile of cloth, and the leather from which she cuts their shoes. When the Lord arrives and meets the handsome children, he blesses them such that they will become the elite and bourgeois rulers of society: a king, a prince, a count, a knight, a nobleman, a burgher, a merchant, and a scholar. Upon hearing the Lord's blessings, Eve fetches her "misshapen" children, and the "entire band of coarse, dirty, scabby, and grimy children" stand before the Lord; he blesses them as well, but their futures will be full of physical labor and servitude: a farmer, a fisherman, a blacksmith, a tanner, a weaver, a shoemaker, a tailor, a potter, a carter, a sailor, a messenger, and "a house servant for the rest of [their lives]" (Zipes 2003, 526–27). When Eve expresses her dismay at the unequal blessings, the Lord reminds her that humanity needs laborers just as much as it needs rulers, to which Eve responds: "Oh, Lord, please forgive my rashness and interference. Let your will be done also with my children" (527).

No matter how respectable these trades, the correlation between Eve's ugly, misshapen, dirty, coarse children and tradesmen, day laborers, and servants only reinforces the profoundly intersectional nature of contemporary human hierarchies, like Meiners's, with their pinnacles in German superiority (of the white, male, and Christian variety). At the same time, "Eve's Unequal Children" does more than bring Meiners's taxonomy of the beautiful and the ugly to life; it also racializes the lower classes by recirculating stereotypes of racial others, especially Jews, Gypsies, and Blacks, in its descriptions of Eve's "ugly" children. Even more, in articulating this racialization with a theory of monogenesis—God reminds Eve that "it is necessary for [him] to populate the entire world with [her] children" (Zipes 2003, 527)—the tale participates in what Hess identifies as an acutely political mode of racial formation: "The exclusion of Jews and/or Judaism from monogenesis's support for a universalist politics is not something that *happens* to race discourse when it enters the political arena. It is arguably the constitutive element of eighteenth-century race thinking itself, a problem inscribed into the very heart of the attempt to salvage and modernize via anthropology the Judeo-Christian narrative of human origins" (Hess 2006, 210). Here, then, "Eve's Unequal Children" not only reinforces the multidimensional implications of late-eighteenth- and nineteenth-century racial taxonomies but also buttresses theories of monogenesis that naturalize, as simply God's will, racist precepts such as Meiners's belief that some people (Africans) have a "natural predisposition to slavery" (quoted in Zantop 1997b, 24).[24]

If women are linked to natives, slaves, and "savages," with Jews and Blacks, criminals and degenerates, in theories and typologies of human difference and white superiority, so too are they positioned as at least partially responsible for racialized otherness and the threats to the patriarchal family and nation posed by that otherness. "Eve's Unequal Children," for instance, seems to insinuate that the differential blessings bestowed on Eve's children originate not only in God's ostensible need to create a laboring and subservient class but also in Eve's inclination to hide her "ugly" children, essentially keeping them from the privileged first blessings. Thus, although late-eighteenth- and nineteenth-century ideologies of race and beauty make it unlikely that presenting all her children at the outset would have changed the calculus of beauty and social superiority inherent in God's blessings, it is nonetheless significant that Eve—symbol of all women and metonymic representation of female sin—is figured as complicit in the racialization of elite white Europe's others. The implicit affiliation of women, sin, and race in "Eve's Unequal Children" is paralleled in "The Rejuvenated Little Old Man," where it takes a much more explicit form. Like "Eve's Unequal Children," "The Rejuvenated Little Old Man" is set in a religious frame and begins when the Lord and Saint Peter take lodging with a blacksmith. There, Saint Peter takes pity on a poor, old, sickly beggar and asks God to alleviate his sufferings. Agreeing to do so, God asks the blacksmith to fire up the forge, after which he places the old man in the fire and then into a tub of water; once the man has cooled, God blesses him, and he emerges from the tub "straight, sound, and fit as a young man of twenty" (Zipes 2003, 462). After God, Saint Peter, and the rejuvenated old man leave, the blacksmith determines that, having watched God's process for transforming the old beggar, he might offer the same to his "old, half-blind, hunch-backed mother-in-law" (Zipes 2003, 462). Once on the fire, she shrieks and screams in pain, which brings the blacksmith's wife and daughter-in-law running to the forge. When the two women, both pregnant, see that the old woman's "wrinkled and shriveled face had lost its shape," they become so upset that they deliver their babies that night; the babies, however, are "not shaped like human beings but like apes," and they escape to the forest. The tale ends as an etiological narrative: "[I]t is from them that we have the race of apes" (463).

The complete disjuncture in narrative logic between the tale and its etiological conclusion highlights the Grimms' (at best) tacit investment in both a gendered racism and a racist sexism, especially when read alongside Basile's version of the tale, "The Old Woman Who Was Skinned." In Basile's tale, two old sisters deceive an eavesdropping king into believing they are beautiful beyond compare; when he invites one of them to his kingdom, she pulls all her wrinkled, loose skin into a knot and secures it behind her head. Unfortunately for her, the king realizes he has been duped and has the old woman thrown from the window, whereupon she lands in a tree, hanging from her hair. In the morning, a passing group of fairies finds the scene so humorous that they reward the woman by blessing her with youth, beauty, wealth, nobility, virtue, love, and luck. When the king comes across the beautiful young woman, he marries her, and she invites her old sister to the celebration. The old sister continues to pester her newly youthful sister about how she accomplished her transformation, and in a moment of frustration at the constant badgering, the now young sister claims to have had herself skinned, which prompts the old sister to run to a barber who, after much cajoling, agrees to skin her, thus bringing about her death. The tale ends with a moral about envy in the form of a verse taken from Iacopo Sannazaro's *Arcadia* (c. 1480): "Envy, my son, destroys itself" (quoted in Canepa 2007a, 125). Basile's version puts the incongruous elements of the Grimms' etiological tale in especially sharp relief, and the absence of a logical bridge connecting the two parts of the "The Rejuvenated Little Old Man" opens the tale to a range of narratives and beliefs about sexual relations between women and primates that circulated in travel literature, natural histories, and Enlightenment philosophy by leading thinkers such as Locke and Voltaire (Hund 2015–16, 46–50). Even more, the two women's birthing the "race" of apes clearly posits a *biological* connection between women and primates, a biological connection that literalizes the association between women and racialized others. Bottigheimer reads this tale as yet another example of *Kinder- und Hausmärchen*'s socialization of violence against women, seeing in the etiological conclusion a justification for a narrative that carries forward the tradition of "seventeenth- and eighteenth-century chapbooks' humorous accounts of wife-beating" (1987, 147), and while the Grimms' collection is certainly replete with "humorous" tales of violence against women, especially wives, the absence of wife-beating and other forms of violence against women in "The Rejuvenated Old Man" only underscores the clearly racialized dimensions of the tale's etiological conclusion.

That apes and raced others shared a deep affinity in early modern and modern pseudoscientific and ethnological theories of human difference is well established (see, e.g., Bindman 2002; Hund, Mills, and Sebastiani 2015–16). Although Moses Maimonides's late-twelfth-century *Guide for the Perplexed* and other medieval associations among monkeys, demons, Satan, and even African "Pygmies" anticipate the racist articulation of Blacks and primates, Charles Mills points out that it is really modernity that "elevates the ape to its current centrality as a signifier of inferiority, whether for Africans (its oldest and most enduring association) or other non-white and 'lesser' white races" (2015–16, 30; Hund 2015–16, 44). By the late eighteenth century, Petrus Camper's purportedly "scientific" studies of facial angles—which "located the heads of blacks 'closer to the lines of apes and dogs than to men'" (Mills 2015–16, 31)—cemented the racist articulation of primates and Europe's most notable others, specifically Blacks and Jews. As Claudia Bruns elaborates in her theorization of transnational racism, Wilhelm Marr, the "founding father of German racial anti-Semitism," invoked this exact racialization in his arguments against granting rights to Jews in Bremen: "'You would not permit ten thousand monkeys to settle in Bremen,' Marr claimed in the letter to Hobelmann," who had sought Marr's endorsement of his proposal for Jewish emancipation (2011, 129).[25]

Yet another example of the convergence of racial antisemitism and anti-Black racism, the facile equation of Blacks, Jews, and primates provides the ideological context for monkeys and apes as avatars, close companions, and connecting metaphors of racialized others in the Grimms' tales. For instance, in "The Robber and His Sons," one of the omitted tales, a gang of robbers is simultaneously simian and cannibalistic: "I saw the monsters coming down from the mountain: they were a gruesome and terrible sight and looked like apes. They were dragging a dead boy after them ... they lit a large fire, tore apart the bloody body with their teeth, and devoured it" (Zipes 2003, 658). In another example, a dwarf in the tale "Strong Hans" "[grins] at Hans like a monkey" (497). Here, primate analogies further the racialization of outsiders—cannibals, dwarves—and reveal the underlying logics that align seemingly fantastic fairy-tale creatures with the Jewish and Black characters that populate the overtly antisemitic and anti-Black tales. Black dwarves, black devils, black ghosts "with horns on their heads and fire coming from their mouths" (665), "twelve black men in chains" who torture, beat, and stab the hero of "The King of the Golden Mountain" (312), a girl "black as a raven and so ugly that people were truly frightened" born to a king who wishes for a child even if it is "the devil himself" (710): on their own, such characters might seem marked only by premodern and early-modern color symbolism; read together and alongside the collection's more explicit antisemitism and anti-Black racism, however, their descriptions are decidedly racialized.

Just as black demons and devils attest to the breadth of anti-Black racial formations in *Kinder- und Hausmärchen*, dwarves expose the magnitude of the collection's racialized antisemitism, especially as they embody, literally, the "ugliness" that Meiners opposes to the "beauty" of Germans' superior corporeality—"taller, slimmer, stronger, and with more beautiful bodies than all the remaining peoples of the earth" (quoted in Bindman 2002, 219). Meiners further refines his taxonomy so as to avoid any possible confusion or ambiguity regarding "small and 'ugly' mountain dwellers in the German or Swiss Alps," who, like "the Wends, Slavs, Jews, Gypsies and other 'non-German' *Fremdlinge* (strangers or foreigners) living in German states," are not likely to be of German blood (Zantop 1997b, 28–29). Michaelis, too, found Jews' bodies to be lacking. For him, Jews were too physically weak to serve Germany militarily, although—paradoxically—he found them well suited for slave labor on his fantasied sugar islands (Hess 2000, 58). Dwarves—by definition opposed to Germans in height, bodily stature, and presumed strength for military service—would absolutely be consigned to Meiners's category of "ugly" racialized others over whom Christian, white, male Germans ought to hold dominion, a position implicitly reiterated in Michaelis's characterization of Jews as physically unable to be incorporated into the German social body.

Building on such stereotypes and distinctions between tall, beautiful, white Germans and small, ugly, dark others, the Grimms add details that further amplify dwarves' racialized Jewishness. In "Rumpelstiltskin," for instance, the eponymous character, although never specifically identified as a dwarf, is referred to as "the little man" throughout. Even more, when he appears to claim the queen's child unless she can guess his name, the first three she proposes are Kaspar, Melchior, and Balzer, the names of the magi who traveled "from the East" to Bethlehem. Although the three wise men had been transformed into common Christian symbols by the medieval period, their names remain distinctly "foreign," an enduring sign of otherness even in the midst of familiarity.[26] That otherness is further exacerbated when on the second day the queen suggests Ribsofbeef, Muttonchops, and Lacedleg—three cooked meats—as names for "the little man," in the process casting him as an irreverent and mocking antithesis to the typically venerated magi. In addition to the otherness and dehumanization implicit in these names, Rumpelstiltskin's description as a little man who ritualistically dances around a fire, sinks into the ground, and rips himself in two suggests an intimate association with the devil, a longstanding antisemitic trope (see, e.g., Trachtenberg 2002 [1943]; Felsenstein 1990).

Individual details like these are certainly suggestive of *Kinder- und Hausmärchen*'s underlying entanglement with the period's dominant racial thinking, but their broader significance only emerges when such details are read together across the full corpus of tales in all their versions—unpublished, published, edited, repeatedly revised, and omitted. As Bottigheimer argues in her analysis of the collection's extensive gender biases, *Kinder- und Hausmärchen*'s motifs and themes must be understood as part of an overarching whole in order to "discern coherent patterns and to ascertain the premises on which the collection rests, which are nowhere articulated but everywhere apparent" (1987, ix). In this case, such a reading method lays bare the magnitude of *Kinder- und Hausmärchen*'s nineteenth-century racial formations. As a pedagogically oriented nation-building project, what Bottigheimer calls "the nation's primer" (1987, 171), the Grimms' collection was also ideologically aligned with the contemporary theories of race, slavery, and colonialism that Zantop sees as "intimately connected to self-perceptions and the search for a 'German' ethnic identity within the European context" (1997a, 80). Thus, with echoes of Meiners's racialized logics and reductive binaries, so easily reproduced (even if subconsciously) in the spare language of the Grimms' tales, *Kinder- und Hausmärchen* extends the political implications driving Meiners's "theory of the natural domination of the white race," a theory that not only "links Africans with children, women, servants, criminals, and Jews" in his articulation of "naturally inferior races, classes, genders, and social groups" but also decries demands for equality—Jewish emancipation and the abolition of slavery—as "impossible" and "unjust" (Zantop 1997a, 83).

In his overview of the racisms of Immanuel Kant, Wulf D. Hund maintains that "[t]he category of race is only one reference point of racism, which has appeared in different historical shapes and has drawn upon several dichotomies, constructing monsters, barbarians, inferiors, the impure, the cursed, savages and eventually coloureds" (2011, 70). Many of Hund's racialized others and their kin—dwarves and devils, cannibals and wild men, witches and stepmothers—populate *Kinder- und Hausmärchen*, and their dichotomized relationship to the Grimms' beautiful, snow-white, morally righteous, and cheerfully industrious protagonists dramatically underscores the ways the marvelous and fantastic have been complicit in the production and proliferation of white racism. Bottigheimer contends that *Kinder- und Hausmärchen* is "a historical document with its roots firmly in nineteenth-century Germany," and while this is absolutely true, the collection also extends its reach well beyond nineteenth-century Germany (1987, x). According to Jack Zipes, despite its initially modest reception, *Kinder- und Hausmärchen* soon became a local, national, and ultimately international success: beginning in the late nineteenth century, the Grimms' tales were included in school curricula, primers, and anthologies for children in Germany and "throughout the Western world," and by the start of the twentieth century, the collection was "second only to the Bible as a best-seller in Germany," a position it has continued to hold (2003, xxxiii). Translated into over 160 languages, the Grimms' collection has been enormously influential not only in its own historical moment but also across time to our contemporary moment, inspiring other nineteenth-century national collecting efforts as well as countless adaptations across a range of media, cultures, and periods. As such, *Kinder- und Hausmärchen* is the collection most responsible for "universalizing" the European fairy tale, and in this way its underlying racial formations have been naturalized and circulated as typical and essential features of "the fairy tale" as a genre.

4

GREAT BRITAIN, 1889–1910

Andrew and Nora Lang's Colored Fairy Books

The extraordinary global reach of the Grimms' fairy tales has its origins not in the brothers' sizable early editions of *Kinder- und Hausmärchen*, as one might expect, but rather in Edgar Taylor's 1823 English translation, *German Popular Stories*, a selection of thirty-one tales from the Grimms' 1819 edition. Followed by a second volume of twenty-four additional tales published in 1826, *German Popular Stories* proved immediately and immensely successful: the first volume was an instantaneous bestseller, reissued in a second run later the same year, then again in each of the next two years (Sutton 1996, 9).[1] Martin Sutton, in his definitive study of nineteenth-century English versions of the Grimms' *Kinder- und Hausmärchen*, notes that *German Popular Stories* was also the source text for translations into other languages, including the first French version in 1830 and, most likely, the first Chinese version in 1909 (1996, 56). Even more, in a rather ironic echo, Taylor's translations also had a profound influence on the Grimms' later editorial choices. Having received a copy of *German Popular Stories* from Taylor and well aware of the first volume's remarkable success in Britain—especially when compared to *Kinder- und Hausmärchen*'s disappointingly modest sales—Wilhelm Grimm proposed a similar single-volume German edition of fifty tales, which was published in 1825 as the *"kleine Ausgabe,"* or "Small Edition" (Sutton 1996, 57; Schacker 2003, 26; Lathey 2010, 89–90). Beyond inspiring the Grimms' more reader-friendly volume, Taylor's translations and editorial interventions also likely shaped some of Wilhelm's subsequent revisions to the tales, including the addition of diegetic explanations and a tempering of some of the more unforgiving and severe endings (Sutton 1996, 57–58).

Despite the Grimms' efforts to reproduce Taylor's paradigm for success, however, the Small Edition never achieved the popularity or profitability that *German Popular Stories* enjoyed in Britain. Indeed, Jennifer Schacker points out that "[t]he true publishing success of the *KHM* in Germany occurred only in the 1890s and the twentieth century—long after the *international* popularity of Grimms' fairy tales had been established" (2003, 26, emphasis in original), a popularity born of the "widespread and long-lasting influence" of *German Popular Stories* on "the 'internationalization' of the *KHM*" (Sutton 1996, 57).[2] As such, Schacker argues, "no one has done more to shape contemporary conceptions of the fairy tale—its content, tone, function, origin, and intended audience—than English solicitor and amateur folklorist Edgar Taylor" (2003, 14). That a relatively unknown "English solicitor and amateur folklorist" lurks in the shadows of the almost universally recognized brothers Grimm, that *Kinder- und Hausmärchen*—the most famous German publication of all time—has deep roots in England, may at first seem quite surprising. And yet, in many ways, the extended Victorian era—stretching from the late Georgian period to the early Edwardian period—might be understood as the century of the fairy tale in Great Britain, with Taylor's watershed *German Popular Stories* at one end, Andrew Lang's now classic Colored Fairy Book series (1889–1910) at the other, and a wealth of collections—regional, "national," and colonial—in between.

Of course, Britain's long nineteenth century is distinguished by much more than its affinity for the fairy tale; it is also marked by a burgeoning market for children's literature, an unprecedented growth of commodity culture, an increasingly professionalized anthropology undergirded by social evolutionary theory, and a robust expansion of imperial conquest. By century's end, the Victorian penchant for the fairy tale was wholly imbricated with these social, cultural, and political phenomena, and nowhere is this convergence of children's popular entertainment, sociocultural change, and racialized imperial ideology clearer than in Andrew Lang's Colored Fairy Books.

Pedagogies of Empire: Adventure, Geography, and the Fairy Tale

During his lifetime, Lang was a prominent public intellectual whose vast oeuvre encompassed everything from classical Greek mythology, poetry, and popular adventure literature to social evolutionary theory, comparative ethnology, and fairy tales, interests that came together in the Colored Fairy Books, the capstone to his career and the works for which he is best known today. And yet, as Andrea Day and others have noted, Lang was not as involved in the production of the twelve-book series as the prominence of his name on the books' covers suggests (Green 1946; Koestenbaum 1989; Lathey 2010; Day 2018, 2019; Teverson 2019). Rather, the series was primarily the work of his wife, Nora Lang, as she explains in a 1912 letter to American journalist Louise Both-Hendrickson: "I also wrote the bulk of all the Fairy Books after the first four & edited and often rewrote those [stories] contributed by other people (I also include the Animal Books & the True Stories.). My husband never saw the stories until they were ready for Press, when he read them through and wrote the Preface" (quoted in Day 2018, 98). Penned a few months after Andrew's death, Nora's letter might be perceived as perhaps overestimating her contributions to the Colored Fairy Books, a representation that Andrew obviously could not then contest. Andrew, however, acknowledged her work in similar terms in the Lilac Fairy Book, the final book in the series:[3] "The fairy books have been almost wholly the work of Mrs. Lang, who has translated and adapted them from the French, German, Portuguese, Italian, Spanish, Catalan, and other languages" (1910, vi–vii).

While Andrew's description of the series as "almost wholly the work of Mrs. Lang" is, of course, "giving credit where credit is due" (vi), his seemingly generous tribute also establishes his distance from what he understands—and further positions—as a feminized genre (see, e.g., Smol 1996, 181; Clark Hillard 2014, 51; Day 2019, 401), a point made undeniably clear in the sentences that follow his celebration of Nora's role: "My part has been that of Adam, according to Mark Twain, in the Garden of Eden. Eve worked, Adam superintended. I also superintend. I find out where the stories are, and advise, and, in short, superintend" (vi–vii).[4] Strikingly sexist as it may be, Andrew's self-presentation as overseer of Nora's labor—and, indirectly, the labor of the many other women who translated tales for the Colored Fairy Books—aligns with the long-standing gendering of narrative production, a system Day references in contextualizing the Langs' collaborative work on the series: "Such divisions reify a system of narrative production in which women labour, men create, and the colonized and rural populations who originated these stories are, if they are acknowledged at all, credited en masse in order to highlight the authenticity of the stories that the (white, middle-class, male) editor has improved" (2019, 412). The profoundly gendered and raced nature of such a system—and the Langs' seemingly unwavering adherence to it across the full set of Colored Fairy Books—necessarily complicates Andrew's claim that the series is "almost wholly the work of Mrs. Lang."

Indeed, as "superintendent" of the Colored Fairy Books, Andrew framed the series—through his prefaces to each volume—so as to privilege his enduring belief in folk and fairy tales as evidence of social evolutionary theory.[5] Thus, for example, in the preface to the *Green Fairy Book* (1892)—the third volume in the series and the first to offer a substantive preface—Lang provides a child-friendly summary of social evolutionary theory as exemplified by the fairy tale:

> However much these nations [those whose tales feature in the volume] differ about trifles, they all agree in liking fairy tales. The reason, no doubt, is that men were much like children in their minds long ago, long, long ago, and so before they took to writing newspapers, and sermons, and novels, and long poems, they told each other stories, such as you read in the fairy books. They believed that witches could turn people into beasts, that beasts could speak, that magic rings could make their owners invisible, and all the other wonders in the stories. Then, as the world became grown-up, the fairy tales which were not written down would have been quite forgotten but that the old grannies remembered them and told them to the little grandchildren: and when they, in turn, became grannies, they remembered them, and told them also. In this way these tales are older than reading and writing, far older than printing. (ix)

This account of the fairy tale recurs, with slight but significant variations, across the remaining Colored Fairy Books. Perhaps most notable is Lang's shift in the representation of the earliest storytellers. In subsequent volumes, the "old grannies" transmitting tales to "little grandchildren" are increasingly distanced in time, space, culture, and class from the presumed reader of the Colored Fairy Books:[6] they are now "naked savage women" sharing stories with "naked savage children," likened to our "naked ancestors, thousands of years ago" (*Violet Fairy Book*, 1901, vii–viii); they are "peasant or savage grandmothers," "some savage grandmother" telling tales to her "savage granddaughter" (*Crimson Fairy Book*, 1903, v–vi). Implicit in this reimagining of the earliest storytellers—a resituating of the fairy tale's origins among "naked savage women" and its continuation among peasant storytellers—is a parallel shift in the cultural origins of the specific tales in each volume. That is, the *Green Fairy Book*, with its "old grannies" and "little grandchildren," primarily comprises tales from European countries: France, Germany, Russia, Italy, Scotland, and England. The only tales from a non-European country are from China, widely recognized as a "civilized" nation during the Victorian era. The later volumes—in which the "old grannies" have been replaced by "naked savage women," "naked ancestors," and "peasants"—bring together tales from a much wider range of cultures, many made available through missionary and imperial contact: among tales from the British Isles and parts of western Europe are tales from Aboriginal Australia, Zanzibar (Swahili), South Africa (Ba-Ronga), indigenous America, India (Punjabi, Pashto), Estonia, Lithuania, Serbia, Armenia, Turkey, Japan, Finland, and Lapland. Lang's association of "naked savage women" with increasingly remote and relatively unfamiliar cultures is certainly no coincidence, a fact made particularly evident in his use of the present tense to characterize the storytelling practices of these "naked savage women": "These stories are as old as anything that men have invented. They *are narrated* by naked savage women to naked savage children" (*Violet Fairy Book*, vii; my emphasis). Here, Lang distinguishes between a fanciful version of history, with "our earliest civilised ancestors, who really *believed* that beasts and trees and stones can talk" (vii; my emphasis), and the present moment in which "naked savage women" continue to narrate the same stories. That distinction is, in many ways, the crux of social evolutionary theory.

While theoretical debates about social evolution were generally limited to academics—anthropologists, philologists, ethnologists—and public intellectuals like Lang, those debates were fundamentally shaped by ideas that emerged alongside, indeed as Diarmuid Ó Giolláin (2022) argues, in conversation with, Britain's imperial policies and historical legacies. As such, they extended beyond the realm of academia and elite public discourse, and their underlying precepts and concerns figured centrally in ongoing, if tacit, efforts to "compile the nation's official narrative" (Clark Hillard 2013). In imagining all cultures "evolving" along the same trajectory, the pinnacle of which resided in the "civilized," educated, adult British man, social evolutionary theory effectively authorized imperial, paternalistic rule at home and abroad.[7] For cultural groups, race was essentially determinative; for individuals, sex, class, and age were deciding factors. Perhaps not surprisingly, the two were also deeply imbricated such that "savages," "peasants," and British children were understood to occupy similar stages of evolutionary development (see, e.g., Bolt 1971, 24–27; McClintock 1995, 51; Castle 1996, 13; Malik 1996, 88; Smith and Do Rozario 2016, 40; for Lang's position, specifically, see De Selms Langstaff 1978, 125, 134–35; Smol 1996; Sundmark 2005, 8; Sands-O'Connor 2009, 178; Teverson 2019, 7).

Lest the obvious racist logics underpinning social evolutionary theory appear to be nothing more than the seemingly inevitable, unquestioned, naturalized racisms of a bygone era, it is worth noting that such attitudes were by no means universally held, even in nineteenth-century Britain. Refusing "ignorance or lack of information" as justification for centuries of racist descriptions of white superiority and Black inferiority, Dorothy Kuya points out that notable figures—the explorer Mungo Park, the abolitionist Thomas Clarkson, and the freed slave Olaudah Equiano, for instance—were "describing Africa and Asia and their inhabitants very positively" as early as the eighteenth century (1980, 28). Beyond such positive portrayals, Kuya notes that others decried the savagery of British imperialism, highlighting its affiliation with racism: "Russell, a reporter for *The Times*, recounted the savagery of the British towards the Indians following the Cawnpore uprising in 1858 and said: 'The British could not govern India justly until they had first learned to repress their own racialist attitudes by governing themselves'" (31). Tensions around race and racism also surfaced in much more explicit ways, with "racists" and "philanthropists"—a common designation for abolitionists, especially, as well as for others such as members of the Aborigines

Protection Society—slinging barbed attacks at each other in a range of public, cultural, and pedagogical contexts. In one example, James Hunt, the first president of the London Anthropological Society, was assailed as a racist because of his belief in "the Negro's place in nature," the idea that "race-subordination" is dictated by natural law (cited in Bolt 1971, 6, 8). In turn, he "[ridiculed] his critics as individuals afflicted by 'rights-of-man mania,'" who made "the gigantic assumption of absolute human equality," an assumption he saw as a sign of their "defective reasoning power" (cited in Bolt 1971, 6), a position echoed by Sir Richard Burton, whose works on Africa had been similarly attacked and who likewise vilified his critics as "ignorant and emotional philanthropists" (Bolt 1971, 6). Christine Bolt concludes her account of this case with a wry commentary on the political perspectives expressed by (pseudo)scientific racists like Hunt and Burton in their rejoinders to the philanthropists who challenged them: "Fortunately, an improved acquaintance with coloured races would still the voice of the abolitionists, for years 'a power steadily influencing national policy,' and diminish the prestige of the Negro" (6).

As the case of Hunt, Burton, and their philanthropist critics suggests, "abolition" stood for much more than a desire to end the slave trade; rather, its meaning encompassed a range of ideological positions associated with race, nation, empire, and the "rights of man." Linda Colley contends, for example, that abolition was critical in the formation of a British "national" identity, in relation first to France and then to America: "Anti-slavery became an emblem of national virtue, a means by which the British could impress foreigners with their innate love of liberty and reassure themselves whenever their own faith was in danger of flagging" (2009 [1992], 361). History textbooks likewise offered self-congratulatory nationalist accounts of Britain's abolitionist movement, although—as tools for the indoctrination of young people—such accounts often bent back around to support colonial rule at home and abroad, as Kathryn Castle establishes in her reading of colonialism in children's literature (1996, 67). Referencing V. G. Kiernan, she points out that "these efforts of Britain in working to free the enslaved and transported African invested the European with a 'treasury of merit,' which helped to justify extending control over the African at home" (67). That debates about the meaning of race and racism thoroughly saturated nineteenth-century cultural and political life is perhaps nowhere clearer than in Harry Blyth's 1894 adventure tale, "Heroes of the Matabele War. A Romance of the Recent Campaign in South Africa," where a character proclaims, "'If *I* had my way I would soon teach the black demons a lesson. If you knew as much as I do about them, Will, you would find it hard to believe that they are human. . . . There's a set of folks in England who would rather see a thousand of their own countrymen massacred in this bush than suffer one of these black fiends to be killed" (quoted in Springhall 1989, 116–17, emphasis in original).

Blyth's "Heroes of the Matabele War" may be especially blunt in its jingoistic, mocking caricature of late-century philanthropists, but the story's sentiments were by no means idiosyncratic. Indeed, adventure fiction for boys was an unwavering mouthpiece for empire, inculcating imperial values in generations of Victorian readers (see, e.g., Green 1979; Rose 1993 [1984]; Dunae 1989; Richards 1989; Springhall 1989; Bristow 2016 [1991]; Castle 1996; Hollingworth 2001; Singh 2004; Knuth 2012). Along these lines, for instance, a brochure promoting the *Union Jack*, a Harmsworth periodical introduced in 1894, suggests that several of the company's publications are responsible for sustaining the nation's armed forces: "It is interesting to learn from recruiting-sergeants that these three journals [*Pluck, Marvel* and *Union Jack*] do more to provide recruits for our Army and Navy and to keep up the estimation of these two services in the eyes of the people of this country than anything else" (quoted in Springhall 1989, 113–14; clarification in original). Even more, adventure fiction for boys was so ubiquitous—appearing in countless halfpenny and penny magazines, propaganda tracts, novels, and textbooks—that it is often seen as a primary driver in the proliferation of nineteenth-century children's literature (Rose 1993 [1984]; Richards 1989; Bristow 2016 [1991]). By the last three decades of the nineteenth century, the market for boys' periodical literature featured anywhere from ten (1870) to twenty-three (1900) simultaneous weeklies and monthlies (Dunae 1989, 17), with overall circulation rates between 125,000 and 200,000 for the weeklies (Springhall 1989, 113). As a child, Lang was one of the hundreds of thousands of boys who cherished such tales, mostly in the form of novels by Sir Walter Scott, Robert Louis Stevenson, James Fennimore Cooper, and Mayne Reid, and his early enthusiasm for romance and adventure persisted throughout his life, proving as foundational to his oeuvre as fairy tales and social evolutionary theory (Green 1946;

De Selms Langstaff 1978). Even more, Lang's unabashed defense of popular romance and adventure fiction—especially read alongside *The World's Desire*, the 1890 novel he coauthored with Rider Haggard—attests to his active engagement with the predominant genre of empire as well as to the ways that his oeuvre is implicated in British imperialism in more than passing fashion.

If Andrew's imperial values were especially gendered, so too were Nora's. As literary helpmate, translator, and adapter of tales for children, Nora's role in shaping the Colored Fairy Books was utterly typical for educated, middle-class women with any degree (even unspoken) of writerly ambition. Together, the nineteenth-century expansion of children's literature and the late imperial preoccupation with mothering as a crucial source of national—and racial—strength opened opportunities for women writers, albeit primarily in the creation of pedagogical materials for young readers and parenting advice for other mothers. Additionally, a growing Victorian interest in works translated from modern languages—and the perception of such languages as less prestigious than "the classical ones over which male translators held dominion"—afforded further possibilities for middle-class women to "enter the literary marketplace and participate in intellectual discourses" (Day 2018, 122).[8] That Nora had a natural affinity for modern languages is obvious in the range of her translations for the Colored Fairy Books, and close friends of the Langs clearly attributed the extensive cultural variation of the series to the fact that "her linguistic abilities opened a wide field" (Christie and Stewart, quoted in Day 2018, 99).[9] Andrew, too, seems to have had some degree of admiration for Nora's facility with languages, although he expressed that admiration not in the prefaces but in private correspondence; in a letter to W. B. Richmond, for instance, Andrew wrote of their recent travels through Italy: "My wife has evolved a knowledge apparently minute of the Italian language.... I can't patter a word of their lingo" (quoted in Green 1946, 192). In the prefaces, by contrast, Andrew downplays the importance of Nora's translations to the overall scope and character of the series. In the first several volumes, "Mrs. Lang" is simply included at the end of each list of female translators; as the series progresses, Andrew gives Nora slightly more credit: "The stories have mainly been adapted or translated by Mrs. Lang" (*Crimson Fairy Book*, vi); following credits for several specific translations, "all the rest are told by Mrs. Lang, who does not give them exactly as they are told by all sorts of outlandish natives, but makes them up in the hope white people will like them, skipping the pieces which they will not like" (*Brown Fairy Book*, 1904, viii); again, after several specific acknowledgments for collecting and translating, "[w]ith these exceptions . . . all the tales have been done, from various sources, by Mrs. Lang, who has modified, where it seemed desirable, all the narratives" (*Orange Fairy Book*, 1906, vii); "Mrs. Lang, except in cases mentioned, has translated and adapted to the conditions of young readers the bulk of the collection" (*Olive Fairy Book*, 1907, ix); "All the stories were translated or adapted by Mrs. Lang, except . . ." (*Lilac Fairy Book*, ix).

As such examples make clear, translation and adaptation are essentially indistinguishable for Andrew. While translation theory is, of course, premised on the fact that translation is always already interpretation and adaptation (see, e.g., Venutti 1995; Pym 1998; Lathey 2006, 2010), Andrew's collapsing of Nora's translation and adaptation practices is of a completely different order and highlights the multiple transformations implicit in each of her tales as she produces English versions for white British children. In addition to his account of Nora altering tales "in the hope that white people will like them," Andrew emphasizes their reworking so as to be appropriate for children: "The stories are not literal, or word by word translations, but have been altered in many ways to make them suitable for children. Much has been left out in places, and the narrative has been broken up into conversations, the characters telling each other how matters stand, and speaking for themselves as children, and some older people, prefer them to do. In many tales, fairly cruel and savage deeds are done, and these have been softened down as much as possible" (*Orange Fairy Book*, vi). Here, the slippage between acknowledgments of Nora's translation-adaptation work and the same work rendered in the passive voice simultaneously inscribes Nora in conventional, nineteenth-century gendered categories—female translator, children's story author—and subsumes the value of such work to Andrew's own editorial role as "superintendent," ensuring the tales are appropriate for middle-class white British children. In another preface, Andrew similarly relies on the passive voice to account for the work of adaptation but asserts his own editorial role in a slightly more direct manner: "When the tales are found they are adapted to the needs of British children by various hands, the Editor doing little beyond guarding the interests of propriety, and toning down to mild reproofs the tortures inflicted on wicked stepmothers, and other naughty characters" (*Crimson Fairy Book*, v). Thus, although Andrew claims to "[give] credit where credit is due" by asserting that "[the] fairy books have been almost wholly the work of Mrs. Lang," such a slippage continually reiterates Andrew's investment in Victorian hierarchies of gendered authorship. Moreover, despite Nora's early self-fashioning as a "Bloomsbury bluestocking," she, too, seems to have understood herself largely as a children's book author and pedagogue, albeit one with authorial agency, both in the Colored Fairy Books and in her single-authored publications (De Selms Langstaff 1978, 30).[10]

Although Nora's literary legacy has been defined almost exclusively by Andrew's attributions in the prefaces to the Colored Fairy Books and the couple's annual Christmas offerings, she published several works of her own, including a three-volume geography primer for children. Geography primers were, in many ways, a female-authored complement to the adventure fiction for boys so popular in the nineteenth and early twentieth centuries. As Megan Norcia explains in her astute and detailed study of the genre and its gendering, such works constituted a "sizeable imperial tradition in which women writers penned geographies that marshaled history, religion, economics, and anecdotal evidence to establish the social and cultural supremacy of England" (2010, 2). Keeping pace with the rapid expansion of the British empire across the nineteenth century—Norcia cites growth rates of approximately 100,000 square miles *per year* between 1815 and 1914 (5)—geography primers satisfied two of the period's increasing, interrelated needs: the demand for "information about far-flung colonies and peoples," especially in the burgeoning domain of children's literature, and the desire, on the part of women writers, for greater (but still appropriately gendered) opportunities (5). Throughout the century, then, women writers often framed their geography primers as modest extensions of their maternal duties. Mary Mister, for instance, claims in the preface to her *Mungo, the Little Traveller* (1814) that the book "was not intended, originally, for the public eye; it was the evening employment of a mother, for the amusement of her child; and as it fully answered that design, she flatters herself it may prove to other children not an unacceptable present" (quoted in Norcia 2010, 4). Motherhood was doubly appropriate in relation to children's geography primers because it encompassed responsibilities for both pedagogy and imperial strength (see, e.g., Davin 1978; Stoler 2002; Rosenman and Klaver 2008).

Although Nora was not herself a mother, her geography primers fully conform to the genre. Published between 1881 and 1883—almost a decade before the first of the Colored Fairy Books appeared in 1889—her three-volume *A Geography: Physical, Political, and Descriptive, for Beginners* seeks to introduce readers to the world according to the generic paradigms established over the course of the century: "[T]hese women spent comparatively little time *locating* territories, concentrating instead on the hermeneutic move of *positioning* them in relation to England, Britain, Europe, and the established colonies," a move that helped instantiate "a meaningful framework of imperialism through which children could come to recognize their own small island as a mighty empire entitled and even morally beholden to rule the rest of the world" (Norcia 2010, 21, emphasis in original). The first volume of *A Geography* is divided into two parts, "The British Isles" and "The British Possessions," and Nora bridges the two by invoking the imperial logic that Norcia identifies as foundational to the genre: "One of the most remarkable facts in English history is, the conquest and possession by the little island of Britain of all the great countries that make up India" (1881, 1:137). Also in keeping with the genre, volume 2, *European Continent*, and volume 3, *Asia, Africa, and America*, move outward from Britain. The three volumes are peppered with "ethnographic" snapshots that might combine—in seemingly random fashion—elements of physical description, cultural practices, beliefs and attitudes, and (over)generalized group-based characteristics. For instance: "Before Europeans colonized Australia the country had no corn, and no domesticated animals, like pigs, sheep, and cows. The natives, therefore, lived by hunting, and on wild roots and grasses; they were cannibals and ate each other" (1881, 1:175); "in Labrador, and along the coasts bordering the Arctic Ocean, live a short, ugly race called the Eskimos, who also inhabit the neighboring great island of Greenland" (1881, 1:212); "They [the 'Annamese branch of the Mongol race'] are lively and brave, but cruel and treacherous, and are great ship builders" (1883, 3:634); "The island [Borneo] is peopled by *Dyaks*, of Malay race, but taller than the generality of Malays, and lively though homicidal" (1883, 3:641). Interspersed among these brief but ostensibly comprehensive descriptions are slightly more detailed treatments of "civilized" cultures as well as superficial explanations of "savage" beliefs; when read together, these "historically" inflected sketches evoke the social evolutionary theory that so thoroughly influenced Andrew's work: "The *Ainus* [of 'the Japanese Empire'] are quick and clever, but more prone to adopt the inventions of others than to invent themselves, and they long ago borrowed their military system from the Chinese" (1883, 3:605); "The natives [of Australia] were chiefly governed by men who pretended to be wizards. They are often called the lowest of savages; but probably they do nothing which our own ancestors did not do long ago, and they are clever in their own way" (1881, 1:177).

Insofar as Nora's "ethnographic" sketches and snapshots "[oscillate] between condescension and explicit racism," they were typical of nineteenth-century geography primers in their imperial tone and attitude (Day 2018, 177). Where her three-volume geography diverged from other geography primers, however, was in its treatment of slavery; as noted above, the British abolition movement and eventual Slavery Abolition Act of 1833 were critical to the formation of a national identity and, as such, featured centrally in history textbooks and much pedagogical literature for children, including geography primers (Norcia 2010).[11] Priscilla Wakefield's *A Family Tour through the British Empire*, for instance, follows oldest son Arthur as he "embarks on his African travels, remarking on trade, settlements, and the evils of slavery" (Norcia 2010, 58),[12] in the process highlighting what Norcia identifies as the pervasive citation of abolition to signal Britain's "superior" imperialism: "These brief, seemingly casual references to inappropriate Dutch colonial practices sprinkled through primers from 1816–1854 demonstrate a consistent conviction about the favorableness of British imperial rule. . . . Britain's duties included the regulation not only of domestic spaces . . . but also commercial loci such as ports in Africa, which needed to be supervised and regulated so that unseemly commerce in human flesh was not undertaken" (61).

Against this backdrop, *A Geography* is particularly notable for its vague and anodyne allusions to the slave trade, most likely lost on her child readers. In one of only a few direct references to slavery throughout the three volumes, Nora explains that "[t]he commerce and prosperity of [Jamaica] have however much diminished since slavery was abolished in 1838, owing to the difficulty of obtaining labor" (1881, 1:220). Elsewhere, she euphemistically recodes the slave trade as an "importation," as if human beings were any other trade good: "Hayti was the first island settled by Columbus, and very soon after the colonization the native Indians were all exterminated, and their places filled by negroes imported from Africa" (1883, 3:720); "The population of Brazil is composed of . . . [among others] imported negroes, who are allowed to buy their freedom for a small sum" (1883, 3:744).[13] In the case of Barbados, the history of slavery is completely effaced—"The cultivation of the sugar-cane can be carried on here successfully owing to the dense population (162,000)" (1881, 1:220–21)—an especially telling obfuscation given her family's multigenerational ownership of a plantation on the island and her own social designation as "Leonora Blanche Alleyne (youngest daughter of C.T. Alleyne of Clifton and Barbadoes)" (Green 1946, 41; see also De Selms Langstaff 1978, 29, and Day 2018, 111). Even more, Day's account of Charles Thomas Alleyne's financial compensation for slaves freed under the 1833 Slavery Abolition Act suggests that Nora would have understood—and benefited from—the extent of slave labor necessary for sugar production on Barbados, even if her family's slaves had been freed prior to her birth: "[B]etween 11 April 1836 and 11 May 1836, Nora's father won five claims against the British government after 717 of his Barbadian slaves were freed. . . . He received £12,411 6S, 6D, an amount that would be worth about £1.3 million today [2018]" (2018, 111). Nora, too, appears to have been complicit in the project of empire, independent of her collaborations with Andrew.

Imperial Whitewashing: Adaptation and Otherness

In many ways, Nora's *A Geography* anticipates the tenor of Andrew's prefaces to the Colored Fairy Books with their pithy "ethnographic" references and often pejorative asides. Where the descriptions of people in the three-volume geography primer generally pertain to adults, however, those in the prefaces to the fairy-tale collections mainly revolve around children. Young readers thus meet "Red Indian children who never go to school, nor see pen and ink," "the Kaffirs in Africa, whose dear papas are not so poor as those in Australia, but have plenty of cattle and milk, and good mealies to eat, and live in houses like very big bee-hives, and wear clothes of a sort, though not very like our own," and "the brown people in the island of New Caledonia, where a boy is never allowed to speak to or even look at his own sisters; nobody knows why, so curious are the manners of this remote island" (*Brown Fairy Book*, vii). Aboriginal Australian children receive the lengthiest introduction, which seamlessly blends description, judgment, and pure fancy:

> [E]ven more uneducated little ones, running about with no clothes at all in the bush, in Australia. . . . They have no lessons except in tracking and catching birds, beasts, fishes, lizards, and snakes, all of which they eat. But when they grow up to be big boys and girls, they are cruelly cut about with stone knives and frightened with sham bogies—"all for their own good" their parents say—and I think they would rather go to school, if they had their choice, and take their chance of being birched and bullied. However, many boys might think it better fun to begin to learn hunting as soon as they can walk. (vii)

At the same time, Andrew encourages readers to explore geography primers to learn more about the regions where the tales originate: "No doubt many children will like to look out these places on the map, and study their mountains, rivers, soil, products, and fiscal policies, in the geography books" (*Crimson Fairy Book*, vi). With this advice, Andrew makes clear the ideological affiliation between Victorian fairy-tale collections—exemplified by the Colored Fairy Books—and children's geography primers, an affiliation not only shaped by but also advancing the work of empire.

As the collaborative work of Andrew and Nora Lang, the Colored Fairy Books consolidate the gendered domains of Victorian children's literature, showcasing the prevailing logics underlying—and unifying—seemingly diverse genres like adventure fiction, didactic narratives intended to cultivate proper British character, and geography primers, whose ultimate goal was, as Norcia pointedly notes, "to prime readers—to prime them for encountering, assessing, understanding, and reacting to peoples from cultures different from their own" (2010, 196; see also Richards 1989; Rose 1993 [1984]; Castle 1996; Singh 2004; Knuth 2012). Jacqueline Rose identifies the nineteenth-century belief in the absolute "knowability" of both the world and the child as one of the foundational logics at the heart of a proliferating children's literature:

> Children's fiction emerges, therefore, out of a conception of both the child and the world as knowable in a direct and unmediated way.... We can see it, in differing forms, in such apparently diverse types of writing as the fairy tale and the adventure story for boys. Andrew Lang published his fairy tales in the nineteenth century as the uncontaminated record of our cultural infancy... to which, it was assumed, the child had a direct and privileged access.... And the boy's adventure story, which came into its own in the mid to late nineteenth century with writers such as Marryat, Kingston, Henty and Stevenson, was always part of an exploratory and colonialist venture which assumed that discovering or seeing the world was the same thing as controlling it. (1993 [1984]: 9)

Simultaneously presenting their tales as the "uncontaminated record of our cultural infancy" while also taking care to frame and adapt the collected tales "to the needs of British children" (*Crimson Fairy Book*, v) and "in the hope white people will like them" (*Brown Fairy Book*, viii), the Langs repeatedly seek to distance their British readers from that world even as they present it as populated by "knowable" imagined others. Of course, exactly how the needs of British children and the preferences of white people are determined and defined is not clear, although I, along with several critics, speculate that the Langs' particular adaptations are driven by their investments in white superiority and British imperialism (see, e.g., Sundmark 2005; Sands-O'Connor 2009; Hines 2010; Day 2018, 2019; Teverson 2019).

The Langs' adaptation of "The Bunyip," an Aboriginal Australian tale, illustrates beautifully how their textual elaborations and omissions, passing editorial comments, and decisions to retain (or not) culturally specific elements all combine to "intervene in the meaning and significance of the story" through "a progrommatic imposition of European sensibilities, and European languages, upon the narrative traditions of others" (Teverson 2019, 8, 9). Originally published in English in the *Journal of the Anthropological Institute of Great Britain and Ireland* (*JAI*) almost fifty years after it was collected by "Mr. W. Dunlop," a colonial settler, the Langs' source tale recounts a village's disastrous encounter with a nearby bunyip, an "amphibious monster supposed to inhabit inland waterways" common in Aboriginal Australian mythology (Hughes 1989, 90; Dunlop and Holmes 1899).[14] The two English versions adhere to the same basic narrative: a group of young men capture a bunyip calf and, after threatening its mother, abscond with it to their village; in retaliation, the mother bunyip floods the village and transforms its inhabitants into black swans. The Langs open their version with an immediate change by situating the narrative within a familiar European fairy-tale frame: "Long, long ago, far, far away on the other side of the world" (*Brown Fairy Book*, 71). Andrew Teverson, in an especially perceptive reading of the Langs' version, notes that the inclusion of such a formulaic opening not only amplifies the story's "otherness" by removing it in time and space from its British readers but also diminishes the agency of the Aboriginal Australian narrators who now become "objects of curiosity" as the "apparent subjects of the story become objects of attention, while the British reader becomes the observing agency" (2019, 9). The appropriation of narrative perspective and agency is further exacerbated by the Langs' editorial comments: "[T]he sun was hot, *but they liked the heat*," "*a strange* weapon called a boomerang," "[i]n that country the people are fond of the roots of bulrushes, *which they think as good as onions*" (71, my emphases; see also Teverson 2019, 9).

In addition to placing the tale within a conventional European fairy-tale frame, the Langs introduce a series of subtle changes that alternately domesticate and amplify cultural differences in order to cultivate a sense of Aboriginal Australian otherness and British superiority (Sands-O'Connor 2009, 181; Teverson 2019, 9). Karen Sands-O'Connor highlights the significant ideological import implicit in one such seemingly minor revision: in the *JAI* version, the young man who catches the bunyip calf is clearly part of a collective so that when he "raised his spear and brandished it" at the raging mother bunyip, "he by degrees infused part of his own courage into the breasts of his companions," who then help him transport the calf back to the village. In the Langs' version, by contrast, the young man acts alone and with more aggression; after "flinging his spear at the mother to keep her back, he threw the little Bunyip on to his shoulders and set out for the camp" (Dunlop and Holmes 1899, 23; *Brown Fairy Book*, 72). Sands-O'Connor's incisive reading of this ostensibly minor revision calls attention to the Langs' promotion of heroic individualism, the violence associated with such an ideology, and the effect of both on the tale's ending:

> Dunlop and Holmes's hero threatens but does not harm the mother, and his companions share the blame for the action of kidnapping the calf; this makes the ending, in which the entire village is punished and redeemed, more psychologically satisfying. Lang, on the other hand, argues for rugged individualism—a prevalent ideology in the Edwardian era—but also an uncomfortable sort of justice, in which innocent bystanders are punished along with the guilty hero. (2009, 180)

Although Sands-O'Connor stops short of articulating the racialized implications of the tale's ending when read through the Langs' revisions, the "uncomfortable sort of justice" that emerges through their version tacitly distances the original storyteller and his culture from the logic of Western modernity in which the destruction of an entire village owing to the transgression of a single individual would seem both irrational and unduly cruel, two commonly invoked beliefs about "savages" during the long Victorian era. Though tangential to Sands-O'Connor's argument,[15] the Langs' emphasis on rugged individualism reproduces many of the dominant tropes of adventure fiction—the brave individual hero confronts a fierce creature with violent action—a genre whose ideological underpinnings are anchored in the same imperial values that Sands-O'Connor contends "[keep] both white child and non-white savage firmly in their places" (2009, 183).

Extending Sands-O'Connor's analysis, "[keeping] both the white child and non-white savage firmly in their places"—the child through an imagined innocence, the "savage" through a fantastically heightened otherness—while also creating an equivalency between them depends on their triangulation with the adult keepers of white British imperialist values. For adult enforcers like the Langs, who never questioned their presumed authority to dictate the boundaries of "proper" knowledge and behavior for "innocent" white children and "heathen" non-white "savages," sexuality was often a central concern insofar as it emblematized both "savage" life and the dangerous knowledge from which children needed protecting. The Langs' adaptations are especially clear in this regard as their versions excise any and all references to sexuality, whether such references are critical to the meaning of the tale or barely noticeable because so oblique.[16] The Langs' version of "The Bunyip," for instance, condenses a lively description of the villagers' fear at the encroaching flood in order to remove even the slightest allusions to sexual desire. In the Dunlop and Holmes version, such allusions not only animate the passage but also emphasize Aboriginal Australian mores around sexual propriety:

> Those that were dearest to each other rushed together in the vain hope of yielding mutual assistance. Mothers clasped their children, husbands their wives, and the young betrothed, who a few hours before would not even have touched each others' [sic] hands, frantically clung together in the hope that they might swim through the water, and save themselves for the happiness they had looked forward to from their earliest years. (Dunlop and Holmes 1899, 24)

The Langs reduce and flatten this passage, stating only that "[p]arents and children clung together, as if by that means they could drive back the advancing flood" (*Brown Fairy Book*, 75). Here, even as the Langs' version omits any sexual innuendo by installing the parent-child relationship in place of all others, their much shorter rendering still manages to expand on the meaning, as Sands-O'Connor notes in her observation that the revision "takes away the agency of the people and makes them appear unscientific; they cling together in a mystical belief that this will make the flood disappear, rather than in hope of offering aid to each other" (2009, 180).

If the Langs severely abridge or delete narrative elements that reference sexuality, "rational" thinking, and cultural customs and mores—especially those that index "civilized" standards of propriety—in order to align their tales with imperial ideologies and assumed white British tastes, they also expand several tales by introducing fanciful elaborations for similar effect. In "The Owl and the Eagle," for instance, the Langs imagine and import extensive background details, conversation and interiority, and character motivations to their source text, "The

Eagle and the Owl," a tale told among the Siciatl of British Columbia and collected and published by Charles Hill-Tout (1904).[17] The Siciatl tale follows the wives of Eagle and Owl as they leave home to search for their lost husbands, who have been captured by the witch-monster Yanēqḗmēkwon. Accompanied by their sons, one of whom is a frog, the women first use magic and the frog-son's help to reach Yanēqḗmēkwon's house and to outwit her ploy to kill them; though outraged that the women survived her attempts on their lives, Yanēqḗmēkwon is distracted by their "long glossy hair," and she asks them how it grows so "luxuriantly" (50). Cleverly taking advantage of the witch-monster's vanity, the women tell her that the "abundance of their tresses" is due to their "putting pitch and hot stones on their heads," and because the process is so painful, one of them must hold her down; they then proceed to cover her head with burning pitch and stones, thereby killing her. The story simply ends with Yanēqḗmēkwon's death, omitting any further mention of Eagle and Owl.

Although both versions begin with the formulaic European opening, "Once upon a time," the rest of the first sentences diverge in dramatic fashion. Hill-Tout's version, based on his word-for-word transcription/translation (also included in the publication), is concise and direct: "Once upon a time Eagle and Owl lived together in the same house" (49). The Langs' version, by contrast, alters not only the length and tone of Hill-Tout's version but also its connotations: "Once upon a time, in a savage country where the snow lies deep for many months in the year, there lived an owl and an eagle" (*Orange Fairy Book*, 236). Here, locating the narrative in an unnamed "savage country" immediately transforms Native storytelling subjects into the objects of stories told about othered Natives, a move Teverson cites with respect to "The Bunyip" and one that the Langs invoke throughout the Colored Fairy Books (2019, 8–9); the remainder of the opening sentence similarly diminishes Siciatl cultural authority by replacing Eagle and Owl, two named characters likely to have their own histories and mythologies, with generic birds—"an owl" and "an eagle." Hill-Tout's version continues in candid fashion, neither downplaying nor overstating the sexuality that motivates the first half of the narrative: "They were great hunters, and always had a goodly supply of meat on hand; but there was one thing that they both lacked and that was the possession of wives"

(49). As luck would have it, Eagle and Owl return from hunting one day to find that two young women have fallen asleep, each in one of their beds; not surprisingly, "[t]hey were delighted to see them and each took one to wife," and "[i]n due course of time each woman gave birth to a son" (49). The tale's straightforward account of events—a desire for wives, the young women asleep in their beds, the birth of sons—implies that Eagle's and Owl's perceived lack is a sexual one readily satisfied by the unexpected arrival of the two young women.

In the Lang version, this series of events occupies nearly two pages and involves a description of the birds' differences, their friendship, their living situation, their hunting schedules, and their thoughts when they find the girls asleep in their house. Beyond these general elaborations, the Langs' story also features several noteworthy changes, including the birds' reason for wanting wives:

> "I really am too tired when I come home in the evening to clean up the house," said the eagle.
> "And I am much too sleepy at dawn after a long night's hunting to begin to sweep and dust," answered the owl. And they both made up their minds that wives they must have. (236)

So eager are the eagle and the owl to find wives to keep house for them that they actively pursue "the young ladies of their acquaintance, but the girls all declared they preferred one husband to two" (236). Once the owl and the eagle discover the girls asleep in their beds and agree that "[t]hey will make capital wives if they will only stay," the birds "[fly] off to give themselves a wash, and to make themselves smart before the girls awoke" (236). When the girls finally awake, the eagle and the owl woo them with food as well as with their "kindness and cleverness" before asking them to marry them (237).

In asserting creative control over the story, the Langs overwrite Eagle's and Owl's sexual motivation for seeking wives in a way that invests the tale with alternative connotations of "savagery." Beginning with their initial substitution—the birds' desire to find wives to keep house (wholly consistent with British ideologies of gender)—the Langs' lengthy introduction foregrounds a need for cleanliness, an exceedingly pervasive trope in the imperial imagination (see, e.g., Davin 1978; McClintock 1995;

Cohen 2004; Van Dijk 2011). Not only is the birds' house in need of cleaning but so too are Eagle and Owl, whose washing figures in their plan to entice the girls to marry them and thus suggests that such grooming is not a regular occurrence. Bridging these two references to the birds' lack of cleanliness is the claim that the young ladies first approached by the owl and the eagle "all declared they preferred one husband to two." Disingenuous as such a claim may be given that the birds are *each* seeking *a* wife, it nonetheless summons the common association between polygamy and "primitive" or "savage" cultures. Relying on precisely this association, the Langs' narrative sequencing makes abundantly clear that "savagery," almost by definition, entails the need for cleanliness.

That "savages" are "dirty" is a familiar refrain in the Colored Fairy Books. "The Story of a Gazelle," for example, begins and ends with a poor man who essentially lives off of a dust-heap. Abridged and adapted from the story "Sultan Darai" in Edward Steere's English 1870 collection of Swahili tales (published as interleaved Swahili and English pages), the Langs' "The Story of a Gazelle" follows the rise and fall of a poor man who finds a coin while scratching for food in a dust-heap and uses it to purchase what turns out to be a magical gazelle; the gazelle, in turn, uses his wits and charm to marry the poor man—in the guise of "Sultan Darai"—to another sultan's daughter, in the process acquiring an excessively grand palace and life of luxury for them. Once installed there, the gazelle, beloved by all, takes ill, only to find that Sultan Darai has become too arrogant and proud to provide proper care for him; appalled by his cruelty, the sultan's wife sends the gazelle to her father for care, but the gazelle dies soon after. Once the mourning period has passed, the wife dreams that she is back at her father's palace and Sultan Darai dreams that he is back at his dust-heap, and they both wake to find that their dreams are, indeed, reality.

Earlier in the story, the gazelle instructs the poor man, filthy from the dust-heap, to clean himself as part of his transformation into "Sultan Darai": "And the gazelle said to him, 'Get up, my master, and bathe in the stream!' and when the man had bathed it said again, 'Now rub yourself well with earth, and rub your teeth well with sand to make them bright and shining'" (*Violet Fairy Book*, 134). Although the Langs' version of this scene reproduces the direct dialogue fairly faithfully, it omits a significant exchange from Steere's version:

And it said, "Get up, master, and bathe." And its master went into the stream. And it said, "Here in the stream there is little water; go there into the pool." And he said, "There in the pool, why I fear is, that there is water exceedingly plenty; and where there is great plenty of water, where there is a pool, there are sure to be noxious animals."

And it said, "What animals, master?" And he said, "First, in lakes there are surely crocodiles, and secondly, there are surely *kenges*, and thirdly, there are surely snakes, and fourthly, whatever there be, there are frogs, and they bite people, and I fear all those things."

"Well, master, bathe just here in the stream." (81, 83)

Given the Langs' tendency to embroider Native tales with exoticizing details like local wildlife and plants in order to exaggerate their cultural otherness, the deletion of this passage—with its colorful enumeration of threatening animals—may seem strange. The direct dialogue in Steere's version privileges the protagonist's perspective, however, and in so doing the animal references point to his logical reasoning, not simply to local color. In addition, the Langs' abridged version of this scene intensifies the effect of the gazelle's command that "Sultan Darai" scrub himself with dirt and his teeth with sand to further clean himself after bathing in the stream. For British readers whose cultural landscape was saturated with advertisements for soap—among the most ubiquitous commodities in a rapidly expanding consumer environment—the idea of cleansing with dirt would have been downright foreign even as it fit with common visual and discursive constructions of dirty colonial others for whom "soap [was] the onset of civilization" (Van Dijk 2011, 1).[18]

Soap was much more than an ever-present commodity in Victorian Britain, however. As Anne McClintock so convincingly establishes in *Imperial Leather*, soap—from its manufacture to its advertising—was central to empire, not only as "a cheap and portable domestic commodity" capable of "[mediating] the Victorian poetics of racial hygiene and imperial progress" but also as a "God-given sign of Britain's evolutionary superiority" and a "technology of social purification, inextricably entwined with the semiotics of imperial racism and class denigration" (1995, 209, 207, 212). Nowhere is the ideological convergence of soap, imperial racism, and British superiority clearer than in Victorian advertisements, an astounding number of which adopt the logic of Unilever's slogan: "Soap is civilization" (207). McClintock argues that "[t]he initial impetus for soap advertising came from the realm of empire," and she presents an impressive array of examples, including a Pears ad in which a white boy holds a mirror before a black boy so he can see that the soap has washed away his body's blackness (apparently he failed to use the soap on his face, which remains black); several Pears ads set in colonial locales, including one featuring a "native," clad only in a loincloth, holding a spear in one hand and a bar of soap, from a Pears crate that has washed ashore, in the other, all beneath the line, "The Birth of Civilization"; and a Bovril ad in which the letters *B O V R I L* track Lord Roberts's military advance, snaking across a map of colonial South Africa, to inscribe, literally, the name of the soap above the line, "How Lord Roberts wrote BOVRIL" (212–27). Such nineteenth-century preoccupations with soap and the Victorian fetishization of "cleaning rituals" lend further context and insight to the Langs' narrative attention to cleanliness and dirt (207). Together with prefatory references to "the Eskimo in their dark dirty winter huts" (*Pink Fairy Book*, 1897, vii) and "the Lapps" as "a people not fond of soap and water" (*Violet Fairy Book*, viii), their editorial focus on tropes of cleanliness and its absence reveals an undeniable complicity in the racialized and racist project of empire.[19]

If, for the Langs, adaptation is also a form of cleansing—of removing the "dirty" presence of sexuality in order to suit "the needs of British children" (*Crimson Fairy Book*, v)—it is, perhaps ironically, one that leaves its own taint. That is, in purging the tales of their sexual innuendo, the Langs also erase some of the most powerful markers of "savagery" and difference, for them a disquieting erasure that must be righted through alternative, often exaggerated, signs of "savagery"—the magical thinking in lieu of mutual aid in "The Bunyip" and the allusions to polygamy and a need for cleanliness in "The Owl and the Eagle," for instance. Ultimately, "[t]hese tendencies, to on the one hand sanitize the 'savage' tales and on the other make them more irrational," suggest that, for the Langs, "the needs of British children" are sutured to the needs of empire with "savage" fantasies (Sands-O'Connor 2009, 181).

The Colored Fairy Books: It's a White, White World

Although Andrew Lang is now remembered almost exclusively for the Colored Fairy Books, he was a prominent public scholar whose centrality to late-nineteenth-century intellectual life far exceeded his contributions to any single topic, including the study and anthologizing of fairy tales. Nathan Hensley—in his edited special issue, "The Andrew Lang Effect: Network, Discipline, Method" (2013)—invokes Bruno Latour's network theory to convey the multiple, entangled ways that Lang not only mediated but also shaped late Victorian thinking about gender, sexuality, race, and imperialism in relation to a wide range of literary genres and cultural arts. Contesting Lang's general relegation to historical "footnote" by literary critics—that is, *simply* "a collaborator, an enabler, a translator, and a compiler"—Hensley argues instead that it is precisely such work that recommends Lang as a quintessential example of Latour's "'mediator': an agent of connection that serves to link various sectors of its network in active, shaping ways," one "'endowed with the capacity to *translate* what they transport, to redefine it, to redeploy it'" (2013, Latour quoted in Hensley, emphasis added by Hensley).

Understanding Lang as the central mediating node in a complex network of academic and public scholars helps to identify and map the intersecting and interpenetrating nature of his various discourse communities, in the process highlighting the depths of his involvement in many of the leading humanistic and social scientific conversations of the period. In this sense, the "Andrew Lang effect" not only draws together conversations that might initially seem divergent, adjacent, perhaps even unrelated—conversations that may not have been considered together previously—but also reframes the "heterogeneous, distributed, wide-ranging quality of his work less as a problem to be managed and more of an important and conceptually vital element of his achievement" (Siegel 2013). Kathy Alexis Psomiades, for example, argues persuasively that centering Lang among Rider Haggard, Sigmund Freud, and Edward Tylor highlights their common investment in an "attempt to define civilized European masculinity against its others—femininity, the 'primitive,' the 'savage'"—and the connections among them "[enabled] Haggard's novel [*She*] to be read as a kind of microcosm of late-nineteenth-century ideologies of race, gender, and empire, its fantastic strangeness ultimately allied to the strangeness of the imperial project itself" (2013). Tracing "the ideas that circulate through the texts [Lang] transmits and enables"—the looping interconnections among Haggard, Freud, and Tylor—Psomiades contends that Lang's work attends to questions at the heart of interpretation, questions about the making of meaning, that proved critical in shaping the eventual fields of anthropology, literary criticism, and psychoanalysis (2013).

Many of the foundational topics and questions associated with the development of anthropology, literary criticism, and psychoanalysis—the social evolution of the different "races"; the relationship of child and "savage" minds to those of "civilized" adults; the cultural meaning of texts and the nature of authorship, for instance—were for Lang writ small in the fairy tale, and Molly Clark Hillard contends that it is the fairy tale that accounts for Lang's central position in a number of overlapping and interconnected Victorian networks (2013). For Clark Hillard, the fairy tale is itself a "networked" genre, characterized by its "hybridizing" work, the way "its language, figures, structure, methods of production, and multiple authors reappear in other forms of cultural production," which was particularly evident during the nineteenth century when fairy tales "could be found in virtually every genre of Victorian literary and visual art" (2013; see also Clark Hillard 2014). As a networked, seemingly ubiquitous form, the Victorian fairy tale inspired questions related to the nature of authorship, and while Clark Hillard privileges Lang's engagements with the fairy tale as paradigmatic of networked cultural production and the pressures it puts on the very notion of "the author" as an individual entity, she also calls attention to the ideological stakes implicit in such tensions between "author" and "network": "who would compile the nation's official narrative; what communities and contents would this narrative encompass (and thus leave out); and what was the value (in use and exchange) of this national story?" (2013).

Although Lang was largely uninterested in "politics"—indeed, his authoritative biographer, Roger Lancelyn Green, claims that "Lang detested politics" (1946, 183)—his enduring passions were by their very nature highly politicized and thus necessarily, if implicitly, part of the contest to articulate "the nation's official narrative." Emerging as they did during a late Victorian moment of heightened imperial anxiety, the Colored Fairy Books can thus be understood as a symbolic response to the pervasive sense of Britain's growing vulnerabilities, as Teverson so persuasively argues (2016). The waning decades of the nineteenth century saw threats to the empire's dominance from competing global powers as well as from shifts in domestic power inspired by the extension of the franchise, turmoil over Irish Home Rule, and mounting xenophobia (Bell 2007). Such threats converged in cultural and political debates over "Greater Britain," an imagined "global British polity" and aspirational "'Anglo-Saxon' empire" whose advocates "proselytized a vision of moral order in which a superior Anglo-Saxon race offered stability and leadership, benevolently but firmly, to a chaotic world" (Bell 2007, 12, 5, 92). Although not directly engaged in these debates, Andrew Lang certainly "felt the anxiety attendant upon the fractures in Empire," according to Teverson, and "resorted to the materials of folklore to stage a symbolic expression of togetherness under one banner" (2016, 16). With the Colored Fairy Books, then, Lang—or the Langs, to be more precise—"creates a symbolic commonwealth of nations, a spell against the disintegratory pressures of an empire in decline" (Teverson 2016, 26; see also Sundmark 2005; Hines 2010; Day 2018).[20]

As a "symbolic commonwealth of nations," the Colored Fairy Books do more than offer a talismanic British empire writ small, however. They also exemplify the nineteenth-century British penchant for collecting, an activity predicated on the removal of "objects"—whether natural, material, cultural, intellectual, or geopolitical—from their native environment in order to recontextualize them in another environment, specifically that of the collection (Stewart 1993). Moreover, as Susan Stewart establishes and as the Colored Fairy Books so clearly demonstrate, collecting is "a mode of control and containment insofar as it is a mode of generation and series," and it is precisely this feature that tethers the Victorian obsession to empire and its ideological underpinnings (159). Drawing on Stewart's theorization of the collection, Sara Hines thus positions the Langs' series among a broad array of Victorian collections—"[f]rom small-scale examples such as private home museums, libraries, and aquariums to larger-scale collections like discussions of taxonomic systems in the biological sciences, national botanical gardens and museums, and the collection of nations and countries through colonial expansion"—and argues that the Colored Fairy Books "effectually allow British readers to collect, possess, and display the empire through ownership of 'outlandish native stories'" (2010, 48, 54). That is, the series allows for the control and containment of Britain's imperial others—and at the hands of children, no less. In this sense, the Colored Fairy Books are not so different from Victorian puzzle maps that likewise put the empire's holdings in the hands of children, whose lessons in piecing together the world also impart "narratives of power and authority which are incumbent in the business of building both nation and empire" and "[foster] what Roderick McGillis has called 'a colonial mentality' (xxii)" (Norcia 2009, 2).[21]

Like children's puzzle maps and geography primers, the Colored Fairy Books consolidate—and thus remake—the world in and through the British empire. In keeping with all collections, the Langs' series seeks "not the restoration of context of origin but rather the creation of a new context," one that "presents a hermetic world" (Stewart 1993, 152). The hermetic world of the collection—the world instantiated by the way "the stories have been collected, translated, and edited specifically so that white people will like them" (Hines 2010, 54)—thus supersedes the cultural worlds in which the tales circulated prior to colonial, missionary, and anthropological contact. The Langs' editorial practices accomplish much more than circumscribing colonial otherness in the self-contained world of the Colored Fairy Books, however. They also succeed in universalizing the *genre* itself. That is, in rewriting tales according to the particular conventions of the British (and European) fairy tale while simultaneously asserting the adapted tales' cultural difference, the Langs convey—and in the process solidify—the idea that the fairy tale is the same the world over, an idea widely disseminated by virtue of the transatlantic and diasporic popularity of the Colored Fairy Books. As a global cultural commodity that purports to showcase the world's diverse fairy tales, the Langs' collection—its hermetic world—ultimately obscures the fact that many of the tales are "[made up] in the hope white people will like them," thus erasing the erasures at the heart of imperial power and notions of white British superiority.

CONCLUSION

Spectral Politics and the Return to Wonder

The Langs' Colored Fairy Books may have been vital to the popular understanding of the European fairy tale as a universal genre, but they were by no means idiosyncratic in cultivating such a belief. Where the Langs' anthologies consolidated the pedagogical genres, the intellectual convictions, and the political ideologies of empire in order to showcase the purportedly universal nature of the fairy tale, nineteenth- and early-twentieth-century scholarly collections—and the tools they inspired for comparative analysis—advanced the colonizing logics of an emergent, decidedly Eurocentric discipline to similar effect. As many fairy-tale scholars have established, early disciplinary frameworks predicated on classification and comparison "tend to promote the universalizing of texts across cultures" because such paradigms—encoded in Antti Aarne's foundational 1910 tale type index, *Verzeichnis der Märchentypen* (translated, updated, and expanded by Stith Thompson in 1928 and 1961 and again by Hans-Jörg Uther in 2004)—privilege the tale type and its constituent elements over the specificity of individual tales (Haase 2010, 27).[1] At the same time, the enduring disciplinary investment in classification and comparison has also entailed, if not demanded, the imposition of European genre categories on narrative traditions with their own cultural designations, an imposition that obviously discounts, dismisses, and/or simply overwrites Native knowledge systems and "naturalizes the *colonial history* of folk and fairy-tale exchange and entanglements across cultures" (Bacchilega 2019, 34, emphasis in original; see also Naithani 2006, 2010; Bacchilega 2013, 2019; Bacchilega and Duggan 2016; Kuwada and Yamashiro 2016; Sasser 2019; Seifert 2019; Teverson 2019; Zobel Marshall 2019).

So deeply embedded are these paradigms and practices in fairy-tale studies that Donald Haase, in his seminal 2008 call to "decolonize" the discipline, begins with what he himself sees as a seemingly obvious reminder that we must "resist the twin urges to universalize traditional narratives at the expense of their specific historical and sociocultural contexts and to generalize the European fairy tale as an ahistorical global genre" (2010, 29). Pushing Haase's call to decolonize the field beyond the immediate realm of academic fairy-tale studies, Hawaiian scholar-artist-activist Bryan Kamaoli Kuwada and ally artist-activist Aiko Yamashiro highlight the ways that critical conversation and mutual learning between Indigenous scholar-artist-activists and fairy-tale scholars might interrupt the long and fraught histories of "Indigenous knowledges being relegated to folk wisdom or fairy tales as a way to undermine their authority in colonial knowledge systems," practices at the center of disciplines like fairy-tale studies, folklore, cultural anthropology, and ethnography (2016, 18). Across the essays in Kuwada and Yamashiro's "Rooted in Wonder," a special issue of the international fairy-tale journal *Marvels and Tales*, wonder is disarticulated from its hegemonic associations with the European fairy tale, freeing readers to "rethink the differences and the affinities of fairy tales and other wonder genres, their ontologies, and the activist uses to which they are put today" (Bacchilega and Duggan 2016, 12). Excavating and foregrounding wonder's affective relationship to sovereignty, land, and bodies, "Rooted in Wonder" necessarily decenters the understanding of wonder at the heart of the ostensibly universal fairy tale; as such, the volume creates opportunities "to build solidarity across disciplines" by contributing to the provincialization of the European fairy tale (12).

What "Rooted in Wonder" makes most evident, however, is that the work of decolonizing fairy-tale studies, of building solidarity across disciplines, of recuperating Indigenous knowledges from their trivialization and marginalization in colonial knowledge systems is all secondary to the essential role that Indigenous wonder stories continue to play in spiritual and political movements for Native sovereignty and land reclamation. Introducing the essays in "Rooted in Wonder" shortly after the start of the Hawaiian movement to protest the construction of the Thirty Meter Telescope atop the sacred mountain Mauna Kea, Kuwada and Yamashiro weave the themes of the special issue—and "moʻolelo (story, legend, tradition, or history)" more generally—together with specific collective actions, public protests, and Indigenous power: "[O]ur moʻolelo have energized us, awakened us, moved us. Part of it is the awe and wonder that we feel at the top of the mountain . . . but also the wonder at the power of our collectivity, what happens when we tell our stories and do our chants, in larger and larger numbers across the world" (18). Such testaments to the ways Indigenous wonder practices are deeply imbricated with real material political actions seeking to overcome white-settler colonialism, capitalist and statist land expropriation, and imperial legacies of allegedly apolitical knowledge production underscore the fact that the need to decolonize fairy-tale studies is motivated by much more than an anodyne political correctness or a facile attempt to expand the range of representations in an inherently European fairy-tale canon. Rather, such work insists that we reckon with the white world of the fairy tale as a way of reckoning with the real world that the European fairy tale helps to instantiate and maintain through empires of white superiority, whether material, political, historical, cultural, and/or scholarly.

Creole Marvels and the Provincial European Fairy Tale

Critical—not to mention obvious and largely overlooked—to the project of decolonizing fairy-tale studies is recognizing and embracing the marginal place of the European fairy-tale tradition in Native, Indigenous, and postcolonial storytelling. Along these lines, Lewis Seifert (2002a, 2019) and Cristina Bacchilega (2008, 2013) have followed the lead of Caribbean writers like Patrick Chamoiseau and Nalo Hopkinson in centering a politics of creolization in contemporary wonder genres, including speculative fiction, tales of the marvelous, and (re)invented local and European folk and fairy tales. In prioritizing the implicit multivocality of Creoleness—a political, pan-Caribbean identification that "aims to put into question the hegemonic status of the West and its writing and to create a new identity and consciousness through this questioning" (Seifert 2002a, 228)—in Chamoiseau's *Creole Folktales* (1994) and Hopkinson's *Skin Folk* (2001), Seifert and Bacchilega disrupt the critical tendency to read postcolonial Caribbean wonder genres as only, or even predominantly, subversive rewritings of European fairy tales, a tendency that perhaps paradoxically celebrates postcolonial resistance while simultaneously reifying the European genre's supposed universality. Instead, they trace the intertextualities at play in Chamoiseau's and Hopkinson's collections across complex networks of Creole tradition and postcolonial literary production, privileging insider knowledge systems often closed to outside readers while also noting occasional European fairy-tale touchstones in order to highlight the European fairy tale's very provincialism.

Hopkinson's story "The Glass Bottle Trick" (2001), together with the fairy-tale scholarship it has inspired, exemplifies the power of creolization and its related critical approaches. Focalized through Beatrice, the young, light-skinned third wife of the older, excessively proper, "molasses-dark" Samuel, the story meanders through past and present as Beatrice prepares to tell Samuel of her pregnancy. The story's main action is set in motion when Beatrice attempts to keep a snake from devouring the eggs a bird has laid in their guava tree, in the process shattering the two blue bottles Samuel has hung there out of (uncharacteristic, according to Beatrice) superstition: "Is just my superstitiousness, darling. . . . You never heard the old people say that if someone dies, you must put a bottle in a tree to hold their spirit, otherwise it will come back as a duppy and haunt you? A blue bottle. To keep the duppy cool, so it won't come at you in hot anger for being dead" (2001, 67). Once shattered, the bottles release their spirits, hot "little dust devils" (69) that lead Beatrice to a locked room where she hopes to find the controls to the air conditioner but where she discovers, instead, the corpses of Samuel's ex-wives, each visibly pregnant; now freed to return to their bodies, the duppies lap at the pooled blood around each corpse, becoming increasingly solid as they do so. The story ends in ambiguity: as Samuel arrives home, Beatrice wonders, "When they had fed, would they come and save her, or would they take revenge on her, their usurper, as well as on Samuel?" (79).

Although "The Glass Bottle Trick" clearly shares motifs with the European "Bluebeard" tradition—and even refers to "glints of the deepest blue in [Samuel's] trim beard" (74)—Bacchilega's Creole-centric reading pivots away from other insightful postcolonial analyses that position Hopkinson's story as primarily engaged in challenging the European "Bluebeard" tradition, a positioning that unintentionally reproduces the genre's assumed universality even as it seeks to undermine its "colonial heritage" (Hennard Dutheil de la Rochère 2009, 213). Thus, where Martine Hennard Dutheil de la Rochère describes "The Glass Bottle Trick" as an "appropriation of the European fairy tale tradition" (213) and Natalie Robinson characterizes it as "[w]riting back to European tales" (2011, 253), Bacchilega contests the "focus on the European *literary* tradition of the fairy tale as an essential place from which Hopkinson's adaptation draws its empowering and hegemonic force" (2013, 42, emphasis in original), arguing instead that "The Glass Bottle Trick" not only "[provincializes] the Perrault and Grimm printed tales" but also underscores the fact that such tales are "hardly central to its intertextual web" (45–46). Hopkinson's reflection on her artistic practice lends further credence to Bacchilega's point: "[M]ore often than not, I start from my native lore, not from the European" (Simpson 2005, 104–5).

And yet Hopkinson encourages the European tradition to haunt "The Glass Bottle Trick," with its allusions to literary versions of "Bluebeard," precisely because such a haunting presence helps animate the story's politics of creolization. That is, for Hopkinson and other Caribbean artist-activists, creolization encapsulates the resistance and survival manifest in the Caribbean's hybrid cultures, cultures forged through violent histories of colonialism, slavery, and indentured labor; creolization and cultural hybridity, Hopkinson explains, provided (and continue to provide) ways of "[using] elements of all the cultures"—including the "alien culture and speech imposed on them"—"in order to continue to exist" ("Code Sliding," n.d.). European cultural legacies obviously contribute to Caribbean hybridities, but as "The Glass Bottle Trick" so powerfully establishes, their contribution is marginal. Drawing on Hopkinson's theorization of hybridity as resistance and survival, then, Bacchilega's privileging of the story's creolization over its engagement with the European "Bluebeard" tradition foregrounds two of the story's critical features: first, "issues of race and sexual power are thematized together" and, second, "racial politics come to inform the traditional Bluebeard abhorrence of pregnancy and reproduction" (2008, 188–89).

Here, creolization enables the thematic coupling of race and sexual power because the Caribbean's colonial history is so profoundly structured by race-based hierarchies of skin color. The absence of such explicit racial framing in the European literary versions—despite the fact that the association between the eponymous "blue beard" and the dusky shadow of facial hair common to dark-skinned men raises specters of race that were fully materialized in Victorian stagings of Bluebeard as a "Turk" in Orientalist pantomimes and illustrated chapbooks (Hermansson 2009; Schacker 2021)—literalizes its provincial nature. What Bacchilega's cogent reading implicitly reveals is the causal relationship between these two critical dimensions of "The Glass Bottle Trick." That is, Hopkinson's thematizing race and sexual power together rationalizes the European Bluebeard tradition by providing the literary tale's missing logic—Bluebeard's motivation for killing the first wife—a logic that makes sense only after "The Glass Bottle Trick" surfaces the literary tale's latent racial codes epitomized in the villain's blue beard. Thus, when Hopkinson creolizes the tale and posits internalized anti-Black racism as Samuel's motivation for killing his pregnant wives, she lays bare the absurdities of the European fairy tale's deracinated legacy.

While the creolization at the heart of "The Glass Bottle Trick" might also be read as a tacit metacritique of the European fairy tale's naturalized racism and racialized violence, such a metacritique comes to the fore in "Precious," the final story in *Skin Folk* (Hopkinson 2001) and one in which the creolization that drives many of the collection's other stories is largely absent. A version of "The Kind and Unkind Girls," "Precious" is narrated in the first person by the "kind girl," whose "reward" of having jewels and flowers fall from her mouth with every word she speaks has led to years of domestic violence at the hands of her greedy lover, Jude. The story culminates when Jude tracks the heroine, breaks into her house, and begins to attack her until she appeases him with the treasures he so desires, precious metals and gems spit out with the surely bitter words of false love so often forced from the mouths of abused women. It is only at the end of her attempt to assuage Jude that the heroine bursts into righteous anger: "'Well, just listen to me, Jude: I am not your treasure trove, and I will not run anymore, and I shall be nice if and when it pleases me, and stop calling me Precious; my name is Isobel!'" (199). With her tirade, Isobel coughs up "a ruby as big as a human heart," an act that simultaneously knocks Jude out and frees her from her cursed "reward" (199). Here, as in "The Glass Bottle Trick," Hopkinson's inspiring and transformative tale of feminine liberation depends on the absurdities of a European fairy-tale tradition blind to the misogynist impracticalities of a value system that renders women—both kind and unkind—incapable of speaking without bodily trauma, whether in the form of flowers and jewels or newts and frogs.² Even without explicit Creole markers, "Precious" conjures the same specters of race and sexual power that propel "The Glass Bottle Trick," only here those specters operate as metacommentary, calling attention to the inherent folly of a fairy-tale tradition that equates whiteness with precious wealth, all the while blind to the fact that the ultimate costs of such a moral system compromise even a kind, white girl's health and bodily integrity. Vividly evoking what the European fairy tale represses, Hopkinson's stories challenge readers to confront the genre's violent and ugly underpinnings as well as the ways such foundational logics facilitate the racism and sexism that sustain what Bacchilega aptly refers to as the European fairy tale's "commodified magic within a Western economy of colonial exploitation and capitalist desire" (2019, 37).

Fairy Books of Another Color

That "colonial exploitation and capitalist desire" are sold alongside the European fairy tale's "commodified magic" is nowhere clearer than in collections, such as the Langs' Colored Fairy Books, that bring together a multiplicity of wonder genres under the singular and purportedly universal sign of "the fairy tale." Despite aspirations and even explicit claims to the universal, however, the reality is that such collections are undeniably Eurocentric in their framing, an elision made especially evident in Bolu Babalola's (2020) story collection, *Love in Color: Mythical Tales from Around the World, Retold*. Simultaneously reimagining ten culturally diverse wonder tales and challenging the Eurocentric orientation of the "worldly" fairy-tale collection, Babalola's beautifully evocative, affectively poignant adaptations draw their inspiration from tales generally excluded from the European fairy-tale canon:

> Osun: Yoruba myth and religion, Nigeria
> Scheherazade: *1,001 Nights*, Persia
> Nefertiti: Ancient Egyptian fact and myth
> Attem: "Ituen and the King's Wife," Calabar peoples, Nigeria
> Yaa: "The Princess's Wedding," Asante tribe, Ghana

> Siya: Ancient Soninke legend, Soninke people, modern Mali, Senegal, Guinea, the Gambia, and southern Mauritania
> Psyche: Eros and Psyche, ancient Greece
> Naleli: "How Khosi Chose a Wife," Lesotho
> Zhinu: "The Cowherd and the Weaver Girl," China
> Thisbe: Pyramus and Thisbe, Mesopotamia (283)

In anchoring her stories to this set of tales, Babalola rearticulates the cultural makeup of "the world" as represented by most English-language collections of international tales, a rearticulation made all the more powerful by the fact that it remains wholly unmarked. That is, even as *Love in Color* rewrites the colonizing dimensions of anthologies that incorporate a wide variety of wonder genres into the category of the fairy tale and even as Babalola alludes, in her acknowledgments, to the erasure of Black women, like herself, in such works, she refuses to frame her collection as a corrective. Instead, the world as she defines it is simply *the* world, and the absence of authorial notes explaining Babalola's choice of source tales along such lines naturalizes her constitution of the world in exactly the same ways that Eurocentric collections naturalize theirs. Even more, Babalola's celebration of love as the collection's unifying thematic—rooted in her desire to "[explore] how the power of love has been expressed within a variety of cultures from around the world" (xi–xii)—furthers this effect by unsettling and displacing the European fairy tale's hegemony as the definitive genre of love.

In many ways, then, Babalola's polysemous title, *Love in Color*, not only condenses the book's interventions but also resonates with specific histories of the European fairy tale and the collections that have sustained its universalizing reach. For starters, the cover art—featuring a Black man and a Black woman closing in on a kiss, their clothing and the abstract backdrop bright with shades of yellows, reds, greens, and blues, colors associated with African art, textiles, and national flags—suggests that at least one meaning of the title's invocation of "color" involves race. Babalola's appreciation of "the young black women who sent me messages telling me what this book means to them, who saw themselves in me" (290) further bolsters that meaning. Of course, the "color" in Babalola's title also conjures the Langs' Colored Fairy Books, and indeed it is not difficult to imagine that Babalola—a British Nigerian writer and cultural critic with a self-proclaimed devotion to love and a fascination with wonder genres—has a deep familiarity with the Langs' series. Most compelling, however, is the intersection of the two, and I read Babalola's declaration that "[t]his book is about being seen in all your iterations, in every dynamic, brightly and in color" (xii) as securing that intersection. As such, Babalola's adaptations restore color—race—to the wonder tale, the universalized European version of which expunges racial referents through increasing metaphorization over time or through editorial decisions driven by the perceived tastes of white readers. In "Psyche," for example, Babalola offers but a single, simple reference to the heroine's skin color—"the sparkling bow-and-arrow necklace that hung from her neck, its gold bringing out the deep copper tones of her skin" (152)—and, yet, that brief description, focalized through Eros in the moment when he and Psyche "see" each other beyond the protective guises of "friendship," invests the story with a naturalized racial significance that calls to mind the north African versions that likely influenced Apuleius's classical myth as well as Basile's "The Padlock" and "The Golden Trunk" (discussed in chapter 1). Challenging the European fairy tale's assumptions of whiteness and sharpening questions of cultural specificity, *Love in Color*—as a title, as a collection—instead privileges those who remain unseen in the white world of the European fairy tale, encouraging readers to seem them, "brightly and in color."

That color features centrally in a spectral politics of wonder is visibly and vividly apparent in Sarindar Dhaliwal's art installation *the green fairy storybook* (2009). Comprising fourteen brightly colored handmade books standing side by side on a table, Dhaliwal's *the green fairy storybook* offers a version of her story, her history, her art across their spines:

> once upon a time there was a little girl who loved learning to read, sitting on the floor between the stacks in the public library, surrounded by piles of books. the green fairy book, the yellow fairy book the red, the blue, the lavender fairy book. she's convinced, many years on, that there was even a violet, lilac and a purple book this early love of colour is reflected in much of her later life "gamboge, heliotrope, rose madder madder lake." this work represents a resolution of sorts: a coming home to the place where all the narratives she has written began.

A citizen of the Indian diaspora—born in Punjab, raised in London and rural Ontario, and now living in Toronto—Dhaliwal describes her work as mediating "childhood memories and the experience of migration" through artistic engagements with "issues of identity, the slippage between 'here' and 'there,' and the intertwining of colonial histories"; as such, her artwork seeks to "'fix' some cultural dissonances that [she] experienced" and to create beauty from past traumas ("Sarindar Dhaliwal," n.d.). As several curators, critics, and reviewers have noted, Dhaliwal's love of color is an essential dimension of her oeuvre as well as her politics (see, e.g., Isherwood 2006, Wirk 2013), a convergence of such signal importance that it frames Dhaliwal's 2023 retrospective, which takes its title from her 2010 mixed-media piece *When I Grow Up I Want to Be a Namer of Paint Colours*, at the Art Gallery of Ontario.

the green fairy storybook showcases Dhaliwal's chromophilia, both visually and narratively, to keenly penetrating effect: invoking the colorful legacy of the Langs' series, Dhaliwal inscribes the surface of her twinned storybooks with another set of colors—"gamboge, heliotrope, rose madder madder lake"—a set of colors born of Western, and especially British, imperialism, exploitation, and colonial violence. As an example, gamboge, the color of traditional robes worn by Buddhist monks, is created from the sap of deciduous trees of the *Garcinia* family, native to Cambodia—a source represented by the color's name, derived from "Camboja," an early form of "Cambodia"—and the pigment was first brought to Europe by the British East India Company in the early seventeenth century (Ball 2009 [2001], 156; St. Clair 2016, 80; Kelleher 2017). Heliotrope's discovery as a color occurred, accidentally, in 1856 with William Perkin's failed attempt to synthesize quinine from coal tar (St. Clair 2016, 169, 172; "Heliotrope," n.d.); the search for quinine was, of course, itself intertwined with British imperialism, not only because the British empire depended on quinine as an antimalarial drug for its soldiers and civil servants in India but also because British expeditions "raided the highland forests of South America, looking for a hot commodity: *Cinchona* seeds," the bark of whose "fever" trees was a source of quinine (Callaway 2022; see also St. Clair 2016, 169). Rose madder is a shade of pink, and "pink, as a concept, arrived in Europe in the late fourteenth century with shipments of brazilwood dye" (Kelleher 2018). Brazilwood (*pau brazil*) extraction, in turn, marks the start of Brazilian colonial history, conferring on the region a name that originates in its first economically exploitable resource; even more, colonial Brazil's export economy was largely powered by slavery, first "Indian slavery to cut brazilwood" and later African slavery ("Colonial Brazil" 2024). While madder lake can be traced to the ancient Egyptians, who used the root of the madder plant (*Rubia tinctorum*) as a dye for textiles, Lytle Shaw emphasizes its prominence as "the color of empire": "Madder lake found its calling when, in the seventeenth century, it became the color of the British army's red coat. As Britain expanded its colonial outposts globally throughout the eighteenth and nineteenth centuries, madder lake grew into the color of empire" (7; see also St. Clair 2016, 152–53).

The histories of conquest, violence, and exploitation associated with these particular colors and the imperial networks that enabled them resonate across time as well. In a 2012 *Radiolab* story titled "The Perfect Yellow," for instance, reporter Jad Abumrad recounts a much more recent case of gamboge's entanglement with war and Western imperialism: in the 1980s, a worker at the British paint manufacturer Winsor & Newton traced a supply of the pigment to the Khmer Rouge killing fields after discovering "dozens of bullets" in the batch he was preparing for sale. In a wry summation of his exchange with a rather rambling Winsor & Newton spokesperson, Abumrad concludes the story with the painful truth that "[c]olors are sometimes soaked in blood. That's just how it is" (quoted in Kelleher 2017; St. Clair 2016, 80). Similarly crafting a story around a color "soaked in blood," Stephen King's 1995 novel, *Rose Madder*, opens with the protagonist, Rose, sitting on the floor and bleeding from a miscarriage, while her "aggressively racist, homophobic, and violent" husband lurks "in the shadowy background" (Kelleher 2018). The image of Rose sitting on the floor, blood pooling around her, calls to mind Dhaliwal's description of sitting on the floor of the library, surrounded by colored fairy books, a mirroring that ties the imperial past to the postcolonial present with colorful—but bloody—bindings, bindings that pull nostalgia, love, and violence into a tight knot with racism, homophobia, and misogyny.

Dhaliwal captures the complex workings of nostalgia, love, and violence in beautiful and intimate fashion as she superimposes her story onto a haunting reincarnation of the Langs' Colored Fairy Books, allowing her early love of color—and what color represented: stories—to grow into the colors of empire, colors whose brutal histories she seeks to reclaim in her collected works. In so doing, Dhaliwal not only calls to the surface—to the books' very covers—the largely unspoken imperial ideologies framing the Langs' series but also identifies the series as "a resolution of sorts: a coming home to the place where all the narratives she has written began" (2009). Here, even more than in the twining of her story with the imperial histories of the colors she will later make her own, Dhaliwal illustrates the seemingly benign but severely cruel and lasting effects of a child's racialized exclusion (even if perhaps unrecognized at the time), such as that facilitated by the Langs in their "[making] up" and editing tales "in the hope that white people will like them" (*Brown Fairy Book*, 1904, viii). Dhaliwal's characterization of the piles of colored fairy books as the origin of "all the narratives she has written" is thus not so much a tribute as an unsettling reminder of harm, even/especially if that harm is perpetrated by an early love. As my friend and colleague Vilashini Cooppan—who, like Dhaliwal, was raised in the transnational Indian diaspora—said with poignant and inspired humor, "I read all twelve Lang collections over and over as a kid, burning the empire deep into my soul" (personal communication, May 22, 2022). Understood alongside such an articulation, Dhaliwal's oeuvre, "all the narratives she has written"—visual, textual, and filmic narratives whose many themes include the arrogance of British imperial cartography; the violent aftereffects of colonial partition; identity, migration, and belonging; exploitative extraction, collecting, and classification in the name of empire—is a welcome balm for the long-lasting burn of the Langs' fairy books.

Bringing down the House (That Race Built)

In "Venus in Two Acts," Saidiya Hartman suggests that stories like Dhaliwal's are much more than just a balm, proposing instead that they might, in fact, serve as "a form of compensation or even reparations" (2008, 4). Reflecting on the place of narrative invention in writing counterhistories of slavery, Hartman experiments with what she calls "critical fabulation," an attempt to animate the silences that constitute slavery's archive and its origination in violence (11). For Hartman, critical fabulation is thus simultaneously an act of imagination and of instantiation, an evocation of slavery's counterhistory together with "a history of the present [that] strives to illuminate the intimacy of our experience with the lives of the dead, to write our now as it is interrupted by the past" (4). While such critical fabulations in relation to the history of slavery may seem of an entirely different order than critical fabulations in relation to the European fairy tale, the two are held together by the racisms and racialized logics that enabled such atrocities as well as their literary legacies, and nowhere is this clearer than in Helen Oyeyemi's fairy-tale novels.[3]

With her extended fairy-tale reimaginings, Oyeyemi exploits European fairy-tale conventions in ways that simultaneously make strange the familiar and normalize the unexpected. In the process, typically inanimate objects become living, active, narrating agents, characters that far exceed the usual fairy-tale magic of enchanted objects, while ethnically and racially diverse human characters are entirely naturalized as part of Oyeyemi's fairy-tale landscapes. As a result, when the novels specifically call attention to race, it is to make visible the operative racisms of the stories—both the implicit racisms of the European tales and the diegetic racisms at play in Oyeyemi's narratives.

Given the ideological power of stories to affect material realities, it can be of little surprise that Oyeyemi's novels convey a certain urgency to contest, defy, and expand the European fairy-tale tradition, often compelled by an ancestral call to narrate, tell stories, testify, to heed what Hartman describes as "the imperative to respect black noise—the shrieks, the moans, the nonsense, and the opacity, which are always in excess of legibility and of the law and which hint at and embody aspirations that are wildly utopian" (2008, 12). In *Mr. Fox* (2011), for instance, the story of Brown and Blue ("Like This") features a woman, Brown, who finds herself in a new home with a room where she is clearly meant to write something, although she is at a loss as to what she is to write. Shortly after her arrival, a note appears under the door: "*Write the stories*" (96). She begins with "*Once upon a time*" but abandons that effort and begins making a list of things she has lost. Another note slides under the door: "*WRITE THE STORIES*" (96, emphasis in original). This pattern of seeming nonsense and opacity ensues for days until she encounters a strange man, made up as a harlequin, who introduces himself as Reynardine before quickly channeling a coterie of her ancestors: "'Can you see us?' And for a moment she saw and felt them all, crowding her. Faces she recognized from family photo albums, some she had never seen before, old ones leaning on walking sticks. They were all familiar" (103). In the ensuing conversation, they demand that she narrate from her Yoruba identity, regardless of the fact that she doesn't know the language and is living in Paris: "Tell the stories. Tell them to us. We want to know all the ways you're still like us, and all the ways you've changed. Talk to us. We're from a different place and time..." (104); when she claims she can't, they reply that she can and must, that the stories belong to them: "It doesn't matter what language they're in, or what they're about; they belong to us. And we gave them to you without looking at them first. So now it's time to see what we've done" (104).

While at first Brown can only conceive of stories that begin with "*Once upon a time*," can only equate story with the dominance of the European fairy tale, her Yoruba ancestors reorient her very definition of story by inserting themselves into the narrative legacy. In turn, Brown writes the stories, story upon story upon story. In exchange, Reynardine returns what she has lost, the lover she walked away from and immediately mourned, but the happy ending requires that she join him in death, albeit a death in which they have the consciousness to appreciate that they can spend an eternity waltzing in their stone house under Père Lachaise. For Oyeyemi, such ancestral stories are obviously entangled with the European fairy-tale tradition—the initial impulse to start with "*Once upon a time*," the slightly twisted happily ever after—but they also push against the boundaries of the genre, exemplified by the fact that Brown's stories include personal narratives, memories of stories she told herself as a child, inventions about imaginary cities (including one that "men were forbidden to enter," 107), tales set in specific locations such as the Okitipupa village.

The American writer Audre Lorde famously claimed that "the master's tools will never dismantle the master's house" (2007 [1984], 112), and Toni Morrison built on Lorde's influential proclamation in her opening address for the 1994 Race Matters conference at Princeton University: "If I had to live in a racial house, it was important, at the least, to rebuild it so that it was not a windowless prison into which I was forced, a thick-walled, impenetrable container from which no cry could be heard, but rather an open house, grounded, yet generous in its supply of windows and doors. Or, at the most, it became imperative for me to transform this house completely" (4). Morrison goes on to describe how her fiction has facilitated this commitment to a complete transformation of the "house that race built," the phrase that became the title of the published proceedings from that conference.

I refer to Lorde and Morrison in closing because their entwined evocation of house metaphors to conceptualize power and dominance—particularly racial dominance—seems like an apt inheritance for Oyeyemi, whose fairy-tale novels regularly feature fantastic and horrifying houses, houses that animate oppressive narrative structures while also suggesting possibilities for radical reconstruction and renewal. In her most recent novel, *Gingerbread*, for instance, Oyeyemi introduces a fanciful house on the move, a house that appears "as if it stands on chicken legs and keeps running away" (2019, 249), one that leads the real estate agent on "a merry dance" (250) and that "seems to have moods" (257). With its wonderfully charming history—built of magical materials by thousands of fireflies in a single night, reminiscent of a classic gingerbread house "straight out of a story," according to a German hiker who caught a glimpse of it (although a group of Japanese tourists argued that it was not made of gingerbread but "thinner, crisper stuff . . . *yatsuhashi*," 257)—this house continually escapes attempts to approach it, attempts to possess it. A sign posted out front reads, in the perhaps make-believe language of Druhástranian: "*Only those who have nothing can enter this place*" (257).

If Oyeyemi's enchanted houses endeavor to dismantle the master's house—the house that European ideas and ideologies of race built with the help of a set of fairy-tale power tools—*Gingerbread*'s delightfully escapist, trickster-like house begins to lay the foundation for a new narrative structure. In *White Is for Witching*, one of Oyeyemi's earlier fairy-tale novels, Miranda's heart is broken when her racist ancestral home, a sentient character in the book, violently disrupts her love for Ore, a Black girl Miranda meets while studying at Cambridge. With the house's destruction of Miranda and Ore's interracial romance, Oyeyemi seems to suggest that the power of the European fairy tale is yet too tight, that the desire for alternative stories—like the one of a girl's escape that Miranda requests of Ore—is still too reliant on the master's tools. In *Gingerbread*, by contrast, the enchanted house provides a site for the reunion of two friends—one worldly (Harriet), one otherworldly (Gretel)—separated for the greater part of their lives but unknowingly (for Harriet) connected through Gretel's caring watch, her desire for Harriet's joy, and her narration of their story as it unfolds: "Harriet Lee, you're right about the house being a last last last last chance for you and Gretel. That it is and that it will be, and a long time from now, when you have nothing left, we'll meet at the house and pass through it . . . Let's talk when we get to the house, that third unhaunted house" (2009, 258). This house can only be built of other tools. It is a celebration. A homecoming. An entirely different happy ending.

A Return to Wonder

As fairy-tale scholars have well established, decolonizing the field depends on historicizing the genre, and I hope that *Specters of the Marvelous* has followed the crucial work by writers, artists, and activists like those discussed here—as well as works by others like Karen King-Aribisala and other works by Oyeyemi, which I have discussed elsewhere (Lau 2016, 2019a)—in contributing to such an effort. At the same time, I want to underscore the fact that while such works offer remarkable and provocative examples of the historicizing necessary to begin the long, multidimensional process of decolonizing fairy-tale studies, they are just as critical to the adjacent project of provincializing "the fairy tale," unraveling the various ways the European literary fairy tale is entangled with empire, colonial histories, and racialized violence. Even more significant than the ways they further efforts to decolonize fairy-tale studies and facilitate the provincialization of the European fairy tale, however, is how they animate the racialized specters haunting the European fairy tale. In so doing, they remind us of the disturbingly dangerous and persistent fantasy of a world—*our* world ostensibly writ small in the white world of the fairy tale—structured by centuries of white supremacy.

But so, too, do they remind us of the wonder in our world, a wonder activated not only in stories but also in ways of living and being with and through stories, as the example of Hawaiians protesting the siting of the Thirty Meter Telescope atop Mauna Kea so beautifully demonstrates. In this sense, the spectral politics I read in these bold, creolized, defiant works return us to the wonder of our world, a wonder that can embolden us in the long battle against relentless legacies of racist hatred and violence, that can continue to inspire hope in a justice capable of sustaining us in rich and colorful ways.

NOTES

Introduction

1. For more on the relationship between the marvelous and the fairy tale, see Todorov (1975 [1973]), Jackson (1981), Röhrich (1991), Seifert (1996), Hoffmann (1997), and Tiffin (2009). Seifert (1996) and Hoffmann (1997) also draw out the particularly gendered dimensions of the relationship between the marvelous and the *contes de fées* of Old Regime France.
2. For a small representation of scholarly attempts to define the genre, see Propp (1968 [1928]), Lüthi (1982), Warner (1994), Zipes (2000), and Jones and Schacker (2013).
3. It is worth noting that queer sexuality is another significant absence in critical and popular understandings of the fairy tale and contributes to a heteronormative fairy-tale world in ways that resonate with the racial reckoning that inspires *Specters of the Marvelous*. There is, however, more work on the fairy tale's heteronormative underpinnings than on its racial underpinnings. See, for instance, Orme (2010), Turner and Greenhill (2012), Duggan (2013), and the articles in the special issue of *Marvels and Tales* devoted to "queering" the fairy tale (Seifert, 2015).
4. The critical literature and historical analyses of *The Arabian Nights* is extensive. For excellent historical overviews, see Haddawy (1990), Irwin (1994), Marzolph and van Leeuwen (2004), and Marzolph (2006). For the relationship of the *Nights* to the European fairy tale, see Marzolph (2014).
5. The exact number of "fairy tales" in Straparola's *Pleasant Nights* depends on interpretation and classification, but there is general agreement among fairy-tale scholars that there are at least a dozen stories that conform to accepted definitions of the European fairy tale.

6 Ruth B. Bottigheimer (2002) argues compellingly—and highly controversially—that Straparola invented the "rise tale," in which a poor young man or young woman marries into royalty, through magical assistance, and consequently gains great wealth. Her claim, based on the complete absence of rise tales in European literary publications prior to Straparola, has been exceedingly controversial because its corollary is that the rise tale, perhaps the most recognizable fairy-tale formula, did not exist in oral tradition prior to Straparola's versions. For a condensed overview of the controversy, see *Journal of American Folklore* 123 (490) (2010), special issue on "The European Fairy-Tale Tradition between Orality and Literacy" with articles by Ben-Amos (2010a, 2010b), Ziolkowski (2010), and Vaz da Silva (2010), as well as Bottigheimer's (2010a) response; see also Zipes (2010).

7 The nine tales Canepa (2007a) identifies as having strong affinities to Straparola's are "Peruonto" (1.3), "The Merchant" (1.7), "Cagliuso" (2.4), "The Two Brothers" (4.2), "The Two Little Pizzas" (4.7), "Pride Punished" (4.10), "The Goose" (5.1), "Sapia" (5.6), and "The Five Sons" (5.7).

8 In the preface to *The Olive Fairy Book* (1907) in his Colored Fairy Books series (Lang 1889–1910), for instance, Lang writes: "Perrault picked up the rustic tales which the nurse of his little boy used to tell, and he told them again in his own courtly, witty way. . . . Naturally Perrault had imitators, such as Madame d'Aulnoy, a wandering lady of more wit than reputation" (vi).

9 ATU numbers are based on the classificatory system first developed and published by Antti Aarne in 1910 as *Verzeichnis der Märchentypen* (*List of Fairy Tale Types*) and translated, revised, and expanded by Stith Thompson in 1928 and 1961. In 2004, Hans-Jörg Uther published an updated and expanded version as *The Types of International Folktales: A Classification and Bibliography*, which led to the revision of the AT numbering system to the ATU numbering system. ATU 425 has three variants worth noting here given that they appear in full or in terms of their significant motifs in Basile's *The Tale of Tales*: 425A (The Animal as Bridegroom), 425B (Son of the Witch), and 425C (Beauty and the Beast). See Lundell (1989 [1986]) for an excellent early critique of the biases implicit in the system; although Uther recognizes these—and other—biases in the revised 2004 edition, he has done little to correct them.

10 Hans Christian Andersen is sometimes included in European fairy-tale canons, and, as I have argued elsewhere, his literary fairy tales are certainly entangled with racial formation projects particular to the nineteenth-century Scandinavian context and to Danish colonialism (Lau 2019b). However, Andersen's explicit authorship meant that his tales lacked a connection to orality and, thus, to the supposed authenticity of "the folk," an increasingly significant quality in the definition of the genre after the publication of the Grimms' *Children's and Household Tales* in the first half of the nineteenth century.

11 Anne Duggan points out that "it needs to be clear that the character isn't 'inherently' Jewish but that Jewish writers have projected this Jewishness back onto the character, particularly after anti-Semitic uses of the character were made by the Nazis. Dwarfs abound in French tales, which influenced German tales, so we need to be careful about 'essentializing' the Jewishness of Rumpelstiltskin in particular or dwarfs in general. . . . We need to separate out Nazi uses of the tale, Jewish writers using the tale in new ways, and what the tale represented in its context" (editorial communication, November 16, 2023). Her point is an important one and adds nuance and broader cultural context to Schanoes's article.

12 I want to thank Anne Duggan for providing this information as well as her translation of the frame narrative.

13 See, for instance and in addition to those cited previously, Conrad (2016), Harris (2017), Joosen (2017), and Zöhrer (2021) for illustration and Richards (2010), Schacker (2018), and Schacker and O'Quinn (2021) for pantomime and stage production.

14 See also Aurora Wolfgang's 2020 critical edition and translation of Villeneuve's *La Jeune Américaine* and "Beauty and the Beast" for a consideration of Saint-Domingue's influence on the relationship between the frame tale and "Beauty and the Beast." Her critical edition was published after an earlier 2016 version of this chapter appeared as "Imperial Marvels: Race and the Colonial Imagination in the Fairy Tales of Madame d'Aulnoy," so I did not have the benefit of her extensive introduction, but our points are much the same.

Chapter 1

1 Although the reader eventually learns, in the collection's conclusion, that the slave is named Lucia, she is only ever referred to as "the slave" (or worse, a "cricket-legged slave girl" [Canepa 2007a, 39], "that mass of black flesh" [39], a "black [thing]" [39], "this bitch" [40], an "ugly slave" [41])—in the introductory section of the frame tale. In the preludes to several of the tales, she is sometimes referred to as "the princess" or by Tadeo as his "wife." It is also worth noting that as a Moor, Lucia is not the name she would have been given at birth; rather, she would have been renamed Lucia by those selling or purchasing her. See Steven Epstein's *Speaking of Slavery* for historical data regarding the (re)naming of slaves (2001, 26–28).
2 Despite the fact that the Kingdom of Italy was not established until March 17, 1871, when Victor Emmanuel II of Sardinia was proclaimed king of Italy, the different states of the Italian peninsula enjoyed a certain cultural cohesion ("History of the Kingdom of Italy" 2023).
3 See also Nettl (1944) for a lengthier description of the racialization of the dances, pantomimes, and music that fall under the label of the "Mauresque" or "Moresca."
4 Scala also highlights the contrast between Basile's Lucia and Dante's: "Indeed, for this particular function [to guide and rescue], Dante's Lucia is the complete opposite of Basile's slave; in fact, in *Lo cunto*, Lucia epitomizes injustice and deceit" (2014, 105). Based on this contrast, Scala reads Basile as parodying Dante (106).
5 In characterizing early modern Mediterranean slavery, Magnanini (2023) emphasizes two important organizing principles that distinguish it from Atlantic slavery: its reciprocity (the fact that different groups enslaved, traded, ransomed, and freed members of other groups) and its temporariness (the fact that slaves were not only ransomed but also frequently manumitted, either through charitable acts or the death of their owners).
6 As Llewelyn Morgan reminds critics, "*Elegi* is before all else a *metrical* denomination," and "[m]uch of the communicative power of elegiac meter . . . lies in the range of conventions that influenced its deployment." She goes on to provide a definition of elegiac meter: "The elegiac couplet or distich is an 'epodic' combination of two dactylic

lengths (a dactyl is ‾ ˘ ˘, a long syllable and two shorts), the 'dactylic hexameter' (or just 'hexameter'; in Latin most often [*uersus*] *herous*) followed by the 'dactylic pentameter' (or plain 'pentameter')" (2012, 205). Throughout this chapter, I am concerned with Roman love elegy's thematic content and not its meter, although I take Morgan's point that meter is fundamental to the genre's communicative power.

7 See Greene (1998; 2012, 370); James (2003a, 2003b); Ancona and Greene (2005); Boyd (2012); Gold (2012, 3); Keith (2012); and Skoie (2012) for examples of readings that question the *domina*'s agency and suggest, instead, that she is under the discursive authority of the male poet-lover.

8 In her discussion of this tale, Nancy Canepa notes that "cruel lady" is a "standard topos in the love lyric," but she stops short of reading it in relation to the *servitium amoris* tradition of Roman love elegy (1999, 136).

9 See Magnanini (2023) for a discussion of several artistic works by Basile's contemporaries that highlight the fluidity of racial markers—skin color, "somatic features," perceptions of beauty—assigned to the designation "Moor." As Magnanini notes, such fluidity is also consistent with the contemporary variability in terminology for skin color, ethnicity, and religion, as is evident in the fact that "'Moor' and 'Saracen' could describe North African or Middle Eastern Muslims, as well as Black Africans who might not be Muslim" (207). Such terminological variability, I would argue, underscores the specifically racialized nature of Basile's consistent suturing of blackness to slaves, Moors, and Saracens.

10 Thorsten Fögen points out that "already in antiquity, elegy was not exclusively conceived of as a lament" (2009, 181), and Sharon James emphasizes the critical debate regarding "[h]ow seriously readers are to take all this misery" (2003a, 99). Nonetheless, both understand weeping as fundamental to the genre.

11 In the notes to her translation, Canepa (2007a) writes that this patois is also found in tales 6, 9, and 10 of day 5, but I have not found evidence of it in 5.6, "Sapia." It also appears in "Penta with the Chopped-Off Hands" (3.2), when Penta requests that the slave Ali remove her hands: "My dear Ali, you cut my hands, me want make nice formula and get more white!" (225). In this case, Canepa cites Michel Rak's

footnote that Penta's request to Ali is "[a]nother example of 'Turkish' speech' (Rak 498)," but she does not connect it to Lucia's and Giorgia's specifically Neapolitan-Moorish patois. I contend that they are of a piece, however, especially given Ali's name and his slave status, a status Penta further highlights by speaking to him in "his" vernacular. Epstein's analysis of the names given to slaves indicates that in the early modern period the majority of slaves were Tartar, Russian, and Circassian (2001, 24–32).

12 Magnanini (2023) argues that the lack of critical attention to Lucia as a Black woman provides an opportunity for students to consider a number of important lessons about race in Renaissance Italy (and, I would argue, in relation to the literary fairy tale more specifically): "how dominant paradigms in our fields might discourage discussions of race; how identity was intersectional in the early modern period as it is today, with gender and race affecting whether a character achieves a happy ending; and how a pluri-vocal text with many narrators and tales might simultaneously possess an openness to the imagined difference of fantastic characters (ogres) and a racist attitude toward characters whose identity is grounded in historical reality (slaves)" (203–4).

13 I use "Berber" here instead of the contemporary "Amazigh" or "Imazighen" because it accords with the common terminology of Apuleius's time.

14 Canepa cross-references Basile's use of "King of Birds" here with a note from a reference in the opening frame tale. The sentence from the tale reads: "Out came a tiny little man, as big as a doll, the most delicious little plaything in the world, who got up on the windowsill and began to sing with so many trills, warbles, and embellishments that he sounded like Compar Biondo, he surpassed Pezzillo, and he left Cieco di Potenza and the King of Birds far behind" (2007a, 40). Her note cites Croce: "*compa'Iunno . . . Pezzillo* (Neap.): 'Two popular singers of humble origins who were famous in Naples at the time. They are also mentioned in tale 6 of day 4, and in other places in the works of Basile, Cortese, and Sgruttendio [other seventeenth-century Neapolitan authors] . . . The other two subsequently mentioned were probably similar figures' (Croce 540)" (40). Given the two contexts in which the "King of Birds" is invoked, I would argue against

cross-referencing them. It seems much more likely that the use of the moniker in "The Golden Trunk" refers to "The Son of the Ogress" variant of ATU 425B and not to a contemporary singer, as Croce suggests and Canepa implicitly reiterates.

15 This particular innovation also reiterates the themes of race, temporary slavery, and mistaken identity that Basile explores in *Del Teagene* (composed in Italian and published posthumously in 1637), his adaptation of Heliodorus's third-century *Aethiopica*, an early romance novel and "great influence on the development of the fairy tale" (Warner 1994, 364; Canepa 1999, 44) in which the queen of Ethiopia sends her white daughter away out of fear that her husband will believe her to have been unfaithful; the main plot centers on the daughter, her chaste lover, their many mistaken identities, and their suffering at the hands of pirates, robbers, priests, and various royalty whose machinations continually foil nearly all attempts to restore them to their proper place.

Canepa contends in a footnote that Heliodorus's *Aethiopica* "presents a suggestive parallel to the 'supplanted bride' motif of the frame tale of *Lo cunto*, in which the fair Zoza, destined bride of Prince Tadeo, is deceitfully substituted by the black slave Lucia, only to regain her rightful position at the close of the tale (and of *Lo cunto*)" (2007a, 270n45). Such a parallel seems a bit of a stretch, however, given that *Aethiopica*'s white heroine, Chariclera, is never supplanted by another woman; her tribulations result from her mother sending her away as an infant and the series of subsequent misfortunes that ensue as a result of piracy, male lust, and mistaken identities. Moreover, the implicit ideology of race is the inverse of that found in *Lo cunto* insofar as blackness, as reified in the king and queen of Aethiopia, is neither denigrated nor dehumanized but rather portrayed as consistent with descriptions of white royalty.

Chapter 2

1 As Christine Jones (2003) and others have argued, d'Aulnoy's title *Les Contes des fées* suggests that her *contes* may be the fairies' stories (i.e., stories *by* fairies) in contrast to the generic term *contes de fées*, which implies that they are stories *about* fairies. For Jones, d'Aulnoy's *Les*

Contes des fées encourages a reading of her tales as "an allegory of the art of writing stories" (67). See also Warner (1994, 234) and Seifert (1996, 197).

2   For detailed readings of d'Aulnoy as responding to Perrault, see Jones (2003, 61–70) and Duggan (2005, 202–16).

3   Here, I mark *race* with quotation marks to emphasize its anachronistic use in the context of the sixteenth and seventeenth centuries since the modern sense of *race* did not emerge until the middle of the eighteenth century. Despite its status as an anachronism, however, *race* is an indispensable term for the argument I am making because it signals in important and condensed ways the early logics of otherness and difference underpinning colonial expansion and the boundaries of the French empire. I will thus use *race* throughout this chapter, unmarked by quotation marks, to refer to these logics and their relation to emergent conceptualizations of race at the end of the seventeenth century and, of course, in the eighteenth century. See also Melzer's summary of Yves Citton's defense of the anachronistic in his *Livre, interpreter, actualiser* and particularly her point, based on Citton's work, that "contemporary categories of thought, if applied with careful attention to relevant historical specificity, can create a meaningful dialogue between past and present" (2012, 4).

4   For more on the debate over the veracity of d'Aulnoy's travel accounts, see Foulché-Delbosc (1926), Roche-Mazon (1927), Courteault (1936), and Adams (1962).

5   See Hannon (1998, 211–14) for a nuanced discussion of representations of luxury in the *contes de fées* of the first fairy tale vogue relative to Paul Hazard's (2013 [1935]) hypothesis that the austerity of the century's close gave rise to a compensatory turn to the marvelous in literature. In addition to reading luxury in the *contes* against Hazard's claims, she also complicates Robert's (1982) and Seifert's (1996) engagements with Hazard on this topic.

6   See, for instance, Dickason (1984), Stuurman (2000), Beasley (2010), and Jones (2013).

7   See Jean LaFaurie and Pierre Prieur, *Les Monnaies des rois de France*, vol. 2, plates XXXI and XXXII, for photographs of the coins.

8   Here, I am using the term *animal* to refer to nonhuman animals because it is less cumbersome than *nonhuman animal*, not because

I want to reinforce the distinction between human and nonhuman animals.
9   Twelve of d'Aulnoy's twenty-five *contes* involve animal-human metamorphosis. See Seifert (2011, 258n4) for a complete list.
10 See, for instance, Hubert (1973), Mitchell (1978), DeGaff (1984), and Warner (1995).
11 While Belmessous readily recognizes that her use of the term *assimilation* is anachronistic for the seventeenth-century French American context, she claims its appropriateness for holding together the French and British colonial projects of inclusion and incorporation that she addresses in her book; in keeping with her work, I also use the term *assimilation* in this context.
12 For detailed overviews of the debates concerning *vraisemblance* in seventeenth-century France and their theoretical implications, see Gérard Genette's "*Vraisemblance* and Motivation" (translated by David Gorman, 2001) and Janet Morgan's "The Meanings of Vraisemblance in French Classical Theory" (1986). For a discussion of *vraisemblance* in relation to fairy tales, especially d'Aulnoy's, see Seifert (1996, 26–36), Hannon (1998, 210–211), and Duggan (2005, 204, 239).
13 While "Prince Marcassin" is often translated as "Prince Wild Boar," I am following the convention of *The Fairy Tales of Madame d'Aulnoy*, translated by "Miss Annie Macdonell" and "Miss Lee" and introduced by Anne Thackeray Ritchie (2003 [1895 (1697 and 1698)]), which leaves *marcassin* untranslated throughout, regardless of whether it is being invoked as a proper noun, common noun, or adjective.
14 The protagonists of "Babiole" and "Prince Marcassin" also seem to be inspired by accounts from d'Aulnoy's ostensible travels in Spain, which suggests an enduring fascination with the "humanization" of monkeys and pigs in the context of a "real" exotic (at the time, Spain was seen to be exotic) as well as the marvelous and exotic world of her *contes*. Kathryn A. Hoffmann recounts an episode from *Relation du voyage d'Espagne* in which d'Aulnoy claims that her daughter was given a "Babiole-like creature" (75) by the archbishop of Burgos: "He sent for a little monkey, which he would needs give my daughter; and though I was troubled at it, I could not resist his instances and the desires of my daughter at accepting it. Every time the Archbishop took tobacco, which he often did, this little ape reached out his paw

to him and he put some on it, which he made as if he would take" (quoted in Hoffmann 2005, 75).

In her introduction to *The Fairy Tales of Madame d'Aulnoy*, Anne Thackeray Ritchie describes a scene from d'Aulnoy's *Mémoires de la cour d'Espagne* in which she is welcomed to Bayonne by ladies "carrying for the most part little sucking pigs, tied up with ribbons, under their arms, which little pigs are set down upon the floor to frolic during the rest of the visit" (2003 [1895], xiv).

15 Jean de La Fontaine, the famous fabulist, was also a central figure in Mme. de Sablière's salon. Like La Fontaine, Bernier, the primary advocate of Gassendi's philosophy, was active in contemporary debates about the nature of animals and animal-human boundaries, and it is difficult to imagine they were not regular interlocutors. In addition, as Seifert (2013, 248, 258) points out by way of Nadine Jasmin's (2002) *Naissance du conte feminine. Mots et merveilles: Les Contes de fées de Madame d'Aulnoy (1690–1698)*, d'Aulnoy was familiar with La Fontaine's animal fables as well as his lexemes and neologisms. These shared interests and influences strongly suggest that d'Aulnoy would have also been familiar with Bernier's writings and philosophies, even if she did not encounter him personally.

16 Annie Macdonell translates *les pagodes* as "pagodas" and "pagodinas," sometimes capitalized when referring to them as a race; this translation creates a particularly marvelous image of miniature anthropomorphized pagodas. However, Jones clarifies that in the late seventeenth and early eighteenth centuries, *pagodes* were actually "a popular Chinese figurine with comic features and a bobbing head" (2013, 185).

17 See Seifert (2002b, 208n52) for seventeenth-century figurative uses of *cochon* and *porc* for humans and the lack of such uses for *marcassin* or *sanglier*.

18 Anne L. Birberick (2011) also reads "Prince Marcassin" as a narrative of the civilizing process, but she compares it to "Babiole" to highlight the gendered differences in the way the two tales relate sexuality and power to that process.

19 "The Pigeon and the Dove" offers the clearest articulation of such a critique when the metamorphosed protagonists choose to remain in their avian forms to "live only for each other in delightful solitude"

(Ritchie 1895 [1697 and 1698], 441) rather than return to "the vanities of the world," which they disdained (442). See also "Fair Goldilocks," "The Blue Bird," "Prince Ariel," "Princess Carpillon," "The Hind in the Wood," "Belle-Belle," and "Belle-Etoile" for critiques of the flattery and empty vanities found at court as well as the use of court politics for duplicitous ends.

20 See also Warner (1995, 273–97) and Birberick (2011).

21 For some, like Bernier, the equation of natives and settlers was based on an assumption that natives live "like our remote ancestors" (quoted in Stuurman 2000, 10), thus anticipating nineteenth-century unilinear social evolutionary theory.

In terms of *mésalliance*, Duggan points out that while Perrault and many of the *conteuses* implicitly embraced such unions in their "rags-to-riches" tales and were frequently accused of promoting *mésalliance*, d'Aulnoy remained staunchly opposed to such relations (2005, 205–9). Such opposition further underscores the importance of colonial New France as part of the ideological context for "Prince Marcassin."

22 Anne Duggan notes that d'Aulnoy was generally opposed to "intermarriage between noble and non-noble. It might matter in d'Aulnoy that Babiole and Marcassin are only 'artificially' savage, and thus redeemable, due to a fairy's curse" (editorial communication, November 16, 2023).

23 See Spear (2003) for a discussion of some of these differences in the cases of native Americans and African slaves in New France and Louisiana.

24 Cooper (1985, 115–16) cites the following examples from the frame tale: "l'intempérie de l'air qu'on respire à l'Amérique" (the poor quality of the air one breathes in America [Villeneuve 2008 (1740), 79]); "L'Amérique est l'endroit du monde où l'on exerce le plus noblemen l'Hospitalité . . . rien n'est cher excepté le temps. On y vit suivant les commodities du pays avec une magnificence et une profusion qui font qu'un hôte et même quatre ne sont jamais à charge dans une Maison. Sans indiscretion, et sans crainte d'être incommodé, on y peut faire une visite de plusieurs années" (America is the place on earth where hospitality is practiced with great care . . . nothing was expensive except time. One lives with the amenities of a country of

such magnificence and abundance that a guest and even four are never expected to pay. Without indiscretion and without worry of being uncomfortable, one can make a trip of several years [80–81]); "lorsque les *Créols* font quelque chose qui force absolument leur inclination, ils tombent dane une maladie incurable qui se nomme communément *piller fantaisie*" (when the Creoles do something that propels their tendencies, they fall ill to an incurable illness, commonly known as *piller fantaisie* [86]); "L'Amérique est un fort beau pays, surtout l'isle de Saint-Domingue, et particulierement Léogane. Mais une maligne influence de temps en temps corrompt l'ai de ce riche climat. Il y règne une maladie, à laquelle les naturels du pays, et les étrangers sont subjet. C'est une espèce de dysenterie, qui dégoûte, affaiblit au dernier point, et qui deviant souvent mortelle" (America is a beautiful country, especially the island of Saint-Domingue, particularly the city of Leogane. However, a malignant influence appeared from time to time, corrupting the air of this rich climate. There reigns an illness that affects both the natives and the foreigners in the country. It is a type of disgusting dysentery, which weakens one to the end, and often becomes fatal [88]); "il n'avoit point besoin comme la plûpart des Amériquains d'en [des grâces] venir chercher en France" (he, unlike most Americans, did not lack those [manners] one comes to find in France [89]). Translations are mine, with the assistance of Alejandra Monteagudo.

25 "Qu'il s'imagine faire le voyage de Saint-Domingue" (Villeneuve 2008 [1740], 94).

26 "Dans l'inviation au voyage de la narratrice, le dépaysment exotique de la traversée se conjugue avec le dépaysment mental du merveilleux" (Villeneuve 2008 [1740], 94).

27 See also Aurora Wolfgang's 2020 critical edition and translation of Villeneuve's *La Jeune Américaine* and "Beauty and the Beast" for a consideration of Saint-Domingue's influence on the relationship between the frame tale and "Beauty and the Beast."

28 The extent to which colonial slavery shaped developing ideas about race is open for debate. Madeleine Dobie captures the underlying difficulties in determining the relationship between the two in her review essay of Andrew Curran's *The Anatomy of Blackness*: "At one point in the book, Curran states that slavery constituted the main

source of scientific evidence in discussions of skin color and related issues (p. ix). I think that this is both true and inaccurate. As I noted earlier, the scientific study of blackness took shape in a context structured by the racial order of the colonial plantation but, at the same time, inflected by the relative invisibility of this universe. The traces of this duality can be read in the perplexing silences and disjunctures of cultural history" (2012, 42).

29 Although the elephant was imported from both the East Indies and Africa, it was perhaps most strongly associated with Africa in the cultural imagination. Curran cites a stanza from a 1733 Jonathan Swift poem in which he "[mocks] cartographers who drew on their imaginations to fill in unexplored lands on their maps: 'Geographers, in *Afric* maps, / With savage pictures fill their gaps, / And o'er uninhabitable downs / Place elephants, for want of towns'" (2011, 7–8). In her book *Elephant Slaves and Pampered Parrots* (2002), Louise Robbins describes the ways that "animal slaves" were invoked in debates about colonial slavery in eighteenth-century France.

30 Some examples from the tale: Beauty's father asks himself, "How can I be so barbaric as to bring her back and undoubtedly see her devoured before my eyes?" (Wolfgang 2020, 98); "'The Beast must be quite famished to put on such a celebration for the arrival of his prey'" (102); Beauty's fear that "he would devour her once he was alone with her" (105), and "Since she had not yet been alone with him, and not knowing how this meeting would unfold, even fearing that he came to devour her, how could she not tremble?" (109). Of course, the terms *cannibal* and *Carib* are intimately intwined, the Caribs having been so named by early Spanish explorers who believed them to be anthropophagous. Peter Hulme further argues that cannibalism was figured racially throughout the colonial period: "The racial dimension of the discourse of cannibalism was never far from the surface during the colonial period: the tendency was to associate cannibalistic practice with darkness of skin, so the Caribs and Melanesians were more likely to be accused than the Arawaks or Polynesians—although, in a familiar colonial trope, suspicion of cannibal practice could land native groups in those supposedly descriptive categories and miraculously darken their skin" (1998, 30).

31 Until Wolfgang's 2020 translation, much of this sexual threat is diminished in the English translations of the tale that consistently render

the Beast's nightly question—"Elle [la Bête] lui [Belle] demanda sans detour si elle voulait la laisser coucher avec elle" (Villeneuve 2008 [1740], 124; "He then asked her directly if she would allow him to sleep with her" [Wolfgang, 2020, 109])—as "he asked her bluntly if she would marry him" (Zipes 1998, 172). For example, Jack Zipes, who himself critiques the bourgeois editing of *Kinder- und Hausmärchen* by the Grimms, bases his translation on J. R. Planché's 1858 translation. In his "A Note on the Translation" that accompanies his 1989 *Beauties, Beasts and Enchantment: Classic French Fairy Tales*, the standard scholarly source of Villeneuve's tale in English prior to Wolfgang's translation, Zipes writes that he decided to "retranslate the tales using Planché's versions as the basis for [his] work since, to his credit, his renditions contained a certain style and idiomatic characteristics that [he] felt helped recapture the highly mannered style of the French authors" (13). While this may certainly be true of Planché's translations, Zipes does not clarify why his own retranslation of Villeneuve's tale keeps so closely to Planché's, particularly in terms of sexuality. For instance, not only does Zipes continue to replace the Beast's more directly sexual question with a question of marriage, but he also omits—following Planché—the entire scene in which Beauty and the Beast sleep together for the first time.

On a related note, Planché's translations were also widely adapted for the stage in nineteenth-century England; such productions often brought to the surface the underlying racialized characterizations of the Beast, first as the Oriental other and later as the African. See Michelle J. Smith and Rebecca-Anne C. Do Rozario (2016) for an extensive discussion of these performances and their racial politics.

32 The following sections of the tale make clear that Beauty is actually the prince's cousin and higher in rank than the prince, as she is the daughter of a fairy and a king who was hidden with a merchant family shortly after her birth.

33 I am not suggesting here that the seventeenth-century expansion of the French empire into the Caribbean did not exert a cultural influence during its earliest phases; rather, I am arguing that the colonization of the North American territories condensed a number of dominant cultural and religious ideologies (e.g., human perfectibility,

civility, *francisation*) and contemporary cultural discourses and phenomena (e.g., early exploration and travel literature, a belief in the New World's natural riches, a belief in *les sauvages* as more similar to Europeans than not) that structured the seventeenth-century imperial imagination, particularly for a writer like d'Aulnoy who, as Seifert (1996) has established, expressed not only a utopian impulse but a particularly *nostalgic* one.

Doris Garraway, in her work on the politics of sexuality and creolization in Saint-Domingue, supports this point about France's shifting colonial priorities and their cultural effects: "When French attempts to settle the Brazilian littoral and other points along the Atlantic coast faltered, Canada emerged as the center of French colonial activity in the seventeenth century.... In the following century, however, Canada was overtaken in geopolitical importance by the Antilles, a fact that is reflected in the number of published works on the island colonies. Whereas in the seventeenth century the total number of books on the French Caribbean did not exceed several dozen, this number increased to over three hundred in the eighteenth century, thus signaling the new centrality of the Caribbean to the Old Regime colonial empire" (2005, 3–4).

34 The first thirty-six volumes were published during this time period; an additional eight volumes were compiled by Bernard Germaine de Lacépède and published between 1789 and 1804.

35 Kathryn R. Bastin (2014) situates her reading of "Babiole" in the context of French empire through the symbolic association of the monkey, its origins in the "colonized spaces of the era," and their ideological relation to "othered, non-white bodies" (83), but her analysis never moves to a more specific sociopolitical colonial context, most likely because her primary interest centers on standards of beauty in the tale, not in race per se. In addition, Anne Duggan suggests that "we can also attribute the popularity of this kind of tale to a society in which arranged marriage was the norm and women were often paired with much older men. D'Aulnoy was married at thirteen to a man some thirty years her senior, so this is a really important component that explains the prevalence of such a tale, particularly for women writers" (editorial communication, November 16, 2023).

Chapter 3

1 Buck-Morss calls attention to the widely acknowledged influence of the French Revolution on Hegel's thinking: "*The Phenomenology of Mind* does not mention Haiti or Saint-Domingue, but it does not mention the French Revolution either, at points where experts are in total agreement in reading the revolution into the text" (2009, 50). Sander Gilman makes a similar case for the importance of "the Black"—whether in Africa or transported into slavery—as fundamental to Hegel's concept of the slave (1982, 93–94).

2 Jost Hermand notes that German intellectual reactions to Napoleon's rise to power and the Confederation of the Rhine were divided: "Whereas many of the older liberals (Wieland, Goethe, Jean Paul, and Hegel, for example) saw in Napoleon a kind of world-historical agent for the advancement of highly progressive ideas, a figure who came not only as Germany's Oppressor but also as its Liberator, the more nationalist and democratic elements in Germany had no interest in such a dialectical perspective and were decidedly negative in their assessments of Napoleon" (1992, 13).

3 For a detailed and nuanced discussion of Herder's work as blending relativism and universalism, see Sonia Sikka (2005).

4 The degree to which the Grimms' antisemitism influences their collection remains an open question. Although there is widespread agreement that several tales in *Kinder- und Hausmärchen* reveal a clear antisemitic bias, the intentionality of that bias is less clear. Some suggest that the collection's antisemitism is more an effect of the culture of the period than a reflection of the brothers' personal beliefs. Others, like Martha Helfer, contend that "a conscious anti-Jewish agenda arguably informs the Grimms' *Kinder- und Hausmärchen* (*Children's and Household Tales*), to a small but significant degree" (2009, 32), a claim that resonates with Ruth B. Bottigheimer's analysis of the editorial history of the collection's explicitly antisemitic tales, which she suggests may derive from Wilhelm's friendship with members of the Christian-German Society, including Clemens Brentano (1987, 140–41). I discuss both Helfer's and Bottigheimer's work in more detail in this chapter.

While the Grimms' close friendship with Brentano, a virulent antisemitist, has been marshaled as evidence of their antisemitic leanings, this assumption is sometimes countered by the fact that the brothers were also good friends with Bettina von Arnim, a vocal critic of antisemitism. Rather than balance each other out, however, I would argue that the Grimms' intimate familiarity with von Arnim's condemnation of antisemitism lends credence to the position that their editorial decisions to represent Jews in the most offensive ways represent more than merely a reflection of the culture of the period.

    The Grimms were also central to the development of German comparative linguistics (*die vergleichende Sprachwissenschaft*)—particularly evident in Grimms' *Geschichte der deutschen Sprache* (History of the German language, 1848), *Deutsche Grammatik* (German grammar, 1819), *Deutsches Wörterbuch* (German dictionary, 1854), and Grimm's law (also known as the First Germanic sound shift)—and Loisa Nygaard notes that "the rise of modern racial categories and thinking in racial terms" are deeply imbricated with the history of the discipline, pointing out that "[l]ike 'Semite,' the loaded term 'Aryan' in its modern usage also came out of the study of comparative linguistics" (personal communication, March 6, 2022).

5 Jonathan M. Hess makes a similar point when he argues that "[f]rom the beginning . . . discussions over the 'civic improvement' of the Jews unfolded in close proximity to contemporary racial theory's concern with the category of 'regeneration'" (2006, 205).

6 The three tales with specifically identified Jewish characters are "The Good Bargain" (KHM 7), "The Jew in the Thornbush" (KHM 110), and "The Bright Sun Will Bring It to Light" (KHM 115).

7 Bottigheimer also observes that Wilhelm's notes "[omit] entirely discussion of the fact that in some versions with a monk instead of a Jew, the monk escapes punishment altogether with no question of his swinging in the servant's stead" (1987, 140). Additionally, she points out that in this nineteenth-century German example, "some versions of the tale in which the monk is a victim end far less violently and destructively, with the monk being taken home by the bailiff to talk it over rather than being hanged as a thief" (140).

8 See "Work, Money, and Anti-Semitism" in Bottigheimer (1987) for additional examples of revisions Wilhelm made to the descriptions of both the servant and the Jew.

9 Loisa Nygaard points out that the debates about antisemitism were also entwined with debates about the rights of women: "[O]ne of the early defenses of Jewish civil rights in Germany by Christian Wilhelm von Dohm was entitled *Über die bürgerliche Verbesserung der Juden* (1781), *On the Civil Improvement of Jews*. Later, another author, Theodor Gottlieb von Lippel, deliberately echoed this title when he urged certain civil rights for women in his *Über die bürgerliche Verbesserung der Frauen* (1792). So writers of the time certainly saw the parallels between the position of women and the position of Jews" (personal communication, March 6, 2022).

10 Susanne Zantop also calls attention to the significance of "German industry" in the writings of Herder and Meiners, who both invoke the idea in order to draw a moral distinction between Germans and other European colonizers—specifically the "'lazy' Spaniard and the 'greedy' Englishman" (1997, 94).

11 See Hess (2006), Bruns (2011), and Davis (2012, esp. 77–132) for additional discussions of Michaelis's sugar island proposal as a condensation of racialized antisemitism and colonial racism.

12 Herder is widely understood to be among the earliest cultural relativists, but his cultural relativism is, of course, also tempered by his contemporary moment, his investment in the idea of a nation's *Geist* (akin to what we might today consider an ethnic group), his explicit German nationalism, and his own racial prejudices. See Zantop (1997a, 75–76, 234–35) for a discussion of some of Herder's personal beliefs and prejudices about African Blacks; Marchand (2009, 26) for a discussion of how Herder's romantic celebration of the Qur'an also imposed on Arabs a "frozen primordiality" (Ian Almond, quoted in Marchand); and Kontje (2004, 64–77) for a nuanced discussion of Herder's understanding of national cultures in relation to Germanic nationalism and the "Aryan myth." See also Feuser (1978), Solbrig (1990), Sikka (2005), and Berlin (2000) for overviews of the complexities of Herder's cultural relativism in relation to his ideas about universal history and human difference.

13 The four tales are "The Three Black Princesses" (KHM 137), "The Prince Who Feared Nothing" (KHM 121), "The White Bride and the Black Bride" (KHM 135), and "Hans My Hedgehog" (KHM 108).

14 East India as the named setting for "The Three Black Princesses" is extraordinary not only among the four tales featuring Black human

characters but also within the collection as a whole. It is one of only five specifically named locations in *Kinder- und Hausmärchen* and the only one to exist outside of German-speaking Europe.

15 The lion as a common symbol of Jesus (see, e.g., Kosloski 2017; "Lion Depiction across Ancient & Modern Religions" 2020; Harris 2022; and Villanueva 2023) and Jesus's common figuration as *both* lamb and lion—or transitioning from lamb to lion (Harris 2022)—further contributes to the tale's specifically Christian underpinnings.

16 While it is quite likely that the Grimms were most familiar with the prevailing characterization of the maiden in Song of Solomon as "black but beautiful," the Hebrew *we-* is ambiguous: it can be understood adversatively (*but*) as well as in the conjunctive form (*and*) (Goldberg 2003, 79–80). As such, the maiden might just as well be interpreted as saying, "I am black and beautiful," as many biblical scholars have recently suggested in their exegeses and translations (Goldberg 2003, 80). The fact that the maiden's assertion has been overwhelmingly translated as "I am black but beautiful"—and almost exclusively so prior to our contemporary moment—and that the Grimms literalize her words in "The Prince Who Feared Nothing" reveals longstanding hermeneutic biases, undergirded by racialized thinking and racist ideologies, and their naturalization in cultural texts like *Kinder- und Hausmärchen*.

17 According to the myth of the curse of Ham, Ham entered Noah's tent and saw him naked and passed out from wine; Ham went and told his brothers, who covered Noah, but with their backs turned to him so as not to see their father's nakedness. When Noah learned of Ham's transgression, he cursed him to blackness and slavery, which God brought about. See David M. Goldberg (2003) for an excellent and detailed exegetical and intellectual history of the myth of the curse of Ham.

18 See chapter 1 for a full discussion of the racialized underpinnings of "The Three Citrons" and *Lo cunto* more generally.

19 See Tuska Benes (2006) for an analysis of the important role that German, as a "mother tongue," played in the articulation of nineteenth-century German nationalism, particularly in relation to German Orientalism and racial understandings of human difference as linked to categories of language and culture.

20 See chapter 2 for a full discussion of d'Aulnoy's "Prince Marcassin" in relation to French imperial racial formation projects.
21 For general discussions of gender bias and sexism in *Kinder- und Hausmärchen*, see, for example, Zipes (1979–80), Bottigheimer (1980, 1986, 1987), Tatar (1992, 2019 [1987]), Warner (1994), and Haase (2000).
22 There is an extensive body of work on the association among Jews, witches, and magic in European history; within that context, I find Owens's overview of the parallels between the fifteenth- and sixteenth-century German persecution of Jews and witches as two groups ruled by Saturn to be particularly relevant to the points I am making here because of her attention to cannibalism as a unique and dominant aspect of Saturnalia:

> The popular trope portraying the Jew as child-eater would have strong associations with the most prevalent charge lodged against the Jews in this period, that of ritual murder. Saturn was also constructed as governing women's bodily humors, especially those of aged, postmenopausal women in whom the venomous "vapors" of menstrual blood were no longer regularly purged. When infanticide, infant cannibalism, blood libel, and desecration of the host were added to the feminine repertoire of "menstrual" disorders associated with witches, accused women could expect no more mercy than could Jews accused of such heinous crimes. (2014, 57)

23 See Melissa Mullins (2017) for an overview and disarticulation of *ogress*, *fairy*, *sorceress*, and *witch* in versions of "Rapunzel" by Basile, Charlotte Rose de la Force, the Grimms, and numerous English translations of the Grimms, which generally translate the German *Zauberin* (sorceress) as "witch," carrying forward assumptions about witches that do not necessarily pertain to sorceresses. Mullins's rich historical lexical analysis is helpful in thinking about the multiple ways in which female characters threatened the heteronormative patriarchal family, even when they may have been more complex and nuanced than *witch* tends to convey.
24 While the eighteenth- and nineteenth-century racial taxonomies referenced in this chapter do not address class explicitly, the hierarchies that they elaborate share a logic and vocabulary with socioeconomic

hierarchies. In this way, they implicitly racialize class relations such that lower classes of all races were often seen as "racially" inferior to upper classes. At the same time, racial hierarchies were implicitly classed such that certain races were assumed to be "innately" suited to particular forms of labor. That is to say, race and class are deeply imbricated in the underlying logics of the racial taxonomies discussed here. Nonetheless, my reading of "Eve's Unequal Children" foregrounds race based on the fact that the Lord *classes* the children because of their physical characteristics (even if it was Eve's initial decision to conceal them).

25 Marr's racialized argument in opposition to granting rights to Jews in Bremen suggests that racial thinking also undergirds the "humorous" descriptions of the "monsters" the robber finds occupying the house in "The Bremen Town Musicians": In addition to the "gruesome witch" in the house and the "man with a knife" at the door, the robber reports that "[i]n the yard there's a black monster who beat me with a wooden club" (Zipes 2003, 98). The rarity of specific place names in *Kinder- und Hausmärchen* and the Grimms' known antisemitism as well as their sociopolitical affiliations with vocal antisemites lends further credence to such an interpretation.

26 Richard Trexler offers an extensive overview of shifting social and political uses of the story of the magi from the Roman era through the late twentieth century, including the Christian "[Europeanization] of a Near Eastern tale" (1997, 6), the range of cultural and religious backgrounds attributed to the magi, their associations with the Jewish prophets in several interpretations in different historical periods, and their presentation and representation in twentieth-century Christian folklore, commercial contexts, and (antisemitic) popular culture.

Chapter 4

1 Of the twenty-four tales in the second volume of *German Popular Stories*, four are from sources other than the Grimms' *Kinder- und Hausmärchen*. Martin Sutton, in his comprehensive study of nineteenth-century English versions of *KHM*, identifies the source of the four tales as Johann Gustav Büsching's 1812 *Volks-Sagen, Märchen*

und Legenden (two tales), Otmar's (Johann Carl Christoph Nachtigall) 1800 *Volks-Sagen*, and Ludwig Tieck's 1812–16 *Phantasus*.

2 Schacker provides further details regarding the sales of *Kinder- und Hausmärchen*: the Small Edition had "average yearly sales of 187"; moreover, "[n]ine additional printings of the Small Edition were published during the Grimms' lifetimes, but they never garnered profits comparable to the English treatment of the collection that had inspired them" (2003, 26).

3 Andrea Day (2018) includes all the Langs' "Christmas books"—published with Andrew as editor—in her designation "Fairy Books," but I follow virtually all other critics in including only the twelve Colored Fairy Books when I refer to "the series" and/or to the "Fairy Books."

4 Elsewhere in the series, Lang disclaims—in expressly gendered fashion—the common perception that he has authored the tales in the Colored Fairy Books. In the *Violet Fairy Book* (1901), for instance, he writes: "The Editor takes this opportunity to repeat what he has often said before, that he is not the author of the stories in the Fairy Books; that he did not invent them 'out of his own head.' He is accustomed to being asked, by ladies, 'Have you written anything else except the Fairy Books?' He is then obliged to explain that he has *not* written the Fairy Books, but, save these, has written almost everything else, except hymns, sermons, and dramatic works" (vii); a bit later, after summarizing his standard account of how tales have been passed and adapted over time, he adds, "This is the whole truth of the matter. I have said so before, and I say so again. But nothing will prevent children from thinking that I invented the stories, or some ladies from being of the same opinion" (viii). He reiterates his position in the next volume, the *Crimson Fairy Book* (1903), in similarly gendered but increasingly grumpy terms: "A sense of literary honesty compels the Editor to keep repeating that he *is* the Editor, and not the author of the Fairy Tales, just as a distinguished man of science is only the Editor, and not the Author of *Nature*. . . . These explanations have frequently been offered already; but, as far as ladies and children are concerned, to no purpose. They still ask the Editor how he can invent so many stories—more than Shakespeare, Dumas, and Charles Dickens could have invented in a century" (v). And, prior to proclaiming the series "almost wholly the work of Mrs. Lang" in the *Lilac Fairy*

Book (1910), Lang begins with a little diatribe about women's ostensible interest in his work:

> "What cases are you engaged in at present?" "Are you stopping many teeth just now?" "What people have you converted lately?" Do ladies put these questions to the men—lawyers, dentists, clergymen, and so forth—who happen to sit next them at dinner parties?
>
> I do not know whether ladies thus indicate their interest in the occupations of their casual neighbours at the hospitable board. But if they do not know me, or do not know me well, they generally ask, "Are you writing anything now?" (as if they should ask a painter "Are you painting anything now?" or a lawyer "Have you any cases at present?"). Sometimes they are more definite and inquire, "What are you writing now?" as if I must be writing something—which, indeed, is the case, though I dislike being reminded of it. It is an awkward question, because the fair being does not care a bawbee what I am writing; nor would she be much enlightened if I replied "Madam, I am engaged on a treatise intended to prove that Normal is prior to Conceptional Totemism"—though that answer would be as true in fact as obscure in significance. The best plan seems to be to answer that I have entirely abandoned mere literature, and am contemplating a book on "The Causes of Early Blight in the Potato," a melancholy circumstance which threatens to deprive us of our chief esculent root. The inquirer would never be undeceived. One nymph who, like the rest, could not keep off the horrid topic of my occupation, said "You never write anything but fairy tale books, do you?" (v–vi).

I cite these lengthy, rather cantankerous excerpts to underscore the pervasive sexism lurking in the gendered division of labor that accounts for the production of the Colored Fairy Books.

5 This is not to suggest that Lang saw social evolutionary theory as a rigid hierarchy in which purportedly "primitive" groups represented entirely distinct cultures with no relation to contemporary Western cultures. Indeed, as Teverson, Warwick, and Wilson note, Lang "departed rather quickly from Edward Tylor's progressivist narrative as proposed in *Primitive Culture* (1871) and consistently suggests both

a continuity of so-called 'primitive thought' and the equal validity of primitive beliefs and practices as ways of representing and interacting with the world" (2015 2:34). It is this sense of continuity that shapes Lang's introductions in profound ways.

6. Lang indirectly recognizes the class dimensions of the Colored Fairy Books' readers in the preface to the Green Fairy Book, where he recommends that "when you have read a fairy book, lend it to other children who have none" (*Green Fairy Book*, 1892, xi). Additionally, in several prefaces he acknowledges the adult values that underlie their choice of children's gift books (e.g., *Olive Fairy Book*, 1907; *Lilac Fairy Book*) and offers unsolicited advice for the adults who shape children's libraries, a class marker in itself ("parents should be urged to purchase it [Thackery's *The Rose and the Ring*] at the first opportunity, as without it no education is complete" [*Yellow Fairy Book*, 1894, xi]).

7. Duncan Bell questions the critical usefulness of the distinction between "home" and "abroad," especially for colonial unionists, because Greater Britain was perceived as "a single political unit, spanning the planet" (2007, 34). While some supporters of social evolutionary theory may have also been colonial unionists, I refer to "home" and "abroad" in this context to underscore the overlapping ideologies that shaped attitudes, discourses, and policies about a range of "others"—colonized peoples, classed and raced others (Irish, Jews, gays and lesbians, peasants, urban poor), women—throughout the British empire and the British Isles.

8. Gillian Lathey provides an extensive history of translation and gender in the shaping of children's literature, including a section on the team of female translators who contributed to the Colored Fairy Books (2010, 102–10).

9. As Ella Christie and Alice Stewart make clear in their collaborative memoir, Nora's proficiency with languages was only one aspect of her influence on the Colored Fairy Books and their success: "To Mrs. Lang we practically owe the larger number of Andrew's collections of Fairy Tales, as her sound and clear judgment could be relied upon and was unerring in what was fitting in the matter of selection, while her linguistic abilities opened a wider field" (quoted in Day 2018, 99).

10. Eleanor De Selms Langstaff offers a specific example of Nora's pedagogical interests with respect to the Colored Fairy Books and other

books in the Langs' "Christmas book" lineup: "Mrs. Lang's role in the production of the Fairy Book and other children's books was extensive. One of her concerns was to control the vocabulary and sentence structure so that a child of average ability might read the stories" (1978, 144).

11 Although the British Parliament passed An Act for the Abolition of the Slave Trade in 1807 (also known as the Slave Trade Act 1807), which prohibited the slave trade in the British empire and called on Britain to encourage other nations to abolish their slave trades, it didn't abolish all slavery in the British empire. It wasn't until the Slavery Abolition Act of 1833 that slavery was gradually abolished throughout the empire, the last occurring in 1843 when the East India Company's original exemption was, essentially, rejected by the Indian Slavery Act, 1843.

12 Wakefield's *A Family Tour through the British Empire* was so popular that it went through fifteen editions between its original publication in 1804 and its fifteenth edition in 1840.

13 Note, too, the quotidian manner in which she refers to the genocide of the native population after Columbus's arrival in Haiti.

14 The etymology of *bunyip* derives from the Wemba-Wemba or Wergaia language (Hughes 1989, 90).

15 Sands-O'Connor's primary argument involves the ways that Lang and Rudyard Kipling engage anthropological theories and discourses to establish an equivalency between white British children and "savages."

16 See, for example, Sands-O'Connor (2009), who provides a lengthy discussion of the Langs' version of "The Sacred Milk of Koumongoé," in which the southern African "Kaffir" tale of broken taboos—not only, but especially, sexual taboos—is revised in such a way that much of the concluding action "no longer makes sense" (181). By substituting "European or 'civilized' marital customs" for the tale's references to concubinage, bride prices, rituals of sexual maturation, and gendered cannibalism (sacrificing girl children), the Langs "[remove] a great deal of the story's sexual significance," thus perpetuating what Stephen Humphries identifies as "middle-class theories of adolescence, which prescribed a prolonged, regulated and institutionalized dependency on adults as essential to normal and healthy sexual development" that would stave off "an orgy of depravity, idles

and crime" (Sands-O'Connor 2009, 182; Humphries quoted in Sands-O'Connor, 182).

17 I attribute the Langs' source text to Hill-Tout—and not the unnamed Siciatl storytellers from whom he collected the tales—because I am drawing (as I believe the Langs were) on Hill-Tout's narrativized version and not the word-for-word transcribed/translated version that precedes each of the tales in his collection.

18 Kees van Dijk reproduces an account of children at a missionary school in colonial Rhodesia who were forced to sing the lines, "We are dirty, We are dirty. We do not know how to wash ourselves. We have not acquired education," as they were shepherded to a stream on the first day of school. He notes that the children were not dirty but rather that they were perceived to be so because they did not use soap, perhaps "[smearing] their bodies with a mixture of soil and oil or fat to repel the dirt," a practice not so different from the sixteenth-century English practice of cleaning clothes "by smearing them 'with mud or scouring them with dung' (Cunnington and Cunnington 1992: 47)" (Van Dijk 2004, 1).

19 In discussing the loss of Tlingit cultural elements in Nora's translation of the story "Blackskin" for *The Strange Story Book* (1913), the last of the Langs' "Christmas books," Day indirectly provides another example of the Langs' preoccupation with dirt and cleanliness in relation to colonial others: "[T]he protagonist and other characters 'bathe for strength'—that is, swim to become stronger—in the Tlingit versions, whereas Nora's Blackskin is believed to be dirty because the others never saw him bathe, 'but in reality he was cleaner than any of them'" (2018, 161).

20 Here I want to acknowledge that Nora likely shared many of these same anxieties about the decline of the British empire. In addition to the earlier section providing context for Nora's contributions to the Colored Fairy Books, Day notes that "Nora should not be absolved from responsibility for the series' colonial appropriations" (2018, 134) and that while "Andrew's prefaces are more explicitly racist than Nora's translations and adaptations . . . she is nonetheless complicit in the series' colonial project; that she is also responsible for *The Strange Story Book*'s imperialist paratexts illuminates both the extent of this complicity and the metaleptic relations between the Fairy Books' framing and their contents" (2018, 158).

21 In a fascinating aside, Megan Norcia notes that Jill Shefrin has identified Madame Le Prince de Beaumont—author of the most well-known literary version of "Beauty and the Beast"—as the "creator of the dissected map" (2009, 5). Given the French imperial framing and ideological underpinnings of Mme. Villeneuve's "La Belle et la Bête" (1740), Beaumont's likely source text, as well as the tacit racist/imperial dimensions of Beaumont's tale and its afterlives in racialized/racist adaptations, performances, and illustrations, the fact that she may have created the first puzzle map has compelling resonances.

Conclusion

1 For a more detailed account of how the Grimms' *Kinder- und Hausmärchen*, together with the various iterations of the tale type index, facilitated an assumption of the European fairy tale as a universal genre, see my previous work on power and the archaeology of the genre (Lau 2021). See Donald Haase (2003) for more on the central role *Kinder- und Hausmärchen* and its translations played in the universalizing process and Cristina Bacchilega (2019) for a nuanced consideration of how postcolonial, settler, and Native are differently positioned in relation to both historical and contemporary approaches to the narrative traditions that have been appropriated, exploited, decontextualized, and in some cases reimagined in and through the fairy-tale canon. For additional history and critiques of the ATU tale type indexes, see Georges (1983), Lundell (1989 [1986]), and Uther (2004, 2008).
2 See Bacchilega (2008) for an analysis of "Precious" in relation to the "woman-centered" web of feminist fairy tales thematizing feminine empowerment through language and orality.
3 Here, I refer to Oyeyemi's *White Is for Witching* (2009), *Mr. Fox* (2011), *Boy, Snow, Bird* (2014), and *Gingerbread* (2019).

REFERENCES

Aarne, Antti. 1910. *Verzeichnis der Märchentypen*. Folklore Fellows Communications 3. Helsinki: Suomalaisen Tiedeakatemian Toimituksia.

Abumrad, Jad. 2012. "The Perfect Yellow." *Radiolab*, May 21, 2012. Podcast. https://radiolab.org/podcast/211193-perfect-yellow.

Adams, Percy G. 1962. *Travelers and Travel Liars, 1660–1800*. Berkeley: University of California Press.

Anacona, Ronnie, and Ellen Greene, eds. 2005. *Gendered Dynamics in Latin Love Poetry*. Baltimore: Johns Hopkins University Press.

Babalola, Bolu. 2020. *Love in Color: Mythical Tales from Around the World, Retold*. New York: William Morrow.

Bacchilega, Cristina. 2008. "Extrapolating from Nalo Hopkinson's *Skin Folk*: Reflections on Transformation and Recent English-Language Fairy-Tale Fiction by Women." In *Contemporary Fiction and the Fairy Tale*, edited by Stephen Benson, 178–203. Detroit: Wayne State University Press.

———. 2013. *Fairy Tales Transformed? Twenty-First-Century Adaptations and the Politics of Wonder*. Detroit: Wayne State University Press.

———. 2019. "'Decolonizing' the Canon: Critical Challenges to Eurocentrism." In *The Fairy Tale World*, edited by Andrew Teverson, 33–44. London: Routledge.

Bacchilega, Cristina, and Anne Duggan. 2016. "From the Editors." *Marvels and Tales* 30 (1): 12–13.

Ball, Philip. 2009 [2001]. *Bright Earth: The Invention of Colour*. New York: Vintage.

Barchilon, Jacques. 2009. "Adaptations of Folktales and Motifs in Madame d'Aulnoy's *Contes*: A Brief Survey of Influence and Diffusion." *Marvels and Tales* 23 (2): 353–64.

Bastin, Kathryn R. 2014. "Le Singe est-il toujours singe? Speculating on Ugliness, Refinement, and Beauty in Marie-Catherine d'Aulnoy's 'Babiole.'" *Cahiers du dix-septième* 15 (2): 82–102.

Beasley, Faith E. 2010. "Versailles Meets the Taj Mahal." In *French Global: A New Approach to Literary History*, edited by Christie McDonald and Susan Rubin Suleiman, 207–22. New York: Columbia University Press.

Beaumont, Jeanne-Marie Leprince de. 1783 [1756]. *The Young Misses Magazine, Containing Dialogues between a Governess and Several Young Ladies of Quality Her Scholars*, 4th ed. London: C. Nourse.

Bell, Duncan. 2007. *The Idea of Greater Britain: Empire and the Future of World Order, 1860–1900*. Princeton: Princeton University Press.

Bellhouse, Mary L. 2006. "Candide Shoots the Monkey Lovers: Representing Black Men in Eighteenth-Century French Visual Culture." *Political Theory* 34 (6): 741–784.

Belmessous, Saliha. 2013. *Assimilation and Empire: Uniformity in French and British Colonies, 1541–1954*. Oxford: Oxford University Press.

Ben-Amos, Dan. 2010a. "Introduction: The European Fairy-Tale Tradition between Orality and Literacy." Special issue, "The European Fairy-Tale Tradition between Orality and Literacy." *Journal of American Folklore* 123 (490): 373–76.

———. 2010b. "Straparola: The Revolution that Was Not." Special issue, "The European Fairy-Tale Tradition between Orality and Literacy." *Journal of American Folklore* 123 (490): 426–46.

Benes, Tuska. 2006. "From Indo-Germans to Aryans: Philology and the Racialization of Salvationist National Rhetoric, 1806–1830." In *The German Invention of Race*, edited by Sara Eigen and Mark Larrimore, 167–81. New York: State University of New York Press.

Berlin, Isaac. 2000. *Three Critics of the Enlightenment: Vico, Hamann, Herder*. Princeton: Princeton University Press.

Berman, Nina. 2011. *German Literature on the Middle East: Discourses and Practices, 1000–1989*. Ann Arbor: University of Michigan Press.

Biancardi, Élisa, ed. 2008. *Bibliothèque des génies et des fées* 15. Paris: Honoré Champion Éditeur.

Bindman, David. 2002. *Ape to Apollo: Aesthetics and the Idea of Race in the Eighteenth Century*. London: Reaktion Books.

Birberick, Anne L. 2011. "Gendering Metamorphosis in d'Aulnoy's 'Babiole.'" *Seventeenth-Century French Studies* 33 (2): 93–102.

Bodmer, George. 2003. "Arthur Hughes, Walter Crane, and Maurice Sendak: The Picture as Literary Fairy Tale." *Marvels and Tales* 17 (1): 120–137.

Bolt, Christine. 1971. *Victorian Attitudes to Race*. Toronto: Routledge and Kegan Paul.
Bottigheimer, Ruth B. 1980. "The Transformed Queen: A Search for the Origins of Negative Female Archetypes in Grimms' Fairy Tales." *Amsterdamer Beiträge zur neuren Germanistik* 10: 1–12.
———. 1986. "Silenced Women in the Grimms' Tales: The 'Fit' between Fairy Tales and Society in Their Historical Context." In *Fairy Tales and Society: Illusion, Allusion, and Paradigm*, edited by Ruth B. Bottigheimer, 115–31. Philadelphia: University of Pennsylvania Press.
———. 1987. *Grimms' Bad Girls and Bold Boys: The Moral and Social Vision of the Tales*. New Haven: Yale University Press.
———. 2002. *Fairy Godfather: Straparola, Venice, and the Fairy Tale Tradition*. Philadelphia: University of Pennsylvania Press.
———. 2010a. "*Fairy Godfather*, Fairy-Tale History, and Fairy-Tale Scholarship: A Response to Dan Ben-Amos, Jan Ziolkowski, and Francisco Vaz da Silva." Special issue, "The European Fairy-Tale Tradition between Orality and Literacy." *Journal of American Folklore* 123 (490): 447–96.
———. 2010b. "Fairy Tale Illustrations and Real World Gender: Function, Conceptualization, and Publication." *Relief* 4 (2): 142–57.
Boulle, Pierre H. 2003. "François Bernier and the Origins of the Modern Concept of Race." In *The Color of Liberty: Histories of Race in France*, edited by Sue Peabody and Tyler Stovall, 11–27. Durham: Duke University Press.
Bowditch, P. Lowell. 2012. "Roman Love Elegy and the Eros of Empire." In *A Companion to Roman Love Elegy*, edited by Barbara K. Gold, 119–33. West Sussex: Wiley-Blackwell.
Boyd, Barbara Weiden. 2012. "Teaching Ovid's Love Elegy." In *A Companion to Roman Love Elegy*, edited by Barbara K. Gold, 526–40. West Sussex: Wiley-Blackwell.
Brauner, Sigrid. 1994. "Cannibals, Witches, and Shrews in the 'Civilizing Process.'" In *"Neue Welt" / "Dritte Welt": Interkulturelle Beziehungen Deutschlands zu Lateinamerika und der Karibik*, edited by Sigrid Bauschinger and Susan L. Cocalis, 1–28. Tübingen: Francke Verlag.
Bristow, Joseph. 2016 [1991]. *Empire Boys: Adventures in a Man's World*. New York: Routledge.
Bruns, Claudia. 2011. "Toward a Transnational History of Racism: Wilhelm Marr and the Interrelationships between Colonial Racism and German Anti-Semitism." In *Racism in the Modern World: Historical Perspectives*

on *Cultural Transfer and Adaptation*, edited by Manfred Berg and Simon Wendt, 122–39. New York: Berghahn Books.

Buck-Morss, Susan. 2009. *Hegel, Haiti, and Universal History*. Pittsburgh: University of Pittsburgh Press.

Callaway, Ewen. 2022. "Invasive Plant Species Carry Legacy of Colonialism." *Nature*, October 18, 2022. https://www.nature.com/articles/d41586-022-03306-2.

Canepa, Nancy L. 1999. *From Court to Forest: Giambattista Basile's "Lo cunto de li cunti" and the Birth of the Literary Fairy Tale*. Detroit: Wayne State University Press.

———, trans. 2007a. *Giambattista Basile's "The Tale of Tales, or Entertainment for Little Ones."* Detroit: Wayne State University Press.

———. 2007b. "Introduction." In *Giambattista Basile's "The Tale of Tales, or Entertainment for Little Ones,"* translated by Nancy Canepa, 1–31. Detroit: Wayne State University Press.

Canepa, Nancy L., and Antonella Ansani. 1997. "Introduction." In *Out of the Woods: The Origins of the Literary Fairy Tale in Italy and France*, edited by Nancy Canepa, 9–33. Detroit: Wayne State University Press.

Castle, Kathryn. 1996. *Britannia's Children: Reading Colonialism through Children's Books and Magazines*. Manchester: Manchester University Press.

Clark Hillard, Molly. 2013. "Trysting Genres: Andrew Lang's Fairy Tale Methodologies." In "The Andrew Lang Effect: Network, Discipline, Method," edited by Nathan Hensley. Special issue, *Romanticism and Victorianism on the Net* 64 (October). https://doi.org/10.7202/1025670ar.

———. 2014. *Spellbound: The Fairy Tale and the Victorians*. Columbus: Ohio State University Press.

Cohen, William A. 2004. "Introduction: Locating Filth." In *Filth: Dirt, Disgust, and Modern Life*, edited by William A. Cohen and Ryan Johnson, vii–xxxvii. Minneapolis: University of Minnesota Press.

Colley, Linda. 2009 [1992]. *Britons: Forging the Nation, 1707–1837*. New Haven: Yale University Press.

"Colonial Brazil." 2024. Wikipedia, last modified February 8, 2024. https://en.wikipedia.org/wiki/Colonial_Brazil.

Conrad, JoAnn. 2016. "Fantasy Imaginaries and Landscapes of Desire: Gustaf Tenggren's Forgotten Decades." *Journal of Children's Literature Research* 39: 1–27.

———. 2018. "Into the 'Land of Snow and Ice': Racial Fantasies in the Fairy-Tale Landscapes of the North." *Narrative Culture* 5 (2): 255–90.

Conte, Gian Biagio. 1994. *Genres and Readers: Lucretius, Love Elegy, Pliny's Encyclopedia*. Translated by G. W. Most. Baltimore: Johns Hopkins University Press.

Cooper, Barbara. 1985. *Madame de Villeneuve: The Author of "La Belle et la Bête" and Her Literary Legacy*. PhD diss. University of Georgia.

Copley, Frank Olin. 1947. "Servitium amoris in the Roman Elegists." *Transactions and Proceedings of the American Philological Association* 78: 285–300.

Cornum, Lou. 2021. *Skin Worlds: Black and Indigenous Science Fiction Theorizing since the 1970s*. PhD diss. The Graduate Center, City University of New York.

Courteault, Paul. 1936. "Le Voyage de Mme. d'Aulnoy en Espagne." *Bulletin Hispanique* 38 (3): 383–84.

Curran, Andrew S. 2011. *The Anatomy of Blackness: Science and Slavery in an Age of Enlightenment*. Baltimore: Johns Hopkins University Press.

d'Aulnoy, Marie-Catherine. 2003 [1895 (1697 and 1698)]. *The Fairy Tales of Madame d'Aulnoy*. Trans. Miss Annie Macdonell and Miss Lee. Introduction by Anne Thackeray Ritchie. Honolulu: University Press of the Pacific.

Davin, Anna. 1978. "Imperialism and Motherhood." *History Workshop* 5 (Spring): 9–65.

Davis, Christian S. 2000. *Colonialism, Antisemitism, and Germans of Jewish Descent in Imperial Germany*. Ann Arbor: University of Michigan Press.

Davis, Jim, ed. 2012. *Victorian Pantomime: A Collection of Critical Essays*. London: Palgrave Macmillan.

Day, Andrea Lynne. 2018. *Citation, Collaboration, and Appropriation in the Works of Andrew and Nora Lang*. PhD diss. University of Toronto.

———. 2019. "'Almost Wholly the Work of Mrs. Lang': Nora Lang, Literary Labour, and the Fairy Books." *Women's Writing* 26 (4): 400–20.

DeGraff, Amy V. 1984. *The Tower and the Well: A Psychological Interpretation of the Fairy Tales of Madame d'Aulnoy*. Birmingham: Summa.

De Selms Langstaff, Eleanor. 1978. *Andrew Lang*. Boston: Twane.

Dhaliwal, Sarindar. 2009. *the green fairy storybook*. Sculpture. Collection of the Robert McLaughlin Gallery. https://rmg.on.ca/tag/liminal/.

Diaconoff, Suellen. 2005. *Through the Reading Glass: Women, Books, and Sex in the French Enlightenment*. Albany: State University of New York Press.

Dickason, Olive Patricia. 1984. *The Myth of the Savage: And the Beginnings of French Colonialism in the Americas.* Edmonton: University of Alberta Press.

Dillon, Grace, ed. 2012. *Walking the Clouds: An Anthology of Indigenous Science Fiction.* Tucson: University of Arizona Press.

Dobie, Madeleine. 2001. *Foreign Bodies: Gender, Language, and Culture in French Orientalism.* Stanford: Stanford University Press.

———. 2012. "Andrew S. Curran, *The Anatomy of Blackness: Science and Slavery in an Age of Enlightenment*: Review Essay." *H-France Forum* 7 (4): 38–43.

Duggan, Anne E. 1998. "Feminine Genealogy, Matriarchy, and Utopia in the Fairy Tale of Marie-Catherine d'Aulnoy." *Neophilologus* 82: 199–208.

———. 2005. *Salonnières, Furies, and Fairies: The Politics of Gender and Cultural Change in Absolutist France.* Newark: University of Delaware Press.

———. 2013. *Queer Enchantments: Gender, Sexuality, and Class in the Fairy-Tale Cinema of Jacques Demy.* Detroit: Wayne State University Press.

———. 2016. "The Frame Narrative of 'Beauty and the Beast.'" In *Folktales and Fairy Tales: Traditions and Texts from Around the World*, edited by Anne E. Duggan, Donald Haase, and Helen J. Callow, 1183–84. New York: Bloomsbury.

Dunae, Patrick A. 1989. "New Grub Street for Boys." In *Imperialism and Juvenile Literature*, edited by Jeffrey Richards, 12–33. Manchester: Manchester University Press.

Dunlop, W., and T. V. Holmes. 1899. "Australian Folklore Stories." *Journal of the Anthropological Institute of Great Britain and Ireland* 28 (1–2): 22–34.

Ellis, John M. 1983. *One Fairy Story Too Many: The Brothers Grimm and Their Tales.* Chicago: University of Chicago Press.

Epstein, Steven A. 2001. *Speaking of Slavery: Color, Ethnicity, and Human Bondage in Italy.* Ithaca: Cornell University Press.

Farrell, Joseph. 2012. "Calling out the Greeks: Dynamics of the Elegiac Canon." In *A Companion to Roman Love Elegy*, edited by Barbara K. Gold, 11–24. West Sussex: Wiley-Blackwell.

Felsenstein, Frank. 1990. "Jews and Devils: Antisemitic Stereotypes of Late Medieval and Renaissance England." *Literature and Theology* 4 (1): 15–28.

Feuser, Willfried F. 1978. "The Image of the Black in the Writings of Johann Gottfried Herder." *Journal of European Studies* 8: 109–28.

Fögen, Thorsten. 2009. "Tears in Propertius, Ovid and Greek Episolographers." In *Tears in the Graeco-Roman World*, edited by Thorsten Fögen, 179–208. Berlin: Walter de Gruyter.

Foulché-Delbosc, Raymond. 1926. "Madame d'Aulnoy et l'Espagne." *Revue Hispanique* 67 (151): 1–152.

"French Coinage for Canada and Louisiana." n.d. Coin and Currency Collections in the Department of Special Collections, University of Notre Dame Libraries. http://www.coins.nd.edu/ColCoin/ColCoinText/French.1.html. Accessed April 5, 2016.

Garraway, Doris. 2005. *The Libertine Colony: Creolization in the Early French Caribbean*. Durham: Duke University Press.

Georges, Robert. 1983. "The Universality of the Tale-Type as Concept and Construct." *Western Folklore* 42 (1): 21–28.

Gilman, Sander. 1982. *On Blackness without Blacks*. Boston: G. K. Hall.

———. 1985. *Difference and Pathology: Stereotypes of Sexuality, Race, and Madness*. Ithaca: Cornell University Press.

Gold, Barbara K. 2012. "Introduction." In *A Companion to Roman Love Elegy*, edited by Barbara K. Gold, 1–7. West Sussex: Wiley-Blackwell.

Goldberg, David M. 2003. *The Curse of Ham: Race and Slavery in Early Judaism, Christianity, and Islam*. Princeton: Princeton University Press.

Grant, W. L., ed. 1954. *Voyages of Samuel de Champlain, 1604–1618*, by Samuel de Champlain. New York: Barnes and Noble.

Green, Martin. 1979. *Dreams of Adventure, Deeds of Empire*. London: Routledge and Kegan Paul.

Green, Roger Lancelyn. 1946. *Andrew Lang: A Critical Biography*. Leicester: Edmund Ward.

Greene, Ellen. 1998. *The Erotics of Domination: Male Desire and the Mistress in Latin Love Poetry*. Baltimore: Johns Hopkins University Press.

———. 2012. "Gender and Elegy." In *A Companion to Roman Love Elegy*, edited by Barbara K. Gold, 357–71. West Sussex: Wiley-Blackwell.

Haase, Donald. 2000. "Feminist Fairy-Tale Scholarship: A Critical Survey and Bibliography." *Marvels and Tales* 14 (1): 15–63.

———. 2003. "Framing the Brothers Grimm: Paratexts and Intercultural Transmission in Postwar English-Language Editions of the *Kinder- und Hausmärchen*." *Fabula* 44 (1–2): 55–69.

———. 2008. "Fairy Tale." In *The Greenwood Encyclopedia of Folktales and Fairy Tales*, edited by Donald Haase, 1:322–25. Westport: Greenwood Press.

———. 2010. "Decolonizing Fairy-Tale Studies." *Marvels and Tales* 24 (1): 17–38.

Haddawy, Husain, trans. 1990. *The Arabian Nights*. New York: W. W. Norton.

Hannon, Patricia. 1998. *Fabulous Identities: Women's Fairy Tales in Seventeenth-Century France*. Amsterdam: Rodopi.

Hare, J. Laurence, and Fabian Link. 2019. "The Idea of *Volk* and the Origins of *Völkisch* Research, 1800–1930s." *Journal of the History of Ideas* 80 (4): 575–96.

Harries, Elizabeth Wanning. 2001. *Twice upon a Time: Women Writers and the History of the Fairy Tale*. Princeton: Princeton University Press.

Harris, Daniel. 2022. "The Slaughtered Lamb Shepherds with a Rod of Iron: The Use of Psalm 2:9 in Revelation." *Journal of Inductive Biblical Studies* 8 (2): 7–29.

Harris, Rachel. 2017. *Picturing Fairyland: Illustrated Fairy Tale Books and the Rise of the Child Reader-Viewer in the Victorian Era*. PhD diss. Concordia University.

Harth, Erica. 1983. *Ideology and Culture in Seventeenth-Century France*. Ithaca: Cornell University Press.

Hartman, Saidiya. 2008. "Venus in Two Acts." *small axe* 26: 1–14.

Hazard, Paul. 2013 [1935]. *The Crisis of the European Mind, 1680–1715*. Trans. J. Lewis May. Introduction by Anthony Grafton. New York: New York Review Books.

Helfer, Martha B. 2009. "The Fairy Tale Jew." In *Neulektüren / New Readings: Festschrift für Gerd Labroisse Zum 80 Geburstag*, edited by Norbert Otto Eke and Gerhard P. Knapp, 31–42. Leiden: Brill.

"Heliotrope." n.d. Turncoat. https://www.turncoatleather.com/color-heliotrope. Accessed April 9, 2023.

Hennard Dutheil de la Rochère, Martine. 2009. "Rattling Perrault's Dry Bones: Nalo Hopkinson's Literary Voodoo in *Skin Folk*." *Les Carnet du Cerpac* 8: 211–33.

Hensley, Nathan, ed. 2013. "What Is a Network? (And Who Is Andrew Lang?)." In "The Andrew Lang Effect: Network, Discipline, Method," edited by Nathan Hensley. Special issue, *Romanticism and Victorianism on the Net* 64 (October). https://doi.org/10.7202/1025668ar.

Hermand, Jost. 1992. *Old Dreams of a New Reich: Volkish Utopias and National Socialism*. Trans. Paul Levesque. Bloomington: Indiana University Press.

Hermansson, Casie. 2009. *Bluebeard: A Reader's Guide to the English Tradition*. Jackson: University Press of Mississippi.

Hess, Jonathan M. 2000. "Johann David Michaelis and the Colonial Imaginary: Orientalism and the Emergence of Racial Antisemitism in Eighteenth-Century Germany." *Jewish Social Studies* 6 (2): 56–101.

———. 2006. "Jewish Emancipation and the Politics of Race." In *The German Invention of Race*, edited by Sara Eigen and Mark Larrimore, 203–12. New York: State University of New York Press.

Hewitt-White, Caitlin. 2003. "The Stepmother in the Grimms' *Children's and Household Tales*." *Journal for the Association for Research on Mothering* 5 (1): 121–34.

Hill-Tout, Charles. 1904. "Report on the Ethnology of the Siciatl of British Columbia, a Coast Division of the Salish Stock." *Journal of the Anthropological Institute of Great Britain and Ireland* 34 (January–June): 20–91.

Hines, Sara. 2010. "Collecting the Empire: Andrew Lang's Fairy Books." *Marvels and Tales* 24 (1): 39–56.

"History of the Kingdom of Italy (1861–1946)." 2023. Wikipedia, last modified December 10, 2023. https://en.wikipedia.org/wiki/History_of_the_Kingdom_of_Italy_(1861%E2%80%931946).

Hoffmann, Kathryn A. 1997. "Matriarchal Desires and Labyrinths of the Marvelous: Fairy Tales by Old Regime Women." In *Women Writers in Pre-Revolutionary France: Strategies of Emancipation*, edited by Colette H. Winn and Donna Kuizenga, 281–97. New York: Garland.

———. 2005. "Of Monkey Girls and a Hog-Faced Gentlewoman: Marvel in Fairy Tales, Fairgrounds, and Cabinets of Curiosity." *Marvels and Tales* 19 (1): 67–85.

Hollingworth, Jacqualine. 2001. "The Cult of Empire: Children's Literature Revisited." *Agora* 36 (4): 27–33.

Hooley, Dan. 2012. "Modernist Reception." In *A Companion to Roman Love Elegy*, edited by Barbara K. Gold, 491–507. West Sussex: Wiley-Blackwell.

Hopkinson, Nalo. 2001. *Skin Folk: Stories*. New York: Open Road.

———. n.d. "Code Sliding." Black Net.Art. http://blacknetart.com/Hopkinson.html. Accessed March 5, 2023.

Hubert, Renée Riese. 1973. "Le Sens du voyage dans quelques contes de Madame d'Aulnoy." *The French Review* 46 (5): 931–37.

Hughes, Joan. 1989. *Australian Words and Their Origins*. Melbourne: Oxford University Press.

Hulme, Peter. 1998. "Introduction: The Cannibal Scene." In *Cannibalism in the Colonial World*, edited by Francis Barker, Peter Hulme, and Margaret Iversen, 1–38. Cambridge: Cambridge University Press.

Hund, Wulf D. 2011. "'It Must Come from Europe': The Racisms of Immanuel Kant." In *Racisms Made in Germany*, edited by Wulf D. Hund, Christian Koller, and Moshe Zimmermann, 69–98. Zürich: LIT Verlag.

———. 2015–16. "Racist King Kong Fantasies: From Shakespeare's Monster to Stalin's Ape-Man." In *Simianization: Apes, Gender, Class, and Race*, edited by Wulf D. Hund, Charles W. Mills, and Silvia Sebastiani, 43–73. Zürich: LIT Verlag.

Hund, Wulf D., Charles W. Mills, and Silvia Sebastiani, eds. 2015–16. *Simianization: Apes, Gender, Class, and Race*. Zürich: LIT Verlag.

Irwin, Robert. 1994. *The Arabian Nights: A Companion*. New York: Viking.

Isherwood, Barbara. 2006. "Sarindar Dhaliwal." *Border Crossings: A Magazine for the Arts* 25 (1): 116–17.

Iton, Richard. 2008. *In Search of the Black Fantastic: Politics and Popular Culture in the Post–Civil Rights Era*. Oxford: Oxford University Press.

Jackson, Rosemary. 1981. *Fantasy: The Literature of Subversion*. London: Routledge.

James, Sharon L. 2003a. "Her Turn to Cry: The Politics of Weeping in Roman Love Elegy." *Transactions of the American Philological Association* 4 (1): 99–122.

———. 2003b. *Learned Girls and Male Persuasion: Gender and Reading in Roman Love Elegy*. Berkeley: University of California Press.

Janan, Micaela. 2012. "Lacanian Psychoanalytic Theory and Roman Love Elegy." In *A Companion to Roman Love Elegy*, edited by Barbara K. Gold, 375–89. West Sussex: Wiley-Blackwell.

Jasmin, Nadine. 2002. *Naissance du conte feminine. Mots et merveilles: Les Contes de fées de Madame d'Aulnoy (1690–1698)*. Lumière Classique, 44. Paris: Honoré Champion.

Jerng, Mark C. 2017. *Racial Worldmaking: The Power of Popular Fiction*. New York: Fordham University Press.

Jones, Christine A. 2003. "The Poetics of Enchantment (1690–1715)." *Marvels and Tales* 17 (1): 55–74.

———. 2008. "Madame d'Aulnoy Charms the British." *Romantic Review* 99 (3–4): 239–56.

———. 2013. *Shapely Bodies: The Image of Porcelain in Eighteenth-Century France*. Newark: University of Delaware Press.

Jones, Christine A., and Jennifer Schacker. 2013. "Genre." In *Marvelous Transformations: An Anthology of Fairy Tales and Contemporary Critical Perspectives*, edited by Christine A. Jones and Jennifer Schacker, 493–98. Peterborough, Ontario: Broadview Press.

Joosen, Vanessa. 2017. "Picturebooks as Adaptations of Fairy Tales." In *The Routledge Companion to Picturebooks*, edited by Bettina Kümmerling-Meibauer, 473–84. New York: Routledge.

Joshel, Sandra R., and Sheila Murnaghan. 1998. "Introduction: Differential Equations." In *Women and Slaves in Greco-Roman Culture: Differential Equations*, edited by Sandra R. Joshel and Sheila Murnaghan, 1–21. New York: Routledge.

Keith, Alison. 2012. "The Domina in Roman Elegy." In *A Companion to Roman Love Elegy*, edited by Barbara K. Gold, 285–302. West Sussex: Wiley-Blackwell.

Kelleher, Katy. 2017. "Gamboge, A Sunny Yellow with a Deadly Past." *The Awl*, November 7, 2017. https://www.theawl.com/2017/11/gamboge-a-sunny-yellow-with-a-deadly-past/.

———. 2018. "Rose Madder, the Pinky Red of Stephen King's Worst Novel and Hieronymus Bosh's Perverted Playground." *The Awl*, January 2, 2018. https://www.theawl.com/2018/01/rose-madder-the-pinky-red-of-stephen-kings-worst-novel-and-hieronymus-boschs-perverted-playground/.

Knuth, Rebecca. 2012. *Children's Literature and British Identity: Imagining a People and a Nation*. Lanham: Scarecrow Press.

Koestenbaum, Wayne. 1989. *Double Talk: The Erotics of Male Literary Collaboration*. New York: Routledge.

Kontje, Todd. 2004. *German Orientalisms*. Ann Arbor: University of Michigan Press.

Kosloski, Philip. 2017. "The Powerful Symbol of the Lion in Christian Art." *Aleteia* (blog). September 5, 2017. https://aleteia.org/2017/09/05/the-powerful-symbolism-of-the-lion-in-christian-art.

Kuwada, Bryan Kamaoli, and Aiko Yamashiro, eds. 2016. Special issue, "Rooted in Wonder: Tales of Indigenous Activism and Community Organizing." *Marvels and Tales* 30 (1): 17–21.

Kuya, Dorothy. 1980. "Racism in Children's Books in Britain." In *The Slant of the Pen: Racism in Children's Books*, edited by Roy Preiswerk, 26–45. Geneva: World Council of Churches.

LaFaurie, Jean, and Pierre Prieur. 1956. *Les Monnaies des rois de France*, vol. 2. Paris: Émile Bourgey.

Lang, Andrew, ed. 1889–1910. Colored Fairy Books series. London: Longmans, Green.

Lang, Leonora Blanche. 1881–83. *A Geography: Physical, Political, and Descriptive, for Beginners*. 3 vols. Edited by M. Creighton. London: Rivingtons.

———. 1913. *The Strange Story Book*. Edited by Andrew Lang. London: Longmans, Green.

Lateiner, Donald. 2009. "Tears in Apuleius' *Metamorphoses*." In *Tears in the Graeco-Roman World*, edited by Thorsten Fögen, 277–95. Berlin: Walter de Gruyter.

Lathey, Gillian. 2006. "Introduction." *The Translation of Children's Literature: A Reader*, edited by Gillian Lathey, 1–16. Bristol: Multilingual Matters / Channel View.

———. 2010. *The Role of Translators in Children's Literature: Invisible Storytellers*. New York: Routledge.

Lau, Kimberly J. 2016. "Snow White and the Trickster: Race and Genre in Helen Oyeyemi's *Boy, Snow, Bird*." *Western Folklore* 75 (3–4): 371–96.

———. 2019a. "Of Genres and Geopolitics: The European Fairy Tale and the Global Novel." In *The Fairy Tale World*, edited by Andrew Teverson, 462–72. London: Routledge.

———. 2019b. "What's Revealed in the Cut: The Articulation of Silenced Imaginaries in Hans Christian Andersen's Papercuts." Paper delivered at the 25th International Research Society for Children's Literature Congress.

———. 2021. "Power: The Archaeology of a Genre." In *The Modern Age*. Edited by Andrew Teverson. Vol. 6 of *A Cultural History of Fairy Tales*, edited by Anne E. Duggan, 181–96. London: Bloomsbury Academic. http://solomon.eena.alexanderstreet.com.oca.ucsc.edu/cgi-bin/asp/philo/navigate.pl?eena.240.

Lea, Charlene A. 1993. "The Christlich-Deutsche Tischgesellschaft: Napoleonic Hegemony Engenders Political Anti-Semitism." In *Crisis and Culture in Post-Enlightenment Germany: Essays in Honour of Peter Heller*, edited by Hans Schulte and David Richards, 89–111. Lanham, MD: University Press of America.

Leach, Eleanor Winsor. 2012. "Rome's Elegiac Cartography: The View from the *Via Sacra*." In *A Companion to Roman Love Elegy*, edited by Barbara K. Gold, 134–51. West Sussex: Wiley-Blackwell.

Le Jeune, Paul. 1901 [1632–33]. *Jesuit Relations and Allied Documents*. Vol. 5. Edited by Reuben Gold Thwaites. Cleveland: Burrows Brothers.

"Lion Depiction across Ancient & Modern Religions." 2020. ALERT. February 20, 2020. https://lionalert.org/lion-depiction-across-ancient-modern-religions/.

Lorde, Audre. 1007 [1984]. *Sister Outsider: Essays and Speeches*. Berkeley, CA: Crossing Press.

Ludwig, W. 1971. "Petrus Lotichius Secundus and the Roman Elegists: Prolegomena to a Study of Neo-Latin Elegy." In *Classical Influences on European Culture A.D. 500–1500*, edited by Robert R. Bolgar, 171–90. Cambridge: Cambridge University Press.

Lundell, Torborg. 1989 [1986]. "Gender-Related Biases in the Type and Motif Indexes of Aarne and Thompson." In *Fairy Tales and Society: Illusion, Allusion, and Paradigm*, edited by Ruth B. Bottigheimer, 149–63. Philadelphia: University of Pennsylvania Press.

Lüthi, Max. 1982. *The European Folktale: Form and Nature*. Trans. John D. Miles. Philadelphia: Institute for the Study of Human Issue.

Lutz, Tom. 1999. *Crying: The Natural and Cultural History of Tears*. New York: W. W. Norton.

Lyne, R.O.A.M. 1979. "Servitium Amoris." *Classical Quarterly* 29 (1): 117–30.

MacMaster, Neil. 2000. "'Black Jew–White Negro': Anti-Semitism and the Construction of Cross-Racial Stereotypes." *Nationalism and Ethnic Politics* 6 (4): 65–82.

Magnanini, Suzanne, ed. and trans. 2015. *The Pleasant Nights*, by Giovan Francesco Straparola. New York: Iter Press.

———. 2023. "Ogres and Slaves: Representations of Race in Giambattista Basile's Fairy Tales." In *Teaching Race in the European Renaissance: A Classroom Guide*, edited by Matthew Chapman and Anna Wainwright, 201–23. Tempe: ACMRS Press.

Malik, Kenan. 1996. *The Meaning of Race: Race, History, and Culture in Western Society*. New York: New York University Press.

Marchand, Suzanne L. 2009. *German Orientalism in the Age of Empire: Religion, Race, and Scholarship*. Cambridge: Cambridge University Press.

Marshall, Joyce, ed. and trans. 1967. *Word from New France: The Selected Letters of Marie de l'Incarnation*. Toronto: Oxford University Press.

Marzolph, Ulrich, ed. 2006. *The Arabian Nights Reader*. Detroit: Wayne State University Press.

———. 2014. "Grimm Nights: Reflections on the Connections between the Grimms' *Household Tales* and the *1001 Nights*." *Marvels and Tales* 28 (1): 75–87.

Marzolph, Ulrich, and Richard van Leeuwen, eds. 2004. *The Arabian Nights Encyclopedia*. Santa Barbara: ABC-Clio.

McClintock, Anne. 1995. *Imperial Leather: Race, Gender and Sexuality in the Colonial Contest*. New York: Routledge.

McLeod, Glenda K. 1989. "Madame d'Aulnoy: Writer of Fantasy." In *Women Writers of the Seventeenth Century*, edited by Katharina M. Wilson and Frank J. Warnke, 91–118. Athens: University of Georgia Press.

Melzer, Sara. 2006. "The *Relation de voyage*: A Forgotten Genre of Seventeenth-Century France." *Biblio* 17 (106): 35–52.

———. 2012. *Colonizer or Colonized: The Hidden Stories of Early Modern French Culture*. Philadelphia: University of Pennsylvania Press.

Miller, Paul Allen. 2012. "Tibullus." In *A Companion to Roman Love Elegy*, edited by Barbara K. Gold, 53–69. West Sussex: Wiley-Blackwell.

Mills, Charles W. 2015–16. "Bestial Inferiority: Locating Simianization within Racism." In *Simianization: Apes, Gender, Class, and Race*, edited by Wulf D. Hund, Charles W. Mills, and Silvia Sebastiani, 19–41. Zürich: LIT Verlag.

Mitchell, Jane Tucker. 1978. *A Thematic Analysis of Mme. d'Aulnoy's contes de fées*. University, MS: Romance Monographs.

Morgan, Llewelyn. 2012. "Elegiac Meter: Opposites Attract." In *A Companion to Roman Love Elegy*, edited by Barbara K. Gold, 204–18. West Sussex: Wiley-Blackwell.

Morrison, Toni. 1988. "Unspeakable Things Unspoken: The Afro-American Presence in American Literature." The Tanner Lectures on Human Values, University of Michigan, Ann Arbor, October 7, 1988.

———. 1993 [1990]. *Playing in the Dark: Whiteness and the Literary Imagination*. The William S. Massey Sr. Lectures in the History of American Civilization, 1990. New York: Vintage.

Mullins, Melissa. 2017. "Ogress, Fairy, Sorceress, Witch: Supernatural Surrogates and the Monstrous Mother in Variants of 'Rapunzel.'" In *The Morals of Monster Stories: Essays on Children's Picture Book Messages*, edited by Leslie Ormandy, 142–57. Jefferson, NC: McFarland.

Murgatroyd, P. 1981. "'Seruitium Amoris' and the Roman Elegists." *Latomus* 40 (3): 589–606.

Naithani, Sadhana. 2006. *In Quest of Indian Folktales: Pandit Ram Gharib Chaube and William Crooke*. Bloomington: Indiana University Press.

———. 2010. *Story-Time of the British Empire: Colonial and Postcolonial Folkloristics*. Jackson: University Press of Mississippi.

Nettl, Paul. 1944. "Traces of the Negroid in the 'Mauresque' of the Sixteenth and Seventeenth Centuries." *Phylon* 5 (2): 105–13.

Norcia, Megan A. 2009. "Puzzling Empire: Early Puzzles and Dissected Maps as Imperial Heuristics." *Children's Literature* 37: 1–32.

---. 2010. *X Marks the Spot: Women Writers Map the Empire for British Children, 1790–1895*. Columbus: Ohio State University Press.

Ó Giolláin, Diarmuid. 2022. *Exotic Dreams in the Science of the Volksgeist: Towards a Global History of European Folklore Studies*. Helsinki: The Kalevala Society.

Origo, Iris. 1955. "The Domestic Enemy: The Eastern Slaves in Tuscany in the Fourteenth and Fifteenth Centuries." *Speculum: A Journal of Medieval Studies* 30 (3): 321–66.

Orme, Jennifer. 2010. "Mouth to Mouth: Queer Desires in Emma Donoghue's *Kissing the Witch*." *Marvels and Tales* 24 (1): 116–30.

Owens, Yvonne. 2014. "The Saturnine History of Jews and Witches." *Preternature: Critical and Historical Studies on the Preternatural* 3 (1): 56–84.

Oyeyemi, Helen. 2009. *White Is for Witching*. New York: Riverhead Books.

---. 2011. *Mr. Fox*. New York: Riverhead Books.

---. 2014. *Boy, Snow, Bird*. New York: Riverhead Books.

---. 2019. *Gingerbread*. New York: Riverhead Books.

Palmer, Melvin D. 1969. *Madame d'Aulnoy in England*. Dissertation. University of Maryland.

---. 1971. "Madame d'Aulnoy's Pseudo-Autobiographical Works on Spain." *Romanische Forschungen* 83 (2/3): 220–29.

---. 1975. "Madame d'Aulnoy in England." *Comparative Literature* 27 (3): 237–53.

Passemore, John. 2000 [1970]. *The Perfectibility of Man*. 3rd ed. Indianapolis: Liberty Fund.

Peabody, Sue. 1996. *There Are No Slaves in France: The Political Culture of Race and Slavery in the Ancien Régime*. Oxford: Oxford University Press.

Perraudin, Michael. 2000. *Literature, the Volk and Revolution in Mid-Nineteenth Century Germany*. New York: Berghahn Books.

Plantade, Emmanuel, and Nedjima Plantade. 2014. "*Libyca Psyche*: Apuleius' Narrative and Berber Folktales." In *Apuleius and Africa*, edited by Benjamin Todd Less, Ellen Finkelpearl, and Luca Graverini, 174–202. New York: Routledge.

Propp, Vladimir. 1968 [1928]. *Morphology of the Folktale*. Trans. Laurence Scott. Austin: University of Texas Press.

Psomiades, Kathy Alexis. 2013. "Hidden Meaning: Andrew Lang, H. Rider Haggard, Sigmund Freud, and Interpretation." In "The Andrew Lang Effect: Network, Discipline, Method," ed. Nathan Hensley. Special issue,

Romanticism and Victorianism on the Net 64 (October). https://doi.org/10.7202/1025669ar.

Pym, Anthony. 1998. *Method in Translation History*. Manchester: St. Jerome.

Revel, Jacques. 1989. "The Uses of Civility." In *A History of Private Life*. Vol. 3, edited by Roger Chartier and translated by Arthur Goldhammer, 167–205. Cambridge: Harvard University Press.

Richards, Jeffrey, ed. 1989. *Imperialism and Juvenile Literature*. Manchester: Manchester University Press.

———. 2010. "E.L. Blanchard and 'The Golden Age of Pantomime.'" In *Victorian Pantomime: A Collection of Critical Essays*, edited by Jim Davis, 21–40. London: Palgrave Macmillan.

Rieder, John. 2008. *Colonialism and the Emergence of Science Fiction*. Middletown: Wesleyan University Press.

Rifkin, Mark. 2019. *Fictions of Land and Flesh: Blackness, Indigeneity, Speculation*. Durham: Duke University Press.

Ritchie, Anne Thackeray. 2003 [1895]. "Introduction," *The Fairy Tales of Madame d'Aulnoy* by Marie-Catherine d'Aulnoy. Trans. Annie Macdonell and Miss Lee. Honolulu: University Press of the Pacific.

Roanhorse, Rebecca, Elizabeth LaPensée, Johnnie Jae, and Darcie Little Badger. 2017. "Decolonizing Science Fiction and Imagining Futures: An Indigenous Futurism Roundtable." *Strange Horizons*, January 30, 2017. http://strangehorizons.com/non-fiction/articles/decolonizing-science-fiction-and-imagining-futures-an-indigenous-futurisms-roundtable/.

Robbins, Louise E. 2002. *Elephant Slaves and Pampered Parrots: Exotic Animals in Eighteenth-Century Paris*. Baltimore: Johns Hopkins University Press.

Robert, Raymonde. 1982. *Le Conte de fées littéraire en France de la fin du XVIIe siècle à la find du XVIIIe siècle*. Nancy: Presses Universitaires de Nancy.

Robinson, Natalie. 2011. "Exploding the Glass Bottles: Constructing the Postcolonial 'Bluebeard' Tale in Nalo Hopkinson's 'The Glass Bottle Trick.'" In *Anti-Tales: The Uses of Disenchantment*, edited by Catriona McAra and David Calvin, 253–61. Newcastle upon Tyne: Cambridge Scholars.

Roche-Mazon, Jeanne. 1927. "Madame d'Aulnoy n'aurait-elle pas été en Espagne?" *Revue de littérature comparée* 7: 724–36.

Röhrich, Lutz. 1991. *Folktales and Reality*. Trans. Peter Tokofsky. Bloomington: Indiana University Press.

Rose, Jacqueline. 1993 [1984]. *The Case of Peter Pan, or The Impossibility of Children's Fiction*. Philadelphia: University of Pennsylvania Press.

Rosenman, Ellen Bayuk, and Claudia C. Klaver, eds. 2008. *Other Mothers: Beyond the Maternal Ideal*. Columbus: Ohio State University Press.

Sands-O'Connor, Karen. 2009. "Primitive Minds: Anthropology, Children, and Savages in Andrew Lang and Rudyard Kipling." In *Childhood in Edwardian Fiction: Worlds Enough and Time*, edited by Adrienne E. Gavin and Andrew F. Humphries, 177–90. New York: Palgrave Macmillan.

"Sarindar Dhaliwal." n.d. Medalta. https://medalta.org/sarindar-dhaliwal/. Accessed April 9, 2023.

Sasser, Kim Anderson. 2019. "West African Magical Realism among the Wonder Genres." In *The Fairy Tale World*, edited by Andrew Teverson, 144–57. London: Routledge.

Sayre, Gordon M. 1997. *Les sauvages américains: Representations of Native Americans in French and English Colonial Literature*. Chapel Hill: University of North Carolina Press.

Scala, Carmela Bernadetta. 2014. *Fairytales—A World between the Imaginary: Metaphor at Play in "Lo cunto de li cunti" by Giambattista Basile*. Newcastle upon Tyne: Cambridge Scholars.

Schacker, Jennifer. 2003. *National Dreams: The Remaking of Fairy Tales in Nineteenth-Century England*. Philadelphia: University of Pennsylvania Press.

———. 2018. *Staging Fairyland: Folklore, Children's Entertainment, and Nineteenth-Century Pantomime*. Detroit: Wayne State University Press.

———. 2021. "Bluebeard; the Old Story Re-told (1879)." In *The Routledge Pantomime Reader: 1800–1900*, edited by Jennifer Schacker and Daniel O'Quinn, 303–50. London: Routledge.

Schacker, Jennifer, and Daniel O'Quinn, eds. 2021. *The Routledge Pantomime Reader: 1800–1900*. New York: Routledge.

Schanoes, Veronica. 2019. "Thorns into Gold: Contemporary Jewish American Responses to Antisemitism in Traditional Fairy Tales." *Journal of American Folklore* 132 (525): 291–309.

Schenda, Rudolf. 1981. "Delphin." *Enzyklopädie des Märchens*. Vol. 3. Berlin: De Gruyter. https://doi.org/10.1515/9783110845921.

Schmiesing, Anne. 2016. "Blackness in the Grimms' Fairy Tales." *Marvels and Tales* 30 (2): 210–33.

Seifert, Lewis C. 1996. *Fairy Tales, Sexuality, and Gender in France, 1690–1715: Nostalgic Utopias*. Cambridge: Cambridge University Press.

———. 2002a. "Orality, History, and 'Creoleness' in Patrick Chamoiseau's Creole Folktales." *Marvels and Tales* 16 (2): 214–30.

———. 2002b. "Pig or Prince: Murat, d'Aulnoy, and the Limits of Civilized Masculinity." In *High Anxiety: Masculinity in Crisis in Early Modern France*, edited by Kathleen P. Long, 183–209. Kirksville, MO: Truman State University Press.

———. 2011. "Animal-Human Hybridity in d'Aulnoy's 'Babiole' and 'Prince Wild Boar.'" *Marvels and Tales* 25 (2): 244–60.

———, ed. 2015. "Introduction: Queer(ing) Fairy Tales." Special Issue, "Queer(ing) Fairy Tales." *Marvels and Tales* 29 (1): 15–20.

———. 2019. "Francophone Fairy Tales in West Africa and the Caribbean: Colonizing and Reclaiming Tradition." In *The Fairy Tale World*, edited by Andrew Teverson, 158–69. London: Routledge.

Sharrock, Alison R. 2012. "Ovid." In *A Companion to Roman Love Elegy*, edited by Barbara K. Gold, 70–85. West Sussex: Wiley-Blackwell.

Shaw, Lytle. 2012. "Colors / Madder Lake: Fierce Blood to Pale Wash." *Cabinet* 45: 7–9.

Siegel, Jonah. 2013. "Lang's Survivals." In "The Andrew Lang Effect: Network, Discipline, Method," edited by Nathan Hensley. Special issue, *Romanticism and Victorianism on the Net* 64 (October). https://doi.org/10.7202/1025673ar.

Sikka, Sonia. 2005. "Enlightened Relativism: The Case of Herder." *Philosophy and Social Criticism* 31 (3): 309–41.

Simpson, Hyacinth M. 2005. "Fantastic Alternatives: Journeys into the Imagination: A Conversation with Nalo Hopkinson." *Journal of West Indian Literature* 14 (1–2): 96–112.

Singh, Rashna B. 2004. *Goodly Is Our Heritage: Children's Literature, Empire, and the Certitude of Character*. Lanham: Scarecrow Press.

Skoie, Mathilde. 2012. "*Corpus Tibullianum*, Book 3." In *A Companion to Roman Love Elegy*, edited by Barbara K. Gold, 86–100. West Sussex: Wiley-Blackwell.

Smith, Michelle J., and Rebecca-Anne Do Rozario. 2016. "Race, Species, and the Other: 'Beauty and the Beast' in Victorian Pantomime and Children's Literature." *Nineteenth-Century Contexts* 38 (1): 37–53.

Smol, Anna. 1996. "The 'Savage' and the 'Civilized': Andrew Lang's Representation of the Child and the Translation of Folklore." *Children's Literature Association Quarterly* 21 (4): 177–183.

Solbrig, Ingeborg H. 1990. "American Slavery in Eighteenth-Century German Literature: The Case of Herder's 'Neger-Idyllen.'" *Monatshefte* 82 (1): 38–49.

Spear, Jennifer M. 2003. "Colonial Intimacies: Legislating Sex in French Louisiana." *William and Mary Quarterly* 60 (1): 75–98.

Springhall, John. 1989. "'Healthy Papers for Manly Boys': Imperialism and Race in the Hamworths' Halfpenny Boys' Papers of the 1890s and 1900s." In *Imperialism and Juvenile Literature*, edited by Jeffrey Richards, 107–25. Manchester: Manchester University Press.

St. Clair, Kassia. 2016. *The Secret Lives of Color*. New York: Penguin.

Steere, Edward. 1870. *Swahili Tales: As Told by Natives of Zanzibar. With an English Translation*. London: Bell and Daldy.

Stewart, Susan. 1993. *On Longing: Narratives of the Miniature, the Gigantic, the Souvenir, the Collection*. Durham: Duke University Press.

Stoler, Ann Laura. 2002. *Carnal Knowledge and Imperial Power: Race and the Intimate in Colonial Rule*. Berkeley: University of California Press.

Straparola, Giovan Francesco. 2015 [1550–55]. *The Pleasant Nights*. Ed. and trans. Suzanne Magnanini. New York: Iter Press.

Stuurman, Siep. 2000. "François Bernier and the Invention of Racial Classification." *History Workshop Journal* 50: 1–21.

Sundmark, Björn. 2005, August. "Andrew Lang and the Colour Fairy Books." Paper presented at the IRSCL (International Research Society for Children's Literature) Congress, Dublin.

Sutton, Martin. 1996. *The Sin-Complex: A Critical Study of English Versions of the Grimms' "Kinder- und Hausmärchen" in the Nineteenth Century*. Kassel: Grimm-Gesellschaft Kassel e.V.

Tatar, Maria. 1992. *Off with Their Heads! Fairy Tales and the Culture of Childhood*. Princeton: Princeton University Press.

———. 2019 [1987]. *The Hard Facts of the Grimms' Fairy Tales*. Princeton: Princeton University Press.

Teverson, Andrew. 2016. "The Fairy-Tale Collections of Andrew Lang and Joseph Jacobs: Identity, Nation, Empire." *Gramarye* 9: 7–17.

———. 2019. "Introduction: The Fairy Tale and the World." In *The Fairy Tale World*, edited by Andrew Teverson, 1–14. New York: Routledge.

Teverson, Andrew, Alexandra Warwick, and Leigh Wilson, eds. 2015. *The Edinburgh Critical Edition of the Selected Writings of Andrew Lang*, vol. 2. Edinburgh: Edinburgh University Press.

Thomas, Ebony Elizabeth. 2019. *The Dark Fantastic: Race and the Imagination from "Harry Potter" to "The Hunger Games."* New York: New York University Press.

Thomas, Sheree, ed. 2000. *Dark Matter: A Century of Speculative Fiction from the African Diaspora*. New York: Warner Aspect.

Thompson, Stith. 1928. *The Types of the Folk-Tale: A Classification and Bibliography*. Folklore Fellows Communications 74. Helsinki: Suomalaisen Tiedeakatemian Toimituksia.

———. 1961. *The Types of the Folk-Tale: A Classification and Bibliography*. 2nd ed. Folklore Fellows Communications 184. Helsinki: Suomalaisen Tiedeakatemian Toimituksia.

Tiffin, Jessica. 2009. *Marvelous Geometry: Narrative and Metafiction in Modern Fairy Tale*. Detroit: Wayne State University Press.

Todorov, Tzvetan. 1975 [1973]. *The Fantastic: A Structural Approach to a Literary Genre*. Trans. Richard Howard. Ithaca: Cornell University Press.

Trachtenberg, Joshua. 2002 [1943]. *The Devil and the Jews: The Medieval Conception of the Jew and Its Relation to Modern Antisemitism*. 2nd ed. Philadelphia: The Jewish Publication Society.

Trexler, Richard C. 1997. *The Journey of the Magi: Meanings in History of a Christian Story*. Princeton: Princeton University Press.

Turner, Kay, and Pauline Greenhill, eds. 2012. *Transgressive Tales: Queering the Grimms*. Detroit: Wayne State University Press.

Uther, Hans-Jörg. 2004. *The Types of International Folktales: A Classification and Bibliography*. Folklore Fellows Communications 284–286. Helsinki: Suomalaisen Tiedeakatemian Toimituksia.

———. 2008. "Tale Type." In *The Greenwood Encyclopedia of Folktales and Fairy Tales*. Vol. 3, edited by Donald Haase, 937–42. Westport: Greenwood Press.

Valladares, Hérica. 2012. "Elegy, Art and the Viewer." In *A Companion to Roman Love Elegy*, edited by Barbara K. Gold, 318–38. West Sussex: Wiley-Blackwell.

Van Dijk, Kees. 2011. "Soap Is the Onset of Civilization." In *Cleanliness and Culture: Indonesian Histories*, edited by Kees van Dijk and Jean Gelman Taylor, 1–39. Leiden: KITLV Press.

Vaz da Silva, Francisco. 2010. "The Invention of Fairy Tales." Special issue, "The European Fairy-Tale Tradition between Orality and Literacy." *Journal of American Folklore*, 123 (490): 398–425.

Venutti, Lawrence. 1995. *The Translator's Invisibility*. New York: Routledge.

Verdier, Gabrielle. 1993. "Figures de la conteuse dans les contes de fées féminins." *XVIIe siècle* 45 (3): 481–99.

Villanueva, Annabelle. 2023. "Three Christian Symbols that Are Thematic Turning Points in *The Chronicles of Narnia: The Lion, the Witch, and the Wardrobe*." *World Journal of Research and Review* 16 (4): 1–3.

Villeneuve, Gabrielle-Suzanne. 2008 [1740]. *La Jeune Américaine et les contes marin*. Édition critique établie par Élisa Biancardi. *Bibliothèque des génies et des fées* 15. Paris: Honoré Champion Éditeur.

Warner, Marina. 1994. *From the Beast to the Blonde: On Fairy Tales and Their Tellers*. New York: Farrar, Straus and Giroux.

Weigel, Sigrid. 1987. "The Near Stranger: The Territory of the 'Feminine' and the Relationship between 'Savages' and 'Women' in the Discourse of the Enlightenment." In *Die andere Welt. Studien zum Exotismus*, edited by Thomas Koebner and Gerhart Pickerodt, 179–99. Frankfurt am Main: Athenäum. Personal translation by Katherine Oden.

Williamson, George S. 2006. "Gods, Titans, and Monsters: Philhellenism, Race, and Religion in Early-Nineteenth-Century Mythography." In *The German Invention of Race*, edited by Sara Eigen and Mark Larrimore, 147–65. New York: State University of New York Press.

Wirk, Mandeep. 2013. "Sarindar Dhaliwal: Narratives from the Beyond Exhibition." *Punjabi Patrika*, December 20, 2013, 54.

Wolfgang, Aurora, ed. and trans. 2020. *"Beauty and the Beast": The Original Story*. Toronto: Iter Press.

Wray, David. 2012. "Catullus the Roman Love Elegist?" In *A Companion to Roman Love Elegy*, edited by Barbara K. Gold, 25–38. West Sussex: Wiley-Blackwell.

Young, Helen. 2016. *Race and Popular Fantasy Literature: Habits of Whiteness*. New York: Routledge.

Zantop, Susanne. 1997a. "The Beautiful, the Ugly, and the German: Race, Gender, and Nationality in Eighteenth-Century Anthropological Discourse." In *Gender and Germanness: Cultural Productions of Nation*, edited by Patricia Herminghouse and Magda Mueller, 21–25. Providence: Berghahn Books.

———. 1997b. *Colonial Fantasies: Conquest, Family, and Nation in Precolonial Germany, 1770–1870*. Durham: Duke University Press.

Ziolkowski, Jan M. 2010. "Straparola and the Fairy Tale: Between Literary and Oral Traditions." Special issue, "The European Fairy-Tale Tradition between Orality and Literacy." *Journal of American Folklore* 123 (490): 377–97.

Zipes, Jack. 1979–80. "Who's Afraid of the Brothers Grimm? Socialization and Politi[ci]zation through Fairy Tales." *The Lion and the Unicorn* 3 (2): 4–56.

———, ed. 1989. *Beauties, Beasts and Enchantment: Classic French Fairy Tales*. New York: New American Library.

———. 1991 [1983]. *Fairy Tales and the Art of Subversion*. New York: Routledge.

———. 2000. "Introduction: Towards a Definition of the Literary Fairy Tale." In *The Oxford Companion to Fairy Tales*, edited by Jack Zipes, xv–xxxii. Oxford: Oxford University Press.

———. 2002. *The Brothers Grimm: From Enchanted Forests to the Modern World*. New York: Palgrave Macmillan.

———, trans. 2003. *The Complete Fairy Tales of the Brothers Grimm*. 3rd ed. New York: Bantam.

———. 2010. "Sensationalist Scholarship: A Putative 'New' History of Fairy Tales." *Cultural Analysis* 9: n.p.

Zoebel Marshall, Emily. 2019. "This Is Not a Fairy Tale: Anansi and the Web of Narrative Power." In *The Fairy Tale World*, edited by Andrew Teverson, 170–83. London: Routledge.

Zöhrer, Marlene. 2021. "Reimagining the Grimms' Fairy Tales: New and Familiar Perspectives in Austrian Picturebook Illustration." *Strenæ: Recherches sur les livres et objets culturels de l'enfance* 18: n.p.

INDEX

Aboriginal Australia, 18, 133, 142–47
Abumrad, Jad, 167
adventure literature, 131, 135–37, 139, 143–44, 146
Alleyne, Charles Thomas, 142
Andersen, Hans Christian, 175n10
animal bridegroom, 8–9, 16–17, 43–44, 80–88
animal-human hybridity, 67–71, 74–78, 86, 181n9
Ansani, Antonella, 6, 11
anti-Black racism: in the Grimms' *Children's and Household Tales*, 10, 17–18, 101–7, 113, 118, 125
antimiscegenation, 17, 80. *See also* miscegenation
antisemitism, 110, 118, 190n11; German, 17–18, 89, 92–96, 102–4, 106–8, 190n9; in the Grimms' *Children's and Household Tales*, 10, 17–18, 96–101, 106–8, 111, 113, 116, 125–27, 188–89n4, 193n25
Apuleius, 47–49, 117, 165, 178n13; "Cupid and Psyche," 47–49, 117, 165; *The Golden Ass*, 48
Aribisala, Karen King, 172
assimilation, 16–17, 67, 88, 181n11; Jewish, 101. *See also* Frenchification (*francisation*)
ATU (Aarne-Thompson-Uther) index, 157, 174n9; ATU 402 (The Animal Bride), 7; ATU 403 (The Black and the White Bride), 7, 9–10, 16; ATU 425 (Search for the Lost Husband), 7, 43–45, 47–50, 117, 174n9; ATU 425A (Animal Bridegroom), 43, 174n9; ATU 425B (Son of the Witch / Cupid and Psyche), 7–8, 16, 43–45, 47–48, 174n9, 178–79n14; ATU 425C (Beauty and the Beast), 16, 43, 45, 174n9; ATU 480 (The Kind and Unkind Girls), 115, 162

Babalola, Bolu, 19, 163–65; *Love in Color: Mythical Tales from Around the World, Retold*, 163–65; "Psyche," 165
Bacchilega, Cristina, 159–61, 163, 199nn1–2
Bandello, Matteo, 42
Barbin, Claude, 54
Barchilon, Jacques, 6–7, 85
Baroque, 35, 51; Baroque excess, 41; Baroque inversion, 25, 34, 37
Basile, Giambattista, 2, 4–9, 15–16, 21–51, 53, 114–17, 123–24, 165, 177–78n11, 178–79n14, 179n15, 192n23; *Aethiopica*, 179n15; "The Crucible," 29; *Del Teagene*, 179n15; "The Dove" (2.7), 29; "The Golden Trunk" (5.4), 7–8, 22–23, 43, 45–49, 117, 165, 178–79n14; "The Green Meadow" (2.2), 23;

Basile, Giambattista (*continued*)
"The Little Slave Girl" (2.8), 22–23, 44; "The Old Woman Who Was Skinned," 123–24; "The Padlock" (2.9), 7–8, 22–23, 43–45, 47–49, 117, 165; "Penta with the Chopped-Off Hands" (3.2), 177–78n11; "Petrosinella" (Rapunzel), 192n23; "Pride Punished" (4.10), 33–35, 40; "Sapia" (5.6), 33, 177–78n11; *The Tale of Tales* (Lo cunto de li cunti), 2, 4–9, 15–16, 21–51, 53, 115–16, 179n15; "The Three Citrons" (5.9), 9, 16, 22–24, 38–43, 115–16; "The Two Little Pizzas" (7.4), 23–24, 115–16
Bastin, Kathryn R., 187n35
Bell, Duncan, 196n7
Bellhouse, Mary, 83
Belmessous, Saliha, 69, 79, 181n11
Benes, Tuska, 191n19
Berber oral tradition, 48–49, 178n13; "The Son of the Ogress," 48–49
Berman, Nina, 93–94, 110
Bernier, François, 68, 72–73, 83–84, 89, 182n15, 183n21; "A New Division of the Earth, according to the Different Species or Races of Men Who Inhabit It," 72–73, 83–84
Biancardi, Élisa, 81
Blackness: as accursed state, 12; association with animality, 8, 23; in Basile's *The Tale of Tales*, 8–9, 22–25, 40–42, 49–50, 177n9, 179n15; in the Grimms' *Children's and Household Tales*, 10, 17–18, 107–18; Jewish "blackness," 102; scientific study of, 184–85n28
Bluebeard, 160–62
Blumenbach, Johann Friedrich, 89, 103

Blyth, Harry: "Heroes of the Matabele War. A Romance of the Recent Campaign in South Africa," 135–36
Boccaccio, Giovanni: *The Decameron*, 21
Bolt, Christine, 135
Bottigheimer, Ruth B., 92, 96–97, 124, 127–28, 174nn7–8
Boulle, Pierre, 72–73, 83–84
Brauner, Sigrid, 119
Brentano, Clemens, 90, 94–96, 188–89n4; "Der Philister vor, in und nach der Geschichte," 95–96; *Des Knaben Wunderhorn*, 90, 94
British empire: decline of, 154–55, 198n20. See also imperialism: British
Bruns, Claudia, 125
Buck-Morss, Susan, 90, 188n1
Burton, Richard, 135
Büsching, Johann Gustav: *Volks-Sagen, Märchen und Legenden*, 193–94n1

Campe, Joachim Heinrich: *Robinson der Jüngere: Ein Lesebuch für Kinder*, 104–6
Camper, Petrus, 124–25
Canepa, Nancy, 5–6, 11, 29, 32, 35, 40, 48, 50–51, 174n7, 177n8, 177–78n11, 178–79n14, 179n15
cannibalism, 119–20, 125, 185n30, 192n22
Caribbean literature, 159–63
Castle, Kathryn, 135
Chamoiseau, Patrick: *Creole Folktales*, 159–60
Christianity: Christian patriarchy, 118–19; Christian Romantic nationalism (*see* nationalism: German); in the Grimms' *Children's and Household Tales*, 110–11, 113–14, 121–23, 126, 191n15

Christlich Deutsche
    Tischgesellschaft, 94–95
Citton, Yves, 180n3
civility, 8, 18–19, 62, 69–71, 74–78, 119,
    133–34, 141, 147, 151–54, 182n18,
    186–87n33, 197n16
Clark Hillard, Molly, 154
Clarkson, Thomas, 134
cleanliness, 149–52, 198nn18–19
Code Noir, 17, 80
Colley, Linda, 135
colonialism: British (*see* imperialism:
    British); colonial history, 157, 161,
    167; French, 16–17, 55–88, 186–
    87n33, 187n35; German, 17–18,
    102–5; Mediterranean, 48. *See also*
    slavery: colonial
color symbolism, 108–9, 115, 125
Columbus, Christopher, 57–58, 197n13
Confederation of the Rhine, 91, 188n1
Conte, Gian Biagio, 27
contes de fées, 2, 4, 6–7, 16–17, 53–88,
    179–80n1, 183n21
conteuses. See *contes de fées*
Cooper, Barbara, 80–81, 84–85,
    183–84n24
Cooper, James Fennimore, 136
Cooppan, Vilashini, 168
Copley, Frank, 28, 30
Cortés, Hernán, 58
Creole fairytale adaptations, 19–20,
    159–63
creolization, 159–63, 172
Croce, Benedetto, 29, 40, 178n14
Curran, Andrew, 82, 184–85n28,
    185n29

Dante, 176n4
Datini, Margherita, 42
d'Aulnoy, Marie-Catherine, 2, 5–9,
    16–17, 53–88, 115, 117, 174n8, 179–
    80n1, 180n4, 181–82n14, 182n15,
    182n18, 182–83n19, 183nn21–22,
    186–87n33, 187n35; "Babiole,"
    59, 68, 70–71, 78, 181–82n14,
    182n18, 183n22, 187n35; "Belle-
    Belle," 182–83n19; "Belle-Etoile,"
    17, 62–64, 66, 182–83n19; "The
    Blue Bird," 78, 182–83n19; "The
    Dolphin," 5, 17, 62, 64–66, 78;
    "Fair Goldilocks," 182–83n19;
    Fairy Tales (*Les Contes des fées*),
    2, 5–8, 16–17, 54, 61, 179–80n1;
    "Finette Cendron," 59; "The
    Golden Branch," 59; "The Green
    Serpent," 8; "The Hind in the
    Wood," 182–83n19; *Mémoires
    de la cour d'Espagne*, 55–56,
    181–82n14; *New Tales, or Fairies
    in Fashion* (*Suites des contes
    nouveaux, ou Des fées à la mode*),
    5–8, 16–17, 54, 61; "The Pigeon
    and the Dove," 182–83n19;
    "Prince Ariel," 59, 182–83n19;
    "Prince Marcassin," 5, 17, 50,
    68, 70–71, 74–78, 117, 181n12,
    181–82n14, 182n18, 183n22;
    "Princess Carpillon," 182–83n19;
    "Prince Wild Boar" (*see* "Prince
    Marcassin"); "The Ram," 17, 60–
    61; *Relation du voyage d'Espagne*,
    55–56, 181–82n14; "Rosette," 115;
    Tales of the Fairies, 9; "The White
    Cat," 59
Davis, Christian S., 102
Day, Andrea, 131–32, 142, 194n3,
    198nn19–20
de Beaumont, Jeanne-Marie
    Leprince: "Beauty and the Beast,"
    8, 14, 50, 80, 86–88, 199n21
de Champlain, Samuel, 60–61
decolonization of fairytale studies, 3,
    20, 158–59, 172
de Denonville, Governor General
    Jacques René des Brisay, 79
Defoe, Daniel: *Robinson Crusoe*, 104

de Fontenelle, Bernard le Bovier: *Lettres galantes du chevalier d'Her*, 83-84
de Gómara, Francisco López, 58
de La Fontaine, Jean, 182n15
de la Force, Charlotte Rose, 192n23
de l'Incarnation, Marie, 67, 71, 75
de Murat, Henriette-Julie: "Le Roi Porc," 74, 77; *Sublime and Allegorical Stories*, 5
Descartes, René, 68
De Simone, Roberto, 24
de Villeneuve, Gabrielle-Suzanne Barbot: "Beauty and the Beast," 8, 17, 50, 80-89, 117, 175n14, 184n27, 185n30, 185-86n31, 186n32, 199n21; *La Jeune Américaine*, 80-82, 175n14
Dhaliwal, Sarindar, 19, 165-68; *the green fairy storybook*, 165-66; *When I Grow Up I Want to Be a Namer of Paint Colours*, 166
Diaconoff, Suellen, 84-85
Dickason, Olive, 57-58, 61-62
Dobie, Madeleine, 81-82, 184-85n28
domina figure, 31-38, 177n7
Do Rozario, Rebecca-Anne, 8-9, 13-14, 185-86n31
Du Buffon, Comte: *Histoire naturelle*, 87, 187n34
Duggan, Anne, 175n11, 183nn21-22, 187n35
Du Tertre, Jean-Baptiste: *Histoire générale des Antilles habitées par les François*, 83
dwarves, 125-27

"East India," 108-11, 113, 190-91n14
Edwardian era, 13, 88, 130, 146
Elias, Norbert, 76
Epstein, Steven, 25-28, 41-42, 50-51, 176n1, 177-78n11

Equiano, Olaudah, 134

fairy tale as genre, 1-11, 15-20, 27, 32, 44, 51, 53-56, 88, 94, 105, 117-18, 128, 156-65, 170-72, 173n2, 175n10, 199n1
Farrell, Joseph, 31
Farrell, Michèle, 76
Fichte, Johann Gottlieb, 89
Fögen, Thorsten, 35-36, 177n10
Ford, Henry J., 11-12
frame narrative: in Basile's *The Tale of Tales*, 7, 9, 16, 21-25, 35, 42-43, 115-16, 176n1, 178n14, 179n15; in de Beaumont's "Beauty and the Beast," 14, 87-88; in de Villeneuve's "Beauty and the Beast," 17, 80, 175n14, 183-84n24, 184n27
French colonies in the Caribbean, 17, 55, 63-64, 79-87, 186-87n33
Frenchification (*francisation*), 16-17, 55, 69-71, 74-79, 186-87n33
French occupation of Germany, 10, 107
French Revolution, 90-92, 188n1
Freud, Sigmund, 153-54

Galland, Antoine: *The Arabian Nights*, 4, 21, 65, 94, 173n4
Gallus, 27
Garraway, Doris, 63-64, 81, 86, 186-87n33
Gassendi, Pierre, 182n15
German comparative linguistics, 188-89n4
Germanistik, 92
German superiority (corporeal), 90, 104-7, 121-22, 126-27
Gilman, Sander, 118-19, 188n1
Gold, Barbara, 27
Görres, Joseph, 94
Green, Roger Lancelyn, 154

Grien, Hans Baldung, 120
Grimm, Jacob and Wilhelm, 2, 5, 7, 9-10, 13, 17-18, 89-130, 161, 188-89n4, 190-91n14, 191n16, 193n25, 194n2, 199n1; "The Bremen Town Musicians," 193n25; "The Bright Sun Will Bring It to Light," 100-101, 111, 189n6; *Children's and Household Tales (Kinder- und Hausmärchen)*, 2, 5, 9-10, 17-18, 89-130, 190-91n14, 191n16, 193n25, 194n2, 199n1; *Deutsche Grammatik*, 188-89n4; *Deutsches Wörterbuch*, 188-89n4; "Eve's Unequal Children," 121-23, 192-93n24; "The Foundling," 120; *Geschichte der Deutschen Sprache*, 188-89n4; "The Good Bargain," 10, 18, 99-100, 189n6; "The Goose Girl," 116; "Hansel and Gretel," 107, 120; "Hans My Hedgehog," 117-18, 190n13; "The Jew in the Thornbush," 10, 18, 96-98, 101, 189n6; "Jorinda and Joringel," 120; "The Juniper Tree," 120; "The King of the Golden Mountain," 125; "Mother Holle," 18, 107, 116; "The Prince Who Feared Nothing," 10, 18, 111-13, 190n13, 191n16; "Rapunzel," 120, 192n23; "The Rejuvenated Little Old Man," 123-24; "The Robber and His Sons," 125; "Rumpelstiltskin," 13, 126-27; "The Singing Springing Lark," 116-17; "Snow White," 107; "Strong Hans," 125; "The Three Black Princesses," 10, 18, 108-11, 113, 190n13, 190-91n14; "The Three Little Gnomes in the Forest," 18, 116-17; "The White Bride and the Black Bride," 18, 114-16, 190n13
Grimm's law, 188-89n4

Haase, Donald, 2, 158, 199n1
Haggard, Rider, 137, 153-54; *The World's Desire*, 137
Haitian Revolution, 90
Hannon, Patricia, 57, 68, 180n5
Hare, J. Laurence, 93
Harth, Erica, 56
Hartman, Saidiya, 14, 168-69
Hazard, Paul, 180n5
Hegel, Georg Wilhelm Friedrich: *The Phenomenology of Mind*, 90, 188n1
Helfer, Martha B., 96, 98-101
Heliodorus: *Aethiopica*, 175n15
Hennard Dutheil de la Rochère, Martine, 161
Hensley, Nathan, 153
Herder, Johann Gottfried, 89, 91-92, 105, 188n3, 190n10, 190n12
Hermand, Jost, 188n2
Hess, Jonathan M., 93, 103, 122, 189n5
Hewitt-White, Caitlin, 106-8, 119
Hill-Tout, Charles: "The Eagle and the Owl," 147-49, 198n17
Hines, Sara, 11-13, 155
Hobbes, Thomas, 68
Hopkinson, Nalo, 19, 159-63; "The Glass Bottle Trick," 160-63; "Precious," 162-63, 199n2; *Skin Folk*, 159-62
Hulme, Peter, 185n30
Humphries, Stephen, 197-98n16
Hund, Wulf D., 127
Hunt, James, 135
hybridity as resistance, 161
hypersexuality, 84-85, 87, 185-86n31

imperialism: British, 19, 133-37, 139-42, 144-47, 151-52, 155-56, 166-68, 197n11, 197n120; epistemological, 11, 18-19; imperial imagination, 55-57, 65-66, 68, 71, 78, 80, 149, 186-87n33. *See also* colonialism

Indigeneity: fairy tale adaptations, 19–20, 159; knowledge systems, 158. *See also* wonder genre
interracial marriage. *See* miscegenation
Itzig, Moritz, 96

James, Sharon, 32–33, 35–36, 177n10
Jesuit Relations, 17, 55–56, 67, 75
Jewishness: in the Grimms' *Children's and Household Tales*, 13, 96–101, 126–27, 175n11; Jewish emancipation, 93, 101–3, 107, 125, 127. *See also* assimilation: Jewish
Jones, Christine, 53, 61, 179–80n1, 182n16

Kant, Immanuel, 89, 103, 105, 127
Kiernan, V. G., 135
King, Stephen: *Rose Madder*, 167
Kletke, Hermann, 11
Kontje, Todd, 92, 110, 190n12
Kramer, Heinrich: *Malleus melficarum*, 119
Kunstmärchen. See *Märchen*
Kuwada, Bryan Kamaoli, 19, 158
Kuya, Dorothy, 134

Lang, Andrew, 2, 5, 9–13, 18–19, 129–57, 163–68, 174n8, 194–95n4, 196n6, 198n20; "Blackskin," 198n19; *Brown Fairy Book*, 138, 142–47, 168; "The Bunyip," 144–48, 152; Colored Fairy Books, 2, 5, 9–13, 18–19, 129–57, 163–68, 194n3, 194–95n4, 196n9, 198n20; *Crimson Fairy Book*, 133, 137, 139, 143–44, 152, 194–95n4; "The Glass Axe," 11–13; *Green Fairy Book*, 132–33, 196n6; *Lilac Fairy Book*, 131, 138, 194–95n4, 196n6; as "mediator," 153–54; *Olive Fairy Book*, 138, 174n8, 196n6; *Orange Fairy Book*, 138, 148; "The Owl and the Eagle," 147–50, 152; *Pink Fairy Book*, 152; "The Sacred Milk of Koumongoé," 197–98n16; "The Story of a Gazelle," 150–51; *The Strange Story Book*, 198nn19–20; *Violet Fairy Book*, 19, 133, 150, 152, 194–95n4; *The World's Desire*, 137; *Yellow Fairy Book*, 11–13, 196n6
Lang, Nora, 131–32, 137–42, 196n9, 196–97n10, 198nn19–20; *A Geography: Physical, Political, and Descriptive, for Beginners*, 140–42
Lateiner, Donald, 36
Lathey, Gillian, 196n8
Latour, Bruno, 153
Lea, Charlene A., 94–95
Le Jeune, Father Paul, 67
Link, Fabian, 93
Locke, John, 124
Lorde, Audre, 170–71
Louis XIV, 61, 65, 81
Lutz, Tom, 36
Lyne, R.O.A.M., 28

MacMaster, Neil, 118
Magnanini, Suzanne, 24, 27, 176n5, 177n9, 178n12
Maimonides, Moses: *Guide for the Perplexed*, 124
Malleus melficarum, 119
Marchand, Suzanne L., 92, 110, 190n12
Märchen, 2, 92, 94
Marr, Wilhelm, 125, 193n25
McClintock, Anne, 151–52
McGillis, Roderick, 156
McLeod, Glenda, 56
Meiners, Christoph, 89–90, 103, 105–6, 109, 116–18, 121–22, 126–27, 190n10; *Grundriß der Geschichte der Menschheit*, 105–6
Melzer, Sara, 55–56, 180n3
merveilleux, 3, 184n26

metamorphosis, 35, 67–71, 74–78, 80, 85, 181n9, 182–83n19. *See also* animal-human hybridity
Michaelis, Johann David, 17–18, 89, 102–3, 107, 126, 190n11; *Mosaisches Recht*, 102; *Orientalische und exegetische Bibliothek*, 103
Mills, Charles, 124
miscegenation, 17, 77–80, 85, 87–88, 102, 171, 183n22
Mister, Mary: *Mungo, the Little Traveller*, 139
monogenesis, 122
Montesquieu, 68, 81, 103; *De l'Esprit de lois*, 81
Morgan, Llewelyn, 176–77n6
Morrison, Toni, 14, 170–71
motherhood, 137, 139–40
Müller, Adam, 94–95
Mullins, Melissa, 192n23
Murgatroyd, P., 28–31

Napoleon, 91, 188n2
Nationalgeist. See *Volksgeist*
nationalism: German, 10, 17–18, 89–96, 104–7, 188n2, 190n12, 191n19
Neapolitan-Moorish patois, 15, 37–39, 43, 177–78n11
Nettl, Paul, 25, 176n3
network theory, 153–54
New France, 16–17, 55, 64–71, 74–80, 86, 183n21, 183n23
"noble savage" trope, 17, 76
Norcia, Megan, 139, 141, 143, 199n21
Novik, Naomi, 13
Nygaard, Loisa, 188–89n4, 190n9

Oexmelin, Alexandre Olivier: *Histoire des aventuriers*, 63
Ó Giolláin, Diarmuid, 134
Orientalism, 4, 8–9, 61–62, 92–94, 102–3, 109–11, 162, 185–86n31, 191n19

Origen, 113
otherness: in Basile's *The Tale of Tales*, 23–25, 39, 43–44, 56–57, 80; in Beauty and the Beast, 8–9, 13–14, 86, 88; in the Grimms' *Children's and Household Tales*, 107, 110, 121–22, 126; in Lang's Colored Fairy Books, 145–46, 151, 156
Otmar: *Volks-Sagen*, 193–94n1
Ovid, 27, 31, 36; *Ars amatoria*, 36
Owens, Yvonne, 120, 192n22
Oyeyemi, Helen, 19, 169–72, 199n3; *Boy, Snow, Bird*, 199n3; *Gingerbread*, 171–72, 199n3; *Mr. Fox*, 169–70, 199n3; *White Is for Witching*, 171–72, 199n3

Palmer, Melvin, 5–6, 55–56
Park, Mungo, 134
Peabody, Sue, 82
Penzer, Norman N., 48
periodical literature, 136
Perraudin, Michael, 91
Perrault, Charles, 4–5, 54, 161, 174n8, 180n2, 183n21; *Tales from Times Past*, 4–5; *Tales of Mother Goose* (*Les Contes de ma mère l'oye*), 54
Petrarch, 32, 42
piracy, 62–64, 179n15
Planché, J. R., 185–86n31
Plantade, Emmanuel and Nedjima, 48–49
postcolonialism, 19–20, 159–60, 167, 199n1
Propertius, 27
Psomiades, Kathy Alexis, 153–54
puella figure, 32–33, 36–37
Puss-in-Boots, 4–5

Quarrel of the Ancients and the Moderns, 54–55
queerness, 173n3

Red Sea, 117–18
Reid, Mayne, 136
relation (French travel narrative), 17, 55–57, 61, 72, 181n14
Richelieu, Cardinal, 69
Ritchie, Anne Thackeray, 181n13, 181–82n14
Robbins, Louise, 83, 185n29
Robinson, Natalie, 161
Robinsonade (genre), 104–5
Roman love elegy, 15–16, 27–38, 44, 50–51, 176–77n6, 177n8
Romanticism: German, 91, 94, 98
Rose, Jacqueline, 143–44

Saint-Domingue, 17, 63, 80–82, 175n14, 183–84n24, 184n25, 184n27, 186–87n33, 188n1
salon literature, 4–5, 53, 56, 73, 83–84, 182n15
salonnières. *See* salon literature
Sands-O'Connor, Karen, 145–47, 197nn15–16
Sannazaro, Jacopo: *Arcadia*, 124
sauvages, 17, 55, 68–71, 75–79, 117, 186–87n33
Sayre, Gordon, 68–69
Scala, Carmela Bernadetta, 25, 38, 176n4
Schacker, Jennifer, 130, 194n2
Schanoes, Veronica, 13
Schenda, Rudolf: *Enzyklopädie des Märchens*, 65
Schlegel, August and Karl, 92
Schmiesing, Ann, 108–10, 115
Scott, Walter, 136
Seifert, Lewis, 3, 53, 57, 67–68, 70, 74, 76–78, 159, 182n17, 186–87n33
servitium amoris (slave to love), 15–16, 27–35, 44, 51, 177n8
sexism: in the Grimms' *Children's and Household Tales*, 118–21, 123–24, 192n20

Shaw, Lytle, 167
Shefrin, Jill, 199n21
Skoie, Mathilde, 30–31
slavery: abolition of, 101–2, 127, 134–35, 141–42, 197n11; "animal slaves," 87, 185n29; in Basile's *The Tale of Tales*, 15–16, 21–51; colonial, 81–83, 85–87, 184–85n28, 185n29; figurative language of, 15–16, 23–35, 51; influence on Italian language, 25–27; Italian, 22–27, 39–44; "Lucia" as generalized moniker for female slaves, 16, 24–25, 35–40, 42–44, 176n1; Mediterranean, 25–26, 41–42, 176n5; plantation, 17, 80–87, 142, 184–85n28; Roman, 26–27, 29; Slavery Abolition Act (1833), 141–42, 197n11. *See also servitium amoris* (slave to love)
Smith, Michelle, 8–9, 13–14, 185–86n31
Snow White, 106
social evolutionary theory, 18, 130–36, 140–41, 183n21, 195–96n5, 196n7
Song of Solomon, 113, 191n16
speciesism, 8
Steere, Edward: "Sultan Darai," 150–51
stepmothers, 106–8, 119–20
Stevenson, Robert Louis, 136
Stewart, Susan, 155
Straparola, Giovan Francesco, 4–6, 74, 77, 173–74n5, 174nn6–7; "Costantino and His Cat" (11.1), 4; "Peter the Fool" (3.1), 5; *Pleasant Nights*, 4–5, 6; "Prince Pig" (2.1), 5, 74, 77
Stuurman, Siep, 72
Sutton, Martin, 129, 193–94n1

Tausch-Täuschung, 98–101
Taylor, Edgar: *German Popular Stories*, 129–30, 193–94n1

tears, 21, 22, 33, 35–37, 38
Teverson, Andrew, 145, 148, 155, 195–96n5
Tibullus, 27
Tieck, Ludwig: *Phantasus*, 193–94n1
translation, 138–39, 196n8
travel narrative, 17, 54–62, 104, 124. See also *relation* (French travel narrative)
Trexler, Richard, 193n26
Tylor, Edward, 153–54, 195–96n5

Union Jack, 136
universalization, 1–2, 10, 15, 18–19, 128, 156–57, 164, 188n3, 199n1
utopianism, 6, 17, 53, 65–71, 80, 88, 94, 169, 186–87n33

Valladares, Hérica, 28
van Dijk, Kees, 198n18
Vaudreuil, Governor, 79
Vespucci, Amerigo: *Mundus Novus*, 120; *Quattuor Americi navigationes*, 120
Victorian era, 9–10, 12–13, 88, 130, 133, 136–39, 143–44, 146, 151–56, 162
Volk, 90–93, 96. See also nationalism: German
Volksgeist, 91–92
Volkslieder, 90, 92
Volksmärchen. See *Märchen*
Voltaire, 124
von Arnim, Bettina, 188–89n4

von Arnim, Ludwig Achim, 90–91, 94–96; *Des Knaben Wunderhorn*, 90, 94; "Von Volksliedern," 90
von Dohm, Christian Konrad Wilhelm, 103
von Goethe, Johann Wolfgang, 94
von Humboldt, Alexander and Wilhelm, 92
von Savigny, Friedrich, 94–95
von Schelling, Friedrich Wilhelm Joseph, 89, 91
voyage literature. See travel narrative
vraisemblance, 70, 181n12

Wackenroder, Wilhelm Heinrich, 94
Wakefield, Priscilla: *A Family Tour through the British Empire*, 141, 197n12
weeping, 35–38, 177n10
Wieland, Christoph Martin, 94
witches, 119–21, 192nn22–23
Wolfgang, Aurora, 82, 175n14, 185–86n31
wonder genre, 158–59, 163–65
Wray, David, 31

Yamashiro, Aiko, 19, 158
Yolen, Jane, 13

Zantop, Susanne, 90, 104–6, 119, 127, 190n10, 190n12
Zaubermärchen. See *Märchen*
Zipes, Jack, 128, 185–86n31